FOUR SHORT NOVELS
BY
D. H. LAWRENCE

BY D. H. LAWRENCE

NOVELS

* Sons and Lovers
* The Rainbow
* Women in Love
* The Lost Girl
* Aaron's Rod
* Kangaroo
  Lady Chatterley's Lover
* Four Short Novels *(Love among the Haystacks,*
    The Ladybird, The Fox, The Captain's Doll)

NONFICTION

* Psychoanalysis and the Unconscious *and*
    Fantasia of the Unconscious
* Studies in Classic American Literature
* Apocalypse
* Sex, Literature and Censorship

COLLECTIONS

  Phoenix
  The Portable D. H. Lawrence
* Selected Poems
* The Complete Short Stories of D. H. Lawrence
* Selected Literary Criticism
  The Collected Letters of D. H. Lawrence
* The Complete Poems of D. H. Lawrence
  The Complete Plays of D. H. Lawrence
* Phoenix II
* D. H. Lawrence and Italy: Twilight in Italy, Sea and
    Sardinia, Etruscan Places

VIKING CRITICAL EDITION

  Sons and Lovers *(edited by Julian Moynahan)*

* Available in Viking Compass edition.

D H Lawrence

FOUR SHORT NOVELS

93 - 128

SPRUCE HOME SCHOOL
SPRUCE HOME, SASK.
S0J 2N0

NEW YORK · THE VIKING PRESS

Copyright 1923, Renewed 1951 by Frieda Lawrence

VIKING COMPASS EDITION
Issued in 1965 by The Viking Press, Inc.
625 Madison Avenue, New York, N.Y. 10022

Eleventh printing April 1972

Distributed in Canada by
The Macmillan Company ot Canada Limited

SBN 670-00180-5

Library of Congress catalog card number: 65-2786

Printed in U.S.A. by the Murray Printing Company

CONTENTS

LOVE AMONG THE HAYSTACKS

LOVE AMONG THE HAYSTACKS

I

THE two large fields lay on a hillside facing south. Being newly cleared of hay, they were golden green, and they shone almost blindingly in the sunlight. Across the hill, half-way up, ran a high hedge, that flung its black shadow finely across the molten glow of the sward. The stack was being built just above the hedge. It was of great size, massive, but so silvery and delicately bright in tone that it seemed not to have weight. It rose dishevelled and radiant among the steady, golden-green glare of the field. A little farther back was another, finished stack.

The empty wagon was just passing through the gap in the hedge. From the far-off corner of the bottom field, where the sward was still striped grey with winrows, the loaded wagon launched forward to climb the hill to the stack. The white dots of the hay-makers showed distinctly among the hay.

The two brothers were having a moment's rest, waiting for the load to come up. They stood wiping their brows with their arms, sighing from the heat and the labour of placing the last load. The stack they rode was high, lifting them up above the hedge-tops, and very broad, a great slightly-hollowed vessel into which the sunlight poured, in which the hot, sweet scent of hay was suffocating. Small and inefficacious the brothers looked, half-submerged in the loose, great trough, lifted high up as if on an altar reared to the sun.

Maurice, the younger brother, was a handsome young fellow of twenty-one, careless and debonair, and full of vigour. His grey eyes, as he taunted his brother, were bright and baffled with a strong emotion. His swarthy face had the same peculiar smile, expectant and glad and nervous, of a young man roused for the first time in passion.

"Tha sees," he said, as he leaned on the pommel of his fork, "tha thowt as tha'd done me one, didna ter?" He smiled as he spoke, then fell again into his pleasant torment of musing.

"I thought nowt—tha knows so much," retorted Geoffrey,

3

with the touch of a sneer. His brother had the better of him. Geoffrey was a very heavy, hulking fellow, a year older than Maurice. His blue eyes were unsteady, they glanced away quickly; his mouth was morbidly sensitive. One felt him wince away, through the whole of his great body. His inflamed self-consciousness was a disease in him.

"Ah, but though, I know tha did," mocked Maurice. "Tha went slinkin' off"—Geoffrey winced convulsively—"thinking as that wor the last night as any of us'ud ha'e ter stop here, an' so tha'd leave me to sleep out, though it wor thy turn——"

He smiled to himself, thinking of the result of Geoffrey's ruse.

"I didna go slinkin' off neither," retorted Geoffrey, in his heavy, clumsy manner, wincing at the phrase. "Didna my feyther send me to fetch some coal——"

"Oh yes, oh yes—we know all about it. But tha sees what tha missed, my lad."

Maurice, chuckling, threw himself on his back in the bed of hay. There was absolutely nothing in his world, then, except the shallow ramparts of the stack, and the blazing sky. He clenched his fists tight, threw his arms across his face, and braced his muscles again. He was evidently very much moved, so acutely that it was hardly pleasant, though he still smiled. Geoffrey, standing behind him, could just see his red mouth, with the young moustache like black fur, curling back and showing the teeth in a smile. The elder brother leaned his chin on the pommel of his fork, looking out across the country.

Far away was the faint blue heap of Nottingham. Between, the country lay under a haze of heat, with here and there a flag of colliery smoke waving. But near at hand, at the foot of the hill, across the deep-hedged high road, was only the silence of the old church and the castle farm, among their trees. The large view only made Geoffrey more sick. He looked away, to the wagons crossing the field below him, the empty cart like a big insect moving down-hill, the load coming up, rocking like a ship, the brown head of the horse ducking, the brown knees lifted and planted strenuously. Geoffrey wished it would be quick.

"Tha didna think——"

Geoffrey started, coiled within himself, and looked down

at the handsome lips moving in speech below the brown arms
of his brother.

"Tha didna think 'er'd be thur wi' me—or tha wouldna
ha' left me to it," Maurice said, ending with a little laugh of
excited memory. Geoffrey flushed with hate, and had an
impulse to set his foot on that moving, taunting mouth,
which was there below him. There was silence for a time,
then, in a peculiar tone of delight, Maurice's voice came
again, spelling out the words, as it were:

> *"Ich bin klein, mein Herz ist rein,*
> *Ist niemand d'rin als Christ allein."*

Maurice chuckled, then, convulsed at a twinge of recollec-
tion, keen as pain, he twisted over, pressed himself into the
hay.

"Can thee say thy prayers in German?" came his muffled
voice.

"I non want," growled Geoffrey.

Maurice chuckled. His face was quite hidden, and in the
dark he was going over again his last night's experiences.

"What about kissing 'er under th' ear, Sonny," he said, in
a curious, uneasy tone. He writhed, still startled and inflamed
by his first contact with love.

Geoffrey's heart swelled within him, and things went dark.
He could not see the landscape.

"An' there's just a nice two-handful of her bosom," came
the low, provocative tones of Maurice, who seemed to be
talking to himself.

The two brothers were both fiercely shy of women, and
until this hay harvest, the whole feminine sex had been
represented by their mother and in presence of any other
women they were dumb louts. Moreover, brought up by a
proud mother, a stranger in the country, they held the
common girls as beneath them, because beneath their mother,
who spoke pure English, and was very quiet. Loud-mouthed
and broad-tongued the common girls were. So these two
young men had grown up virgin but tormented.

Now again Maurice had the start of Geoffrey, and the elder
brother was deeply mortified. There was a danger of his
sinking into a morbid state, from sheer lack of living, lack
of interest. The foreign governess at the Vicarage, whose

garden lay beside the top field, had talked to the lads through the hedge, and had fascinated them. There was a great elder bush, with its broad creamy flowers crumbling on to the garden path, and into the field. Geoffrey never smelled elder-flower without starting and wincing, thinking of the strange foreign voice that had so startled him as he mowed out with the scythe in the hedge bottom. A baby had run through the gap, and the Fräulein, calling in German, had come brushing down the flowers in pursuit. She had started so on seeing a man standing there in the shade, that for a moment she could not move: and then she had blundered into the rake which was lying by his side. Geoffrey, forgetting she was a woman when he saw her pitch forward, had picked her up carefully, asking: "Have you hurt you?"

Then she had broken into a laugh, and answered in German, showing him her arms, and knitting her brows. She was nettled rather badly.

"You want a dock leaf," he said. She frowned in a puzzled fashion.

"A dock leaf?" she repeated. He had rubbed her arms with the green leaf.

And now, she had taken to Maurice. She had seemed to prefer himself at first. Now she had sat with Maurice in the moonlight, and had let him kiss her. Geoffrey sullenly suffered, making no fight.

Unconsciously, he was looking at the Vicarage garden. There she was, in a golden-brown dress. He took off his hat, and held up his right hand in greeting to her. She, a small, golden figure, waved her hand negligently from among the potato rows. He remained, arrested, in the same posture, his hat in his left hand, his right arm upraised, thinking. He could tell by the negligence of her greeting that she was waiting for Maurice. What did she think of himself? Why wouldn't she have him?

Hearing the voice of the wagoner leading the load, Maurice rose. Geoffrey still stood in the same way, but his face was sullen, and his upraised hand was slack with brooding. Maurice faced up-hill. His eyes lit up and he laughed. Geoffrey dropped his own arm, watching.

"Lad!" chuckled Maurice. "I non knowed 'er wor there." He waved his hand clumsily. In these matters Geoffrey did better. The elder brother watched the girl. She ran to the

end of the path, behind the bushes, so that she was screened
from the house. Then she waved her handkerchief wildly.
Maurice did not notice the manœuvre. There was the cry
of a child. The girl's figure vanished, reappeared holding up
a white childish bundle, and came down the path. There she
put down her charge, sped up-hill to a great ash tree, climbed
quickly to a large horizontal bar that formed the fence there,
and, standing poised, blew kisses with both her hands, in
a foreign fashion that excited the brothers. Maurice laughed
aloud, as he waved his red handkerchief.

"Well, what's the danger?" shouted a mocking voice from
below. Maurice collapsed, blushing furiously.

"Nowt!" he called.

There was a hearty laugh from below.

The load rode up, sheered with a hiss against the stack,
then sank back again upon the scotches. The brothers
ploughed across the mass of hay, taking the forks. Presently
a big burly man, red and glistening, climbed to the top of
the load. Then he turned round, scrutinised the hillside from
under his shaggy brows. He caught sight of the girl under
the ash tree.

"Oh, that's who it is," he laughed. "I thought it was some
such bird, but I couldn't see her."

The father laughed in a hearty, chaffing way, then began
to teem the load. Geoffrey, on the stack above, received his
great forkfuls, and swung them over to Maurice, who took
them, placed them, building the stack. In the intense sunlight,
the three worked in silence, knit together in a brief passion
of work. The father stirred slowly for a moment, getting
the hay from under his feet. Geoffrey waited, the blue tines
of his fork glittering in expectation: the mass rose, his fork
swung beneath it, there was a light clash of blades, then the
hay was swept on to the stack, caught by Maurice, who
placed it judiciously. One after another, the shoulders of the
three men bowed and braced themselves. All wore light blue,
bleached shirts, that stuck close to their backs. The father
moved mechanically, his thick, rounded shoulders bending
and lifting dully: he worked monotonously. Geoffrey flung
away his strength. His massive shoulders swept and flung the
hay extravagantly.

"Dost want to knock me ower?" asked Maurice angrily.
He had to brace himself against the impact. The three men

worked intensely, as if some will urged them. Maurice was light and swift at the work, but he had to use his judgment. Also, when he had to place the hay along the far ends, he had some distance to carry it. So he was too slow for Geoffrey. Ordinarily, the elder would have placed the hay as far as possible where his brother wanted it. Now, however, he pitched his forkfuls into the middle of the stack. Maurice strode swiftly and handsomely across the bed, but the work was too much for him. The other two men, clenched in their receive and deliver, kept up a high pitch of labour. Geoffrey still flung the hay at random. Maurice was perspiring heavily with heat and exertion, and was getting worried. Now and again, Geoffrey wiped his arm across his brow, mechanically, like an animal. Then he glanced with satisfaction at Maurice's moiled condition, and caught the next forkful.

"Wheer dost think thou'rt hollin' it, fool!" panted Maurice, as his brother flung a forkful out of reach.

"Wheer I've a mind," answered Geoffrey.

Maurice toiled on, now very angry. He felt the sweat trickling down his body: drops fell into his long black lashes, blinding him, so that he had to stop and angrily dash his eyes clear. The veins stood out in his swarthy neck. He felt he would burst, or drop, if the work did not soon slacken off. He heard his father's fork dully scrape the cart bottom.

"There, the last," the father panted. Geoffrey tossed the last light lot at random, took off his hat, and, steaming in the sunshine as he wiped himself, stood complacently watching Maurice struggle with clearing the bed.

"Don't you think you've got your bottom corner a bit far out?" came the father's voice from below. "You'd better be drawing in now, hadn't you?"

"I thought you said next load," Maurice called sulkily.

"Aye! All right. But isn't this bottom corner——?"

Maurice, impatient, took no notice.

Geoffrey strode over the stack, and stuck his fork in the offending corner. "What—here?" he bawled in his great voice.

"Aye—isn't it a bit loose?" came the irritating voice.

Geoffrey pushed his fork in the jutting corner, and, leaning his weight on the handle, shoved. He thought it shook. He thrust again with all his power. The mass swayed.

"What art up to, tha fool!" cried Maurice, in a high voice.

"Mind who tha'rt callin' a fool," said Geoffrey, and he prepared to push again. Maurice sprang across, and elbowed his brother aside. On the yielding, swaying bed of hay, Geoffrey lost his foothold and fell grovelling. Maurice tried the corner.

"It's solid enough," he shouted angrily.

"Aye—all right," came the conciliatory voice of the father; "you do get a bit of rest now there's such a long way to cart it," he added reflectively.

Geoffrey had got to his feet.

"Tha'll mind who tha'rt nudging, I can tell thee," he threatened heavily; adding, as Maurice continued to work, "an' tha non ca's him a fool again, dost hear?"

"Not till next time," sneered Maurice.

As he worked silently round the stack, he neared where his brother stood like a sullen statue, leaning on his fork-handle, looking out over the countryside. Maurice's heart quickened in its beat. He worked forward, until a point of his fork caught in the leather of Geoffrey's boot, and the metal rang sharply.

"Are ter going ta shift thysen?" asked Maurice threateningly. There was no reply from the great block. Maurice lifted his upper lip like a dog. Then he put out his elbow and tried to push his brother into the stack, clear of his way.

"Who are ter shovin'?" came the deep, dangerous voice.

"Thaïgh," replied Maurice, with a sneer, and straightway the two brothers set themselves against each other, like opposing bulls, Maurice trying his hardest to shift Geoffrey from his footing, Geoffrey leaning all his weight in resistance. Maurice, insecure in his footing, staggered a little, and Geoffrey's weight followed him. He went slithering over the edge of the stack.

Geoffrey turned white to the lips, and remained standing, listening. He heard the fall. Then a flush of darkness came over him, and he remained standing only because he was planted. He had not strength to move. He could hear no sound from below, was only faintly aware of a sharp shriek from a long way off. He listened again. Then he filled with sudden panic.

"Feyther!" he roared, in his tremendous voice: "Feyther! Feyther!"

The valley re-echoed with the sound. Small cattle on the hillside looked up. Men's figures came running from the bottom field, and much nearer a woman's figure was racing across the upper field. Geoffrey waited in terrible suspense.

"Ah-h!" he heard the strange, wild voice of the girl cry out. "Ah-h!"—and then some foreign wailing speech. Then: "Ah-h! Are you dea-ed!"

He stood sullenly erect on the stack, not daring to go down, longing to hide in the hay, but too sullen to stoop out of sight. He heard his eldest brother come up, panting:

"Whatever's amiss!" and then the labourer, and then his father.

"Whatever have you been doing?" he heard his father ask, while yet he had not come round the corner of the stack. And then, in a low, bitter tone:

"Eh, he's done for! I'd no business to ha' put it all on that stack."

There was a moment or two of silence, then the voice of Henry, the eldest brother, said crisply:

"He's not dead—he's coming round."

Geoffrey heard, but was not glad. He had as lief Maurice were dead. At least that would be final: better than meeting his brother's charges, and of seeing his mother pass to the sick-room. If Maurice was killed, he himself would not explain, no, not a word, and they could hang him if they liked. If Maurice were only hurt, then everybody would know, and Geoffrey could never lift his face again. What added torture, to pass along, everybody knowing. He wanted something that he could stand back to, something definite, if it were only the knowledge that he had killed his brother. He *must* have something firm to back up to, or he would go mad. He was so lonely, he who above all needed the support of sympathy.

"No, he's commin' to; I tell you he is," said the labourer.

"He's not dea-ed, he's not dea-ed," came the passionate, strange sing-song of the foreign girl. "He's not dead—no-o."

"He wants some brandy—look at the colour of his lips," said the crisp, cold voice of Henry. "Can you fetch some?"

"Wha-at? Fetch?" Fräulein did not understand.

"Brandy," said Henry, very distinct.

"Brrandy!" she re-echoed.

"You go, Bill," groaned the father.

"Aye, I'll go," replied Bill, and he ran across the field.

Maurice was not dead, nor going to die. This Geoffrey now

realised. He was glad after all that the extreme penalty was revoked. But he hated to think of himself going on. He would always shrink now. He had hoped and hoped for the time when he would be careless, bold as Maurice, when he would not wince and shrink. Now he would always be the same, coiling up in himself like a tortoise with no shell.

"Ah-h! He's getting better!" came the wild voice of the Fräulein, and she began to cry, a strange sound, that startled the men, made the animal bristle within them. Geoffrey shuddered as he heard, between her sobbing, the impatient moaning of his brother as the breath came back.

The labourer returned at a run, followed by the Vicar. After the brandy, Maurice made more moaning, hiccuping noise. Geoffrey listened in torture. He heard the Vicar asking for explanations. All the united, anxious voices replied in brief phrases.

"It was that other," cried the Fräulein. "He knocked him over—Ha!"

She was shrill and vindictive.

"I don't think so," said the father to the Vicar, in a quite audible but private tone, speaking as if the Fräulein did not understand his English.

The Vicar addressed his children's governess in bad German. She replied in a torrent which he would not confess was too much for him. Maurice was making little moaning, sighing noises.

"Where's your pain, boy, eh?" the father asked pathetically.

"Leave him alone a bit," came the cool voice of Henry. "He's winded, if no more."

"You'd better see that no bones are broken," said the anxious Vicar.

"It wor a blessing as he should a dropped on that heap of hay just there," said the labourer. "If he'd happened to ha' catched hisself on this nog o' wood 'e wouldna ha' stood much chance."

Geoffrey wondered when he would have courage to venture down. He had wild notions of pitching himself head foremost from the stack: if he could only extinguish himself, he would be safe. Quite frantically, he longed not to be. The idea of going through life thus coiled up within himself in morbid self-consciousness, always lonely, surly, and a misery, was enough to make him cry out. What would they all think when they knew he had knocked Maurice off that high stack?

They were talking to Maurice down below. The lad had recovered in great measure, and was able to answer faintly.

"Whatever was you doin'?" the father asked gently. "Was you playing about with our Geoffrey?—Aye, and where is he?"

Geoffrey's heart stood still.

"I dunno," said Henry, in a curious, ironic tone.

"Go an' have a look," pleaded the father, infinitely relieved over one son, anxious now concerning the other. Geoffrey could not bear that his eldest brother should climb up and question him in his high-pitched drawl of curiosity. The culprit doggedly set his feet on the ladder. His nailed boots slipped a rung.

"Mind yourself," shouted the over-wrought father.

Geoffrey stood like a criminal at the foot of the ladder, glancing furtively at the group. Maurice was lying, pale and slightly convulsed, upon a heap of hay. The Fräulein was kneeling beside his head. The Vicar had the lad's shirt full open down the breast, and was feeling for broken ribs. The father kneeled on the other side, the labourer and Henry stood aside.

"I can't find anything broken," said the Vicar, and he sounded slightly disappointed.

"There's nowt broken to find," murmured Maurice, smiling.

The father started. "Eh?" he said. "Eh?" and he bent over the invalid.

"I say it's not hurt me," repeated Maurice.

"What were you doing?" asked the cold, ironic voice of Henry. Geoffrey turned his head away: he had not yet raised his face.

"Nowt as I know on," he muttered in a surly tone.

"Why!" cried Fräulein in a reproachful tone. "I see him— knock him over!" She made a fierce gesture with her elbow. Henry curled his long moustache sardonically.

"Nay lass, niver," smiled the wan Maurice. "He was fur enough away from me when I slipped."

"Oh, ah!" cried the Fräulein, not understanding.

"Yi," smiled Maurice indulgently.

"I think you're mistaken," said the father, rather pathetically, smiling at the girl as if she were 'wanting'.

"Oh no," she cried. "I *see* him."

"Nay, lass," smiled Maurice quietly.

She was a Pole, named Paula Jablonowsky: young, only twenty years old, swift and light as a wild cat, with a strange, wild-cat way of grinning. Her hair was blonde and full of life, all crisped into many tendrils with vitality, shaking round her face. Her fine blue eyes were peculiarly lidded, and she seemed to look piercingly, then languorously, like a wild cat. She had somewhat Slavonic cheek-bones, and was very much freckled. It was evident that the Vicar, a pale, rather cold man, hated her.

Maurice lay pale and smiling in her lap, whilst she cleaved to him like a mate. One felt instinctively that they were mated. She was ready at any minute to fight with ferocity in his defence, now he was hurt. Her looks at Geoffrey were full of fierceness. She bowed over Maurice and caressed him with her foreign-sounding English.

"You say what you lai-ike," she laughed, giving him lord-ship over her.

"Hadn't you better be going and looking what has become of Margery?" asked the Vicar in tones of reprimand.

"She is with her mother—I heared her. I will go in a whai-ile," smiled the girl coolly.

"Do you feel as if you could stand?" asked the father, still anxiously.

"Aye, in a bit," smiled Maurice.

"You want to get up?" caressed the girl, bowing over him, till her face was not far from his.

"I'm in no hurry," he replied, smiling brilliantly.

This accident had given him quite a strange new ease, an authority. He felt extraordinarily glad. New power had come to him all at once.

"You in no hurry," she repeated, gathering his meaning. She smiled tenderly: she was in his service.

"She leaves us in another month—Mrs. Inwood could stand no more of her," apologised the Vicar quietly to the father.

"Why, is she——"

"Like a wild thing—disobedient and insolent."

"Ha!"

The father sounded abstract.

"No more foreign governesses for me."

Maurice stirred, and looked up at the girl.

"You stand up?" she asked brightly. "You well?"

He laughed again, showing his teeth winsomely. She lifted his head, sprang to her feet, her hands still holding his head, then she took him under the armpits and had him on his feet before anyone could help. He was much taller than she. He grasped her strong shoulders heavily, leaned against her, and, feeling her round, firm breast doubled up against his side, he smiled, catching his breath.

"You see, I'm all right," he gasped. "I was only winded."

"You all raïght?" she cried, in great glee.

"Yes, I am."

He walked a few steps after a moment.

"There's nowt ails me, father," he laughed.

"Quite well, you?" she cried in a pleading tone. He laughed outright, looked down at her, touching her cheek with his fingers.

"That's it—if tha likes."

"If I lai-ike!" she repeated, radiant.

"She's going at the end of three weeks," said the Vicar consolingly to the farmer.

II

While they were talking, they heard the far-off hooting of a pit.

"There goes th' loose 'a," said Henry coldly. "We're *not* going to get that corner up to-day."

The father looked round anxiously.

"Now, Maurice, are you sure you're all right?" he asked.

"Yes, I'm all right. Haven't I told you?"

"Then you sit down there, and in a bit you can be getting dinner out. Henry, you go on the stack. Wheer's Jim? Oh, he's minding the hosses. Bill, and you, Geoffrey, you can pick while Jim loads."

Maurice sat down under the wych elm to recover. The Fräulein had fled back. He made up his mind to ask her to marry him. He had got fifty pounds of his own, and his mother would help him. For a long time he sat musing, thinking what he would do. Then, from the float he fetched a big basket covered with a cloth, and spread the dinner. There was an immense rabbit-pie, a dish of cold potatoes, much bread, a great piece of cheese, and a solid rice pudding.

These two fields were four miles from the home farm. But they had been in the hands of the Wookeys for several generations, therefore the father kept them on, and everyone looked forward to the hay harvest at Greasley: it was a kind of picnic. They brought dinner and tea in the milk-float, which the father drove over in the morning. The lads and the labourers cycled. Off and on, the harvest lasted a fortnight. As the high road from Alfreton to Nottingham ran at the foot of the fields, someone usually slept in the hay under the shed to guard the tools. The sons took it in turns. They did not care for it much, and were for that reason anxious to finish the harvest on this day. But work went slack and disjointed after Maurice's accident.

When the load was teemed, they gathered round the white cloth, which was spread under a tree between the hedge and the stack, and, sitting on the ground, ate their meal. Mrs. Wookey sent always a clean cloth, and knives and forks and plates for everybody. Mr. Wookey was always rather proud of this spread: everything was so proper.

"There now," he said, sitting down jovially. "Doesn't this look nice now—eh?"

They all sat round the white spread, in the shadow of the tree and the stack, and looked out up the fields as they ate. From their shady coolness, the gold sward seemed liquid, molten with heat. The horse with the empty wagon wandered a few yards, then stood feeding. Everything was still as a trance. Now and again, the horse between the shafts of the load that stood propped beside the stack, jingled his loose bit as he ate. The men ate and drank in silence, the father reading the newspaper, Maurice leaning back on a saddle, Henry reading the *Nation*, the others eating busily.

Presently "Helloa! 'Er's 'ere again!" exclaimed Bill. All looked up. Paula was coming across the field carrying a plate.

"She's bringing something to tempt your appetite, Maurice," said the eldest brother ironically. Maurice was midway through a large wedge of rabbit-pie and some cold potatoes.

"Aye, bless me if she's not," laughed the father. "Put that away, Maurice, it's a shame to disappoint her."

Maurice looked round very shamefaced, not knowing what to do with his plate.

"Give it over here," said Bill. "I'll polish him off."

"Bringing something for the invalid?" laughed the father to the Fräulein. "He's looking up nicely."

"I bring him some chicken, him!" She nodded her head at Maurice childishly. He flushed and smiled.

"Tha doesna mean ter bust 'im," said Bill.

Everybody laughed aloud. The girl did not understand, so she laughed also. Maurice ate his portion very sheepishly.

The father pitied his son's shyness.

"Come here and sit by me," he said. "Eh, Fräulein! Is that what they call you?"

"I sit by you, father," she said innocently.

Henry threw his head back and laughed long and noiselessly.

She settled near to the big, handsome man.

"My name," she said, "is Paula Jablonowsky."

"Is what?" said the father, and the other men went into roars of laughter.

"Tell me again," said the father. "Your name———"

"Paula."

"Paula? Oh—well, it's a rum sort of name, eh? His name———" he nodded at his son.

"Maurice—I know." She pronounced it sweetly, then laughed into the father's eyes. Maurice blushed to the roots of his hair.

They questioned her concerning her history, and made out that she came from Hanover, that her father was a shop-keeper, and that she had run away from home because she did not like her father. She had gone to Paris.

"Oh," said the father, now dubious. "And what did you do there?"

"In school—in a young ladies' school."

"Did you like it?"

"Oh no—no laïfe—no life!"

"What?"

"When we go out—two and two—all together—no more. Ah, no life, no life."

"Well, that's a winder!" exclaimed the father. "No life in Paris! And have you found much life in England?"

"No—ah no. I don't like it." She made a grimace at the Vicarage.

"How long have you been in England?"

"Chreestmas—so."

"And what will you do?"

"I will go to London, or to Paris. Ah, Paris!—Or get married!" She laughed into the father's eyes.

The father laughed heartily.

"Get married, eh? · And who to?"

"I don't know. I am going away."

"The country's too quiet for you?" asked the father.

"Too quiet—hm!" she nodded in assent.

"You wouldn't care for making butter and cheese?"

"Making butter—hm!" She turned to him with a glad, bright gesture. "I like it."

"Oh," laughed the father. "You would, would you?"

She nodded vehemently, with glowing eyes.

"She'd like anything in the shape of a change," said Henry judicially.

"I think she would," agreed the father. It did not occur to them that she fully understood what they said. She looked at them closely, then thought with bowed head.

"Hullo!" exclaimed Henry, the alert. A tramp was slouching towards them through the gap. He was a very seedy, slinking fellow, with a tang of horsey braggadocio about him. Small, thin, and ferrety, with a week's red beard bristling on his pointed chin, he came slouching forward.

"Have yer got a bit of a job goin'?" he asked.

"A bit of a job," repeated the father. "Why, can't you see as we've a'most done?"

"Aye—but I noticed you was a hand short, an' I thowt as 'appen you'd gie me half a day."

"What, are *you* any good in a hay close?" asked Henry, with a sneer.

The man stood slouching against the haystack. All the others were seated on the floor. He had an advantage.

"I could work aside any on yer," he bragged.

"Tha looks it," laughed Bill.

"And what's your regular trade?" asked the father.

"I'm a jockey by rights. But I did a bit o' dirty work for a boss o' mine, an' I was landed. '*E* got the benefit, *I* got kicked out. '*E* axed me—an' then 'e looked as if 'e'd never seed me."

"Did he, though!" exclaimed the father sympathetically.

"'E did that!" asserted the man.

"But we've got nothing for you," said Henry coldly.

"What does the boss say?" asked the man, impudent.

"No, we've no work you can do," said the father. "You can have a bit o' something to eat, if you like."

"I should be glad of it," said the man.

He was given the chunk of rabbit-pie that remained. This he ate greedily. There was something debased, parasitic, about him, which disgusted Henry. The others regarded him as a curiosity.

"That was nice and tasty," said the tramp, with gusto.

"Do you want a piece of bread 'n' cheese?" asked the father.

"It'll help to fill up," was the reply.

The man ate this more slowly. The company was embarrassed by his presence, and could not talk. All the men lit their pipes, the meal over.

"So you dunna want any help?" said the tramp at last.

"No—we can manage what bit there is to do."

"You don't happen to have a fill of bacca to spare, do you?"

The father gave him a good pinch.

"You're all right here," he said, looking round. They resented this familiarity. However, he filled his clay pipe and smoked with the rest.

As they were sitting silent, another figure came through the gap in the hedge, and noiselessly approached. It was a woman. She was rather small and finely made. Her face was small, very ruddy, and comely, save for the look of bitterness and aloofness that it wore. Her hair was drawn tightly back under a sailor hat. She gave an impression of cleanness, of precision and directness.

"Have you got some work?" she asked of her man. She ignored the rest. He tucked his tail between his legs.

"No, they haven't got no work for me. They've just gave me a draw of bacca."

He was a mean crawl of a man.

"An' am I goin' to wait for you out there on the lane all day?"

"You needn't if you don't like. You could go on."

"Well, are you coming?" she asked contemptuously. He rose to his feet in a rickety fashion.

"You needn't be in such a mighty hurry," he said. "If you'd wait a bit you might get summat."

She glanced for the first time over the men. She was quite

young, and would have been pretty, were she not so hard and callous-looking.

"Have you had your dinner?" asked the father.

She looked at him with a kind of anger and turned away. Her face was so childish in its contours, contrasting strangely with her expression.

"Are you coming?" she said to the man.

"He's had his tuck-in. Have a bit, if you want it," coaxed the father.

"What have you had?" she flashed to the man.

"He's had all what was left o' th' rabbit-pie," said Geoffrey, in an indignant, mocking tone, "and a great hunk o' bread an' cheese."

"Well, it was gave me," said the man.

The young woman looked at Geoffrey, and he at her. There was a sort of kinship between them. Both were at odds with the world. Geoffrey smiled satirically. She was too grave, too deeply incensed even to smile.

"There's a cake here, though—you can have a bit o' that," said Maurice blithely.

She eyed him with scorn.

Again she looked at Geoffrey. He seemed to understand her. She turned, and in silence departed. The man remained obstinately sucking at his pipe. Everybody looked at him with hostility.

"We'll be getting to work," said Henry, rising, pulling off his coat. Paula got to her feet. She was a little bit confused by the presence of the tramp.

"I go," she said, smiling brilliantly. Maurice rose and followed her sheepishly.

"A good grind, eh?" said the tramp, nodding after the Fräulein. The men only half understood him, but they hated him.

"Hadn't you better be getting off?" said Henry.

The man rose obediently. He was all slouching, parasitic insolence. Geoffrey loathed him, longed to exterminate him. He was exactly the worst foe of the hypersensitive: insolence without sensibility, preying on sensibility.

"Aren't you goin' to give me summat for her? It's nowt she's had all day, to my knowin'. She'll 'appen eat it if I take it 'er—though she gets more than I've any knowledge of"—this with a lewd wink of jealous spite. "And then tries to keep a tight hand on me," he sneered, taking the bread and cheese, and stuffing it in his pocket.

III

Geoffrey worked sullenly all the afternoon, and Maurice did the horse-raking. It was exceedingly hot. So the day wore on, the atmosphere thickened, and the sunlight grew blurred. Geoffrey was picking with Bill—helping to load the wagons from the winrows. He was sulky, though extra-ordinarily relieved: Maurice would not tell. Since the quarrel neither brother had spoken to the other. But their silence was entirely amicable, almost affectionate. They had both been deeply moved, so much so that their ordinary inter-course was interrupted: but underneath, each felt a strong regard for the other. Maurice was peculiarly happy, his feel-ing of affection swimming over everything. But Geoffrey was still sullenly hostile to the most part of the world. He felt isolated. The free and easy inter-communication between the other workers left him distinctly alone. And he was a man who could not bear to stand alone, he was too much afraid of the vast confusion of life surrounding him, in which he was helpless. Geoffrey mistrusted himself with every-body.

The work went on slowly. It was unbearably hot, and everyone was disheartened.

"We s'll have getting-on-for another day of it," said the father at tea-time, as they sat under the tree.

"Quite a day," said Henry.

"Somebody'll have to stop, then," said Geoffrey. "It 'ud better be me."

"Nay, lad, I'll stop," said Maurice, and he hid his head in confusion.

"Stop again to-night!" exclaimed the father. "I'd rather you went home."

"Nay, I'm stoppin'," protested Maurice.

"He wants to do his courting," Henry enlightened them.

The father thought seriously about it.

"I don't know . . ." he mused, rather perturbed.

But Maurice stayed. Towards eight o'clock, after sun-down, the men mounted their bicycles, the father put the horse in the float, and all departed. Maurice stood in the gap of the hedge and watched them go, the cart rolling and swinging down-hill, over the grass stubble, the cyclists dipping swiftly like shadows in front. All passed through the gate, there was a quick clatter of hoofs on the roadway under the lime trees, and they were gone. The young man was very much excited, almost afraid, at finding himself alone.

Darkness was rising from the valley. Already, up the steep hill the cart-lamps crept indecisively, and the cottage windows were lit. Everything looked strange to Maurice, as if he had not seen it before. Down the hedge a large lime tree teemed with scent that seemed almost like a voice speaking. It startled him. He caught a breath of the over-sweet fragrance, then stood still, listening expectantly.

Up-hill, a horse whinneyed. It was the young mare. The heavy horses went thundering across to the far hedge.

Maurice wondered what to do. He wandered round the deserted stacks restlessly. Heat came in wafts, in thick strands. The evening was a long time cooling. He thought he would go and wash himself. There was a trough of pure water in the hedge bottom. It was filled by a tiny spring that filtered over the brim of the trough down the lush hedge bottom of the lower field. All round the trough, in the upper field, the land was marshy, and there the meadow-sweet stood like clots of mist, very sickly-smelling in the twilight. The night did not darken, for the moon was in the sky, so that as the tawny colour drew off the heavens they remained pallid with a dimmed moon. The purple bell-flowers in the hedge went black, the ragged robin turned its pink to a faded white, the meadow-sweet gathered light as if it were phosphorescent, and it made the air ache with scent.

Maurice kneeled on the slab of stone bathing his hands and arms, then his face. The water was deliciously cool. He had still an hour before Paula would come: she was not due till nine. So he decided to take his bath at night instead of waiting till morning. Was he not sticky, and was not Paula coming to talk to him? He was delighted the thought had occurred to him. As he soused his head in the trough, he wondered what the little creatures that lived in the velvety silt at the bottom would think of the taste of soap. Laughing to himself, he squeezed his cloth into the water. He washed himself from head to foot, standing in the fresh, forsaken corner of the field, where no one could see him by daylight, so that now, in the veiled grey tinge of moonlight, he was no more noticeable than the crowded flowers. The night had on a new look: he never remembered to have seen the lustrous grey sheen of it before, nor to have noticed how vital the lights looked, like live folk inhabiting the silvery spaces. And the tall trees, wrapped obscurely in their mantles, would not have surprised him had they begun to move in converse. As he dried himself, he discovered little wanderings in the air, felt on his sides soft touches and caresses that were peculiarly delicious: sometimes they startled him, and he laughed as if he were not alone. The flowers, the meadow-sweet particularly, haunted him. He reached to put his hand over their fleeciness. They touched his thighs. Laughing, he gathered them and dusted himself all over with their cream dust and fragrance. For a moment he hesitated in wonder at himself: but the subtle glow in the hoary and black night reassured him. Things never had looked so personal and full of beauty, he had never known the wonder in himself before.

At nine o'clock he was waiting under the elder bush, in a state of high trepidation, but feeling that he was worthy, having a sense of his own wonder. She was late. At a quarter-past nine she came, flitting swiftly, in her own eager way.

"No, she would *not* go to sleep," said Paula, with a world of wrath in her tone. He laughed bashfully. They wandered out into the dim, hill-side field.

"I have sat—in that bedroom—for an hour, for hours," she cried indignantly. She took a deep breath: "Ah, breathe!" she smiled.

She was very intense, and full of energy.

"I want"—she was clumsy with the language—"I want—I should laike—to run—there!" She pointed across the field.

"Let's run, then," he said curiously.

"Yes!"

And in an instant she was gone. He raced after her. For all he was so young and limber, he had difficulty in catching her. At first he could scarcely see her, though he could hear the rustle of her dress. She sped with astonishing fleetness. He overtook her, caught her by the arm, and they stood panting, facing one another with laughter.

"I could win," she asserted blithely.

"Tha couldna," he replied, with a peculiar, excited laugh.

They walked on, rather breathless. In front of them suddenly appeared the dark shapes of the three feeding horses.

"We ride a horse?" she said.

"What, bareback?" he asked.

"You say?" She did not understand.

"With no saddle?"

"No saddle—yes—no saddle."

"Coop, lass!" he said to the mare, and in a minute he had her by the forelock, and was leading her down to the stacks, where he put a halter on her. She was a big, strong mare. Maurice seated the Fräulein, clambered himself in front of the girl, using the wheel of the wagon as a mount, and together they trotted uphill, she holding lightly round his waist. From the crest of the hill they looked round.

The sky was darkening with an awning of cloud. On the left the hill rose black and wooded, made cosy by a few lights from cottages along the highway. The hill spread to the right, and tufts of trees shut round. But in front was a great vista of night, a sprinkle of cottage candles, a twinkling cluster of lights, like an elfish fair in full swing, at the colliery, an encampment of light at a village, a red flare on the sky far off, above an iron-foundry, and in the farthest distance the dim breathing of town lights. As they watched the night stretch far out, her arms tightened round his waist, and he pressed his elbows to his side, pressing her arms closer still. The horse moved restlessly. They clung to each other.

"Tha daesna want to go right away?" he asked the girl behind him.

"I stay with you," she answered softly, and he felt her crouching close against him. He laughed curiously. He was afraid to kiss her, though he was urged to do so. They remained still, on the restless horse, watching the small lights lead deep into the night, an infinite distance.

"I don't want to go," he said, in a tone half pleading.

She did not answer. The horse stirred restlessly.

"Let him run," cried Paula, "fast!"

She broke the spell, startled him into a little fury. He kicked the mare, hit her, and away she plunged down-hill. The girl clung tightly to the young man. They were riding bareback down a rough, steep hill. Maurice clung hard with hands and knees. Paula held him fast round the waist, leaning her head on his shoulders, and thrilling with excitement.

"We shall be off, we shall be off," he cried, laughing with excitement; but she only crouched behind and pressed tight to him. The mare tore across the field. Maurice expected every moment to be flung on to the grass. He gripped with all the strength of his knees. Paula tucked herself behind him, and often wrenched him almost from his hold. Man and girl were taut with effort.

At last the mare came to a standstill, blowing. Paula slid off, and in an instant Maurice was beside her. They were both highly excited. Before he knew what he was doing, he had her in his arms, fast, and was kissing her, and laughing. They did not move for some time. Then, in silence, they walked towards the stacks.

It had grown quite dark, the night was thick with cloud. He walked with his arm round Paula's waist, she with her arm round him. They were near the stacks when Maurice felt a spot of rain.

"It's going to rain," he said.

"Rain!" she echoed, as if it were trivial.

"I s'll have to put the stack-cloth on," he said gravely. She did not understand.

When they got to the stacks, he went round to the shed, to return staggering in the darkness under the burden of the immense and heavy cloth. It had not been used once during the hay harvest.

"What are you going to do?" asked Paula, coming close to him in the darkness.

"Cover the top of the stack with it," he replied. "Put it over the stack, to keep the rain out."

"Ah!" she cried, "up there!" He dropped his burden. "Yes," he answered.

Fumblingly he reared the long ladder up the side of the stack. He could not see the top.

"I hope it's solid," he said softly.

A few smart drops of rain sounded drumming on the cloth. They seemed like another presence. It was very dark indeed between the great buildings of hay. She looked up the black wall and shrank to him.

"You carry it up there?" she asked.

"Yes," he answered.

"I help you?" she said.

And she did. They opened the cloth. He clambered first

up the steep ladder, bearing the upper part, she followed closely, carrying her full share. They mounted the shaky ladder in silence, stealthily.

IV

As they climbed the stacks a light stopped at the gate on the high road. It was Geoffrey, come to help his brother with the cloth. Afraid of his own intrusion, he wheeled his bicycle silently towards the shed. This was a corrugated iron erection, on the opposite side of the hedge from the stacks. Geoffrey let his light go in front of him, but there was no sign from the lovers. He thought he saw a shadow slinking away. The light of the bicycle lamp sheered yellowly across the dark, catching a glint of raindrops, a mist of darkness, shadow of leaves and strokes of long grass. Geoffrey entered the shed— no one was there. He walked slowly and doggedly round to the stacks. He had passed the wagon, when he heard something sheering down upon him. Starting back under the wall of hay, he saw the long ladder slither across the side of the stack, and fall with a bruising ring.

"What wor that?" he heard Maurice, aloft, ask cautiously.

"Something fall," came the curious, almost pleased voice of the Fräulein.

"It wor niver th' ladder," said Maurice. He peered over the side of the stack. He lay down, looking.

"It is an' a'!" he exclaimed. "We knocked it down with the cloth, dragging it over."

"We fast up here?" she exclaimed with a thrill.

"We are that—without I shout and make 'em hear at the Vicarage."

"Oh no," she said quickly.

"I don't want to," he replied, with a short laugh. There came a swift clatter of raindrops on the cloth. Geoffrey crouched under the wall of the other stack.

"Mind where you tread—here, let me straighten this end," said Maurice, with a peculiar intimate tone—a command and an embrace. "We s'll have to sit under it. At any rate, we shan't get wet."

"Not get wet!" echoed the girl, pleased, but agitated.

Geoffrey heard the slide and rustle of the cloth over the top of the stack, heard Maurice telling her to "Mind!"

"Mind!" she repeated. "Mind! you say 'Mind!'"

"Well, what if I do?" he laughed. "I don't want you to fall over th' side, do I?" His tone was masterful, but he was not quite sure of himself.

There was silence a moment or two.

"Maurice!" she said plaintively.

"I'm here," he answered tenderly, his voice shaky with excitement that was near to distress. "There, I've done. Now should we—we'll sit under this corner."

"Maurice!" she was rather pitiful.

"What? You'll be all right," he remonstrated, tenderly indignant.

"I be all raïght," she repeated, "I be all raïght, Maurice?"

"Tha knows tha will—I canna ca' thee Powla. Should I ca' thee Minnie?"

It was the name of a dead sister.

"Minnie?" she exclaimed in surprise.

"Aye, should I?"

She answered in full-throated German. He laughed shakily.

"Come on—come on under. But do yer wish you was safe in th' Vicarage? Should I shout for somebody?" he asked.

"I don't wish, no!" She was vehement.

"Art sure?" he insisted, almost indignantly.

"Sure—I quite sure." She laughed.

Geoffrey turned away at the last words. Then the rain beat heavily. The lonely brother slouched miserably to the hut, where the rain played a mad tattoo. He felt very miserable, and jealous of Maurice.

His bicycle lamp, downcast, shone a yellow light on the stark floor of the shed or hut with one wall open. It lit up the trodden earth, the shafts of tools lying piled under the beam, beside the dreary grey metal of the building. He took off the lamp, shone it round the hut. There were piles of harness, tools, a big sugar-box, a deep bed of hay—then the beams across the corrugated iron, all very dreary and stark. He shone the lamp into the night: nothing but the furtive glitter of raindrops through the mist of darkness, and black shapes hovering round.

Geoffrey blew out the light and flung himself on to the hay. He would put the ladder up for them in a while, when they would be wanting it. Meanwhile he sat and gloated

over Maurice's felicity. He was imaginative, and now he had
something concrete to work upon. Nothing in the whole of
life stirred him so profoundly, and so utterly, as the thought
of this woman. For Paula was strange, foreign, different from
the ordinary girls: the rousing, feminine quality seemed in
her concentrated, brighter, more fascinating than in anyone
he had known, so that he felt most like a moth near a
candle. He would have loved her wildly—but Maurice
had got her. His thoughts beat the same course, round
and round. What was it like when you kissed her, when
she held you tight round the waist, how did she feel towards
Maurice, did she love to touch him, was he fine and attractive
to her; what did she think of himself—she merely disregarded
him, as she would disregard a horse in a field; why would she
do so, why couldn't he make her regard himself, instead of
Maurice: he would never command a woman's regard like
that, he always gave in to her too soon; if only some woman
would come and take him for what he was worth, though
he was such a stumbler and showed to such disadvantage,
ah, what a grand thing it would be; how he would kiss her.
Then round he went again in the same course, brooding
almost like a madman. Meanwhile the rain drummed deep
on the shed, then grew lighter and softer. There came the
drip, drip of the drops falling outside.

Geoffrey's heart leaped up his chest, and he clenched himself, as a black shape crept round the post of the shed and,
bowing, entered silently. The young man's heart beat so
heavily in plunges, he could not get his breath to speak. It
was shock, rather than fear. The form felt towards him. He
sprang up, gripped it with his great hands panting "Now,
then!"

There was no resistance, only a little whimper of despair.

"Let me go," said a woman's voice.

"What are you after?" he asked, in deep, gruff tones.

"I thought 'e was 'ere," she wept despairingly, with little,
stubborn sobs.

"An' you've found what you didn't expect, have you?"

At the sound of his bullying she tried to get away from
him.

"Let me go," she said.

"Who did you expect to find here?" he asked, but more his
natural self.

"I expected my husband—him as you saw at dinner. Let me go."

"Why, is it you?" exclaimed Geoffrey. "Has he left you?"

"Let me go," said the woman sullenly, trying to draw away. He realised that her sleeve was very wet, her arm slender under his grasp. Suddenly he grew ashamed of himself: he had no doubt hurt her, gripping her so hard. He relaxed, but did not let her go.

"An' are you searching round after that snipe as was here at dinner?" he asked. She did not answer.

"Where did he leave you?"

"I left him—here. I've seen nothing of him since."

"I s'd think it's good riddance," he said. She did not answer. He gave a short laugh, saying:

"I should ha' thought you wouldn't ha' wanted to clap eyes on him again."

"He's my husband—an' he's not goin' to run off if I can stop him."

Geoffrey was silent, not knowing what to say.

"Have you got a jacket on?" he asked at last.

"What do you think? You've got hold of it."

"You're wet through, aren't you?"

"I shouldn't be dry, comin' through that teemin' rain. But 'e's not here, so I'll go."

"I mean," he said humbly, "are you wet through?"

She did not answer. He felt her shiver.

"Are you cold?" he asked, in surprise and concern.

She did not answer. He did not know what to say.

"Stop a minute," he said, and he fumbled in his pocket for his matches. He struck a light, holding it in the hollow of his large, hard palm. He was a big man, and he looked anxious. Shedding the light on her, he saw she was rather pale, and very weary looking. Her old sailor hat was sodden and drooping with rain. She wore a fawn-coloured jacket of smooth cloth. This jacket was black-wet where the rain had beaten, her skirt hung sodden, and dripped on to her boots. The match went out.

"Why, you're wet through!" he said.

She did not answer.

"Shall you stop in here while it gives over?" he asked. She did not answer.

" 'Cause if you will, you'd better take your things off, an'
have th' rug. There's a horse-rug in the box."

He waited, but she would not answer. So he lit his bicycle
lamp, and rummaged in the box, pulling out a large brown
blanket, striped with scarlet and yellow. She stood stock still.
He shone the light on her. She was very pale, and trembling
fitfully.

"Are you that cold?" he asked in concern. "Take your
jacket off, and your hat, and put this right over you."

Mechanically, she undid the enormous fawn-coloured
buttons, and unpinned her hat. With her black hair drawn
back from her low, honest brow, she looked little more than
a girl, like a girl driven hard with womanhood by stress of
life. She was small, and natty, with neat little features. But
she shivered convulsively.

"Is something a-matter with you?" he asked.

"I've walked to Bulwell and back," she quivered, "looking
for him—an' I've not touched a thing since this morning."
She did not weep—she was too dreary-hardened to cry. He
looked at her in dismay, his mouth half open: "Gormin"
as Maurice would have said.

" 'Aven't you had nothing to eat?" he said.

Then he turned aside to the box. There, the bread remaining was kept, and the great piece of cheese, and such things as
sugar and salt, with all table utensils: there was some butter.

She sat down drearily on the bed of hay. He cut her a
piece of bread and butter, and a piece of cheese. This she
took, but ate listlessly.

"I want a drink," she said.

"We 'aven't got no beer," he answered. "My father doesn't
have it."

"I want water," she said.

He took a can and plunged through the wet darkness,
under the great black hedge, down to the trough. As he came
back he saw her in the half-lit little cave sitting bunched
together. The soaked grass wet his feet—he thought of her.
When he gave her a cup of water, her hand touched his and
he felt her fingers hot and glossy. She trembled so she spilled
the water.

"Do you feel badly?" he asked.

"I can't keep myself still—but it's only with being tired
and having nothing to eat."

He scratched his head contemplatively, waited while she ate her piece of bread and butter. Then he offered her another piece.

"I don't want it just now," she said.

"You'll have to eat summat," he said.

"I couldn't eat any more just now."

He put the piece down undecidedly on the box. Then there was another long pause. He stood up with bent head. The bicycle, like a restful animal, glittered behind him, turning towards the wall. The woman sat hunched on the hay, shivering.

"Can't you get warm?" he asked.

"I shall by an' by—don't you bother. I'm taking your seat —are you stopping here all night?"

"Yes."

"I'll be goin' in a bit," she said.

"Nay, I non want you to go. I'm thinkin' how you could get warm."

"Don't you bother about me," she remonstrated, almost irritably.

"I just want so see as the stacks is all right. You take your shoes an' stockin's an' all your wet things off: you can easy wrap yourself all over in that rug, there's not so much of you."

"It's raining—I s'll be all right—I s'll be going in a minute."

"I've got to see as the stacks is safe. Take your wet things off."

"Are you coming back?" she asked.

"I mightn't, not till morning."

"Well, I s'll be gone in ten minutes, then. I've no rights to be here, an' I s'll not let anybody be turned out for me."

"You won't be turning me out."

"Whether or no, I shan't stop."

"Well, shall you if I come back?" he asked. She did not answer.

He went. In a few moments, she blew the light out. The rain was falling steadily, and the night was a black gulf. All was intensely still. Geoffrey listened everywhere: no sound save the rain. He stood between the stacks, but only heard the trickle of water, and the light swish of rain. Everything was lost in blackness. He imagined death was like that, many things dissolved in silence and darkness, blotted out, but

existing. In the dense blackness he felt himself almost extin-
guished. He was afraid he might not find things the same.
Almost frantically, he stumbled, feeling his way, till his hand
touched the wet metal. He had been looking for a gleam of
light.

"Did you blow the lamp out?" he asked, fearful lest the
silence should answer him.

"Yes," she answered humbly. He was glad to hear her
voice. Groping into the pitch-dark shed, he knocked against
the box, part of whose cover served as table. There was a
clatter and a fall.

"That's the lamp, an' the knife, an' the cup," he said. He
struck a match.

"Th' cup's not broke." He put it into the box.

"But th' oil's spilled out o' th' lamp. It always was a rotten
old thing." He hastily blew out his match, which was burning
his fingers. Then he struck another light.

"You don't want a lamp, you know you don't, and I s'll be
going directly, so you come an' lie down an' get your night's
rest. I'm not taking any of your place."

He looked at her by the light of another match. She was
a queer little bundle, all brown, with gaudy border folding
in and out, and her little face peering at him. As the match
went out she saw him beginning to smile.

"I can sit right at this end," she said. "You lie down."

He came and sat on the hay, at some distance from her.
After a spell of silence:

"Is he really your husband?" he asked.

"He is!" she answered grimly.

"Hm!" Then there was silence again.

After a while: "Are you warm now?"

"Why do you bother yourself?"

"I don't bother myself—do you follow him because you
like him?" He put it very timidly. He wanted to know.

"I don't—I wish he was dead," this with bitter contempt.
Then doggedly: "But he's my husband."

He gave a short laugh.

"By Gad!" he said.

Again, after a while: "Have you been married long?"

"Four years."

"Four years—why, how old are you?"

"Twenty-three."

"Are you turned twenty-three?"

"Last May."

"Then you're four month older than me." He mused over it. They were only two voices in the pitch-black night. It was eerie silence again.

"And do you just tramp about?" he asked.

"He reckons he's looking for a job. But he doesn't like work in any shape or form. He was a stableman when I married him, at Greenhalgh's, the horse-dealers, at Chester-field, where I was housemaid. He left that job when the baby was only two months, and I've been badgered about from pillar to post ever sin'. They say a rolling stone gathers no moss. . . ."

"An' where's the baby?"

"It died when it was ten months old."

Now the silence was clinched between them. It was quite a long time before Geoffrey ventured to say sympathetically: "You haven't much to look forward to."

"I've wished many a score time when I've started shiverin' an' shakin' at nights, as I was taken bad for death. But we're not that handy at dying."

He was silent. "But whatever shall you do?" he faltered.

"I s'll find him, if I drop by th' road."

"Why?" he asked, wondering, looking her way, though he saw nothing but solid darkness.

"Because I shall. He's not going to have it all his own road."

"But why don't you leave him?"

"Because he's *not goin' to have it all his own road*."

She sounded very determined, even vindictive. He sat in wonder, feeling uneasy, and vaguely miserable on her behalf. She sat extraordinarily still. She seemed like a voice only, a presence.

"Are you warm now?" he asked, half afraid.

"A bit warmer—but my feet!" She sounded pitiful.

"Let me warm them with my hands," he asked her. "I'm hot enough."

"No, thank you," she said coldly.

Then, in the darkness, she felt she had wounded him. He was writhing under her rebuff, for his offer had been pure kindness.

"They're 'appen dirty," she said, half mocking.

"Well—mine is—an' I have a bath a'most every day," he answered.

"I don't know when they'll get warm," she moaned to herself.

"Well, then, put them in my hands."

She heard him faintly rattling the match-box, and then a phosphorescent glare began to fume in his direction. Presently he was holding two smoking, blue-green blotches of light towards her feet. She was afraid. But her feet ached so, and the impulse drove her on, so she placed her soles lightly on the two blotches of smoke. His large hands clasped over her instep, warm and hard.

"They're like ice!" he said, in deep concern.

He warmed her feet as best he could, putting them close against him. Now and again convulsive tremors ran over her. She felt his warm breath on the balls of her toes, that were bunched up in his hands. Leaning forward, she touched his hair delicately with her fingers. He thrilled. She fell to gently stroking his hair, with timid, pleading finger-tips.

"Do they feel any better?" he asked, in a low voice, suddenly lifting his face to her. This sent her hand sliding softly over his face, and her finger-tips caught on his mouth. She drew quickly away. He put his hand out to find hers, in his other palm holding both her feet. His wandering hand met her face. He touched it curiously. It was wet. He put his big fingers cautiously on her eyes, into two little pools of tears.

"What's a matter?" he asked in a low, choked voice.

She leaned down to him and gripped him tightly round the neck, pressing him to her bosom in a little frenzy of pain. Her bitter disillusionment with life, her unalleviated shame and degradation during the last four years, had driven her into loneliness, and hardened her till a large part of her nature was caked and sterile. Now she softened again, and her spring might be beautiful. She had been in a fair way to make an ugly old woman.

She clasped the head of Geoffrey to her breast, which heaved and fell, and heaved again. He was bewildered, full of wonder. He allowed the woman to do as she would with him. Her tears fell on his hair, as she wept noiselessly; and he breathed deep as she did. At last she let go her clasp. He put his arms round her.

"Come and let me warm you," he said, folding up on his knee and lapping her with his heavy arms against himself. She was small and *câline*. He held her very warm and close. Presently she stole her arms round him.

"You *are* big," she whispered.

He gripped her hard, started, put his mouth down wanderingly, seeking her out. His lips met her temple. She slowly, deliberately turned her mouth to his, and with opened lips, met him in a kiss, his first love kiss.

V

It was breaking cold dawn when Geoffrey woke. The woman was still sleeping in his arms. Her face in sleep moved all his tenderness: the tight shutting of her mouth, as if in resolution to bear what was very hard to bear, contrasted so pitifully with the small mould of her features. Geoffrey pressed her to his bosom: having her, he felt he could bruise the lips of the scornful, and pass on erect, unabateable. With her to complete him, to form the core of him, he was firm and whole. Needing her so much, he loved her fervently.

Meanwhile the dawn came like death, one of those slow, livid mornings that seem to come in a cold sweat. Slowly, and painfully, the air began to whiten. Geoffrey saw it was not raining. As he was watching the ghastly transformation outside, he felt aware of something. He glanced down: she was open-eyed, watching him; she had golden-brown, calm eyes, that immediately smiled into his. He also smiled, bowed softly down and kissed her. They did not speak for some time. Then:

"What's thy name?" he asked curiously.

"Lydia," she said.

"Lydia!" he repeated wonderingly. He felt rather shy.

"Mine's Geoffrey Wookey," he said.

She merely smiled at him.

They were silent for a considerate time. By morning light, things look small. The huge trees of the evening were dwindled to hoary, small, uncertain things, trespassing in the sick pallor of the atmosphere. There was a dense mist, so that the light could scarcely breathe. Everything seemed to quiver with cold and sickliness.

"Have you often slept out?" he asked her.

"Not so very," she answered.

"You won't go after *him?*" he asked.

"I s'll have to," she replied, but she nestled in to Geoffrey. He felt a sudden panic.

"You mustn't," he exclaimed, and she saw he was afraid for himself. She let it be, was silent.

"We couldn't get married?" he asked thoughtfully.

"No."

He brooded deeply over this. At length:

"Would you go to Canada with me?"

"We'll see what you think in two months' time," she replied quietly, without bitterness.

"I s'll think the same," he protested, hurt.

She did not answer, only watched him steadily. She was there for him to do as he liked with; but she would not injure his fortunes; no, not to save his soul.

"Haven't you got no relations?" he asked.

"A married sister at Crick."

"On a farm?"

"No—married a farm labourer—but she's very comfortable. I'll go there, if you want me to, just till I can get another place in service."

He considered this.

"Could you get on a farm?" he asked wistfully.

"Greenhalgh's was a farm."

He saw the future brighten: she would be a help to him. She agreed to go to her sister, and to get a place of service— until spring, he said, when they would sail for Canada. He waited for her assent.

"You will come with me, then?" he asked.

"When the time comes," she said.

Her want of faith made him bow his head: she had reason for it.

"Shall you walk to Crick, or go from Langley Mill to Ambergate? But it's only ten mile to walk. So we can go together up Hunt's Hill—you'd have to go past our lane-end, then I could easy nip down an' fetch you some money," he said humbly.

"I've got half a sovereign by me—it's more than I s'll want."

"Let's see it," he said.

After a while, fumbling under the blanket, she brought out

the piece of money. He felt she was independent of him. Brooding rather bitterly, he told himself she'd forsake him. His anger gave him courage to ask:

"Shall you go in service in your maiden name?"

"No."

He was bitterly wrathful with her—full of resentment.

"I bet I s'll niver see you again," he said, with a short, hard laugh. She put her arms round him, pressed him to her bosom, while the tears rose to her eyes. He was reassured, but not satisfied.

"Shall you write to me to-night?"

"Yes, I will."

"And can I write to you—who shall I write to?"

"Mrs. Bredon."

" 'Bredon'!" he repeated bitterly.

He was exceedingly uneasy.

The dawn had grown quite wan. He saw the hedges drooping wet down the grey mist. Then he told her about Maurice.

"Oh, you *shouldn't!*" she said. "You should ha' put the ladder up for them, you *should.*"

"Well—I don't care."

"Go and do it now—and I'll go."

"No, don't you. Stop an' see our Maurice; go on, stop an' see him—then I'll be able to tell him."

She consented in silence. He had her promise she would not go before he returned. She adjusted her dress, found her way to the trough, where she performed her toilet.

Geoffrey wandered round to the upper field. The stacks looked wet in the mist, the hedge was drenched. Mist rose like steam from the grass, and the near hills were veiled almost to a shadow. In the valley, some peaks of black poplar showed fairly definite, jutting up. He shivered with chill.

There was no sound from the stacks, and he could see nothing. After all, he wondered, were they up there? But he reared the ladder to the place whence it had been swept, then went down the hedge to gather dry sticks. He was breaking off thin dead twigs under a holly tree when he heard, on the perfectly still air: "Well, I'm dashed!"

He listened intently. Maurice was awake.

"Sithee here!" the lad's voice exclaimed. Then, after a while, the foreign sound of the girl:

"What—oh, thair!"

"Aye, th' ladder's there, right enough."

"You said it had fall down."

"Well, I heard it drop—an' I couldna feel it nor see it."

"You said it had fall down—you lie, you liar."

"Nay, as true as I'm here——"

"You tell me lies—make me stay here—you tell me lies——" She was passionately indignant.

"As true as I'm standing here——" he began.

"Lies!—lies!—lies!" she cried. "I don't believe you, never. You *mean*, you *mean*, *mean*, *mean!*"

"A' raïght, then!" He was now incensed, in his turn.

"You are bad, mean, mean, mean."

"Are ter commin' down?" asked Maurice coldly.

"No—I will not come with you—mean, to tell me lies."

"Are ter commin' down?"

"No, I don't want you."

"A' raïght, then!"

Geoffrey, peering through the holly tree, saw Maurice negotiating the ladder. The top rung was below the brim of the stack, and rested on the cloth, so it was dangerous to approach. The Fräulein watched him from the end of the stack, where the cloth thrown back showed the light, dry hay. He slipped slightly, she screamed. When he had got on to the ladder, he pulled the cloth away, throwing it back, making it easy for her to descend.

"Now are ter commin'?" he asked.

"No!" She shook her head violently, in a pet.

Geoffrey felt slightly contemptuous of her. But Maurice waited.

"Are ter commin'?" he called again.

"No," she flashed, like a wild cat.

"All right, then I'm going."

He descended. At the bottom, he stood holding the ladder.

"Come on, while I hold it steady," he said.

There was no reply. For some minutes he stood patiently with his foot on the bottom rung of the ladder. He was pale, rather washed-out in his appearance, and he drew himself together with cold.

"Are ter commin', or aren't ter?" he asked at length. Still there was no reply.

"Then stop up till tha'rt ready," he muttered, and he went away. Round the other side of the stacks he met Geoffrey.

"What, are thaïgh here?" he exclaimed.

"Bin here a' naïght," replied Geoffrey. "I come to help thee wi' th' cloth, but I found it on, an' th' ladder down, so I thowt tha'd gone."

"Did ter put th' ladder up?"

"I did a bit sin'."

Maurice brooded over this, Geoffrey struggled with himself to get out his own news. At last he blurted:

"Tha knows that woman as wor here yis'day dinner—'er come back, an' stopped i' th' shed a' night, out o' th' rain."

"Oh—ah!" said Maurice, his eye kindling, and a smile crossing his pallor.

"An' I s'll gi'e her some breakfast."

"Oh—ah!" repeated Maurice.

"It's th' man as is good-for-nowt, not her," protested Geoffrey. Maurice did not feel in a position to cast stones.

"Tha pleases thysen," he said, "what ter does." He was very quiet, unlike himself. He seemed bothered and anxious, as Geoffrey had not seen him before.

"What's up wi' thee?" asked the elder brother, who in his own heart was glad, and relieved.

"Nowt," was the reply.

They went together to the hut. The woman was folding the blanket. She was fresh from washing, and looked very pretty. Her hair, instead of being screwed tightly back, was coiled in a knot low down, partly covering her ears. Before she had deliberately made herself plain-looking: now she was neat and pretty, with a sweet, womanly gravity.

"Hello. I didn't think to find you here," said Maurice, very awkwardly, smiling. She watched him gravely without reply. "But it was better in shelter than outside last night," he added.

"Yes," she replied.

"Shall you get a few more sticks?" Geoffrey asked him. It was a new thing for Geoffrey to be leader. Maurice obeyed. He wandered forth into the damp, raw morning. He did not go to the stack, as he shrank from meeting Paula.

At the mouth of the hut, Geoffrey was making the fire. The woman got out coffee from the box: Geoffrey set the tin to boil. They were arranging breakfast when Paula appeared. She was hatless. Bits of hay stuck in her hair, and she was white-faced—altogether, she did not show to advantage.

"Ah—you!" she exclaimed, seeing Geoffrey.

"Hello!" he answered. "You're out early."

"Where's Maurice?"

"I dunno, he should be back directly."

Paula was silent.

"When have you come?" she asked.

"I come last night, but I could see nobody about. I got up half an hour sin', an' put th' ladder up ready to take the stack-cloth up."

Paula understood, and was silent. When Maurice returned with the faggots, she was crouched warming her hands. She looked up at him, but he kept his eyes averted from her. Geoffrey met the eyes of Lydia, and smiled. Maurice put his hands to the fire.

"You cold?" asked Paula tenderly.

"A bit," he answered, quite friendly, but reserved. And all the while the four sat round the fire, drinking their smoked coffee, eating each a small piece of toasted bacon, Paula watched eagerly for the eyes of Maurice, and he avoided her. He was gentle, but would not give his eyes to her looks. And Geoffrey smiled constantly to Lydia, who watched gravely.

The German girl succeeded in getting safely into the Vicarage, her escapade unknown to anyone save the house-maid. Before a week was out, she was openly engaged to Maurice, and when her month's notice expired, she went to live at the farm.

Geoffrey and Lydia kept faith one with the other.

THE LADYBIRD

THE LADYBIRD

How many swords had Lady Beveridge in her pierced heart!
Yet there always seemed room for another. Since she had
determined that her heart of pity and kindness should never
die. If it had not been for this determination she herself might
have died of sheer agony, in the years 1916 and 1917, when
her boys were killed, and her brother, and death seemed to
be mowing with wide swaths through her family. But let us
forget.

Lady Beveridge loved humanity, and come what might, she
would continue to love it. Nay, in the human sense, she would
love her enemies. Not the criminals among the enemy, the
men who committed atrocities. But the men who were
enemies through no choice of their own. She would be swept
into no general hate.

Somebody had called her the soul of England. It was not
ill said, though she was half Irish. But of an old, aristocratic,
loyal family famous for its brilliant men. And she, Lady
Beveridge, had for years as much influence on the tone of
English politics as any individual alive. The close friend of
the real leaders in the House of Lords and in the Cabinet, she
was content that the men should act, so long as they breathed
from her as from the rose of life the pure fragrance of truth
and genuine love. She had no misgiving regarding her own
spirit.

She, she would never lower her delicate silken flag. For
instance, throughout all the agony of the war she never forgot
the enemy prisoners; she was determined to do her best for
them. During the first years she still had influence. But
during the last years of the war power slipped out of the
hands of her and her sort, and she found she could do nothing
any more: almost nothing. Then it seemed as if the many
swords had gone home into the heart of this little, unyielding
Mater Dolorosa. The new generation jeered at her. She was
a shabby, old-fashioned little aristocrat, and her drawing-room
was out of date.

But we anticipate. The years 1916 and 1917 were the years

when the old spirit died for ever in England. But Lady Beveridge struggled on. She was being beaten.

It was in the winter of 1917—or in the late autumn. She had been for a fortnight sick, stricken, paralysed by the fearful death of her youngest boy. She felt she *must* give in, and just die. And then she remembered how many others were lying in agony.

So she rose, trembling, frail, to pay a visit to the hospital where lay the enemy sick and wounded, near London. Countess Beveridge was still a privileged woman. Society was beginning to jeer at this little, worn bird of an out-of-date righteousness and æsthetic. But they dared not think ill of her.

She ordered the car and went alone. The Earl, her husband, had taken his gloom to Scotland. So, on a sunny, wan November morning Lady Beveridge descended at the hospital, Hurst Place. The guard knew her, and saluted as she passed. Ah, she was used to such deep respect! It was strange that she felt it so bitterly, when the respect became shallower. But she did. It was the beginning of the end to her.

The matron went with her into the ward. Alas, the beds were all full, and men were even lying on pallets on the floor. There was a desperate, crowded dreariness and helplessness in the place: as if nobody wanted to make a sound or utter a word. Many of the men were haggard and unshaven, one was delirious, and talking fitfully in the Saxon dialect. It went to Lady Beveridge's heart. She had been educated in Dresden, and had had many dear friendships in the city. Her children also had been educated there. She heard the Saxon dialect with pain.

She was a little, frail, bird-like woman, elegant, but with that touch of the blue-stocking of the 'Nineties which was unmistakable. She fluttered delicately from bed to bed, speaking in perfect German, but with a thin, English intonation: and always asking if there was anything she could do. The men were mostly officers and gentlemen. They made little requests which she wrote down in a book. Her long, pale, rather worn face, and her nervous little gestures somehow inspired confidence.

One man lay quite still, with his eyes shut. He had a black beard. His face was rather small and sallow. He might be dead. Lady Beveridge looked at him earnestly, and fear came into her face.

"Why, Count Dionys!" she said, fluttered. "Are you asleep?"

It was Count Johann Dionys Psanek, a Bohemian. She had known him when he was a boy, and only in the spring of 1914 he and his wife had stayed with Lady Beveridge in her country house in Leicestershire.

His black eyes opened: large, black, unseeing eyes, with curved black lashes. He was a small man, small as a boy, and his face too was rather small. But all the lines were fine, as if they had been fired with a keen male energy. Now the yellowish swarthy paste of his flesh seemed dead, and the fine black brows seemed drawn on the face of one dead. The eyes, however, were alive: but only just alive, unseeing and unknowing.

"You know me, Count Dionys? You know me, don't you?" said Lady Beveridge, bending forward over the bed.

There was no reply for some time. Then the black eyes gathered a look of recognition, and there came the ghost of a polite smile.

"Lady Beveridge." The lips formed the words. There was practically no sound.

"I am so glad you can recognise me. And I am so sorry you are hurt. I am so sorry."

The black eyes watched her from that terrible remoteness of death, without changing.

"There is nothing I can do for you? Nothing at all?" she said, always speaking German.

And after a time, and from a distance, came the answer from his eyes, a look of weariness, of refusal, and a wish to be left alone; he was unable to strain himself into consciousness. His eyelids dropped.

"I am so sorry," she said. "If ever there is anything I can do——"

The eyes opened again, looking at her. He seemed at last to hear, and it was as if his eyes made the last weary gesture of a polite bow. Then slowly his eyelids closed again.

Poor Lady Beveridge felt another sword-thrust of sorrow in her heart, as she stood looking down at the motionless face, and at the black fine beard. The black hairs came out of his skin thin and fine, not very close together. A queer, dark, aboriginal little face he had, with a fine little nose: not an Aryan, surely. And he was going to die.

He had a bullet through the upper part of his chest, and another bullet had broken one of his ribs. He had been in hospital five days.

Lady Beveridge asked the matron to ring her up if anything happened. Then she drove away, saddened. Instead of going to Beveridge House, she went to her daughter's flat near the park—near Hyde Park. Lady Daphne was poor. She had married a commoner, son of one of the most famous politicians in England, but a man with no money. And Earl Beveridge had wasted most of the large fortune that had come to him, so that the daughter had very little, comparatively.

Lady Beveridge suffered, going in the narrow doorway into the rather ugly flat. Lady Daphne was sitting by the electric fire in the small yellow drawing-room, talking to a visitor. She rose at once, seeing her little mother.

"Why, mother, ought you to be out? I'm sure not."

"Yes, Daphne darling. Of course I ought to be out."

"How are you?" The daughter's voice was slow and sonorous, protective, sad. Lady Daphne was tall, only twenty-five years old. She had been one of the beauties, when the war broke out, and her father had hoped she would make a splendid match. Truly, she had married fame: but without money. Now, sorrow, pain, thwarted passion had done her great damage. Her husband was missing in the East. Her baby had been born dead. Her two darling brothers were dead. And she was ill, always ill.

A tall, beautifully-built girl, she had the fine stature of her father. Her shoulders were still straight. But how thin her white throat! She wore a simple black frock stitched with coloured wool round the top, and held in a loose coloured girdle: otherwise no ornaments. And her face was lovely, fair, with a soft exotic white complexion and delicate pink cheeks. Her hair was soft and heavy, of a lovely pallid gold colour, ash-blond. Her hair, her complexion were so perfectly cared for as to be almost artificial, like a hot-house flower.

But alas, her beauty was a failure. She was threatened with phthisis, and was far too thin. Her eyes were the saddest part of her. They had slightly reddened rims, nerve-worn, with heavy, veined lids that seemed as if they did not want to keep up. The eyes themselves were large and of a beautiful green-blue colour. But they were full, languid, almost glaucous.

Standing as she was, a tall, finely-built girl, looking down with affectionate care on her mother, she filled the heart with ashes. The little pathetic mother, so wonderful in her way, was not really to be pitied for all her sorrow. Her life was in her sorrows, and her efforts on behalf of the sorrows of others. But Daphne was not born for grief and philanthropy. With her splendid frame, and her lovely, long, strong legs, she was Artemis or Atalanta rather than Daphne. There was a certain width of brow and even of chin that spoke a strong, reckless nature, and the curious, distraught slant of her eyes told of a wild energy dammed up inside her.

That was what ailed her: her own wild energy. She had it from her father, and from her father's desperate race. The earldom had begun with a riotous, dare-devil border soldier, and this was the blood that flowed on. And alas, what was to be done with it?

Daphne had married an adorable husband: truly an adorable husband. Whereas she needed a dare-devil. But in her *mind* she hated all dare-devils: she had been brought up by her mother to admire only the good.

So, her reckless, anti-philanthropic passion could find no outlet—and *should* find no outlet, she thought. So her own blood turned against her, beat on her own nerves, and destroyed her. It was nothing but frustration and anger which made her ill, and made the doctors fear consumption. There it was, drawn on her rather wide mouth: frustration, anger, bitterness. There it was the same in the roll of her green-blue eyes, a slanting, averted look: the same anger furtively turning back on itself. This anger reddened her eyes and shattered her nerves. And yet her whole will was fixed in her adoption of her mother's creed, and in condemnation of her handsome, proud, brutal father, who had made so much misery in the family. Yes, her will was fixed in the determination that life should be gentle and good and benevolent. Whereas her blood was reckless, the blood of dare-devils. Her will was the stronger of the two. But her blood had its revenge on her. So it is with strong natures to-day: shattered from the inside.

"You have no news, darling?" asked the mother.

"No. My father-in-law had information that British prisoners had been brought into Hasrun, and that details would be forwarded by the Turks. And there was a rumour

from some Arab prisoners that Basil was one of the British
brought in wounded."

"When did you hear this?"

"Primrose came in this morning."

"Then we can hope, dear."

"Yes."

Never was anything more dull and bitter than Daphne's
affirmative of hope. Hope had become almost a curse to her.
She wished there need be no such thing. Ha, the torment of
hoping, and the *insult* to one's soul. Like the importunate
widow dunning for her deserts. Why could it not all be just
clean disaster, and have done with it? This dilly-dallying
with despair was worse than despair. She had hoped so
much: ah, for her darling brothers she had hoped with such
anguish. And the two she loved best were dead. So were
most others she had hoped for, dead. Only this uncertainty
about her husband still rankling.

"You feel better, dear?" said the little, unquenched mother.

"Rather better," came the resentful answer.

"And your night?"

"No better."

There was a pause.

"You are coming to lunch with me, Daphne darling?"

"No, mother dear. I promised to lunch at the Howards
with Primrose. But I needn't go for a quarter of an hour.
Do sit down."

Both women seated themselves near the electric fire. There
was that bitter pause, neither knowing what to say. Then
Daphne roused herself to look at her mother.

"Are you sure you were fit to go out?" she said. "What took
you out so suddenly?"

"I went to Hurst Place, dear. I had the men on my mind,
after the way the newspapers have been talking."

"Why ever do you read the newspapers!" blurted Daphne,
with a certain burning, acid anger. "Well," she said, more
composed. "And do you feel better now you've been?"

"So many people suffer besides ourselves, darling."

"I know they do. Makes it all the worse. It wouldn't matter
if it were only just us. At least, it would matter, but one
could bear it more easily. To be just one of a crowd all in
the same state."

"And some even worse, dear."

"Oh, quite! And the worse it is for all, the worse it is for one."

"Is that so, darling? Try not to see too darkly. I feel if I can give just a little bit of myself to help the others—you know—it alleviates me. I feel that what I can give to the men lying there, Daphne, I give to my own boys. I can only help them now through helping others. But I can still do that, Daphne, my girl."

And the mother put her little white hand into the long, white, cold hand of her daughter. Tears came to Daphne's eyes, and a fearful stony grimace to her mouth.

"It's so wonderful of you that you can feel like that," she said.

"But you feel the same, my love. I know you do."

"No, I don't. Everyone I see suffering these same awful things, it makes me wish more for the end of the world. And I quite see that the world won't end——"

"But it will get better, dear. This time it's like a great sickness—like a terrible pneumonia tearing the breast of the world."

"Do you believe it will get better? I don't."

"It will get better. Of course it will get better. It is perverse to think otherwise, Daphne. Remember what *has* been before, even in Europe. Ah, Daphne, we must take a bigger view."

"Yes, I suppose we must."

The daughter spoke rapidly, from the lips, in a resonant, monotonous tone. The mother spoke from the heart.

"And Daphne, I found an old friend among the men at Hurst Place."

"Who?"

"Little Count Dionys. You remember him?"

"Quite. What's wrong?"

"Wounded rather badly—through the chest. So ill."

"Did you speak to him?"

"Yes. I recognised him in spite of his beard."

"Beard!"

"Yes—a black beard. I suppose he could not be shaven. It seems strange that he is still alive, poor man."

"Why strange? He isn't old. How old is he?"

"Between thirty and forty. But so ill, so wounded, Daphne. And so small. So small, so sallow—*smorto*, you know the

Italian word. The way dark people look. There is something so distressing in it."

"Does he look *very* small now—uncanny?" asked the daughter.

"No, not uncanny. Something of the terrible far-awayness of a child that is very ill and can't tell you what hurts it. Poor Count Dionys, Daphne. I didn't know, dear, that his eyes were so black, and his lashes so curved and long. I had never thought of him as beautiful."

"Nor I. Only a little comical. Such a dapper little man."

"Yes. And yet now, Daphne, there is something remote and in a sad way heroic in his dark face. Something primitive."

"What did he say to you?"

"He couldn't speak to me. Only with his lips, just my name."

"So bad as that?"

"Oh yes. They are afraid he will die."

"Poor Count Dionys. I liked him. He was a bit like a monkey, but he had his points. He gave me a thimble on my seventeenth birthday. Such an amusing thimble."

"I remember, dear."

"Unpleasant wife, though. Wonder if he minds dying far away from her. Wonder if she knows."

"I think not. They didn't even know his name properly. Only that he was a colonel of such and such a regiment."

"Fourth Cavalry," said Daphne. "Poor Count Dionys. Such a lovely name, I always thought: Count Johann Dionys Psanek. Extraordinary dandy he was. And an amazingly good dancer, small, yet electric. Wonder if he minds dying."

"He was so full of life, in his own little animal way. They say small people are always conceited. But he doesn't look conceited now, dear. Something ages old in his face—and, yes, a certain beauty, Daphne."

"You mean long lashes."

"No. So still, so solitary—and ages old, in his race. I suppose he must belong to one of those curious little aboriginal races of Central Europe. I felt quite new beside him."

"How nice of you," said Daphne.

Nevertheless, next day Daphne telephoned to Hurst Place to ask for news of him. He was about the same. She telephoned every day. Then she was told he was a little stronger. The day she received the message that her husband was wounded and a prisoner in Turkey, and that his wounds were healing, she forgot to telephone for news of the little enemy Count. And the following day she telephoned that she was coming to the hospital to see him.

He was awake, more restless, more in physical excitement. They could see the nausea of pain round his nose. His face seemed to Daphne curiously hidden behind the black beard, which nevertheless was thin, each hair coming thin and fine, singly, from the sallow, slightly translucent skin. In the same way his moustache made a thin black line round his mouth. His eyes were wide open, very black, and of no legible expression. He watched the two women coming down the crowded, dreary room, as if he did not see them. His eyes seemed too wide.

It was a cold day, and Daphne was huddled in a black seal-skin coat with a skunk collar pulled up to her ears, and a dull gold cap with wings pulled down on her brow. Lady Beveridge wore her sable coat, and had that odd, untidy elegance which was natural to her, rather like a ruffled chicken.

Daphne was upset by the hospital. She looked from right to left in spite of herself, and everything gave her a dull feeling of horror: the terror of these sick, wounded enemy men. She loomed tall and obtrusive in her furs by the bed, her little mother at her side.

"I hope you don't mind my coming!" she said in German to the sick man. Her tongue felt rusty, speaking the language.

"Who is it then?" he asked.

"It is my daughter, Lady Daphne. You remembered *me*, Lady Beveridge! This is my daughter, whom you knew in Saxony. She was so sorry to hear you were wounded."

The black eyes rested on the little lady. Then they returned to the looming figure of Daphne. And a certain fear grew on the low, sick brow. It was evident the presence loomed and frightened him. He turned his face aside. Daphne noticed how his fine black hair grew uncut over his small, animal ears.

"You don't remember me, Count Dionys?" she said dully.

"Yes," he said. But he kept his face averted.

She stood there feeling confused and miserable, as if she had made a *faux pas* in coming.

"Would you rather be left alone?" she said. "I'm sorry."

Her voice was monotonous. She felt suddenly stifled in her

closed furs, and threw her coat open, showing her thin white throat and plain black slip dress on her flat breast. He turned again unwillingly to look at her. He looked at her as if she were some strange creature standing near him.

"Good-bye," she said. "Do get better."

She was looking at him with a queer, slanting, downward look of her heavy eyes as she turned away. She was still a little red round the eyes, with nervous exhaustion.

"You are so tall," he said, still frightened.

"I was always tall," she replied, turning half to him again.

"And I, small," he said.

"I am so glad you are getting better," she said.

"I am not glad," he said.

"Why? I'm sure you are. Just as we are glad because we want you to get better."

"Thank you," he said. "I have wished to die."

"Don't do that, Count Dionys. Do get better," she said, in the rather deep, laconic manner of her girlhood. He looked at her with a farther look of recognition. But his short, rather pointed nose was lifted with the disgust and weariness of pain, his brows were tense. He watched her with that curious flame of suffering which is forced to give a little outside attention, but which speaks only to itself.

"Why did they not let me die?" he said. "I wanted death now."

"No," she said. "You mustn't. You must live. If we *can* live we must."

"I wanted death," he said.

"Ah, well," she said, "even death we can't have when we want it, or when we think we want it."

"That is true," he said, watching her with the same wide black eyes. "Please to sit down. You are too tall as you stand."

It was evident he was a little frightened still by her looming, overhanging figure.

"I am sorry I am too tall," she said, taking a chair which a man-nurse had brought her. Lady Beveridge had gone away to speak with the men. Daphne sat down, not knowing what to say further. The pitch-black look in the Count's wide eyes puzzled her.

"Why do you come here? Why does your lady mother come?" he said.

"To see if we can do anything," she answered.

"When I am well, I will thank your ladyship."

"All right," she replied. "When you are well I will let my lord the Count thank me. Please do get well."

"We are enemies," he said.

"Who? You and I and my mother?"

"Are we not? The most difficult thing is to be sure of anything. If they had let me die!"

"That is at least ungrateful, Count Dionys."

"*Lady Daphne!* Yes. *Lady Daphne!* Beautiful, the name is. You are always called Lady Daphne? I remember you were so bright a maiden."

"More or less," she said, answering his question.

"Ach! We should all have new names now. I thought of a name for myself, but I have forgotten it. No longer Johann Dionys. That is shot away. I am Karl or Wilhelm or Ernst or Georg. Those are names I hate. Do you hate them?"

"I don't like them—but I don't hate them. And you mustn't leave off being Count Johann Dionys. If you do I shall have to leave off being Daphne. I like your name so much."

"Lady Daphne! Lady Daphne!" he repeated. "Yes, it rings well, it sounds beautiful to me. I think I talk foolishly. I hear myself talking foolishly to you." He looked at her anxiously.

"Not at all," she said.

"Ach! I have a head on my shoulders that is like a child's windmill, and I can't prevent its making foolish words. Please to go away, not to hear me. I can hear myself."

"Can't I do anything for you?" she asked.

"No, no! No, no! If I could be buried deep, very deep down, where everything is forgotten! But they draw me up, back to the surface. I would not mind if they buried me alive, if it were very deep, and dark, and the earth heavy above."

"Don't say that," she replied, rising.

"No, I am saying it when I don't wish to say it. Why am I here? Why am I here? Why have I survived into this? Why can I not stop talking?"

He turned his face aside. The black, fine, elfish hair was so long, and pushed up in tufts from the smooth brown nape of his neck. Daphne looked at him in sorrow. He could not turn his body. He could only move his head. And he lay with his face hard averted, the fine hair of his beard coming up strange from under his chin and from his throat, up to the socket of his ear. He lay quite still in this position. And she turned away, looking for her mother. She had suddenly realised that the bonds, the connections between him and his life in the world had broken, and he lay there a bit of loose, palpitating humanity, shot away from the body of humanity.

It was ten days before she went to the hospital again. She had wanted never to go again, to forget him, as one tries to forget incurable things. But she could not forget him. He came again and again into her mind. She had to go back. She had heard that he was recovering very slowly.

He looked really better. His eyes were not so wide open, they had lost that black, inky exposure which had given him such an unnatural look, unpleasant. He watched her guardedly. She had taken off her furs, and wore only her dress and a dark, soft feather toque.

"How are you?" she said, keeping her face averted, unwilling to meet his eyes.

"Thank you, I am better. The nights are not so long."

She shuddered, knowing what long nights meant. He saw the worn look in her face too, the reddened rims of her eyes.

"Are you not well? Have you some trouble?" he asked her.

"No, no," she answered.

She had brought a handful of pinky, daisy-shaped flowers.

"Do you care for flowers?" she asked.

He looked at them. Then he slowly shook his head.

"No," he said. "If I am on horseback, riding through the marshes or through the hills, I like to see them below me. But not here. Not now. Please do not bring flowers into this grave. Even in gardens, I do not like them. When they are upholstery to human life."

"I will take them away again," she said.

"Please do. Please give them to the nurse."

Daphne paused.

"Perhaps," she said, "you wish I would not come to disturb you."

He looked into her face.

"No," he said. "You are like a flower behind a rock, near an icy water. No, you do not live too much. I am afraid I cannot talk sensibly. I wish to hold my mouth shut. If I open it, I talk this absurdity. It escapes from my mouth."

"It is not so very absurd," she said.

But he was silent—looking away from her.

"I want you to tell me if there is really nothing I can do for you," she said.

"Nothing," he answered.

"If I can write any letter for you."

"None," he answered.

"But your wife and your two children. Do they know where you are?"

"I should think not."

"And where are they?"

"I do not know. Probably they are in Hungary."

"Not at your home?"

"My castle was burnt down in a riot. My wife went to Hungary with the children. She has her relatives there. She went away from me. I wished it too. Alas for her, I wished to be dead. Pardon me the personal tone."

Daphne looked down at him—the queer, obstinate little fellow.

"But you have somebody you wish to tell—somebody you want to hear from?"

"Nobody. Nobody. I wish the bullet had gone through my heart. I wish to be dead. It is only I have a devil in my body that will not die."

She looked at him as he lay with closed, averted face.

"Surely it is not a devil which keeps you alive," she said. "It is something good."

"No, a devil," he said.

She sat looking at him with a long, slow, wondering look.

"Must one hate a devil that makes one live?" she asked.

He turned his eyes to her with a touch of a satiric smile.

"If one lives, no," he said.

She looked away from him the moment he looked at her. For her life she could not have met his dark eyes direct.

She left him, and he lay still. He neither read nor talked throughout the long winter nights and the short winter days. He only lay for hours with black, open eyes, seeing everything around with a touch of disgust, and heeding nothing.

Daphne went to see him now and then. She never forgot him for long. He seemed to come into her mind suddenly, as if by sorcery.

One day he said to her:

"I see you are married. May I ask you who is your husband?"

She told him. She had had a letter also from Basil. The Count smiled slowly.

"You can look forward," he said, "to a happy reunion and new, lovely children, Lady Daphne. Is it not so?"

"Yes, of course," she said.

"But you are ill," he said to her.

"Yes—rather ill."

"Of what?"

"Oh!" she answered fretfully, turning her face aside. "They talk about lungs." She hated speaking of it. "Why, how do you know I am ill?" she added quickly.

Again he smiled slowly.

"I see it in your face, and hear it in your voice. One would say the Evil One had cast a spell on you."

"Oh no," she said hastily. "But do I look ill?"

"Yes. You look as if something had struck you across the face, and you could not forget it."

"Nothing has," she said. "Unless it's the war."

"The war!" he repeated.

"Oh, well, don't let us talk of it," she said.

Another time he said to her:

"The year has turned—the sun must shine at last, even in England. I am afraid of getting well too soon. I am a prisoner, am I not? But I wish the sun would shine. I wish the sun would shine on my face."

"You won't always be a prisoner. The war will end. And the sun *does* shine even in the winter in England," she said.

"I wish it would shine on my face," he said.

So that when in February there came a blue, bright morning, the morning that suggests yellow crocuses and the smell of a mezereon tree and the smell of damp, warm earth, Daphne hastily got a taxi and drove out to the hospital.

"You have come to put me in the sun," he said the moment he saw her.

"Yes, that's what I came for," she said.

She spoke to the matron, and had his bed carried out where there was a big window that came low. There he was put full in the sun. Turning, he could see the blue sky and the twinkling tops of purplish, bare trees.

"The world! The world!" he murmured.

He lay with his eyes shut, and the sun on his swarthy, transparent, immobile face. The breath came and went through his nostrils invisibly. Daphne wondered how he could lie so still, how he could look so immobile. It was true as her mother had said: he looked as if he had been cast in the mould when the metal was white hot, all his lines were so clean. So small, he was, and in his way perfect.

Suddenly his dark eyes opened and caught her looking.

"The sun makes even anger open like a flower," he said.

"Whose anger?" she said.

"I don't know. But I can make flowers, looking through my eyelashes. Do you know how?"

"You mean rainbows?"

"Yes, flowers."

And she saw him, with a curious smile on his lips, looking through his almost closed eyelids at the sun.

"The sun is neither English nor German nor Bohemian," he said. "I am a subject of the sun. I belong to the fire-worshippers."

"Do you?" she replied.

"Yes, truly, by tradition." He looked at her smiling. "You stand there like a flower that will melt," he added.

She smiled slowly at him with a slow, cautious look of her eyes, as if she feared something.

"I am much more solid than you imagine," she said.

Still he watched her.

"One day," he said, "before I go, let me wrap your hair round my hands, will you?" He lifted his thin, short, dark hands. "Let me wrap your hair round my hands, like a bandage. They hurt me. I don't know what it is. I think it is all the gun explosions. But if you let me wrap your hair round my hands. You know, it is the hermetic gold—but so much of water in it, of the moon. That will soothe my hands. One day, will you?"

"Let us wait till the day comes," she said.

"Yes," he answered, and was still again.

"It troubles me," he said after a while, "that I complain like a child, and ask for things. I feel I have lost my manhood for the time being. The continual explosions of guns and shells! It seems to have driven my soul out of me like a bird frightened away at last. But it will come back, you know. And I am so grateful to you; you are good to me when I am soulless, and you don't take advantage of me. Your soul is quiet and heroic."

"Don't," she said. "Don't talk!"

The expression of shame and anguish and disgust crossed his face.

"It is because I can't help it," he said. "I have lost my soul, and I can't stop talking to you. I can't stop. But I don't talk to anyone else. I try not to talk, but I can't prevent it. Do you draw the words out of me?"

Her wide, green-blue eyes seemed like the heart of some curious, full-open flower, some Christmas rose with its petals of snow and flush. Her hair glinted heavy, like water-gold. She stood there passive and indomitable with the wide-eyed persistence of her wintry, blond nature.

Another day when she came to see him, he watched her for a time, then he said:

"Do they all tell you you are lovely, you are beautiful?"

"Not quite all," she replied.

"But your husband?"

"He has said so."

"Is he gentle? Is he tender? Is he a dear lover?"

She turned her face aside, displeased.

"Yes," she replied curtly.

He did not answer. And when she looked again he was lying with his eyes shut, a faint smile seeming to curl round his short, transparent nose. She could faintly see the flesh through his beard, as water through reeds. His black hair was brushed smooth as glass, his black eyebrows glinted like a curve of black glass on the swarthy opalescence of his brow.

Suddenly he spoke, without opening his eyes.

"You have been very kind to me," he said.

"Have I? Nothing to speak of."

He opened his eyes and looked at her.

"Everything finds its mate," he said. "The ermine and the pole-cat and the buzzard. One thinks so often that only the dove and the nightingale and the stag with his antlers have gentle mates. But the pole-cat and the ice-bears of the north have their mates. And a white she-bear lies with her cubs under a rock as a snake lies hidden, and the male bear slowly swims back from the sea, like a clot of snow or a shadow of a white cloud passing on the speckled sea. I have seen her too, and I did not shoot her, nor him when he landed with fish in his mouth, wading wet and slow and yellow-white over the black stones."

"You have been in the North Sea?"

"Yes. And with the Eskimo in Siberia, and across the Tundras. And a white sea-hawk makes a nest on a high stone, and sometimes looks out with her white head over the edge of the rocks. It is not only a world of men, Lady Daphne."

"Not by any means," said she.

"Else it were a sorry place."

"It is bad enough," said she.

"Foxes have their holes. They have even their mates, Lady Daphne, that they bark to and are answered. And an adder finds his female. Psanek means an outlaw; did you know?"

"I did not."

"Outlaws, and brigands, have often the finest woman-mates."

"They do," she said.

"I will be Psanek, Lady Daphne. I will not be Johann Dionys any more. I will be Psanek. The law has shot me through."

"You might be Psanek and Johann and Dionys as well," she said.

"With the sun on my face? Maybe," he said, looking to the sun.

There were some lovely days in the spring of 1918. In March the Count was able to get up. They dressed him in a simple, dark-blue uniform. He was not very thin, only swarthy-transparent, now his beard was shaven and his hair was cut. His smallness made him noticeable, but he was masculine, perfect in his small stature. All the smiling dapperness that had made him seem like a monkey to Daphne when she was a girl had gone now. His eyes were dark and haughty; he seemed to keep inside his own reserves, speaking to nobody if he could help it, neither to the nurses nor the visitors nor to his fellow-prisoners, fellow-officers. He seemed to put a shadow between himself and them, and from across this shadow he looked with his dark, beautifully-fringed eyes, as a proud little beast from the shadow of its lair. Only to Daphne he laughed and chatted.

She sat with him one day in March on the terrace of the hospital, on a morning when white clouds went endlessly and magnificently about a blue sky, and the sunshine felt warm after the blots of shadow.

"When you had a birthday, and you were seventeen, didn't I give you a thimble?" he asked her.

"Yes. I have it still."

"With a gold snake at the bottom, and a Mary-beetle of green stone at the top, to push the needle with."

"Yes."

"Do you ever use it?"

"No. I sew so rarely."

"Would it displease you to sew something for me?"

"You won't admire my stitches. What would you wish me to sew?"

"Sew me a shirt that I can wear. I have never before worn shirts from a shop, with a maker's name inside. It is very distasteful to me."

She looked at him—his haughty little brows.

"Shall I ask my maid to do it?" she said.

"Oh, please, no! Oh, please, no, do not trouble. No, please, I would not want it unless you sewed it yourself, with the Psanek thimble."

She paused before she answered. Then came her slow:
"Why?"

He turned and looked at her with dark, searching eyes.

"I have no reason," he said, rather haughtily.

She left the matter there. For two weeks she did not go to see him. Then suddenly one day she took the bus down Oxford Street and bought some fine white flannel. She decided he must wear flannel.

That afternoon she drove out to Hurst Place. She found him sitting on the terrace, looking across the garden at the red suburb of London smoking fumily in the near distance, interrupted by patches of uncovered ground and a flat, tin-roofed laundry.

"Will you give me measurements for your shirt?" she said.

"The number of the neck-band of this English shirt is fifteen. If you ask the matron she will give you the measurement. It is a little too large, too long in the sleeves, you see," and he shook his shirt cuff over his wrist. "Also too long altogether."

"Mine will probably be unwearable when I've made them," said she.

"Oh no. Let your maid direct you. But please do not let her sew them."

"Will you tell me why you want me to do it?"

"Because I am a prisoner, in other people's clothes, and I have nothing of my own. All the things I touch are distasteful to me. If your maid sews for me, it will still be the same. Only you might give me what I want, something that buttons round my throat and on my wrists."

"And in Germany—or in Austria?"

"My mother sewed for me. And after her, my mother's sister, who was the head of my house."

"Not your wife?"

"Naturally not. She would have been insulted. She was never more than a guest in my house. In my family there are old traditions—but with me they have come to an end. I had best try to revive them."

"Beginning with traditions of shirts?"

"Yes. In our family the shirt should be made and washed by a woman of our own blood: but when we marry, by the wife. So when I married I had sixty shirts, and many other things—sewn by my mother and my aunt, all with my initial, and the ladybird, which is our crest."

"And where did they put the initial?"

"Here!" He put his finger on the back of his neck, on the swarthy, transparent skin. "I fancy I can feel the embroidered ladybird still. On our linen we had no crown: only the ladybird."

She was silent, thinking.

"You will forgive what I ask you?" he said, "since I am a prisoner and can do no other, and since fate has made you so that you understand the world as I understand it. It is not really indelicate, what I ask you. There will be a ladybird on your finger when you sew, and those who wear the ladybird understand."

"I suppose," she mused, "it is as bad to have your bee in your shirt as in your bonnet."

He looked at her with round eyes.

"Don't you know what it is to have a bee in your bonnet?" she said.

"No."

"To have a bee buzzing among your hair! To be out of your wits," she smiled at him.

"So!" he said. "Ah, the Psaneks have had a ladybird in their bonnets for many hundred years."

"Quite, quite mad," she said.

"It may be," he answered. "But with my wife I was quite sane for ten years. Now give me the madness of the ladybird. The world I was sane about has gone raving. The ladybird I was mad with is wise still."

"At least, when I sew the shirts, if I sew them," she said, "I shall have the ladybird at my finger's end."

"You want to laugh at me."

"But surely you know you are funny, with your family insect."

"My family insect? Now you want to be rude to me."

"How many spots must it have?"

"Seven."

"Three on each wing. And what do I do with the odd one?"

"You put that one between its teeth, like the cake for Cerberus."

"I'll remember that."

When she brought the first shirt, she gave it to the matron. Then she found Count Dionys sitting on the terrace. It was a beautiful spring day. Near at hand were tall elm trees and some rooks cawing.

"What a lovely day!" she said. "Are you liking the world any better?"

"The world?" he said, looking up at her with the same old discontent and disgust on his fine, transparent nose.

"Yes," she replied, a shadow coming over her face.

"Is this the world—all those little red-brick boxes in rows, where couples of little people live, who decree my destiny?"

"You don't like England?"

"Ah, England! Little houses like little boxes, each with its domestic Englishman and his domestic wife, each ruling the world because all are alike, so alike."

"But England isn't all houses."

"Fields then! Little fields with innumerable hedges. Like a net with an irregular mesh, pinned down over this island and everything under the net. Ah, Lady Daphne, forgive me. I am ungrateful. I am so full of bile, of spleen, you say. My only wisdom is to keep my mouth shut."

"Why do you hate everything?" she said, her own face going bitter.

"Not everything. If I were free! If I were outside the law. Ah, Lady Daphne, how does one get outside the law?"

"By going inside oneself," she said. "Not outside."

His face took on a greater expression of disgust.

"No, no. I am a man, I am a man, even if I am little. I am not a spirit, that coils itself inside a shell. In my soul is anger, anger, anger. Give me room for my anger. Give me room for that."

His black eyes looked keenly into hers. She rolled her eyes as if in a half-trance. And in a monotonous, tranced voice she said:

"Much better get over your anger. And *why* are you angry?"

"There is no why. If it were love, you would not ask me, *why do you love?* But it is anger, anger, anger. What else can I call it? And there is no why."

Again he looked at her with his dark, sharp, questioning, tormented eyes.

"Can't you get rid of it?" she said, looking aside.

"If a shell exploded and blew me into a thousand fragments," he said, "it would not destroy the anger that is in me. I know that. No, it will never dissipate. And to die is no release. The anger goes on gnashing and whimpering in death. Lady Daphne, Lady Daphne, we have used up all the love, and this is what is left."

"Perhaps *you* have used up all your love," she replied. "You are not everybody."

"I know it. I speak for me and you."

"Not for me," she said rapidly.

He did not answer, and they remained silent.

At length she turned her eyes slowly to him.

"Why do you say you speak for me?" she said, in an accusing tone.

"Pardon me. I was hasty."

But a faint touch of superciliousness in his tone showed he meant what he had said. She mused, her brow cold and stony.

"And why do you tell *me* about your anger?" she said. "Will that make it better?"

"Even the adder finds his mate. And she has as much poison in her mouth as he."

She gave a little sudden squirt of laughter.

"Awfully poetic thing to say about me," she said.

He smiled, but with the same corrosive quality.

"Ah," he said, "you are not a dove. You are a wild-cat with open eyes, half dreaming on a bough, in a lonely place, as I have seen her. And I ask myself—What are her memories, then?"

"I wish I were a wild-cat," she said suddenly.

He eyed her shrewdly, and did not answer.

"You want more war?" she said to him bitterly.

"More trenches? More Big Berthas, more shells and poison-gas, more machine-drilled science-manœuvred so-called armies? Never. Never. I would rather work in a factory that makes boots and shoes. And I would rather deliberately starve to death than work in a factory that makes boots and shoes."

"Then what do you want?"

"I want my anger to have room to grow."

"How?"

"I do not know. That is why I sit here, day after day. I wait."

"For your anger to have room to grow?"

"For that."

"Good-bye, Count Dionys."

"Good-bye, Lady Daphne."

She had determined never to go and see him again. She had no sign from him. Since she had begun the second shirt, she went on with it. And then she hurried to finish it, because she was starting a round of visits that would end in the summer sojourn in Scotland. She intended to post the shirt. But after all, she took it herself.

She found Count Dionys had been removed from Hurst Place to Voynich Hall, where other enemy officers were interned. The being thwarted made her more determined. She took the train next day to go to Voynich Hall.

When he came into the ante-room where he was to receive her, she felt at once the old influence of his silence and his subtle power. His face had still that swarthy-transparent look of one who is unhappy, but his bearing was proud and reserved. He kissed her hand politely, leaving her to speak.

"How are you?" she said. "I didn't know you were here. I am going away for the summer."

"I wish you a pleasant time," he said. They were speaking English.

"I brought the other shirt," she said. "It is finished at last."

"That is a greater honour than I dared expect," he said.

"I'm afraid it may be more honourable than useful. The other didn't fit, did it?"

"Almost," he said. "It fitted the spirit, if not the flesh," he smiled.

"I'd rather it had been the reverse, for once," she said. "Sorry."

"I would not have it one stitch different."

"Can we sit in the garden?"

"I think we may."

They sat on a bench. Other prisoners were playing croquet not far off. But these two were left comparatively alone.

"Do you like it better here?" she said.

"I have nothing to complain of," he said.

"And the anger?"

"It is doing well, I thank you," he smiled.

"You mean getting better?"

"Making strong roots," he said, laughing.

"Ah, so long as it only makes roots!" she said.

"And your ladyship, how is she?"

"My ladyship is rather better," she replied.

"Much better, indeed," he said, looking into her face.

"Do you mean I *look* much better?" she asked quickly.

"Very much. It is your beauty you think of. Well, your beauty is almost itself again."

"Thanks."

"You brood on your beauty as I on my anger. Ah, your ladyship, be wise, and make friends with your anger. That is the way to let your beauty blossom."

"I was not unfriendly with you, was I?" she said.

"With me?" His face flickered with a laugh. "Am I your anger? Your vicar in wrath? So then, be friends with the angry me, your ladyship. I ask nothing better."

"What is the use," she said, "being friends with the *angry* you? I would much rather be friends with the happy you."

"That little animal is extinct," he laughed. "And I am glad of it."

"But what remains? Only the angry you? Then it is no use my trying to be friends."

"You remember, dear Lady Daphne, that the adder does not suck his poison all alone, and the pole-cat knows where to find his she-pole-cat. You remember that each one has his own dear mate," he laughed. "Dear, deadly mate."

"And what if I do remember those bits of natural history, Count Dionys?"

"The she-adder is dainty, delicate, and carries her poison lightly. The wild-cat has wonderful green eyes that she closes with memory like a screen. The ice-bear hides like a snake with her cubs, and her snarl is the strangest thing in the world."

"Have you ever heard me snarl?" she asked suddenly.

He only laughed, and looked away.

They were silent. And immediately the strange thrill of secrecy was between them. Something had gone beyond sadness into another, secret, thrilling communion which she would never admit.

"What do you do all day here?" she asked.

"Play chess, play this foolish croquet, play billiards, and read, and wait, and remember."

"What do you wait for?"

"I don't know."

"And what do you remember?"

"Ah, that. Shall I tell you what amuses me? Shall I tell you a secret?"

"Please don't, if it's anything that matters."

"It matters to nobody but me. Will you hear it?"

"If it does not implicate me in any way."

"It does not. Well, I am a member of a certain old secret society—no, don't look at me, nothing frightening—only a society like the free-masons."

"And?"

"And—well, as you know, one is initiated into certain so-called secrets and rites. My family has always been initiated. So I am an initiate too. Does it interest you?"

"Why, of course."

"Well. I was always rather thrilled by these secrets. Or some of them. Some seemed to me far-fetched. The ones that thrilled me even never had any relation to actual life. When you knew me in Dresden and Prague, you would not have thought me a man invested with awful secret knowledge, now would you?"

"Never."

"No. It was just a little exciting side-show. And I was a grimacing little society man. But now they become true. It becomes true."

"The secret knowledge?"

"Yes."

"What, for instance?"

"Take actual fire. It will bore you. Do you want to hear?"

"Go on."

"This is what I was taught. The true fire is invisible. Flame, and the red fire we see burning, has its back to us. It is running away from us. Does that mean anything to you?"

"Yes."

"Well then, the yellowness of sunshine—light itself—that is only the glancing aside of the real original fire. You know that is true. There would be no light if there was no refraction, no bits of dust and stuff to turn the dark fire into visibility. You know that's a fact. And that being so, even the sun is dark. It is only his jacket of dust that makes him visible. You know that too. And the true sunbeams coming towards us flow darkly, a moving darkness of the genuine fire. The sun is dark, the sunshine flowing to us is dark. And light is only the inside-turning away of the sun's directness that was coming to us. Does that interest you at all?"

"Yes," she said dubiously.

"Well, we've got the world inside out. The true living world of fire is dark, throbbing, darker than blood. Our luminous world that we go by is only the reverse of this."

"Yes, I like that," she said.

"Well! Now listen. The same with love. This white love that we have is the same. It is only the reverse, the whited sepulchre of the true love. True love is dark, a throbbing together in darkness, like the wild-cat in the night, when the green screen opens and her eyes are on the darkness."

"No, I don't see that," she said in a slow, clanging voice.

"You, and your beauty—that is only the inside-out of you. The real you is the wild-cat invisible in the night, with red fire perhaps coming out of its wide, dark eyes. Your beauty is your whited sepulchre."

"You mean cosmetics," she said. "I've got none on to-day—not even powder."

He laughed.

"Very good," he said. "Consider me. I used to think myself small but handsome, and the ladies used to admire me moderately, never very much. A trim little fellow, you know. Well, that was just the inside-out of me. I am a black tom-cat howling in the night, and it is then that fire comes out of me. This me you look at is my whited sepulchre. What do you say?"

She was looking into his eyes. She could see the darkness swaying in the depths. She perceived the invisible, cat-like fire stirring deep inside them, felt it coming towards her. She turned her face aside. Then he laughed, showing his strong white teeth, that seemed a little too large, rather dreadful.

She rose to go.

"Well," she said. "I shall have the summer in which to think about the world inside-out. Do write if there is anything to say. Write to Thoresway. Good-bye!"

"Ah, your eyes!" he said. "They are like jewels of stone."

Being away from the Count, she put him out of her mind. Only she was sorry for him a prisoner in that sickening Voynich Hall. But she did not write. Nor did he.

As a matter of fact, her mind was now much more occupied with her husband. All arrangements were being made to effect his exchange. From month to month she looked for his return. And so she thought of him.

Whatever happened to her, she thought about it, thought and thought a great deal. The consciousness of her mind was like tablets of stone weighing her down. And whoever would make a new entry into her must break these tablets of stone piece by piece. So it was that in her own way she thought often enough of the Count's world inside-out. A curious latency stirred in her consciousness that was not yet an idea.

He said her eyes were like jewels of stone. What a horrid thing to say! What did he want her eyes to be like? He wanted them to dilate and become all black pupil, like a cat's at night. She shrank convulsively from the thought, and tightened her breast.

He said her beauty was her whited sepulchre. Even that, she knew what he meant. The invisibility of her he wanted to love. But ah, her pearl-like beauty was so dear to her, and it was so famous in the world.

He said her white love was like moonshine, harmful, the reverse of love. He meant Basil, of course. Basil always said she was the moon. But then Basil loved her for that. The ecstasy of it! She shivered, thinking of her husband. But it had also made her nerve-worn, her husband's love. Ah, nerve-worn.

What then would the Count's love be like? Something so

secret and different. She would not be lovely and a queen to him. He hated her loveliness. The wild-cat has its mate. The little wild-cat that he was. Ah!

She caught her breath, determined not to think. When she thought of Count Dionys she felt the world slipping away from her. She would sit in front of a mirror, looking at her wonderful cared-for face that had appeared in so many society magazines. She loved it so, it made her feel so vain. And she looked at her blue-green eyes—the eyes of the wild-cat on a bough. Yes, the lovely blue-green iris drawn tight like a screen. Supposing it should relax. Supposing it should unfold, and open out the dark depths, the dark, dilated pupil! Supposing it should?

Never! She always caught herself back. She felt she might be killed before she could give way to that relaxation that the Count wanted of her. She could not. She just could not. At the very thought of it some hypersensitive nerve started with a great twinge in her breast; she drew back, forced to keep her guard. Ah no, Monsieur le Comte, you shall never take her ladyship off her guard.

She disliked the thought of the Count. An impudent little fellow. An impertinent little fellow! A little madman, really. A little outsider. No, no. She would think of her husband: an adorable, tall, well-bred Englishman, so easy and simple, and with the amused look in his blue eyes. She thought of the cultured, casual trail of his voice. It set her nerves on fire. She thought of his strong, easy body—beautiful, white-fleshed, with the fine springing of warm-brown hair like tiny flames. He was the Dionysos, full of sap, milk and honey, and northern golden wine: he, her husband. Not that little unreal Count. Ah, she dreamed of her husband, of the love-days, and the honeymoon, the lovely, simple intimacy. Ah, the marvellous revelation of that intimacy, when he left himself to her so generously. Ah, she was his wife for this reason, that he had given himself to her so greatly, so generously. Like an ear of corn he was there for her gathering—her husband, her own, lovely, English husband. Ah, when would he come again, when would he come again!

She had letters from him—and how he loved her. Far away, his life was all hers. All hers, flowing to her as the beam flows from a white star right down to us, to our heart. Her lover, her husband.

He was now expecting to come home soon. It had all been
arranged. "I hope you won't be disappointed in me when I
do get back," he wrote. "I am afraid I am no longer the plump
and well-looking young man I was. I've got a big scar at the
side of my mouth, and I'm as thin as a starved rabbit, and my
hair's going grey. Doesn't sound attractive, does it? And it
isn't attractive. But once I can get out of this infernal place,
and once I can be with you again, I shall come in for my
second blooming. The very thought of being quietly in the
same house with you, quiet and in peace, makes me realise
that if I've been through hell, I have known heaven on earth
and can hope to know it again. I am a miserable brute to look
at now. But I have faith in you. You will forgive my appearance, and that alone will make me feel handsome."

She read this letter many times. She was not afraid of his
scar or his looks. She would love him all the more.

Since she had started making shirts—those two for the Count
had been an enormous labour, even though her maid had come
to her assistance forty times: but since she had started making
shirts, she thought she might continue. She had some good
suitable silk: her husband liked silk underwear.

But still she used the Count's thimble. It was gold outside
and silver inside, and was too heavy. A snake was coiled
round the base, and at the top, for pressing the needle, was
inlet a semi-translucent apple-green stone, perhaps jade, carved
like a scarab, with little dots. It was too heavy. But then she
sewed so slowly. And she liked to feel her hand heavy,
weighted. And as she sewed she thought about her husband,
and she felt herself in love with him. She thought of him, how
beautiful he was, and how she would love him now he was
thin: she would love him all the more. She would love to
trace his bones, as if to trace his living skeleton. The thought
made her rest her hands in her lap, and drift into a muse. Then
she felt the weight of the thimble on her finger, and took it off,
and sat looking at the green stone. The ladybird. The ladybird. And if only her husband would come soon, soon. It was
wanting him that made her so ill. Nothing but that. She had
wanted him so badly. She wanted now. Ah, if she could go
to him now, and find him, wherever he was, and see him and
touch him and take all his love.

As she mused, she put the thimble down in front of her,
took up a little silver pencil from her work-basket, and on a

bit of blue paper that had been the band of a small skein of silk she wrote the lines of the silly little song:

"Wenn ich ein Vöglein wär'
Und auch zwei Flüglein hätt'
Flög' ich zu dir——"

That was all she could get on her bit of pale-blue paper.

"If I were a little bird
And had two little wings
I'd fly to thee——"

Silly enough, in all conscience. But she did not translate it, so it did not seem quite so silly.

At that moment her maid announced Lady Bingham—her husband's sister. Daphne crumpled up the bit of paper in a flurry, and in another minute Primrose, his sister, came in. The newcomer was not a bit like a primrose, being long-faced and clever, smart, but not a bit elegant, in her new clothes.

"Daphne dear, what a domestic scene! I suppose it's rehearsal. Well, you may as well rehearse, he's with Admiral Burns on the *Ariadne*. Father just heard from the Admiralty: quite fit. He'll be here in a day or two. Splendid, isn't it? And the war is going to end. At least it seems like it. You'll be safe of your man now, dear. Thank heaven when it's all over. What are you sewing?"

"A shirt," said Daphne.

"A shirt! Why, how clever of you. I should never know which end to begin. Who showed you?"

"Millicent."

"And how did *she* know? She's no business to know how to sew shirts: nor cushions nor sheets either. Do let me look. Why, how perfectly marvellous you are!—every bit by hand too. Basil isn't worth it, dear, really he isn't. Let him order his shirts in Oxford Street. Your business is to be beautiful, not to sew shirts. What a dear little pin-poppet, or rather needle-woman! I say, a satire on us, that is. But what a darling, with mother-of-pearl wings to her skirts! And darling little gold-eyed needles inside her. You screw her head off, and you find she's full of pins and needles. Woman for you! Mother says won't you come to lunch to-morrow. And won't you come to Brassey's to tea with me at this minute. Do, there's a dear. I've got a taxi."

Daphne bundled her sewing loosely together.

When she tried to do a bit more, two days later, she could not find her thimble. She asked her maid, whom she could absolutely trust. The girl had not seen it. She searched everywhere. She asked her nurse—who was now her housekeeper—and footman. No, nobody had seen it. Daphne even asked her sister-in-law.

"Thimble, darling? No, I don't remember a thimble. I remember a dear little needle-lady, whom I thought such a precious satire on us women. I didn't notice a thimble."

Poor Daphne wandered about in a muse. She did not want to believe it lost. It had been like a talisman to her. She tried to forget it. Her husband was coming, quite soon, quite soon. But she could not raise herself to joy. She had lost her thimble. It was as if Count Dionys accused her in her sleep of something, she did not quite know what.

And though she did not really want to go to Voynich Hall, yet like a fatality she went, like one doomed. It was already late autumn, and some lovely days. This was the last of the lovely days. She was told that Count Dionys was in the small park, finding chestnuts. She went to look for him. Yes, there he was in his blue uniform stooping over the brilliant yellow leaves of the sweet chestnut tree, that lay around him like a fallen nimbus of glowing yellow, under his feet, as he kicked and rustled, looking for the chestnut burrs. And with his short, brown hands he was pulling out the small chestnuts and putting them in his pockets. But as she approached he peeled a nut to eat it. His teeth were white and powerful.

"You remind me of a squirrel laying in a winter store," said she.

"Ah, Lady Daphne—I was thinking, and did not hear you."

"I thought you were gathering chestnuts—even eating them."

"Also!" he laughed. He had a dark, sudden charm when he laughed, showing his rather large white teeth. She was not quite sure whether she found him a little repulsive.

"Were you *really* thinking?" she said, in her slow, resonant way.

"Very truly."

"And weren't you enjoying the chestnut a bit?"

"Very much. Like sweet milk. Excellent, excellent." He had the fragments of the nut between his teeth, and bit them finely. "Will you take one too." He held out the little, pointed brown nuts on the palm of his hand.

She looked at them doubtfully.

"Are they as tough as they always were?" she said.

"No, they are fresh and good. Wait, I will peel one for you."

They strayed about through the thin clump of trees.

"You have had a pleasant summer; you are strong?"

"Almost *quite* strong," said she. "Lovely summer, thanks. I suppose it's no good asking you if you have been happy?"

"Happy?" He looked at her direct. His eyes were black, and seemed to examine her. She always felt he had a little contempt of her. "Oh yes," he said, smiling. "I have been very happy."

"So glad."

They drifted a little farther, and he picked up an apple-green chestnut burr out of the yellow-brown leaves, handling it with sensitive fingers that still suggested paws to her.

"How did you succeed in being happy?" she said.

"How shall I tell you? I felt that the same power which put up the mountains could pull them down again—no matter how long it took."

"And was that all?"

"Was it not enough?"

"I should say decidedly too little."

He laughed broadly, showing the strong, negroid teeth.

"You do not know all it means," he said.

"The thought that the mountains were going to be pulled down?" she said. "It will be so long after my day."

"Ah, you are bored," he said. "But I—I found the God who pulls things down: especially the things that men have put up. Do they not say that life is a search after God, Lady Daphne? I have found my God."

"The god of destruction," she said, blanching.

"Yes—not the devil of destruction, but the god of destruction. The blessed god of destruction. It is strange"—he stood before her, looking up at her—"but I have found my God. The god of anger, who throws down the steeples and the factory chimneys. Ah, Lady Daphne, he is a man's God, he is a man's God. I have found my God, Lady Daphne."

"Apparently. And how are you going to serve him?"

A naïve glow transfigured his face.

"Oh, I will help. With my heart I will help while I can do nothing with my hands. I say to my heart: Beat, hammer, beat with little strokes. Beat, hammer of God, beat them down. Beat it all down."

Her brows knitted, her face took on a look of discontent.

"Beat what down?" she asked harshly.

"The world, the world of man. Not the trees—these chestnuts, for example"—he looked up at them, at the tufts and loose pinions of yellow—"not these—nor the chattering sorcerers, the squirrels—nor the hawk that comes. Not those."

"You mean beat England?" she said.

"Ah, no. Ah, no. Not England any more than Germany—perhaps not as much. Not Europe any more than Asia."

"Just the end of the world?"

"No, no. No, no. What grudge have I against a world where little chestnuts are so sweet as these! Do you like yours? Will you take another?"

"No, thanks."

"What grudge have I against a world where even the hedges are full of berries, bunches of black berries that hang down, and red berries that thrust up. Never would I hate the world. But the world of man. Lady Daphne"—his voice sank to a whisper—"*I hate it.* Zzz!" he hissed. "Strike, little heart! Strike, strike, hit, smite! Oh, Lady Daphne!"—his eyes dilated with a ring of fire.

"What?" she said, scared.

"I believe in the power of my red, dark heart. God has put the hammer in my breast—the little eternal hammer. Hit—hit—hit! It hits on the world of man. It hits, it hits! And it hears the thin sound of cracking. The thin sound of cracking. Hark!"

He stood still and made her listen. It was late afternoon. The strange laugh of his face made the air seem dark to her. And she could easily have believed that she heard a faint, fine shivering, cracking, through the air, a delicate crackling noise.

"You hear it? Yes? Oh, may I live long! May I live long, so that my hammer may strike and strike, and the cracks go deeper, deeper! Ah, the world of man! Ah, the joy, the passion in every heart-beat! Strike home, strike true, strike sure. Strike to destroy it. Strike! Strike! To destroy the world of man. Ah, God. Ah, God, prisoner of peace. Do I not know you, Lady Daphne? Do I not? Do I not?"

She was silent for some moments, looking away at the twinkling lights of a station beyond.

"Not the white plucked lily of your body. I have gathered no flower for my ostentatious life. But in the cold dark, your lily root, Lady Daphne. Ah, yes, you will know it all your life, that I know where your root lies buried, with its sad, sad quick of life. What does it matter!"

They had walked slowly towards the house. She was silent. Then at last she said, in a peculiar voice:

"And you would never want to kiss me?"

"Ah, no!" he answered sharply.

She held out her hand.

"Good-bye, Count Dionys," she drawled, fashionably. He bowed over her hand, but did not kiss it.

"Good-bye, Lady Daphne."

She went away, with her brow set hard. And henceforth she thought only of her husband, of Basil. She made the Count die out of her. Basil was coming, he was near. He was coming back from the East, from war and death. Ah, he had been through awful fire of experience. He would be something new, something she did not know. He was something new, a stronger lover who had been through terrible fire, and had come out strange and new, like a god. Ah, new and terrible his love would be, pure and intensified by the awful fire of suffering. A new lover—a new bridegroom—a new, supernatural wedding-night. She shivered in anticipation, waiting for her husband. She hardly noticed the wild excitement of the Armistice. She was waiting for something more wonderful to her.

And yet the moment she heard his voice on the telephone, her heart contracted with fear. It was his well-known voice, deliberate, diffident, almost drawling, with the same subtle suggestion of deference, and the rather exaggerated Cambridge intonation, up and down. But there was a difference, a new icy note that went through her veins like death.

"Is that you, Daphne? I shall be with you in half an hour. Is that all right for you? Yes, I've just landed, and shall come straight to you. Yes, a taxi. Shall I be too sudden for you, darling? No? Good, oh, good! Half an hour, then! I say, Daphne? There won't be anyone else there, will there? Quite alone! Good! I can ring up Dad afterwards. Yes, splendid, splendid. Sure you're all right, my darling? I'm at death's door till I see you. Yes. Good-bye—half an hour. Good-bye."

When Daphne had hung up the receiver she sat down almost in a faint. What was it that so frightened her? His terrible, terrible altered voice, like cold, blue steel. She had no time to think. She rang for her maid.

"Oh, my lady, it isn't bad news?" cried Millicent, when she caught sight of her mistress white as death.

"No, good news. Major Apsley will be here in half an hour. Help me to dress. Ring to Murry's first to send in some roses, red ones, and some lilac-coloured iris—two dozen of each, at once."

Daphne went to her room. She didn't know what to wear, she didn't know how she wanted her hair dressed. She spoke hastily to her maid. She chose a violet-coloured dress. She did not know what she was doing. In the middle of dressing the flowers came, and she left off to put them in the bowls. So that when she heard his voice in the hall, she was still standing in front of the mirror reddening her lips and wiping it away again.

"Major Apsley, my lady!" murmured the maid, in excitement.

"Yes, I can hear. Go and tell him I shall be *one* minute."

Daphne's voice had become slow and sonorous, like bronze, as it always did when she was upset. Her face looked almost haggard, and in vain she dabbed with the rouge.

"How does he look?" she asked curtly, when her maid came back.

"A long scar here," said the maid, and she drew her finger from the left-hand corner of her mouth into her cheek, slanting downwards.

"Make him look very different?" asked Daphne.

"Not so *very* different, my lady," said Millicent gently. "His eyes are the same, I think." The girl also was distressed.

"All right," said Daphne. She looked at herself a long, last look as she turned away from the mirror. The sight of her own face made her feel almost sick. She had seen so much of herself. And yet even now she was fascinated by the heavy droop of her lilac-veined lids over her slow, strange, large, green-blue eyes. They *were* mysterious-looking. And she gave herself a long, sideways glance, curious and Chinese.

How was it possible there was a touch of the Chinese in her face?—she so purely an English blonde, an Aphrodite of the foam, as Basil had called her in poetry. Ah well! She left off her thoughts and went through the hall to the drawing-room.

He was standing nervously in the middle of the room in his uniform. She hardly glanced at his face—and saw only the scar.

"Hullo, Daphne," he said, in a voice full of the expected emotion. He stepped forward and took her in his arms, and kissed her forehead.

"So glad! So glad it's happened at last," she said, hiding her tears.

"So glad what has happened, darling?" he asked, in his deliberate manner.

"That you're back." Her voice had the bronze resonance, she spoke rather fast.

"Yes, I'm back, Daphne darling—as much of me as there is to bring back."

"Why?" she said. "You've come back whole, surely?" She was frightened.

"Yes, apparently I have. Apparently. But don't let's talk of that. Let's talk of you, darling. How are you? Let me look at you. You are thinner, you are older. But you are more wonderful than ever. Far more wonderful."

"How?" said she.

"I can't exactly say how. You were only a girl. Now you are a woman. I suppose it's all that's happened. But you are wonderful as a woman, Daphne darling—more wonderful than all that's happened. I couldn't have believed you'd be so wonderful. I'd forgotten—or else I'd never known. I say, I'm a lucky chap really. Here I am, alive and well, and I've got you for a wife. It's brought you out like a flower. I say, darling, there is more now than Venus of the foam—grander. How beautiful you are! But you look like the beauty of all life—as if you were moon-mother of the world—Aphrodite. God is good to me after all, darling. I ought never to utter a single complaint. How lovely you are—how lovely you are, my darling! I'd forgotten you—and I thought I knew you so well. Is it true that you belong to me? Are you really mine?"

They were seated on the yellow sofa. He was holding her hand, and his eyes were going up and down, from her face to her throat and her breast. The sound of his words, and the strong, cold desire in his voice excited her, pleased her, and made her heart freeze. She turned and looked into his light blue eyes. They had no longer the amused light, nor the young look. They burned with a hard, focused light, whitish.

"It's all right. You are mine, aren't you, Daphne darling?" came his cultured, musical voice, that had always the well-bred twang of diffidence.

She looked back into his eyes.

"Yes, I am yours," she said, from the lips.

"Darling! Darling!" he murmured, kissing her hand.

Her heart beat suddenly so terribly, as if her breast would be ruptured, and she rose in one movement and went across the room. She leaned her hand on the mantelpiece and looked down at the electric fire. She could hear the faint, faint noise of it. There was silence for a few moments.

Then she turned and looked at him. He was watching her intently. His face was gaunt, and there was a curious deathly sub-pallor, though his cheeks were not white. The scar ran livid from the side of his mouth. It was not so very big. But it seemed like a scar in him himself, in his brain, as it were. In his eyes was that hard, white, focused light that fascinated her and was terrible to her. He was different. He was like death; like risen death. She felt she dared not touch him. White death was still upon him. She could tell that he shrank with a kind of agony from contact. "Touch me not, I am not yet ascended unto the Father." Yet for contact he had come. Something, someone seemed to be looking over his shoulder. His own young ghost looking over his shoulder. Oh, God! She closed her eyes, seeming to swoon. He remained leaning forward on the sofa, watching her.

"Aren't you well, darling?" he asked. There was a strange, incomprehensible coldness in his very fire. He did not move to come near her.

"Yes, I'm well. It is only that after all it is so sudden. Let me get used to you," she said, turning aside her face from him. She felt utterly like a victim of his white, awful face.

"I suppose I must be a bit of a shock to you," he said. "I hope you won't leave off loving me. It won't be that, will it?"

The strange coldness in his voice! And yet the white, un-canny fire.

"No, I shan't leave off loving you," she admitted, in a low

tone, as if almost ashamed. She *dared* not have said otherwise. And the saying it made it true.

"Ah, if you're sure of that," he said. "I'm a pretty unlovely sight to behold, I know, with this wound-scar. But if you can forgive it me, darling. Do you think you can?" There was something like compulsion in his tone.

She looked at him, and shivered slightly.

"I love you—more than before," she said hurriedly.

"Even the scar?" came his terrible voice, inquiring.

She glanced again, with that slow, Chinese side-look, and felt she would die.

"Yes," she said, looking away at nothingness. It was an awful moment to her. A little, slightly imbecile smile widened on his face.

He suddenly knelt at her feet, and kissed the toe of her slipper, and kissed the instep, and kissed the ankle in the thin, black stocking.

"I knew," he said in a muffled voice. "I knew you would make good. I knew if I had to kneel, it was before you. I knew you were divine, you were the one—Cybele—Isis. I knew I was your slave. I knew. It has all been just a long initiation. I had to learn how to worship you."

He kissed her feet again and again, without the slightest self-consciousness, or the slightest misgiving. Then he went back to the sofa, and sat there looking at her, saying:

"It isn't love, it is worship. Love between me and you will be a sacrament, Daphne. That's what I had to learn. You are beyond me. A mystery to me. My God, how great it all is. How marvellous!"

She stood with her hand on the mantelpiece, looking down and not answering. She was frightened—almost horrified: but she was thrilled deep down to her soul. She really felt she could glow white and fill the universe like the moon, like Astarte, like Isis, like Venus. The grandeur of her own pale power. The man religiously worshipped her, not merely amorously. She was ready for him—for the sacrament of his supreme worship.

He sat on the sofa with his hands spread on the yellow brocade and pushing downwards behind him, down between the deep upholstery of the back and the seat. He had long, white hands with pale freckles. And his fingers touched something. With his long white fingers he groped and brought it out. It was the lost thimble. And inside it was the bit of screwed-up blue paper.

"I say, is that *your* thimble?" he asked.

She started, and went hurriedly forward for it.

"Where was it?" she said, agitated.

But he did not give it to her. He turned it round and pulled out the bit of blue paper. He saw the faint pencil marks on the screwed-up ball, and unrolled the band of paper, and slowly deciphered the verse.

> *"Wenn ich ein Vöglein wär'*
> *Und auch zwei Flüglein hätt'*
> *Flög' ich zu dir——"*

"How awfully touching that is," he said. "A *Vöglein* with two little *Flüglein*! But what a precious darling child you are! Whom did you want to fly to, if you were a *Vöglein*?" He looked up at her with a curious smile.

"I can't remember," she said, turning aside her head.

"I hope it was to me," he said. "Anyhow, I shall consider it was, and shall love you all the more for it. What a darling child! A *Vöglein* if you please, with two little wings! Why, how beautifully absurd of you, darling!"

He folded the scrap of paper carefully, and put it in his pocket-book, keeping the thimble all the time between his knees.

"Tell me when you lost it, Daphne," he said, examining the bauble.

"About a month ago—or two months."

"About a month ago—or two months. And what were you sewing? Do you mind if I ask? I like to think of you then. I was still in that beastly El Hasrun. What were you sewing, darling, two months ago, when you lost your thimble?"

"A shirt."

"I say, a shirt! Whose shirt?"

"Yours."

"There. Now we've run it to earth. Were you really sewing a shirt for me! Is it finished? Can I put it on at this minute?"

"That one isn't finished, but the first one is."

"I say, darling, let me go and put it on. To think I should have it next my skin! I shall feel you all round me, all over me. I say how marvellous that will be! Won't you come?"

"Won't you give me the thimble?" she said.

"Yes, of course. What a noble thimble too! Who gave it you?"

"Count Dionys Psanek."

"Who was he?"

"A Bohemian Count, in Dresden. He once stayed with us in Thoresway—with a tall wife. Didn't you meet them?"

"I don't think I did. I don't think I did. I don't remember. What was he like?"

"A little man with black hair and a rather low, dark forehead—rather dressy."

"No, I don't remember him at all. So he gave it you. Well, I wonder where he is now? Probably rotted, poor devil."

"No, he's interned in Voynich Hall. Mother and I have been to see him several times. He was awfully badly wounded."

"Poor little beggar! In Voynich Hall! I'll look at him before he goes. Odd thing, to give you a thimble. Odd gift! You were a girl then, though. Do you think he had it made, or do you think he found it in a shop?"

"I think it belonged to the family. The ladybird at the top is part of their crest—and the snake as well, I think."

"A ladybird! Funny thing for a crest. Americans would call it a bug. I must look at him before he goes. And you were sewing a shirt for me! And then you posted me this little letter into the sofa. Well, I'm awfully glad I received it, and that it didn't go astray in the post, like so many things. 'Wenn ich ein Vöglein wär' '—you perfect child! But that is the beauty of a woman like you: you are so superb and beyond worship, and then such an exquisite naïve child. Who could help worshipping you and loving you: immortal and mortal together. What, you want the thimble? Here! Wonderful, wonderful white fingers. Ah, darling, you are more goddess than child, you long, limber Isis with sacred hands. White, white, and immortal! Don't tell me your hands could die, darling: your wonderful Proserpine fingers. They are immortal as February and snowdrops. If you lift your hands the spring comes. I can't help kneeling before you, darling. I am no more than a sacrifice to you, an offering. I wish I could die in giving myself to you, give you all my blood on your altar, for ever."

She looked at him with a long, slow look, as he turned his face to her. His face was white with ecstasy. And she was not afraid. Somewhere, saturnine, she knew it was absurd. But she chose not to know. A certain swoon-sleep was on her. With her slow, green-blue eyes she looked down on his ecstasised face, almost benign. But in her right hand unconsciously she held the thimble fast, she only gave him her left hand. He took her hand and rose to his feet in that curious priestly ecstasy which made him more than a man or a soldier, far, far more than a lover to her.

Nevertheless, his home-coming made her begin to be ill again. Afterwards, after his love, she had to bear herself in torment. To her shame and her heaviness, she knew she was not strong enough, or pure enough, to bear this awful outpouring adoration-lust. It was not her fault she felt weak and fretful afterwards, as if she wanted to cry and be fretful and petulant, wanted someone to save her. She could not turn to Basil, her husband. After his ecstasy of adoration-lust for her, she recoiled from him. Alas, she was not the goddess, the superb person he named her. She was flawed with the fatal humility of her age. She could not harden her heart and burn her soul pure of this humility, this misgiving. She could not finally believe in her own woman-godhead—only in her own female mortality.

That fierce power of being alone, even with your lover, the fierce power of the woman *in excelsis*—alas, she could not keep it. She could rise to the height for the time, the incandescent, transcendent, moon-fierce womanhood. But alas, she could not stay intensified and resplendent in her white, womanly powers, her female mystery. She relaxed, she lost her glory, and became fretful. Fretful and ill and never to be soothed. And then naturally her man became ashy and somewhat acrid, while she ached with nerves, and could not eat.

Of course she began to dream about Count Dionys: to yearn wistfully for him. And it was absolutely a fatal thought to her that he was going away. When she thought that—that he was leaving England soon—going away into the dark for ever—then the last spark seemed to die in her. She felt her soul perish, whilst she herself was worn and soulless like a prostitute. A prostitute goddess. And her husband, the gaunt, white, intensified priest of her, who never ceased from being before her like a lust.

"To-morrow," she said to him, gathering her last courage

and looking at him with a side look, "I want to go to Voynich Hall."

"What, to see Count Psanek? Oh, good! Yes, very good! I'll come along as well. I should like very much to see him. I suppose he'll be getting sent back before long."

It was a fortnight before Christmas, very dark weather. Her husband was in khaki. She wore her black furs and a black lace veil over her face, so that she seemed mysterious. But she lifted the veil and looped it behind, so that it made a frame for her face. She looked very lovely like that—her face pure like the most white hellebore flower, touched with winter pink, amid the blackness of her drapery and furs. Only she was rather too much like the picture of a modern beauty: too much the actual thing. She had half an idea that Dionys would hate her for her effective loveliness. He would see it and hate it. The thought was like a bitter balm to her. For herself, she loved her loveliness almost with obsession.

The Count came cautiously forward, glancing from the lovely figure of Lady Daphne to the gaunt well-bred Major at her side. Daphne was so beautiful in her dark furs, the black lace of her veil thrown back over her close-fitting, dull-gold-threaded hat, and her face fair like a winter flower in a cranny of darkness. But on her face, that was smiling with a slow self-satisfaction of beauty and of knowledge that she was dangling the two men, and setting all the imprisoned officers wildly on the alert, the Count could read that acridity of dissatisfaction and of inefficiency. And he looked away to the livid scar on the Major's cheek.

"Count Dionys, I wanted to bring my husband to see you. May I introduce him to you? Major Apsley—Count Dionys Psanek."

The two men shook hands rather stiffly.

"I can sympathise with you being fastened up in this place," said Basil in his slow, easy fashion. "I hated it, I assure you, out there in the East."

"But your conditions were much worse than mine," smiled the Count.

"Well, perhaps they were. But prison is prison, even if it were heaven itself."

"Lady Apsley has been the one angel of my heaven," smiled the Count.

"I'm afraid I was as inefficient as most angels," said she.

The small smile never left the Count's dark face. It was true as she said, he was low-browed, the black hair growing low on his brow, and his eyebrows making a thick bow above his dark eyes, which had again long black lashes. So that the upper part of his face seemed very dusky-black. His nose was small and somewhat translucent. There was a touch of mockery about him, which was intensified even by his small, energetic stature. He was still carefully dressed in the dark-blue uniform, whose shabbiness could not hinder the dark flame of life which seemed to glow through the cloth from his body. He was not thin—but still had a curious swarthy translucency of skin in his low-browed face.

"What would you have been more?" he laughed, making equivocal dark eyes at her.

"Oh, of course, a delivering angel—a cinema heroine," she replied, closing her eyes and turning her face aside.

All the while the white-faced, tall Major watched the little man with a fixed, half-smiling scrutiny. The Count seemed to notice. He turned to the Englishman.

"I am glad that I can congratulate you, Major Apsley, on your safe and happy return to your home."

"Thanks. I hope I may be able to congratulate you in the same way before long."

"Oh yes," said the Count. "Before long I shall be shipped back."

"Have you any news of your family?" interrupted Daphne.

"No news," he replied briefly, with sudden gravity.

"It seems you'll find a fairish mess out in Austria," said Basil.

"Yes, probably. It is what we had to expect," replied the Count.

"Well, I don't know. Sometimes things do turn out for the best. I feel that's as good as true in my case," said the Major.

"Things have turned out for the best?" said the Count, with an intonation of polite enquiry.

"Yes. Just for me personally, I mean—to put it quite selfishly. After all, what we've learned is that a man can only speak for himself. And I feel it's been dreadful, but it's not been lost. It was like an ordeal one had to go through," said Basil.

"You mean the war?"

"The war and everything that went with it."

"And when you've been through the ordeal?" politely enquired the Count.

"Why, you arrive at a higher state of consciousness, and therefore of life. And so, of course, at a higher plane of love. A surprisingly higher plane of love, that you had never suspected the existence of before."

The Count looked from Basil to Daphne, who was posing her head a little self-consciously.

"Then indeed the war has been a valuable thing," he said.

"Exactly!" cried Basil. "I am another man."

"And Lady Apsley?" queried the Count.

"Oh"—her husband faced round to her—"she is *absolutely* another woman—and *much* more wonderful, more marvellous."

The Count smiled and bowed slightly.

"When we knew her ten years ago, we should have said then that it was impossible," said he, "for her to be more wonderful."

"Oh, quite!" returned the husband. "It always seems impossible. And the impossible is always happening. As a matter of fact, I think the war has opened another circle of life to us—a wider ring."

"It may be so," said the Count.

"You don't feel it so yourself?" The Major looked with his keen, white attention into the dark, low-browed face of the other man. The Count looked smiling at Daphne.

"I am only a prisoner still, Major, therefore I feel my ring quite small."

"Yes, of course you do. Of course. Well, I do hope you won't be a prisoner much longer. You must be dying to get back into your own country."

"Yes, I shall be glad to be free. Also," he smiled. "I shall miss my prison and my visits from the angels."

Even Daphne could not be sure he was mocking her. It was evident the visit was unpleasant to him. She could see he did not like Basil. Nay, more, she could feel that the presence of her tall, gaunt, idealistic husband was hateful to the little swarthy man. But he passed it all off in smiles and polite speeches.

On the other hand, Basil was as if fascinated by the Count. He watched him absorbedly all the time, quite forgetting

Daphne. She knew this. She knew that she was quite gone out of her husband's consciousness, like a lamp that has been carried away into another room. There he stood completely in the dark, as far as she was concerned, and all his attention focused on the other man. On his pale, gaunt face was a fixed smile of amused attention.

"But don't you get awfully bored," he said, "between the visits?"

The Count looked up with an affectation of frankness.

"No, I do not," he said. "I can brood, you see, on the things that come to pass."

"I think that's where the harm comes in," replied the Major. "One sits and broods, and is cut off from everything, and one loses one's contact with reality. That's the effect it had on me, being a prisoner."

"Contact with reality—what is that?"

"Well—contact with anybody, really—or anything."

"Why must one have contact?"

"Well, because one must," said Basil.

The Count smiled slowly.

"But I can sit and watch fate flowing, like black water, deep down in my own soul," he said. "I feel that there, in the dark of my own soul, things are happening."

"That may be. But whatever happens, it is only one thing, really. It is a contact between your own soul and the soul of one other being, or of many other beings. Nothing else can happen to man. That's how I figured it out for myself. I may be wrong. But that's how I figured it out when I was wounded and a prisoner."

The Count's face had gone dark and serious.

"But is this contact an aim in itself?" he asked.

"Well"—said the Major—he had taken his degree in philosophy—"it seems to me it is. It results inevitably in some form of activity. But the cause and the origin and the life-impetus of all action, activity, whether constructive or destructive, seems to me to be in the dynamic contact between human beings. You bring to pass a certain dynamic contact between men, and you get war. Another sort of dynamic contact, and you get them all building a cathedral, as they did in the Middle Ages."

"But was not the war, or the cathedral, the real aim, and the emotional contact just the means?" said the Count.

"I don't think so," said the Major, his curious white passion beginning to glow through his face. The three were seated in a little card-room, left alone by courtesy by the other men. Daphne was still draped in her dark, too-becoming drapery. But alas, she sat now ignored by both men. She might just as well have been an ugly little nobody, for all the notice that was taken of her. She sat in the window-seat of the dreary small room with a look of discontent on her exotic, rare face, that was like a delicate white and pink hot-house flower. From time to time she glanced with long, slow looks from man to man: from her husband, whose pallid, intense, white glowing face was pressed forward across the table to the Count, who sat back in his chair, as if in opposition, and whose dark face seemed clubbed together in a dark, unwilling stare. Her husband was *quite* unaware of anything but his own white identity. But the Count still had a grain of secondary consciousness which hovered round and remained aware of the woman in the window-seat. The whole of his face, and his forward-looking attention was concentrated on Basil. But somewhere at the back of him he kept track of Daphne. She sat uneasy, in discontent, as women always do sit when men are locked together in a combustion of words. At the same time, she followed the argument. It was curious that, while her sympathy at this moment was with the Count, it was her husband whose words she believed to be true. The contact, the emotional contact was the real thing, the so-called 'aim' was only a by-product. Even wars and cathedrals, in her mind, were only by-products. The real thing was what the warriors and cathedral-builders had had in common, as a great uniting feeling: the thing they felt for one another, and for their women in particular, of course.

"There are a great many kinds of contact, nevertheless," said Dionys.

"Well, do you know," said the Major, "it seems to me there is really only one supreme contact, the contact of love. Mind you, the love may take on an infinite variety of forms. And in my opinion, no form of love is wrong, so long as it *is* love, and you yourself *honour* what you are doing. Love has an extraordinary variety of forms! And that is all that there is in life, it seems to me. But I grant you, if you deny the *variety* of love you deny love altogether. If you try to specialise love into one set of accepted feelings, you wound the very soul of love. Love *must* be multiform, else it is just tyranny, just death."

"But why call it all *love?*" said the Count.

"Because it seems to me it *is* love: the great power that draws human beings together, no matter what the result of the contact may be. Of course there is hate, but hate is only the recoil of love."

"Do you think the old Egypt was established on love?" asked Dionys.

"Why, of course! And perhaps the most multiform, the most comprehensive love that the world has seen. All that we suffer from now is that our way of love is narrow, exclusive, and therefore not love at all; more like death and tyranny."

The Count slowly shook his head, smiling slowly and as if sadly.

"No," he said. "No. It is no good. You must use another word than love."

"I don't agree at all," said Basil.

"What word then?" blurted Daphne.

The Count looked at her.

"Obedience, submission, faith, belief, responsibility, power," he said slowly, picking out the words slowly, as if searching for what he wanted, and never quite finding it. He looked with his quiet dark eyes into her eyes. It was curious, she disliked his words intensely, but she liked him. On the other hand, she believed absolutely what her husband said, yet her physical sympathy was against him.

"Do you agree, Daphne?" asked Basil.

"Not a bit," she replied, with a heavy look at her husband.

"Nor I," said Basil. "It seems to me, if you love, there is no obedience nor submission, except to the soul of love. If you mean obedience, submission, and all the rest, to the soul of love itself, I quite agree. But if you mean obedience, submission of one person to another, and one man having power over others—I don't agree, and never shall. It seems to me just there where we have gone wrong. Kaiser Wilhelm II wanted power——"

"No, no," said the Count. "He was a mountebank. He had no conception of the sacredness of power."

"He proved himself very dangerous."

"Oh yes. But peace can be even more dangerous still."

"Tell me, then. Do you believe that you, as an aristocrat,

should have feudal power over a few hundreds of other men, who happen to be born serfs, or not aristocrats?"

"Not as a hereditary aristocrat, but as a *man* who is by nature an aristocrat," said the Count, "it is my sacred duty to hold the lives of other men in my hands, and to shape the issue. But I can never fulfil my destiny till men will willingly put their lives in my hands."

"You don't expect them to, do you?" smiled Basil.

"At this moment, no."

"Or at any moment!" The Major was sarcastic.

"At a certain moment the men who are really living will come beseeching to put their lives into the hands of the greater men among them, beseeching the greater men to take the sacred responsibility of power."

"Do you think so? Perhaps you mean men will at last begin to choose leaders whom they will *love*," said Basil. "I wish they would."

"No, I mean that they will at last yield themselves before men who are greater than they: become vassals by choice."

"Vassals!" exclaimed Basil, smiling. "You are still in the feudal ages, Count."

"Vassals. Not to any hereditary aristocrat—Hohenzollern or Hapsburg or Psanek," smiled the Count. "But to the man whose soul is born single, able to be alone, to choose and to command. At last the masses will come to such men and say: 'You are greater than we. Be our lords. Take our life and our death in your hands, and dispose of us according to your will. Because we see a light in your face, and a burning on your mouth.'"

The Major smiled for many moments, really piqued and amused, watching the Count, who did not turn a hair.

"I say, you must be awfully naïve, Count, if you believe the modern masses are ever going to behave like that. I assure you, they never will."

"If they did," said the Count, "would you call it a new reign of love, or something else?"

"Well, of course, it would contain an element of love. There would have to be an element of love in their feeling for their leaders."

"Do you think so? I thought that love assumed an equality in difference. I thought that love gave to every man the right to judge the acts of other men—'This was not an act of love, therefore it was wrong.' Does not democracy, and love, give to every man this right?"

"Certainly," said Basil.

"Ah, but my chosen aristocrat would say to those who chose him: 'If you choose me, you give up forever your right to judge me. If you have truly chosen to follow me, you have thereby rejected all your right to criticise me. You can no longer either approve or disapprove of me. You have performed the sacred act of choice. Henceforth you can only obey.'"

"They wouldn't be able to help criticising, for all that," said Daphne, blurting in her say.

He looked at her slowly, and for the first time in her life she was doubtful of what she was saying.

"The day of Judas," he said, "ends with the day of love."

Basil woke up from a sort of trance.

"I think, of course, Count," he said, "that it's an awfully amusing idea. A retrogression slap back to the Dark Ages."

"Not so," said the Count. "Men—the mass of men—were never before free to perform the sacred act of choice. To-day—soon—they may be free."

"Oh, I don't know. Many tribes chose their kings and chiefs."

"Men have never before been quite free to choose: and to know what they are doing."

"You mean they've only made themselves free in order voluntarily to saddle themselves with new lords and masters?"

"I do mean that."

"In short, life is just a vicious circle?"

"Not at all. An ever-widening circle, as you say. Always more wonderful."

"Well, it's all frightfully interesting and amusing—don't you think so, Daphne? By the way, Count, where would women be? Would they be allowed to criticise their husbands?"

"Only before marriage," smiled the Count. "Not after."

"Splendid!" said Basil. "I'm all for that bit of your scheme, Count. I hope you're listening, Daphne."

"Oh yes. But then I've only married *you*. I've got my right to criticise all the other men," she said in a dull, angry voice.

"Exactly. Clever of you! So the Count won't get off! Well now, what do you think of the Count's aristocratic scheme for the future, Daphne? Do you approve?"

"Not at all. But then little men have always wanted power," she said cruelly.

"Oh, big men as well, for that matter," said Basil, conciliatory.

"I have been told before," smiled the Count, "little men are always bossy. I am afraid I have offended Lady Daphne?"

"No," she said. "Not really. I'm amused, really. But I always dislike any suggestion of bullying."

"Indeed, so do I," said he.

"The Count didn't mean bullying, Daphne," said Basil. "Come, there is really an allowable distinction between responsible power and bullying."

"When men put their heads together about it," said she.

She was haughty and angry, as if she were afraid of losing something. The Count smiled mischievously at her.

"You are offended, Lady Daphne? But why? You are safe from any spark of my dangerous and extensive authority."

Basil burst into a roar of laughter.

"It *is* rather funny, you to be talking of power and of not being criticised," he said. "But I should like to hear more: I would like to hear more."

As they drove home, he said to his wife:

"You know I like that little man. He's a quaint little bantam. And he sets one thinking."

Lady Daphne froze to four degrees below zero, under the north wind of this statement, and not another word was to be thawed out of her.

Curiously enough, it was now Basil who was attracted by the Count, and Daphne who was repelled. Not that she was so bound up in her husband. Not at all. She was feeling rather sore against men altogether. But as so often happens, in this life based on the wicked triangle, Basil could only follow his enthusiasm for the Count in his wife's presence. When the two men were alone together, they were awkward, resistant, they could hardly get out a dozen words to one another. When Daphne was there, however, to complete the circuit of the opposing currents, things went like a house on fire.

This, however, was not much consolation to Lady Daphne. Merely to sit as a passive medium between two men who are

squibbing philosophical nonsense to one another: no, it was
not good enough! She almost hated the Count: low-browed
little fellow, belonging to the race of prehistoric slaves. But
her grudge against her white-faced, spiritually intense husband
was sharp as vinegar. Let down: she was let down between
the pair of them.

What next? Well, what followed was entirely Basil's fault.
The winter was passing: it was obvious the war was really
over, that Germany was finished. The Hohenzollern had
fizzled out like a very poor squib, the Hapsburg was popping
feebly in obscurity, the Romanov was smudged out without a
sputter. So much for imperial royalty. Henceforth democratic
peace.

The Count, of course, would be shipped back now like returned goods that had no market any more. There was a world
peace ahead. A week or two, and Voynich Hall would be
empty.

Basil, however, could not let matters follow their simple
course. He was awfully intrigued by the Count. He wanted
to entertain him as a guest before he went. And Major Apsley
could get anything in reason, at this moment. So he obtained
permission for the poor little Count to stay a fortnight at
Thoresway, before being shipped back to Austria. Earl
Beveridge, whose soul was black as ink since the war, would
never have allowed the little alien enemy to enter his house,
had it not been for the hatred which had been aroused in
him, during the last two years, by the degrading spectacle of
the so-called patriots who had been howling their mongrel in-
decency in the public face. These mongrels had held the Press
and the British public in abeyance for almost two years. Their
one aim was to degrade and humiliate anything that was proud
or dignified remaining in England. It was almost the worst
nightmare of all, this coming to the top of a lot of public filth
which was determined to suffocate the souls of all dignified
men.

Hence, the Earl, who never intended to be swamped by un-
clean scum, whatever else happened to him, stamped his heels
in the ground and stood on his own feet. When Basil said to
him, would he allow the Count to have a fortnight's decent
peace in Thoresway before all was finished, Lord Beveridge
gave a slow consent, scandal or no scandal. Indeed, it was
really to defy scandal that he took such a step. For the

thought of his dead boys was bitter to him: and the thought of England fallen under the paws of smelly mongrels was bitterer still.

Lord Beveridge was at Thoresway to receive the Count, who arrived escorted by Basil. The English Earl was a big, handsome man, rather heavy, with a dark, sombre face that would have been haughty if haughtiness had not been made so ridiculous. He was a passionate man, with a passionate man's sensitiveness, generosity, and instinctive overbearing. But *his* dark passionate nature, and his violent sensitiveness had been subjected now to fifty-five years' subtle repression, condemnation, repudiation, till he had almost come to believe in his own wrongness. His little, frail wife, all love for humanity, she was the genuine article. Himself, he was labelled selfish, sensual, cruel, etc., etc. So by now he always seemed to be standing aside, in the shadow, letting himself be obliterated by the pallid rabble of the democratic hurry. That was the impression he gave, of a man standing back, half-ashamed, half-haughty, semi-hidden in the dark background.

He was a little on the defensive as Basil came in with the Count.

"Ah—how do you do, Count Psanek?" he said, striding largely forward and holding out his hand. Because he was the father of Daphne, the Count felt a certain tenderness for the taciturn Englishman.

"You do me too much honour, my lord, receiving me in your house," said the small Count proudly.

The Earl looked at him slowly, without speaking: seemed to look down on him, in every sense of the words.

"We are still men, Count. We are not beasts altogether."

"You wish to say that my countrymen are so very nearly beasts, Lord Beveridge?" smiled the Count, curling his fine nose.

Again the Earl was slow in replying.

"You have a low opinion of my manners, Count Psanek."

"But perhaps a just appreciation of your meaning, Lord Beveridge," smiled the Count, with the same reckless little look of contempt on his nose.

Lord Beveridge flushed dark, with all his native anger offended.

"I am glad Count Psanek makes my own meaning clear to me," he said.

"I beg your pardon a thousand times, my lord, if I give offence in doing so," replied the Count.

The Earl went black, and felt a fool. He turned his back on the Count. And then he turned round again, offering his cigarcase.

"Will you smoke?" he said. There was kindness in his tone.

"Thank you," said the Count, taking a cigar.

"I dare say," said Lord Beveridge, "that all men are beasts in some way. I am afraid I have fallen into the common habit of speaking by rote, and not what I really mean. Won't you take a seat?"

"It is only as a prisoner that I have learned that I am *not* truly a beast. No, I am myself. I am not a beast," said the Count, seating himself.

The Earl eyed him curiously.

"Well," he said, smiling, "I suppose it is best to come to a decision about it."

"It is necessary, if one is to be safe from vulgarity."

The Earl felt a twinge of accusation. With his agate-brown, hard-looking eyes he watched the black-browed little Count.

"You are probably right," he said.

But he turned his face aside.

They were five people at dinner—Lady Beveridge was there as hostess.

"Ah, Count Dionys," she said with a sigh, "do you really feel that the war is over?"

"Oh yes," he replied quickly. "This war is over. The armies will go home. *Their* cannon will not sound any more. Never again like this."

"Ah, I hope so," she sighed.

"I am sure," he said.

"You think there'll be no more war?" said Daphne.

For some reason she had made herself very fine, in her newest dress of silver and black and pink-chenille, with bare shoulders, and her hair fashionably done. The Count in his shabby uniform turned to her. She was nervous, hurried. Her slim white arm was near him, with the bit of silver at the shoulder. Her skin was white like a hot-house flower. Her lips moved hurriedly.

"Such a war as this there will never be again," he said.

"What makes you so sure?" she replied, glancing into his eyes.

"The machine of war has got out of our control. We shall never start it again, till it has fallen to pieces. We shall be afraid."

"Will everybody be afraid?" said she, looking down and pressing back her chin.

"I think so."

"We will hope so," said Lady Beveridge.

"Do you mind if I ask you, Count," said Basil, "what you feel about the way the war has ended? The way it has ended for *you*, I mean."

"You mean that Germany and Austria have lost the war? It was bound to be. We have all lost the war. All Europe."

"I agree there," said Lord Beveridge.

"We've all lost the war?" said Daphne, turning to look at him.

There was pain on his dark, low-browed face. He suffered having the sensitive woman beside him. Her skin had a hot-house delicacy that made his head go round. Her shoulders were broad, rather thin, but the skin was white and so sensitive, so hot-house delicate. It affected him like the perfume of some white, exotic flower. And she seemed to be sending her heart towards him. It was as if she wanted to press her breast to his. From the breast she loved him, and sent out love to him. And it made him unhappy; he wanted to be quiet, and to keep his honour before these hosts.

He looked into her eyes, his own eyes dark with knowledge and pain. She, in her silence and her brief words seemed to be holding them all under her spell. She seemed to have cast a certain muteness on the table, in the midst of which she remained silently master, leaning forward to her plate, and silently mastering them all.

"Don't I think we've all lost the war?" he replied, in answer to her question. "It was a war of suicide. Nobody could win it. It was suicide for all of us."

"Oh, I don't know," she replied. "What about America and Japan?"

"They don't count. They only helped *us* to commit suicide. They did not enter vitally."

There was such a look of pain on his face, and such a sound of pain in his voice, that the other three closed their ears, shut off from attending. Only Daphne was making him speak. It was she who was drawing the soul out of him, trying to read the future in him as the augurs read the future in the quivering entrails of the sacrificed beast. She looked direct into his face, searching his soul.

"You think Europe has committed suicide?" she said.

"Morally."

"Only morally?" came her slow, bronze-like words, so fatal.

"That is enough," he smiled.

"Quite," she said, with a slow droop of her eyelids. Then she turned away her face. But he felt the heart strangling inside his breast. What was she doing now? What was she thinking? She filled him with uncertainty and with uncanny fear.

"At least," said Basil, "those infernal guns are quiet."

"For ever," said Dionys.

"I wish I could believe you, Count," said the Major.

The talk became more general—or more personal. Lady Beveridge asked Dionys about his wife and family. He knew nothing save that they had gone to Hungary in 1916, when his own house was burnt down. His wife might even have gone to Bulgaria with Prince Bogorik. He did not know.

"But your children, Count!" cried Lady Beveridge.

"I do not know. Probably in Hungary, with their grandmother. I will go when I get back."

"But have you never *written?*—never enquired?"

"I could not write. I shall know soon enough—everything."

"You have no son?"

"No. Two girls."

"Poor things!"

"Yes."

"I say, isn't it an odd thing to have a ladybird on your crest?" asked Basil, to cheer up the conversation.

"Why queer? Charlemagne had bees. And it is a Marienkäfer—a Mary-beetle. The beetle of Our Lady. I think it is quite a heraldic insect, Major," smiled the Count.

"You're proud of it?" said Daphne, suddenly turning to look at him again, with her slow, pregnant look.

"I am, you know. It has such a long genealogy—our spotted beetle. Much longer than the Psaneks. I think, you know, it is a descendant of the Egyptian scarabeus, which is a very mysterious emblem. So I connect myself with the Pharaohs: just through my ladybird."

"You feel your ladybird has crept through so many ages," she said.

"Imagine it!" he laughed.

"The scarab *is* a piquant insect," said Basil.

"Do you know Fabre?" put in Lord Beveridge. "He suggests that the beetle rolling a little ball of dung before him, in a dry old field, must have suggested to the Egyptians the First Principle that set the globe rolling. And so the scarab became the symbol of the creative principle—or something like that."

"That the earth is a tiny ball of dry dung is good," said Basil.

"Between the claws of a ladybird," added Daphne.

"That is what it is, to go back to one's origin," said Lady Beveridge.

"Perhaps they meant that it was the principle of decomposition which first set the ball rolling," said the Count.

"The ball would have to be *there* first," said Basil.

"Certainly. But it hadn't started to roll. Then the principle of decomposition started it." The Count smiled as if it were a joke.

"I am no Egyptologist," said Lady Beveridge, "so I can't judge."

The Earl and Countess Beveridge left next day. Count Dionys was left with the two young people in the house. It was a beautiful Elizabethan mansion, not very large, but with those magical rooms that are all a twinkle of small-paned windows, looking out from the dark panelled interior. The interior was cosy, panelled to the ceiling, and the ceiling moulded and touched with gold. And then the great square bow of the window with its little panes intervening like magic between oneself and the world outside, the crest in stained glass crowning its colour, the broad window-seat cushioned in faded green. Dionys wandered round the house like a little ghost, through the succession of small and large twinkling sitting-rooms and lounge rooms in front, down the long, wide corridor with the wide stair-head at each end, and up the narrow stairs to the bedrooms above, and on to the roof.

It was early spring, and he loved to sit on the leaded, pale-grey roof that had its queer seats and slopes, a little pale world in itself. Then to look down over the garden and the sloping lawn to the ponds massed round with trees, and away to the elms and furrows and hedges of the shires. On the left of

the house was the farmstead, with ricks and great-roofed
barns and dark-red cattle. Away to the right, beyond the
park, was a village among trees, and the spark of a grey
church spire.

He liked to be alone, feeling his soul heavy with its own
fate. He would sit for hours watching the elm trees standing
in rows like giants, like warriors across the country. The
Earl had told him that the Romans had brought these elms to
Britain. And he seemed to see the spirit of the Romans in them
still. Sitting there alone in the spring sunshine, in the solitude
of the roof, he saw the glamour of this England of hedgerows
and elm trees, and the labourers with slow horses slowly drill-
ing the sod, crossing the brown furrow: and the roofs of the
village, with the church steeple rising beside a big black yew
tree: and the chequer of fields away to the distance.

And the charm of the old manor around him, the garden
with its grey stone walls and yew hedges—broad, broad yew
hedges—and a peacock pausing to glitter and scream in the
busy silence of an English spring, when celandines open their
yellow under the hedges, and violets are in the secret, and by
the broad paths of the garden polyanthus and crocuses vary
the velvet and flame, and bits of yellow wallflower shake
raggedly, with a wonderful triumphance, out of the cracks of
the wall. There was a fold somewhere near, and he could hear
the treble bleat of the growing lambs, and the deeper, con-
tented baa-ing of the ewes.

This was Daphne's home, where she had been born. She
loved it with an ache of affection. But now it was hard to
forget her dead brothers. She wandered about in the sun,
with two old dogs paddling after her. She talked with everybody—gardener, groom, stableman, with the farm-hands. That
filled a large part of her life—straying round talking with the
work-people. They were, of course, respectful to her—but not
at all afraid of her. They knew she was poor, that she could
not afford a car, nor anything. So they talked to her very
freely: perhaps a little too freely. Yet she let it be. It was her
one passion at Thoresway to hear the dependants talk and
talk—about everything. The curious feeling of intimacy across
a breach fascinated her. Their lives fascinated her: what
they thought, what they *felt*. These, what they felt. That
fascinated her. There was a gamekeeper she could have loved—
an impudent, ruddy-faced, laughing, ingratiating fellow; she

could have loved him, if he had not been isolated beyond the breach of his birth, her culture, her consciousness. Her *consciousness* seemed to make a great gulf between her and the lower classes, the unconscious classes. She accepted it as her doom. She could never meet in real contact anyone but a super-conscious, finished being like herself: or like her husband. Her father had some of the unconscious blood-warmth of the lower classes. But he was like a man who is damned. And the Count, of course. The Count had something that was hot and invisible, a dark flame of life that might warm the cold white fire of her own blood. But——

They avoided each other. All three, they avoided one another. Basil, too, went off alone. Or he immersed himself in poetry. Sometimes he and the Count played billiards. Sometimes all three walked in the park. Often Basil and Daphne walked to the village, to post. But truly, they avoided one another, all three. The days slipped by.

At evening they sat together in the small west room that had books and a piano and comfortable shabby furniture of faded rose-coloured tapestry: a shabby room. Sometimes Basil read aloud: sometimes the Count played the piano. And they talked. And Daphne stitch by stitch went on with a big embroidered bedspread, which she might finish if she lived long enough. But they always went to bed early. They were nearly always avoiding one another.

Dionys had a bedroom in the east bay—a long way from the rooms of the others. He had a habit, when he was quite alone, of singing, or rather crooning to himself the old songs of his childhood. It was only when he felt he was quite alone: when other people seemed to fade out of him, and all the world seemed to dissolve into darkness, and there was nothing but himself, his own soul, alive in the middle of his own small night, isolate for ever. Then, half unconscious, he would croon in a small, high-pitched, squeezed voice, a sort of high dream-voice, the songs of his childhood dialect. It was a curious noise: the sound of a man who is alone in his own blood: almost the sound of a man who is going to be executed.

Daphne heard the sound one night when she was going downstairs again with the corridor lantern to find a book. She was a bad sleeper, and her nights were a torture to her. She, too, like a neurotic, was nailed inside her own fretful self-consciousness. But she had a very keen ear. So she started as she heard the small, bat-like sound of the Count's singing to himself. She stood in the midst of the wide corridor, that was wide as a room, carpeted with a faded lavender-coloured carpet, with a piece of massive dark furniture at intervals by the wall, and an oak arm-chair and sometimes a faded, reddish Oriental rug. The big horn lantern which stood at nights at the end of the corridor she held in her hand. The intense 'peeping' sound of the Count, like a witchcraft, made her forget everything. She could not understand a word, of course. She could not understand the noise even. After listening for a long time, she went on downstairs. When she came back again he was still, and the light was gone from under his door.

After this, it became almost an obsession to her to listen for him. She waited with fretful impatience for ten o'clock, when she could retire. She waited more fretfully still for the maid to leave her, and for her husband to come and say good-night. Basil had the room across the corridor. And then in resentful impatience she waited for the sounds of the house to become still. Then she opened her door to listen.

And far away, as if from far, far away in the unseen, like a ventriloquist sound or a bat's uncanny peeping, came the frail, almost inaudible sound of the Count's singing to himself before he went to bed. It *was* inaudible to anyone but herself. But she, by concentration, seemed to hear supernaturally. She had a low arm-chair by the door, and there, wrapped in a huge old black silk shawl, she sat and listened. At first she could not hear. That is, she could hear the sound. But it was only a sound. And then, gradually, gradually she began to follow the thread of it. It was like a thread which she followed out of the world: out of the world. And as she went, slowly, by degrees, far, far away, down the thin thread of his singing, she knew peace—she knew forgetfulness. She could pass beyond the world, away beyond where her soul balanced like a bird on wings, and was perfected.

So it was, in her upper spirit. But underneath was a wild, wild yearning, actually to go, actually to be given. Actually to go, actually to die the death, actually to cross the border and be gone, to be gone. To be gone from this herself, from this Daphne, to be gone from father and mother, brothers and husband, and home and land and world: to be gone. To be gone to the call from the beyond: the call. It was the Count calling. He was calling her. She was sure he was calling her. Out of herself, out of her world, he was calling her.

Two nights she sat just inside her room, by the open door, and listened. Then when he finished she went to sleep, a queer, light, bewitched sleep. In the day she was bewitched. She felt strange and light, as if pressure had been removed from around her. Some pressure had been clamped round her all her life. She had never realised it till now; now it was removed, and her feet felt so light, and her breathing delicate and exquisite. There had always been a pressure against her breathing. Now she breathed delicate and exquisite, so that it was a delight to breathe. Life came in exquisite breaths, quickly, as if it delighted to come to her.

The third night he was silent—though she waited and waited till the small hours of the morning. He was silent, he did not sing. And then she knew the terror and blackness of the feeling that he might never sing any more. She waited like one doomed, throughout the day. And when the night came she trembled. It was her greatest nervous terror, lest her spell should be broken, and she should be thrown back to what she was before.

Night came, and the kind of swoon upon her. Yes, and the call from the night. The call! She rose helplessly and hurried down the corridor. The light was under his door. She sat down in the big oak arm-chair that stood near his door, and huddled herself tight in her black shawl. The corridor was dim with the big, star-studded, yellow lantern-light. Away down she could see the lamp-light in her doorway; she had left her door ajar.

But she saw nothing. Only she wrapped herself close in the black shawl, and listened to the sound from the room. It called. Oh, it called her! Why could she not go? Why could she not cross through the closed door.

Then the noise ceased. And then the light went out, under the door of his room. Must she go back? Must she go back? Oh, impossible. As impossible as that the moon should go back on her tracks, once she has risen. Daphne sat on, wrapped in her black shawl. If it must be so, she would sit on through eternity. Return she never could.

And then began the most terrible song of all. It began with a rather dreary, slow, horrible sound, like death. And then

suddenly came a real call—fluty, and a kind of whistling and
a strange whirr at the changes, most imperative, and utterly
inhuman. Daphne rose to her feet. And at the same moment
up rose the whistling throb of a summons out of the death
moan.

Daphne tapped low and rapidly at the door. "Count!
Count!" she whispered. The sound inside ceased. The door
suddenly opened. The pale, obscure figure of Dionys.

"Lady Daphne!" he said in astonishment, automatically
standing aside.

"You called," she murmured rapidly, and she passed intent
into his room.

"No, I did not call," he said gently, his hand on the door
still.

"Shut the door," she said abruptly.

He did as he was bid. The room was in complete darkness.
There was no moon outside. She could not see him.

"Where can I sit down?" she said abruptly.

"I will take you to the couch," he said, putting out his hand
and touching her in the dark. She shuddered.

She found the couch and sat down. It was quite dark.

"What are you singing?" she said rapidly.

"I am so sorry. I did not think anyone could hear."

"What was it you were singing?"

"A song of my country."

"Had it any words?"

"Yes, it is a woman who was a swan, and who loved a
hunter by the marsh. So she became a woman and married
him and had three children. Then in the night one night the
king of the swans called to her to come back, or else he
would die. So slowly she turned into a swan again, and slowly
she opened her wide, wide wings, and left her husband and
her children."

There was silence in the dark room. The Count had been
really startled, startled out of his mood of the song into the
day-mood of human convention. He was distressed and
embarrassed by Daphne's presence in his dark room. She,
however, sat on and did not make a sound. He, too, sat down
in a chair by the window. It was everywhere dark. A wind
was blowing in gusts outside. He could see nothing inside his
room: only the faint, faint strip of light under the door. But
he could feel her presence in the darkness. It was uncanny,

to feel her near in the dark, and not to see any sign of her, nor to hear any sound.

She had been wounded in her bewitched state by the contact with the every-day human being in him. But now she began to relapse into her spell, as she sat there in the dark. And he, too, in the silence, felt the world sinking away from him once more, leaving him once more alone on a darkened earth, with nothing between him and the infinite dark space. Except now her presence. Darkness answering to darkness, and deep answering to deep. An answer, near to him, and invisible.

But he did not know what to do. He sat still and silent as she was still and silent. The darkness inside the room seemed alive like blood. He had no power to move. The distance between them seemed absolute.

Then suddenly, without knowing, he went across in the dark, feeling for the end of the couch. And he sat beside her on the couch. But he did not touch her. Neither did she move. The darkness flowed about them thick like blood, and time seemed dissolved in it. They sat with the small, invisible distance between them, motionless, speechless, thoughtless.

Then suddenly he felt her finger-tips touch his arm, and a flame went over him that left him no more a man. He was something seated in flame, in flame unconscious, seated erect, like an Egyptian King-god in the statues. Her finger-tips slid down him, and she herself slid down in a strange, silent rush, and he felt her face against his closed feet and ankles, her hands pressing his ankles. He felt her brow and hair against his ankles, her face against his feet, and there she clung in the dark, as if in space below him. He still sat erect and motionless. Then he bent forward and put his hand on her hair.

"Do you come to me?" he murmured. "Do you come to me?"

The flame that enveloped him seemed to sway him silently.

"Do you really come to me?" he repeated. "But we have nowhere to go."

He felt his bare feet wet with her tears. Two things were struggling in him, the sense of eternal solitude, like space, and the rush of dark flame that would throw him out of his solitude towards her.

He was thinking too. He was thinking of the future. He had no future in the world: of that he was conscious. He had no future in this life. Even if he lived on, it would only be a kind of enduring. But he felt that in the after-life the inheritance was his. He felt the after-life belonged to him.

Future in the world he could not give her. Life in the world he had not to offer her. Better go on alone. Surely better go on alone.

But then the tears on his feet: and her face that would face him as he left her! No, no. The next life was his. He was master of the after-life. Why fear for this life? Why not take the soul she offered him? Now and for ever, for the life that would come when they both were dead. Take her into the underworld. Take her into the dark Hades with him, like Francesca and Paolo. And in hell hold her fast, queen of the underworld, himself master of the underworld. Master of the life to come. Father of the soul that would come after.

"Listen," he said to her softly. "Now you are mine. In the dark you are mine. And when you die you are mine. But in the day you are not mine, because I have no power in the day. In the night, in the dark, and in death, you are mine. And that is for ever. No matter if I must leave you. I shall come again from time to time. In the dark you are mine. But in the day I cannot claim you. I have no power in the day, and no place. So remember. When the darkness comes, I shall always be in the darkness of you. And as long as I live, from time to time I shall come to find you, when I am able to, when I am not a prisoner. But I shall have to go away soon. So don't forget—you are the night wife of the ladybird, while you live and even when you die."

Later, when he took her back to her room, he saw her door still ajar.

"You shouldn't leave a light in your room," he murmured.

In the morning there was a curious remote look about him. He was quieter than ever, and seemed very far away. Daphne slept late. She had a strange feeling as if she had slipped off all her cares. She did not care, she did not grieve, she did not fret any more. All that had left her. She felt she could sleep, sleep, sleep—for ever. Her face, too, was very still, with a delicate look of virginity that she had never had before. She had always been Aphrodite, the self-conscious one. And her eyes, the green-blue, had been like slow, living jewels, resistant. Now they had unfolded from the hard flower-bud, and had the wonder, and the stillness of a quiet night.

Basil noticed it at once.

"You're different, Daphne," he said. "What are you thinking about?"

"I wasn't thinking," she said, looking at him with candour.

"What were you doing then?"

"What does one do when one doesn't think? Don't make me puzzle it out, Basil."

"Not a bit of it, if you don't want to."

But he was puzzled by her. The sting of his ecstatic love for her seemed to have left him. Yet he did not know what else to do but to make love to her. She went very pale. She submitted to him, bowing her head because she was his wife. But she looked at him with fear, with sorrow, with real suffering. He could feel the heaving of her breast, and knew she was weeping. But there were no tears on her face, she was only death-pale. Her eyes were shut.

"Are you in pain?" he asked her.

"No, no!" She opened her eyes, afraid lest she had disturbed him. She did not want to disturb him.

He was puzzled. His own ecstatic, deadly love for her had received a check. He was out of the reckoning.

He watched her when she was with the Count. Then she seemed so meek—so maidenly—so different from what he had known of her. She was so still, like a virgin girl. And it was this quiet, intact quality of virginity in her which puzzled him most, puzzled his emotions and his ideas. He became suddenly ashamed to make love to her. And because he was ashamed, he said to her as he stood in her room that night:

"Daphne, are you in love with the Count?"

He was standing by the dressing-table, uneasy. She was seated in a low chair by the tiny dying wood fire. She looked up at him with wide, slow eyes. Without a word, with wide, soft, dilated eyes she watched him. What was it that made him feel all confused. He turned his face aside, away from her wide, soft eyes.

"Pardon me, dear. I didn't intend to ask such a question. Don't take any notice of it," he said. And he strode away and picked up a book. She lowered her head and gazed abstractedly into the fire, without a sound. Then he looked at her again, at her bright hair that the maid had plaited for the night. Her plait hung down over her soft pinkish wrap.

His heart softened to her as he saw her sitting there. She seemed like his sister. The excitement of desire had left him, and now he seemed to see clear and feel true for the first time in his life. She was like a dear, dear sister to him. He felt that she was his blood-sister, nearer to him than he had imagined any woman could be. So near—so dear—and all the sex and the desire gone. He didn't want it—he hadn't wanted it. This new pure feeling was so much more wonderful.

He went to her side.

"Forgive me, darling," he said, "for having questioned you."

She looked up at him with the wide eyes, without a word. His face was good and beautiful. Tears came to her eyes.

"You have the right to question me," she said sadly.

"No," he said. "No, darling. I have no right to question you. Daphne! Daphne, darling! It shall be as *you* wish, between us. Shall it? Shall it be as you wish?"

"You are the husband, Basil," she said sadly.

"Yes, darling. But"—he went on his knees beside her—"perhaps, darling, something has changed in us. I feel as if I ought never to touch you again—as if I never *wanted* to touch you—in that way. I feel it was wrong, darling. Tell me what you think."

"Basil, don't be angry with me."

"It isn't anger; it's pure love, darling—it is."

"Let us not come any nearer to one another than this, Basil—physically—shall we?" she said. "And don't be angry with me, will you?"

"Why," he said. "I think myself the sexual part has been a mistake. I had rather love you—as I love now. I *know* that this is true love. The other was always a bit whipped up. I *know* I love you now, darling: now I'm free from that other. But what if it comes upon me, that other, Daphne?"

"I am always your wife," she said quietly. "I am always your wife. I want always to obey you, Basil: what you wish."

"Give me your hand, dear."

She gave him her hand. But the look in her eyes at the same time warned him and frightened him. He kissed her hand and left her.

It was to the Count she belonged. This had decided itself in her down to the depths of her soul. If she could not marry him and be his wife in the world, it had nevertheless happened to her for ever. She could no more question it. Question had gone out of her.

Strange how different she had become—a strange new quiescence. The last days were slipping past. He would be going away—Dionys: he with the still remote face, the man she belonged to in the dark and in the light, for ever. He would be going away. He said it must be so. And she acquiesced. The grief was deep, deep inside her. He must go away. Their lives could not be one life, in this world's day. Even in her anguish she knew it was so. She knew he was right. He was for her infallible. He spoke to the deepest soul in her.

She never *saw* him as a lover. When she saw him, he was the little officer, a prisoner, quiet, claiming nothing in all the world. And when she went to him as his lover, his wife, it was always dark. She only knew his voice and his contact in darkness. "My wife in darkness," he said to her. And in this too she believed him. She would not have contradicted him, no, not for anything on earth: lest, contradicting him she should lose the dark treasure of stillness and bliss which she kept in her breast even when her heart was wrung with the agony of knowing he must go.

No, she had found this wonderful thing after she had heard him singing: she had suddenly collapsed away from her old self into this darkness, this peace, this quiescence that was like a full dark river flowing eternally in her soul. She had gone to sleep from the *nuit blanche* of her days. And Basil, wonderful, had changed almost at once. She feared him, lest he might change back again. She would always have him to fear. But deep inside her she only feared for this love of hers for the Count: this dark, everlasting love that was like a full river flowing for ever inside her. Ah, let that not be broken.

She was so still inside her. She could sit so still, and feel the day slowly, richly changing to night. And she wanted nothing, she was short of nothing. If only Dionys need not go away! If only he need not go away!

But he said to her, the last morning:

"Don't forget me. Always remember me. I leave my soul in your hands and your womb. Nothing can ever separate us, unless we betray one another. If you have to give yourself to your husband, do so, and obey him. If you are true to me, innerly, innerly true, he will not hurt us. He is generous, be generous to him. And never fail to believe in me. Because even on the other side of death I shall be watching for you. I shall be king in Hades when I am dead. And you will be at my side. You will never leave me any more, in the after-death. So don't be afraid in life. Don't be afraid. If you have to cry tears, cry them. But in your heart of hearts know that I shall come again, and that I have taken you for ever. And so, in your heart of hearts be still, be still, since you are the wife of the ladybird." He laughed as he left her, with his own beautiful, fearless laugh. But they were strange eyes that looked after him.

He went in the car with Basil back to Voynich Hall.

"I believe Daphne will miss you," said Basil.

The Count did not reply for some moments.

"Well, if she does," he said, "there will be no bitterness in it."

"Are you sure?" smiled Basil.

"Why—if we are sure of anything," smiled the Count.

"She's changed, isn't she?"

"Is she?"

"Yes, she's quite changed since you came, Count."

"She does not seem to me so very different from the girl of seventeen whom I knew."

"No—perhaps not. I didn't know her then. But she's very different from the wife I have known."

"A regrettable difference?"

"Well—no, not as far as she goes. She is much quieter inside herself. You know, Count, something of me died in the war. I feel it will take me an eternity to sit and think about it all."

"I hope you may think it out to your satisfaction, Major."

"Yes, I hope so too. But that is how it has left me—feeling as if I needed eternity now to brood about it all, you know. Without the need to act—or even to love, really. I suppose love is action."

"Intense action," said the Count.

"Quite so. I know really how I feel. I only ask of life to spare me from further effort of action of any sort—even love. And then to fulfil myself, brooding through eternity. Of course, I don't mind *work*, mechanical action. That in itself is a form of inaction."

"A man can only be happy following his own inmost need," said the Count.

"Exactly!" said Basil. "I will lay down the law for nobody, not even for myself. And live my day——"

"Then you will be happy in your own way. I find it so difficult to keep from laying the law down for myself," said the Count. "Only the thought of death and the after life saves me from doing it any more."

"As the thought of eternity helps me," said Basil. "I suppose it amounts to the same thing."

THE FOX

THE FOX

THE two girls were usually known by their surnames, Banford and March. They had taken the farm together, intending to work it all by themselves: that is, they were going to rear chickens, make a living by poultry, and add to this by keeping a cow, and raising one or two young beasts. Unfortunately, things did not turn out well.

Banford was a small, thin, delicate thing with spectacles. She, however, was the principal investor, for March had little or no money. Banford's father, who was a tradesman in Islington, gave his daughter the start, for her health's sake, and because he loved her, and because it did not look as if she would marry. March was more robust. She had learned carpentry and joinery at the evening classes in Islington. She would be the man about the place. They had, moreover, Banford's old grandfather living with them at the start. He had been a farmer. But unfortunately the old man died after he had been at Bailey Farm for a year. Then the two girls were left alone.

They were neither of them young: that is, they were near thirty. But they certainly were not old. They set out quite gallantly with their enterprise. They had numbers of chickens, black Leghorns and white Leghorns, Plymouths and Wyandottes; also some ducks; also two heifers in the fields. One heifer, unfortunately, refused absolutely to stay in the Bailey Farm closes. No matter how March made up the fences, the heifer was out, wild in the woods, or trespassing on the neighbouring pasture, and March and Banford were away, flying after her, with more haste than success. So this heifer they sold in despair. Then, just before the other beast was expecting her first calf, the old man died, and the girls, afraid of the coming event, sold her in a panic, and limited their attentions to fowls and ducks.

In spite of a little chagrin, it was a relief to have no more cattle on hand. Life was not made merely to be slaved away. Both girls agreed in this. The fowls were quite enough trouble. March had set up her carpenter's bench at the end of the open shed. Here she worked, making coops and doors and other appurtenances. The fowls were housed in the bigger building, which had served as barn and cow-shed in old days. They had a beautiful home, and should have been perfectly content. Indeed, they looked well enough. But the girls were disgusted at their tendency to strange illnesses, at their exacting way of life, and at their refusal, obstinate refusal to lay eggs.

March did most of the outdoor work. When she was out and about, in her puttees and breeches, her belted coat and her loose cap, she looked almost like some graceful, loose-balanced young man, for her shoulders were straight, and her movements easy and confident, even tinged with a little indifference or irony. But her face was not a man's face, ever. The wisps of her crisp dark hair blew about her as she stooped, her eyes were big and wide and dark, when she looked up again, strange, startled, shy and sardonic at once. Her mouth, too, was almost pinched as if in pain and irony. There was something odd and unexplained about her. She would stand balanced on one hip, looking at the fowls pattering about in the obnoxious fine mud of the sloping yard, and calling to her favourite white hen, which came in answer to her name. But there was an almost satirical flicker in March's big, dark eyes as she looked at her three-toed flock pottering about under her gaze, and the same slight dangerous satire in her voice as she spoke to the favoured Patty, who pecked at March's boot by way of friendly demonstration.

Fowls did not flourish at Bailey Farm, in spite of all that March did for them. When she provided hot food for them in the morning, according to rule, she noticed that it made them heavy and dozy for hours. She expected to see them lean against the pillars of the shed in their languid processes of digestion. And she knew quite well that they ought to be busily scratching and foraging about, if they were to come to any good. So she decided to give them their hot food at night, and let them sleep on it. Which she did. But it made no difference.

War conditions, again, were very unfavourable to poultry-keeping. Food was scarce and bad. And when the Daylight Saving Bill was passed, the fowls obstinately refused to go to bed as usual, about nine o'clock in the summer-time. That was late enough, indeed, for there was no peace till they were shut up and asleep. Now they cheerfully walked around, without so much as glancing at the barn, until ten o'clock or later.

Both Banford and March disbelieved in living for work alone. They wanted to read or take a cycle-ride in the evening, or perhaps March wished to paint curvilinear swans on porcelain, with green background, or else make a marvellous fire-screen by processes of elaborate cabinet work. For she was a creature of odd whims and unsatisfied tendencies. But from all these things she was prevented by the stupid fowls.

One evil there was greater than any other. Bailey Farm was a little homestead, with ancient wooden barn and low-gabled farm-house, lying just one field removed from the edge of the wood. Since the war the fox was a demon. He carried off the hens under the very noses of March and Banford. Banford would start and stare through her big spectacles with all her eyes, as another squawk and flutter took place at her heels. Too late! Another white Leghorn gone. It was disheartening.

They did what they could to remedy it. When it became permitted to shoot foxes, they stood sentinel with their guns, the two of them, at the favoured hours. But it was no good. The fox was too quick for them. So another year passed, and another, and they were living on their losses, as Banford said. They let their farm-house one summer, and retired to live in a railway-carriage that was deposited as a sort of out-house in a corner of the field. This amused them, and helped their finances. None the less, things looked dark.

Although they were usually the best of friends, because Banford, though nervous and delicate, was a warm, generous soul, and March, though so odd and absent in herself, had a strange magnanimity, yet, in the long solitude, they were apt to become a little irritable with one another, tired of one another. March had four-fifths of the work to do, and though she did not mind, there seemed no relief, and it made her eyes flash curiously sometimes. Then Banford, feeling more nerve-worn than ever, would become despondent, and March would speak sharply to her. They seemed to be losing ground, some-how, losing hope as the months went by. There alone in the fields by the wood, with the wide country stretching hollow and dim to the round hills of the White Horse, in the far distance, they seemed to have to live too much off themselves. There was nothing to keep them up—and no hope.

The fox really exasperated them both. As soon as they had let the fowls out, in the early summer mornings, they had to take their guns and keep guard: and then again as soon as evening began to mellow, they must go once more. And he was so sly. He slid along in the deep grass; he was difficult as a serpent to see. And he seemed to circumvent the girls deliberately. Once or twice March had caught sight of the white tip of his brush, or the ruddy shadow of him in the deep grass, and she had let fire at him. But he made no account of this.

One evening March was standing with her back to the sunset, her gun under her arm, her hair pushed under her cap. She was half watching, half musing. It was her constant state. Her eyes were keen and observant, but her inner mind took no notice of what she saw. She was always lapsing into this odd, rapt state, her mouth rather screwed up. It was a question whether she was there, actually consciously present, or not.

The trees on the wood-edge were a darkish, brownish green in the full light—for it was the end of August. Beyond, the naked, copper-like shafts and limbs of the pine trees shone in the air. Nearer the rough grass, with its long, brownish stalks all agleam, was full of light. The fowls were round about— the ducks were still swimming on the pond under the pine trees. March looked at it all, saw it all, and did not see it. She heard Banford speaking to the fowls in the distance—and she did not hear. What was she thinking about? Heaven knows. Her consciousness was, as it were, held back.

She lowered her eyes, and suddenly saw the fox. He was looking up at her. His chin was pressed down, and his eyes were looking up. They met her eyes. And he knew her. She was spellbound—she knew he knew her. So he looked into her eyes, and her soul failed her. He knew her, he was not daunted.

She struggled, confusedly she came to herself, and saw him making off, with slow leaps over some fallen boughs, slow, impudent jumps. Then he glanced over his shoulder, and ran smoothly away. She saw his brush held smooth like a feather, she saw his white buttocks twinkle. And he was gone, softly, soft as the wind.

She put her gun to her shoulder, but even then pursed her mouth, knowing it was nonsense to pretend to fire. So she began to walk slowly after him, in the direction he had gone, slowly, pertinaciously. She expected to find him. In her heart she was determined to find him. What she would do when she saw him again she did not consider. But she was determined to find him. So she walked abstractedly about on the edge of the wood, with wide, vivid dark eyes, and a faint flush in her cheeks. She did not think. In strange mindlessness she walked hither and thither.

At last she became aware that Banford was calling her. She made an effort of attention, turned, and gave some sort of screaming call in answer. Then again she was striding off towards the homestead. The red sun was setting, the fowls were retiring towards their roost. She watched them, white creatures, black creatures, gathering to the barn. She watched them spellbound, without seeing them. But her automatic intelligence told her when it was time to shut the door.

She went indoors to supper, which Banford had set on the table. Banford chatted easily. March seemed to listen, in her distant, manly way. She answered a brief word now and then. But all the time she was as if spellbound. And as soon as supper was over, she rose again to go out, without saying why.

She took her gun again and went to look for the fox. For he had lifted his eyes upon her, and his knowing look seemed to have entered her brain. She did not so much think of him: she was possessed by him. She saw his dark, shrewd, unabashed eye looking into her, knowing her. She felt him invisibly master her spirit. She knew the way he lowered his chin as he looked up, she knew his muzzle, the golden brown, and the greyish white. And again she saw him glance over his shoulder at her, half inviting, half contemptuous and cunning. So she went, with her great startled eyes glowing, her gun under her arm, along the wood edge. Meanwhile the night fell, and a great moon rose above the pine trees. And again Banford was calling.

So she went indoors. She was silent and busy. She examined her gun, and cleaned it, musing abstractedly by the lamplight. Then she went out again, under the great moon, to see if everything was right. When she saw the dark crests of the pine trees against the blood-red sky, again her heart beat to the fox, the fox. She wanted to follow him, with her gun.

It was some days before she mentioned the affair to Banford. Then suddenly one evening she said:

"The fox was right at my feet on Saturday night."

"Where?" said Banford, her eyes opening behind her spectacles.

"When I stood just above the pond."

"Did you fire?" cried Banford.

"No, I didn't."

"Why not?"

"Why, I was too much surprised, I suppose."

It was the same old, slow, laconic way of speech March always had. Banford. stared at her friend for a few moments.

"You saw him?" she cried.

"Oh yes! He was looking up at me, cool as anything."

"I tell you," cried Banford—"the cheek! They're not afraid of us, Nellie."

"Oh no," said March.

"Pity you didn't get a shot at him," said Banford.

"Isn't it a pity! I've been looking for him ever since. But I don't suppose he'll come so near again."

"I don't suppose he will," said Banford.

And she proceeded to forget about it, except that she was more indignant than ever at the impudence of the beggar. March also was not conscious that she thought of the fox. But whenever she fell into her half-musing, when she was half rapt and half intelligently aware of what passed under her vision, then it was the fox which somehow dominated her unconsciousness, possessed the blank half of her musing. And so it was for weeks, and months. No matter whether she had been climbing the trees for the apples, or beating down the last of the damsons, or whether she had been digging out the ditch from the duck-pond, or clearing out the barn, when she had finished, or when she straightened herself, and pushed the wisps of hair away again from her forehead, and pursed up her mouth again in an odd, screwed fashion, much too old for her years, there was sure to come over her mind the old spell of the fox, as it came when he was looking at her. It was as if she could smell him at these times. And it always recurred, at unexpected moments, just as she was going to sleep at night, or just as she was pouring the water into the tea-pot to make tea—it was the fox, it came over her like a spell.

So the months passed. She still looked for him unconsciously when she went towards the wood. He had become a settled effect in her spirit, a state permanently established, not continuous, but always recurring. She did not know what she felt or thought: only the state came over her, as when he looked at her.

The months passed, the dark evenings came, heavy, dark November, when March went about in high boots, ankle deep in mud, when the night began to fall at four o'clock, and the day never properly dawned. Both girls dreaded these times. They dreaded the almost continuous darkness that enveloped them on their desolate little farm near the wood. Banford was physically afraid. She was afraid of tramps, afraid lest someone should come prowling around. March was not so much afraid as uncomfortable, and disturbed. She felt discomfort and gloom in all her physique.

Usually the two girls had tea in the sitting-room. March lighted a fire at dusk, and put on the wood she had chopped and sawed during the day. Then the long evening was in front, dark, sodden, black outside, lonely and rather oppressive inside, a little dismal. March was content not to talk, but Banford could not keep still. Merely listening to the wind in the pines outside, or the drip of water, was too much for her.

One evening the girls had washed up the tea-cups in the kitchen, and March had put on her house-shoes, and taken up a roll of crochet-work, which she worked at slowly from time to time. So she lapsed into silence. Banford stared at the red fire, which, being of wood, needed constant attention. She was afraid to begin to read too early, because her eyes would not bear any strain. So she sat staring at the fire, listening to the distant sounds, sound of cattle lowing, of a dull, heavy moist wind, of the rattle of the evening train on the little railway not far off. She was almost fascinated by the red glow of the fire.

Suddenly both girls started, and lifted their heads. They heard a footstep—distinctly a footstep. Banford recoiled in fear. March stood listening. Then rapidly she approached the door that led into the kitchen. At the same time they heard the footsteps approach the back door. They waited a second. The back door opened softly. Banford gave a loud cry. A man's voice said softly:

"Hello!"

March recoiled, and took a gun from a corner.

"What do you want?" she cried, in a sharp voice.

Again the soft, softly-vibrating man's voice said:

"Hello! What's wrong?"

"I shall shoot!" cried March. "What do you want?"

"Why, what's wrong? What's wrong?" came the soft,

wondering, rather scared voice: and a young soldier, with his heavy kit on his back, advanced into the dim light.

"Why," he said, "who lives here then?"

"We live here," said March. "What do you want?"

"Oh!" came the long, melodious, wonder-note from the young soldier. "Doesn't William Grenfel live here then?"

"No—you know he doesn't."

"Do I? Do I? I don't, you see. He *did* live here, because he was my grandfather, and I lived here myself five years ago. What's become of him then?"

The young man—or youth, for he would not be more than twenty—now advanced and stood in the inner doorway. March, already under the influence of his strange, soft, modulated voice, stared at him spellbound. He had a ruddy, roundish face, with fairish hair, rather long, flattened to his forehead with sweat. His eyes were blue, and very bright and sharp. On his cheeks, on the fresh ruddy skin were fine, fair hairs, like a down, but sharper. It gave him a slightly glistening look. Having his heavy sack on his shoulders, he stooped, thrusting his head forward. His hat was loose in one hand. He stared brightly, very keenly from girl to girl, particularly at March, who stood pale, with great dilated eyes, in her belted coat and puttees, her hair knotted in a big crisp knot behind. She still had the gun in her hand. Behind her, Banford, clinging to the sofa-arm, was shrinking away, with half-averted head.

"I thought my grandfather still lived here? I wonder if he's dead."

"We've been here for three years," said Banford, who was beginning to recover her wits, seeing something boyish in the round head with its rather long, sweaty hair.

"Three years! You don't say so! And you don't know who was here before you?"

"I know it was an old man, who lived by himself."

"Ay! Yes, that's him! And what became of him then?"

"He died. I know he died."

"Ay! He's dead then!"

The youth stared at them without changing colour or expression. If he had any expression, besides a slight baffled look of wonder, it was one of sharp curiosity concerning the two girls; sharp, impersonal curiosity, the curiosity of that round young head.

But to March he was the fox. Whether it was the thrusting forward of his head, or the glisten of fine whitish hairs on the ruddy cheek-bones, or the bright, keen eyes, that can never be said: but the boy was to her the fox, and she could not see him otherwise.

"How is it you didn't know if your grandfather was alive or dead?" asked Banford, recovering her natural sharpness.

"Ay, that's it," replied the softly-breathing youth. "You see, I joined up in Canada, and I hadn't heard for three or four years. I ran away to Canada."

"And now have you just come from France?"

"Well—from Salonika really."

There was a pause, nobody knowing quite what to say.

"So you've nowhere to go now?" said Banford rather lamely.

"Oh, I know some people in the village. Anyhow, I can go to the 'Swan'."

"You came on the train, I suppose. Would you like to sit down a bit?"

"Well—I don't mind."

He gave an odd little groan as he swung off his kit. Banford looked at March.

"Put the gun down," she said. "We'll make a cup of tea."

"Ay," said the youth. "We've seen enough of rifles."

He sat down rather tired on the sofa, leaning forward.

March recovered her presence of mind, and went into the kitchen. There she heard the soft young voice musing:

"Well, to think I should come back and find it like this!" He did not seem sad, not at all—only rather interestedly surprised.

"And what a difference in the place, eh?" he continued, looking round the room.

"You see a difference, do you?" said Banford.

"Yes—don't I!"

His eyes were unnaturally clear and bright, though it was the brightness of abundant health.

March was busy in the kitchen preparing another meal. It was about seven o'clock. All the time, while she was active, she was attending to the youth in the sitting-room, not so much listening to what he said as feeling the soft run of his voice. She primmed up her mouth tighter and tighter, puckering it as if it were sewed, in her effort to keep her will upper-

most. Yet her large eyes dilated and glowed in spite of her;
she lost herself. Rapidly and carelessly she prepared the meal,
cutting large chunks of bread and margarine—for there was
no butter. She racked her brain to think of something else to
put on the tray—she had only bread, margarine, and jam, and
the larder was bare. Unable to conjure anything up, she went
into the sitting-room with her tray.

She did not want to be noticed. Above all, she did not want
him to look at her. But when she came in, and was busy setting the table just behind him, he pulled himself up from his
sprawling, and turned and looked over his shoulder. She
became pale and wan.

The youth watched her as she bent over the table, looked at
her slim, well-shapen legs, at the belted coat dropping around
her thighs, at the knot of dark hair, and his curiosity, vivid
and widely alert, was again arrested by her.

The lamp was shaded with a dark-green shade, so that the
light was thrown downwards and the upper half of the room
was dim. His face moved bright under the light, but March
loomed shadowy in the distance.

She turned round, but kept her eyes sideways, dropping and
lifting her dark lashes. Her mouth unpuckered as she said to
Banford:

"Will you pour out?"

Then she went into the kitchen again.

"Have your tea where you are, will you?" said Banford to
the youth—"unless you'd rather come to the table."

"Well," said he, "I'm nice and comfortable here, aren't I?
I will have it here, if you don't mind."

"There's nothing but bread and jam," she said. And she put
his plate on a stool by him. She was very happy now, waiting
on him. For she loved company. And now she was no more
afraid of him than if he were her own younger brother. He
was such a boy.

"Nellie," she called. "I've poured you a cup out."

March appeared in the doorway, took her cup, and sat down
in a corner, as far from the light as possible. She was very
sensitive in her knees. Having no skirts to cover them, and
being forced to sit with them boldly exposed, she suffered.
She shrank and shrank, trying not to be seen. And the youth,
sprawling low on the couch, glanced up at her, with long,
steady, penetrating looks, till she was almost ready to dis-

appear. Yet she held her cup balanced, she drank her tea, screwed up her mouth and held her head averted. Her desire to be invisible was so strong that it quite baffled the youth. He felt he could not see her distinctly. She seemed like a shadow within the shadow. And ever his eyes came back to her, searching, unremitting, with unconscious fixed attention.

Meanwhile he was talking softly and smoothly to Banford, who loved nothing so much as gossip, and who was full of perky interest, like a bird. Also he ate largely and quickly and voraciously, so that March had to cut more chunks of bread and margarine, for the roughness of which Banford apologised.

"Oh, well," said March, suddenly speaking, "if there's no butter to put on it, it's no good trying to make dainty pieces."

Again the youth watched her, and he laughed, with a sudden, quick laugh, showing his teeth and wrinkling his nose.

"It isn't, is it," he answered in his soft, near voice.

It appeared he was Cornish by birth and upbringing. When he was twelve years old he had come to Bailey Farm with his grandfather, with whom he had never agreed very well. So he had run away to Canada, and worked far away in the West. Now he was here—and that was the end of it.

He was very curious about the girls, to find out exactly what they were doing. His questions were those of a farm youth; acute, practical, a little mocking. He was very much amused by their attitude to their losses: for they were amusing on the score of heifers and fowls.

"Oh, well," broke in March, "we don't believe in living for nothing but work."

"Don't you?" he answered. And again the quick young laugh came over his face. He kept his eyes steadily on the obscure woman in the corner.

"But what will you do when you've used up all your capital?" he said.

"Oh, I don't know," answered March laconically. "Hire ourselves out for land-workers, I suppose."

"Yes, but there won't be any demand for women land-workers now the war's over," said the youth.

"Oh, we'll see. We shall hold on a bit longer yet," said March, with a plangent, half-sad, half-ironical indifference.

"There wants a man about the place," said the youth softly. Banford burst out laughing.

"Take care what you say," she interrupted. "We consider ourselves quite efficient."

"Oh," came March's slow plangent voice, "it isn't a case of efficiency, I'm afraid. If you're going to do farming you must be at it from morning till night, and you might as well be a beast yourself."

"Yes, that's it," said the youth. "You aren't willing to put yourselves into it."

"We aren't," said March, "and we know it."

"We want some of our time for ourselves," said Banford.

The youth threw himself back on the sofa, his face tight with laughter, and laughed silently but thoroughly. The calm scorn of the girls tickled him tremendously.

"Yes," he said, "but why did you begin then?"

"Oh," said March, "we had a better opinion of the nature of fowls then than we have now."

"Of Nature altogether, I'm afraid," said Banford. "Don't talk to me about Nature."

Again the face of the youth tightened with delighted laughter.

"You haven't a very high opinion of fowls and cattle, have you?" he said.

"Oh no—quite a low one," said March.

He laughed out.

"Neither fowls nor heifers," said Banford, "nor goats nor the weather."

The youth broke into a sharp yap of laughter, delighted. The girls began to laugh too, March turning aside her face and wrinkling her mouth in amusement.

"Oh, well," said Banford, "we don't mind, do we, Nellie?"

"No," said March, "we don't mind."

The youth was very pleased. He had eaten and drunk his fill. Banford began to question him. His name was Henry Grenfel—no, he was not called Harry, always Henry. He continued to answer with courteous simplicity, grave and charming. March, who was not included, cast long, slow glances at him from her recess, as he sat there on the sofa, his hands clasping his knees, his face under the lamp bright and alert, turned to Banford. She became almost peaceful at last. He was identified with the fox—and he was here in full presence.

She need not go after him any more. There in the shadow of her corner she gave herself up to a warm, relaxed peace, almost like sleep, accepting the spell that was on her. But she wished to remain hidden. She was only fully at peace whilst he forgot her, talking to Banford. Hidden in the shadow of the corner, she need not any more be divided in herself, trying to keep up two planes of consciousness. She could at last lapse into the odour of the fox.

For the youth, sitting before the fire in his uniform, sent a faint but distinct odour into the room, indefinable, but something like a wild creature. March no longer tried to reserve herself from it. She was still and soft in her corner like a passive creature in its cave.

At last the talk dwindled. The youth relaxed his clasp of his knees, pulled himself together a little, and looked round. Again he became aware of the silent, half-invisible woman in the corner.

"Well," he said unwillingly, "I suppose I'd better be going, or they'll be in bed at the 'Swan'."

"I'm afraid they're in bed, anyhow," said Banford. "They've all got this influenza."

"Have they!" he exclaimed. And he pondered. "Well," he continued, "I shall find a place somewhere."

"I'd say you could stay here, only——" Banford began.

He turned and watched her, holding his head forward.

"What?" he asked.

"Oh, well," she said, "propriety, I suppose." She was rather confused.

"It wouldn't be improper, would it?" he said, gently surprised.

"Not as far as we're concerned," said Banford.

"And not as far as I'm concerned," he said, with grave naiveté. "After all, it's my own home, in a way."

Banford smiled at this.

"It's what the village will have to say," she said.

There was a moment's blank pause.

"What do you say, Nellie?" asked Banford.

"I don't mind," said March, in her distinct tone. "The village doesn't matter to me, anyhow."

"No," said the youth, quick and soft. "Why should it? I mean, what should they say?"

"Oh, well," came March's plangent, laconic voice, "they'll

easily find something to say. But it makes no difference what they say. We can look after ourselves."

"Of course you can," said the youth.

"Well then, stop if you like," said Banford. "The spare room is quite ready."

His face shone with pleasure.

"If you're quite sure it isn't troubling you too much," he said, with that soft courtesy which distinguished him.

"Oh, it's no trouble," they both said.

He looked, smiling with delight, from one to another.

"It's awfully nice not to have to turn out again, isn't it?" he said gratefully.

"I suppose it is," said Banford.

March disappeared to attend to the room. Banford was as pleased and thoughtful as if she had her own young brother home from France. It gave her just the same kind of gratification to attend on him, to get out the bath for him, and everything. Her natural warmth and kindliness had now an outlet. And the youth luxuriated in her sisterly attention. But it puzzled him slightly to know that March was silently working for him too. She was so curiously silent and obliterated. It seemed to him he had not really seen her. He felt he should not know her if he met her in the road.

That night March dreamed vividly. She dreamed she heard a singing outside which she could not understand, a singing that roamed round the house, in the fields, and in the darkness. It moved her so that she felt she must weep. She went out, and suddenly she knew it was the fox singing. He was very yellow and bright, like corn. She went nearer to him, but he ran away and ceased singing. He seemed near, and she wanted to touch him. She stretched out her hand, but suddenly he bit her wrist, and at the same instant, as she drew back, the fox, turning round to bound away, whisked his brush across her face, and it seemed his brush was on fire, for it seared and burned her mouth with a great pain. She awoke with the pain of it, and lay trembling as if she were really seared.

In the morning, however, she only remembered it as a distant memory. She arose and was busy preparing the house and attending to the fowls. Banford flew into the village on her bicycle to try and buy food. She was a hospitable soul. But alas, in the year 1918 there was not much food to buy.

The youth came downstairs in his shirt-sleeves. He was young and fresh, but he walked with his head thrust forward, so that his shoulders seemed raised and rounded, as if he had a slight curvature of the spine. It must have been only a manner of bearing himself, for he was young and vigorous. He washed himself and went outside, whilst the women were preparing breakfast.

He saw everything, and examined everything. His curiosity was quick and insatiable. He compared the state of things with that which he remembered before, and cast over in his mind the effect of the changes. He watched the fowls and the ducks, to see their condition; he noticed the flight of wood-pigeons overhead: they were very numerous; he saw the few apples high up, which March had not been able to reach; he remarked that they had borrowed a draw-pump, presumably to empty the big soft-water cistern which was on the north side of the house.

"It's a funny, dilapidated old place," he said to the girls, as he sat at breakfast.

His eyes were wise and childish, with thinking about things. He did not say much, but ate largely. March kept her face averted. She, too, in the early morning could not be aware of him, though something about the glint of his khaki reminded her of the brilliance of her dream-fox.

During the day the girls went about their business. In the morning he attended to the guns, shot a rabbit and a wild duck that was flying high towards the wood. That was a great addition to the empty larder. The girls felt that already he had earned his keep. He said nothing about leaving, however. In the afternoon he went to the village. He came back at tea-time. He had the same alert, forward-reaching look on his roundish face. He hung his hat on a peg with a little swinging gesture. He was thinking about something.

"Well," he said to the girls, as he sat at table. "What am I going to do?"

"How do you mean—what are you going to do?" said Banford.

"Where am I going to find a place in the village to stay?" he said.

"I don't know," said Banford. "Where do you think of staying?"

"Well"—he hesitated—"at the 'Swan' they've got this 'flu,

and at the 'Plough and Harrow' they've got the soldiers who
are collecting the hay for the army: besides, in the private
houses, there's ten men and a corporal altogether billeted in
the village, they tell me. I'm not sure where I could get a bed."

He left the matter to them. He was rather calm about it.
March sat with her elbows on the table, her two hands sup-
porting her chin, looking at him unconsciously. Suddenly he
lifted his clouded blue eyes, and unthinking looked straight
into March's eyes. ·He was startled as well as she. He, too,
recoiled a little. March felt the same sly, taunting, knowing
spark leap out of his eyes, as he turned his head aside, and
fall into her soul, as had fallen from the dark eyes of the
fox. She pursed her mouth as if in pain, as if asleep too.

"Well, I don't know," Banford was saying. She seemed
reluctant, as if she were afraid of being imposed upon. She
looked at March. But, with her weak, troubled sight, she only
saw the usual semi-abstraction on her friend's face. "Why
don't you speak, Nellie?" she said.

But March was wide-eyed and silent, and the youth, as if
fascinated, was watching her without moving his eyes.

"Go on—answer something," said Banford. And March
turned her head slightly aside, as if coming to consciousness,
or trying to come to consciousness.

"What do you expect me to say?" she asked automatically.

"Say what you think," said Banford.

"It's all the same to me," said March.

And again there was silence. A pointed light seemed to be
on the boy's eyes, penetrating like a needle.

"So it is to me," said Banford. "You can stop on here if
you like."

A smile like a cunning little flame came over his face, suddenly and involuntarily. He dropped his head quickly to hide
it, and remained with his head dropped, his face hidden.

"You can stop on here if you like. You can please yourself,
Henry," Banford concluded.

Still he did not reply, but remained with his head dropped.
Then he lifted his face. It was bright with a curious light, as
if exultant, and his eyes were strangely clear as he watched
March. She turned her face aside, her mouth suffering as if
wounded, and her consciousness dim.

Banford became a little puzzled. She watched the steady,
pellucid gaze of the youth's eyes as he looked at March, with

the invisible smile gleaming on his face. She did not know
how he was smiling, for no feature moved. It seemed only in
the gleam, almost the glitter of the fine hairs on his cheeks.
Then he looked with quite a changed look at Banford.

"I'm sure," he said in his soft, courteous voice, "you're
awfully good. You're too good. You don't want to be
bothered with me, I'm sure."

"Cut a bit of bread, Nellie," said Banford uneasily, adding:
"It's no bother, if you like to stay. It's like having my own
brother here for a few days. He's a boy like you are."

"That's awfully kind of you," the lad repeated. "I should
like to stay ever so much, if you're sure I'm not a trouble to
you."

"No, of course you're no trouble. I tell you, it's a pleasure
to have somebody in the house besides ourselves," said warm-
hearted Banford.

"But Miss March?" he said in his soft voice, looking at her.

"Oh, it's quite all right as far as I'm concerned," said March
vaguely.

His face beamed, and he almost rubbed his hands with
pleasure.

"Well then," he said, "I should love it, if you'd let me pay
my board and help with the work."

"You've no need to talk about board," said Banford.

One or two days went by, and the youth stayed on at the
farm. Banford was quite charmed by him. He was so soft
and courteous in speech, not wanting to say much himself,
preferring to hear what she had to say, and to laugh in his
quick, half-mocking way. He helped readily with the work—
but not too much. He loved to be out alone with the gun in
his hands, to watch, to see. For his sharp-eyed, impersonal
curiosity was insatiable, and he was most free when he was
quite alone, half-hidden, watching.

Particularly he watched March. She was a strange character
to him. Her figure, like a graceful young man's, piqued him.
Her dark eyes made something rise in his soul, with a curious
elate excitement, when he looked into them, an excitement
he was afraid to let be seen, it was so keen and secret. And
then her odd, shrewd speech made him laugh outright. He
felt he must go further, he was inevitably impelled. But he
put away the thought of her and went off towards the wood's
edge with the gun.

The dusk was falling as he came home, and with the dusk, a fine, late November rain. He saw the fire-light leaping in the window of the sitting-room, a leaping light in the little cluster of the dark buildings. And he thought to himself it would be a good thing to have this place for his own. And then the thought entered him shrewdly: Why not marry March? He stood still in the middle of the field for some moments, the dead rabbit hanging still in his hand, arrested by this thought. His mind waited in amazement—it seemed to calculate—and then he smiled curiously to himself in acquiescence. Why not? Why not indeed? It was a good idea. What if it was rather ridiculous? What did it matter? What if she was older than he? It didn't matter. When he thought of her dark, startled, vulnerable eyes he smiled subtly to himself. He was older than she, really. He was master of her.

He scarcely admitted his intention even to himself. He kept it as a secret even from himself. It was all too uncertain as yet. He would have to see how things went. Yes, he would have to see how things went. If he wasn't careful, she would just simply mock at the idea. He knew, sly and subtle as he was, that if he went to her plainly and said: "Miss March, I love you and want you to marry me," her inevitable answer would be: "Get out. I don't want any of that tomfoolery." This was her attitude to men and their 'tomfoolery'. If he was not careful, she would turn round on him with her savage, sardonic ridicule, and dismiss him from the farm and from her own mind for ever. He would have to go gently. He would have to catch her as you catch a deer or a woodcock when you go out shooting. It's no good walking out into the forest and saying to the deer: "Please fall to my gun." No, it is a slow, subtle battle. When you really go out to get a deer, you gather yourself together, you coil yourself inside yourself, and you advance secretly, before dawn, into the mountains. It is not so much what you do, when you go out hunting, as how you feel. You have to be subtle and cunning and absolutely fatally ready. It becomes like a fate. Your own fate over-takes and determines the fate of the deer you are hunting. First of all, even before you come in sight of your quarry, there is a strange battle, like mesmerism. Your own soul, as a hunter, has gone out to fasten on the soul of the deer, even before you see any deer. And the soul of the deer fights to

escape. Even before the deer has any wind of you, it is so. It
is a subtle, profound battle of wills which takes place in the
invisible. And it is a battle never finished till your bullet goes
home. When you are *really* worked up to the true pitch, and
you come at last into range, you don't then aim as you do
when you are firing at a bottle. It is your own *will* which
carries the bullet into the heart of your quarry. The bullet's
flight home is a sheer projection of your own fate into the
fate of the deer. It happens like a supreme wish, a supreme
act of volition, not as a dodge of cleverness.

He was a huntsman in spirit, not a farmer, and not a soldier
stuck in a regiment. And it was as a young hunter that he
wanted to bring down March as his quarry, to make her his
wife. So he gathered himself subtly together, seemed to with-
draw into a kind of invisibility. He was not quite sure how
he would go on. And March was suspicious as a hare. So he
remained in appearance just the nice, odd stranger-youth,
staying for a fortnight on the place.

He had been sawing logs for the fire in the afternoon. Darkness came very early. It was still a cold, raw mist. It was getting almost too dark to see. A pile of short sawed logs lay
beside the trestle. March came to carry them indoors, or into
the shed, as he was busy sawing the last log. He was working
in his shirt-sleeves, and did not notice her approach; she came
unwillingly, as if shy. He saw her stooping to the bright-
ended logs, and he stopped sawing. A fire like lightning flew
down his legs in the nerves.

"March?" he said in his quiet, young voice.

She looked up from the logs she was piling.

"Yes!" she said.

He looked down on her in the dusk. He could see her not
too distinctly.

"I wanted to ask you something," he said.

"Did you? What was it?" she said. Already the fright was
in her voice. But she was too much mistress of herself.

"Why"—his voice seemed to draw out soft and subtle, it
penetrated her nerves—"why, what do you think it is?"

She stood up, placed her hands on her hips, and stood looking at him transfixed, without answering. Again he burned
with a sudden power.

"Well," he said, and his voice was so soft it seemed rather
like a subtle touch, like the merest touch of a cat's paw, a

feeling rather than a sound. "Well—I wanted to ask you to marry me."

March felt rather than heard him. She was trying in vain to turn aside her face. A great relaxation seemed to have come over her. She stood silent, her head slightly on one side. He seemed to be bending towards her, invisibly smiling. It seemed to her fine sparks came out of him.

Then very suddenly she said:

"Don't try any of your tomfoolery on me."

A quiver went over his nerves. He had missed. He waited a moment to collect himself again. Then he said, putting all the strange softness into his voice, as if he were imperceptibly stroking her:

"Why, it's not tomfoolery. It's not tomfoolery. I mean it. I mean it. What makes you disbelieve me?"

He sounded hurt. And his voice had such a curious power over her; making her feel loose and relaxed. She struggled somewhere for her own power. She felt for a moment that she was lost—lost—lost. The word seemed to rock in her as if she were dying. Suddenly again she spoke.

"You don't know what you are talking about," she said, in a brief and transient stroke of scorn. "What nonsense! I'm old enough to be your mother."

"Yes, I do know what I'm talking about. Yes, I do," he persisted softly, as if he were producing his voice in her blood. "I know quite well what I'm talking about. You're not old enough to be my mother. That isn't true. And what does it matter even if it was? You can marry me whatever age we are. What is age to me? And what is age to you! Age is nothing."

A swoon went over her as he concluded. He spoke rapidly —in the rapid Cornish fashion—and his voice seemed to sound in her somewhere where she was helpless against it. "Age is nothing!" The soft, heavy insistence of it made her sway dimly out there in the darkness. She could not answer.

A great exultance leaped like fire over his limbs. He felt he had won.

"I want to marry you, you see. Why shouldn't I?" he proceeded, soft and rapid. He waited for her to answer. In the dusk he saw her almost phosphorescent. Her eyelids were dropped, her face half-averted and unconscious. She seemed to be in his power. But he waited, watchful. He dared not yet touch her.

"Say then," he said, "say then you'll marry me. Say—say!" He was softly insistent.

"What?" she asked, faint, from a distance, like one in pain. His voice was now unthinkably near and soft. He drew very near to her.

"Say yes."

"Oh, I can't," she wailed helplessly, half-articulate, as if semi-conscious, and as if in pain, like one who dies. "How can I?"

"You can," he said softly, laying his hand gently on her shoulder as she stood with her head averted and dropped, dazed. "You can. Yes, you can. What makes you say you can't? You can. You can." And with awful softness he bent forward and just touched her neck with his mouth and his chin.

"Don't!" she cried, with a faint mad cry like hysteria, starting away and facing round on him. "What do you mean?" But she had no breath to speak with. It was as if she was killed.

"I mean what I say," he persisted softly and cruelly. "I want you to marry me. I want you to marry me. You know that, now, don't you? You know that, now? Don't you? Don't you?"

"What?" she said.

"Know," he replied.

"Yes," she said. "I know you say so."

"And you know I mean it, don't you?"

"I know you say so."

"You believe me?" he said.

She was silent for some time. Then she pursed her lips.

"I don't know what I believe," she said.

"Are you out there?" came Banford's voice, calling from the house.

"Yes, we're bringing in the logs," he answered.

"I thought you'd gone lost," said Banford disconsolately. "Hurry up, do, and come and let's have tea. The kettle's boiling."

He stooped at once to take an armful of little logs and carry them into the kitchen, where they were piled in a corner. March also helped, filling her arms and carrying the logs on her breast as if they were some heavy child. The night had fallen cold.

When the logs were all in, the two cleaned their boots noisily on the scraper outside, then rubbed them on the mat. March shut the door and took off her old felt hat—her farm-girl hat. Her thick, crisp, black hair was loose, her face was pale and strained. She pushed back her hair vaguely and washed her hands. Banford came hurrying into the dimly-lighted kitchen, to take from the oven the scones she was keeping hot.

"Whatever have you been doing all this time?" she asked fretfully. "I thought you were never coming in. And it's ages since you stopped sawing. What were you doing out there?"

"Well," said Henry, "we had to stop that hole in the barn to keep the rats out."

"Why, I could see you standing there in the shed. I could see your shirt-sleeves," challenged Banford.

"Yes, I was just putting the saw away."

They went in to tea. March was quite mute. Her face was pale and strained and vague. The youth, who always had the same ruddy, self-contained look on his face, as though he were keeping himself to himself, had come to tea in his shirt-sleeves as if he were at home. He bent over his plate as he ate his food.

"Aren't you cold?" said Banford spitefully. "In your shirt-sleeves."

He looked up at her, with his chin near his plate, and his eyes very clear, pellucid, and unwavering as he watched her.

"No, I'm not cold," he said with his usual soft courtesy. "It's much warmer in here than it is outside, you see."

"I hope it is," said Banford, feeling nettled by him. He had a strange, suave assurance and a wide-eyed bright look that got on her nerves this evening.

"But perhaps," he said softly and courteously, "you don't like me coming to tea without my coat. I forgot that."

"Oh, I don't mind," said Banford: although she *did*.

"I'll go and get it, shall I?" he said.

March's dark eyes turned slowly down to him

"No, don't you bother," she said in her queer, twanging tone. "If you feel all right as you are, stop as you are." She spoke with a crude authority.

"Yes," said he, "I *feel* all right, if I'm not rude."

"It's usually considered rude," said Banford. "But we don't mind."

"Go along, 'considered rude'," ejaculated March. "Who considers it rude?"

"Why, you do, Nellie, in anybody else," said Banford, bridling a little behind her spectacles, and feeling her food stick in her throat.

But March had again gone vague and unheeding, chewing her food as if she did not know she was eating at all. And the youth looked from one to another, with bright, watching eyes.

Banford was offended. For all his suave courtesy and soft voice, the youth seemed to her impudent. She did not like to look at him. She did not like to meet his clear, watchful eyes, she did not like to see the strange glow in his face, his cheeks with their delicate fine hair, and his ruddy skin that was quite dull and yet which seemed to burn with a curious heat of life. It made her feel a little ill to look at him: the quality of his physical presence was too penetrating, too hot.

After tea the evening was very quiet. The youth rarely went into the village. As a rule, he read: he was a great reader, in his own hours. That is, when he did begin, he read absorbedly. But he was not very eager to begin. Often he walked about the fields and along the hedges alone in the dark at night, prowling with a queer instinct for the night, and listening to the wild sounds.

To-night, however, he took a Captain Mayne Reid book from Banford's shelf and sat down with knees wide apart and immersed himself in his story. His brownish fair hair was long, and lay on his head like a thick cap, combed sideways. He was still in his shirt-sleeves, and bending forward under the lamp-light, with his knees stuck wide apart and the book in his hand and his whole figure absorbed in the rather strenuous business of reading, he gave Banford's sitting-room the look of a lumber-camp. She resented this. For on her sitting-room floor she had a red Turkey rug and dark stain round, the fire-place had fashionable green tiles, the piano stood open with the latest dance music: she played quite well: and on the walls were March's hand-painted swans and water-lilies. Moreover, with the logs nicely, tremulously burning in the grate, the thick curtains drawn, the doors all shut, and the pine trees hissing and shuddering in the wind outside, it was cosy, it was refined and nice. She resented the big, raw,

long-legged youth sticking his khaki knees out and sitting
there with his soldier's shirt-cuffs buttoned on his thick red
wrists. From time to time he turned a page, and from time to
time he gave a sharp look at the fire, settling the logs. Then
he immersed himself again in the intense and isolated business
of reading.

March, on the far side of the table, was spasmodically
crochetting. Her mouth was pursed in an odd way, as when
she had dreamed the fox's brush burned it, her beautiful, crisp
black hair strayed in wisps. But her whole figure was absorbed
in its bearing, as if she herself was miles away. In a sort of
semi-dream she seemed to be hearing the fox singing round
the house in the wind, singing wildly and sweetly and like
a madness. With red but well-shaped hands she slowly
crochetted the white cotton, very slowly, awkwardly.

Banford was also trying to read, sitting in her low chair.
But between those two she felt fidgetty. She kept moving and
looking round and listening to the wind, and glancing secretly
from one to the other of her companions. March, seated on a
straight chair, with her knees in their close breeches crossed,
and slowly, laboriously crochetting, was also a trial.

"Oh dear!" said Banford. "My eyes are bad to-night." And
she pressed her fingers on her eyes.

The youth looked up at her with his clear, bright look, but
did not speak.

"Are they, Jill?" said March absently.

Then the youth began to read again, and Banford perforce
returned to her book. But she could not keep still. After a
while she looked up at March, and a queer, almost malignant
little smile was on her thin face.

"A penny for them, Nell," she said suddenly.

March looked round with big, startled black eyes, and went
pale as if with terror. She had been listening to the fox singing so tenderly, so tenderly, as he wandered round the house.

"What?" she said vaguely.

"A penny for them," said Banford sarcastically. "Or two-
pence, if they're as deep as all that."

The youth was watching with bright, clear eyes from
beneath the lamp.

"Why," came March's vague voice, "what do you want to
waste your money for?"

"I thought it would be well spent," said Banford.

"I wasn't thinking of anything except the way the wind was blowing," said March.

"Oh dear," replied Banford, "I could have had as original thoughts as that myself. I'm afraid I *have* wasted my money this time."

"Well, you needn't pay," said March.

The youth suddenly laughed. Both women looked at him: March rather surprised-looking, as if she had hardly known he was there.

"Why, do you ever pay up on these occasions?" he asked.

"Oh yes," said Banford. "We always do. I've sometimes had to pass a shilling a week to Nellie, in the winter-time. It costs much less in summer."

"What, paying for each other's thoughts?" he laughed.

"Yes, when we've absolutely come to the end of everything else."

He laughed quickly, wrinkling his nose sharply like a puppy and laughing with quick pleasure, his eyes shining.

"It's the first time I ever heard of that," he said.

"I guess you'd hear of it often enough if you stayed a winter on Bailey Farm," said Banford lamentably.

"Do you get so tired, then?" he asked.

"So bored," said Banford.

"Oh!" he said gravely. "But why should you be bored?"

"Who wouldn't be bored?" said Banford.

"I'm sorry to hear that," he said gravely.

"You must be, if you were hoping to have a lively time here," said Banford.

He looked at her long and gravely.

"Well," he said, with his odd, young seriousness, "it's quite lively enough for me."

"I'm glad to hear it," said Banford.

And she returned to her book. In her thin, frail hair were already many threads of grey, though she was not yet thirty. The boy did not look down, but turned his eyes to March, who was sitting with pursed mouth laboriously crochetting, her eyes wide and absent. She had a warm, pale, fine skin and a delicate nose. Her pursed mouth looked shrewish. But the shrewish look was contradicted by the curious lifted arch of her dark brows, and the wideness of her eyes; a look of startled wonder and vagueness. She was listening again for the fox, who seemed to have wandered farther off into the night.

From under the edge of the lamp-light the boy sat with his face looking up, watching her silently, his eyes round and very clear and intent. Banford, biting her fingers irritably, was glancing at him under her hair. He sat there perfectly still, his ruddy face tilted up from the low level under the light, on the edge of the dimness, and watching with perfect abstract intentness. March suddenly lifted her great, dark eyes from her crochetting and saw him. She started, giving a little exclamation.

"There he is!" she cried involuntarily, as if terribly startled.

Banford looked around in amazement, sitting up straight.

"Whatever has got you, Nellie?" she cried.

But March, her face flushed a delicate rose colour, was looking away to the door.

"Nothing! Nothing!" she said crossly. "Can't one speak?"

"Yes, if you speak sensibly," said Banford. "Whatever did you mean?"

"I don't know what I meant," cried March testily.

"Oh, Nellie, I hope you aren't going jumpy and nervy. I feel I can't stand another *thing*! Whoever did you mean? Did you mean Henry?" cried poor, frightened Banford.

"Yes. I suppose so," said March laconically. She would never confess to the fox.

"Oh dear, my nerves are all gone for to-night," wailed Banford.

At nine o'clock March brought in a tray with bread and cheese and tea—Henry had confessed that he liked a cup of tea. Banford drank a glass of milk and ate a little bread. And soon she said:

"I'm going to bed, Nellie. I'm all nerves to-night. Are you coming?"

"Yes, I'm coming the minute I've taken the tray away," said March.

"Don't be long then," said Banford fretfully. "Good-night, Henry. You'll see the fire is safe, if you come up last, won't you?"

"Yes, Miss Banford, I'll see it's safe," he replied in his re-assuring way.

March was lighting the candle to go to the kitchen. Banford took her candle and went upstairs. When March came back to the fire, she said to him:

"I suppose we can trust you to put out the fire and everything?" She stood there with her hand on her hip, and one knee loose, her head averted shyly, as if she could not look at him. He had his face lifted, watching her.

"Come and sit down a minute," he said softly.

"No, I'll be going. Jill will be waiting, and she'll get upset, if I don't come."

"What made you jump like that this evening?" he asked.

"When did I jump?" she retorted, looking at him.

"Why, just now you did," he said. "When you cried out."

"Oh!" she said. "Then!—Why, I thought you were the fox!" And her face screwed into a queer smile, half-ironic.

"The fox! Why the fox?" he asked softly.

"Why, one evening last summer when I was out with the gun I saw the fox in the grass nearly at my feet, looking straight up at me. I don't know—I suppose he made an impression on me." She turned aside her head again and let one foot stray loose, self-consciously.

"And did you shoot him?" asked the boy.

"No, he gave me such a start, staring straight at me as he did, and then stopping to look back at me over his shoulder with a laugh on his face."

"A laugh on his face!" repeated Henry, also laughing. "He frightened you, did he?"

"No, he didn't frighten me. He made an impression on me, that's all."

"And you thought I was the fox, did you?" he laughed, with the same queer, quick little laugh, like a puppy wrinkling his nose.

"Yes, I did, for the moment," she said. "Perhaps he'd been in my mind without my knowing."

"Perhaps you think I've come to steal your chickens or something," he said, with the same young laugh.

But she only looked at him with a wide, dark, vacant eye.

"It's the first time," he said, "that I've ever been taken for a fox. Won't you sit down for a minute?" His voice was very soft and cajoling.

"No," she said. "Jill will be waiting." But still she did not go, but stood with one foot loose and her face turned aside, just outside the circle of light.

"But won't you answer my question?" he said, lowering his voice still more.

"I don't know what question you mean."

"Yes, you do. Of course you do. I mean the question of you marrying me."

"No, I shan't answer that question," she said flatly.

"Won't you?" The queer, young laugh came on his nose again. "Is it because I'm like the fox? Is that why?" And still he laughed.

She turned and looked at him with a long, slow look.

"I wouldn't let that put you against me," he said. "Let me turn the lamp low, and come and sit down a minute."

He put his red hand under the glow of the lamp and suddenly made the light very dim. March stood there in the dimness quite shadowy, but unmoving. He rose silently to his feet, on his long legs. And now his voice was extraordinarily soft and suggestive, hardly audible.

"You'll stay a moment," he said. "Just a moment." And he put his hand on her shoulder. She turned her face from him. "I'm sure you don't really think I'm like the fox," he said, with the same softness and with a suggestion of laughter in his tone, a subtle mockery. "Do you now?" And he drew her gently towards him and kissed her neck, softly. She winced and trembled and hung away. But his strong, young arm held her, and he kissed her softly again, still on the neck, for her face was averted.

"Won't you answer my question? Won't you now?" came his soft, lingering voice. He was trying to draw her near to kiss her face. And he kissed her cheek softly, near the ear.

At that moment Banford's voice was heard calling fretfully, crossly from upstairs.

"There's Jill!" cried March, starting and drawing erect.

And as she did so, quick as lightning he kissed her on the mouth, with a quick, brushing kiss. It seemed to burn through her every fibre. She gave a queer little cry.

"You will, won't you? You will?" he insisted softly.

"Nellie! *Nellie!* Whatever are you so long for?" came Banford's faint cry from the outer darkness.

But he held her fast, and was murmuring with that intolerable softness and insistency:

"You will, won't you? Say yes! Say yes!"

March, who felt as if the fire had gone through her and scathed her, and as if she could do no more, murmured:

"Yes! Yes! Anything you like! Anything you like! Only let me go! Only let me go! Jill's calling."

"You know you've promised," he said insidiously.

"Yes! Yes! I do!" Her voice suddenly rose into a shrill cry. "All right, Jill, I'm coming."

Startled, he let her go, and she went straight upstairs.

In the morning at breakfast, after he had looked round the place and attended to the stock and thought to himself that one could live easily enough here, he said to Banford:

"Do you know what, Miss Banford?"

"Well, what?" said the good-natured, nervy Banford.

He looked at March, who was spreading jam on her bread.

"Shall I tell?" he said to her.

She looked up at him, and a deep pink colour flushed over her face.

"Yes, if you mean Jill," she said. "I hope you won't go talking all over the village, that's all." And she swallowed her dry bread with difficulty.

"Whatever's coming?" said Banford, looking up with wide, tired, slightly reddened eyes. She was a thin, frail little thing, and her hair, which was delicate and thin, was bobbed, so it hung softly by her worn face in its faded brown and grey.

"Why, what do you think?" he said, smiling like one who has a secret.

"How do I know!" said Banford.

"Can't you guess?" he said, making bright eyes and smiling, pleased with himself.

"I'm sure I can't. What's more, I'm not going to try."

"Nellie and I are going to be married."

Banford put down her knife out of her thin, delicate fingers, as if she would never take it up to eat any more. She stared with blank, reddened eyes.

"You what?" she exclaimed.

"We're going to get married. Aren't we, Nellie?" and he turned to March.

"You say so, anyway," said March, laconically. But again she flushed with an agonised flush. She, too, could swallow no more.

Banford looked at her like a bird that has been shot: a poor, little sick bird. She gazed at her with all her wounded soul in her face, at the deep-flushed March.

"Never!" she exclaimed, helpless.

"It's quite right," said the bright and gloating youth.

Banford turned aside her face, as if the sight of the food on

the table made her sick. She sat like this for some moments,
as if she were sick. Then, with one hand on the edge of the
table, she rose to her feet.

"I'll *never* believe it, Nellie," she cried. "It's absolutely
impossible!"

Her plaintive, fretful voice had a thread of hot anger and
despair.

"Why? Why shouldn't you believe it?" asked the youth,
with all his soft, velvety impertinence in his voice.

Banford looked at him from her wide, vague eyes, as if he
were some creature in a museum.

"Oh," she said languidly, "because she can never be such a
fool. She can't lose her self-respect to such an extent." Her
voice was cold and plaintive, drifting.

"In what way will she lose her self-respect?" asked the boy.

Banford looked at him with vague fixity from behind her
spectacles.

"If she hasn't lost it already," she said.

He became very red, vermilion, under the slow, vague stare
from behind the spectacles.

"I don't see it at all," he said.

"Probably you don't. I shouldn't expect you would," said
Banford, with that straying mild tone of remoteness which
made her words even more insulting.

He sat stiff in his chair, staring with hot, blue eyes from his
scarlet face. An ugly look had come on his brow.

"My word, she doesn't know what she's letting herself in
for," said Banford, in her plaintive, drifting, insulting voice.

"What has it got to do with you, anyway?" said the youth,
in a temper.

"More than it has to do with you, probably," she replied,
plaintive and venomous.

"Oh, has it! I don't see that at all," he jerked out.

"No, you wouldn't," she answered, drifting.

"Anyhow," said March, pushing back her hair and rising un-
couthly. "It's no good arguing about it." And she seized the
bread and the tea-pot and strode away to the kitchen.

Banford let her fingers stray across her brow and along her
hair, like one bemused. Then she turned and went away upstairs.

Henry sat stiff and sulky in his chair, with his face and his
eyes on fire. March came and went, clearing the table. But

Henry sat on, stiff with temper. He took no notice of her. She had regained her composure and her soft, even, creamy complexion. But her mouth was pursed up. She glanced at him each time as she came to take things from the table, glanced from her large, curious eyes, more in curiosity than anything. Such a long, red-faced, sulky boy! That was all he was. He seemed as remote from her as if his red face were a red chimney-pot on a cottage across the fields, and she looked at him just as objectively, as remotely.

At length he got up and stalked out into the fields with the gun. He came in only at dinner-time, with the devil still in his face, but his manners quite polite. Nobody said anything particular; they sat each one at the sharp corner of a triangle, in obstinate remoteness. In the afternoon he went out again at once with the gun. He came in at nightfall with a rabbit and a pigeon. He stayed in all the evening, but hardly opened his mouth. He was in the devil of a temper, feeling he had been insulted.

Banford's eyes were red, she had evidently been crying. But her manner was more remote and supercilious than ever; the way she turned her head if he spoke at all, as if he were some tramp or inferior intruder of that sort, made his blue eyes go almost black with rage. His face looked sulkier. But he never forgot his polite intonation, if he opened his mouth to speak.

March seemed to flourish in this atmosphere. She seemed to sit between the two antagonists with a little wicked smile on her face, enjoying herself. There was even a sort of complacency in the way she laboriously crochetted this evening.

When he was in bed, the youth could hear the two women talking and arguing in their room. He sat up in bed and strained his ears to hear what they said. But he could hear nothing, it was too far off. Yet he could hear the soft, plaintive drip of Banford's voice, and March's deeper note.

The night was quiet, frosty. Big stars were snapping outside, beyond the ridge-tops of the pine trees. He listened and listened. In the distance he heard a fox yelping: and the dogs from the farms barking in answer. But it was not that he wanted to hear. It was what the two women were saying.

He got stealthily out of bed and stood by his door. He could hear no more than before. Very, very carefully he began to lift the door latch. After quite a time he had his door open. Then he stepped stealthily out into the passage. The old oak

planks were cold under his feet, and they creaked pre-
posterously. He crept very, very gently up the one step, and
along by the wall, till he stood outside their door. And there
he held his breath and listened. Banford's voice:

"No, I simply couldn't stand it. I should be dead in a month.
Which is just what he would be aiming at, of course. That
would just be his game, to see me in the churchyard. No,
Nellie, if you were to do such a thing as to marry him, you
could never stop here. I couldn't, I couldn't live in the same
house with him. Oh!—h! I feel quite sick with the smell of
his clothes. And his red face simply turns me over. I can't
eat my food when he's at the table. What a fool I was ever
to let him stop. One ought *never* to try to do a kind action.
It always flies back in your face like a boomerang."

"Well, he's only got two more days," said March.

"Yes, thank heaven. And when he's gone he'll never come
in this house again. I feel so bad while he's here. And I know,
I know he's only counting what he can get out of you. I
know that's all it is. He's just a good-for-nothing, who doesn't
want to work, and who thinks he'll live on us. But he won't
live on me. If you're such a fool, then it's your own look-
out. Mrs. Burgess knew him all the time he was here. And
the old man could never get him to do any steady work. He
was off with the gun on every occasion, just as he is now.
Nothing but the gun! Oh, I do hate it. You don't know what
you're doing, Nellie, you don't. If you marry him he'll just
make a fool of you. He'll go off and leave you stranded. I
know he will, if he can't get Bailey Farm out of us—and he's
not going to, while I live. While I live he's never going to set
foot here. I know what it would be. He'd soon think he was
master of both of us, as he thinks he's master of you already."

"But he isn't," said Nellie.

"He thinks he is, anyway. And that's what he wants: to
come and be master here. Yes, imagine it! That's what we've
got the place together for, is it, to be bossed and bullied by a
hateful, red-faced boy, a beastly labourer. Oh, we *did* make
a mistake when we let him stop. We ought never to have
lowered ourselves. And I've had such a fight with all the
people here, not to be pulled down to their level. No, he's not
coming here. And then you see—if he can't have the place,
he'll run off to Canada or somewhere again, as if he'd never
known you. And here you'll be, absolutely ruined and made

a fool of. I know I shall never have any peace of mind again."

"We'll tell him he can't come here. We'll tell him that," said March.

"Oh, don't you bother; I'm going to tell him that, and other things as well, before he goes. He's not going to have all his own way while I've got the strength left to speak. Oh, Nellie, he'll despise you, he'll despise you, like the awful little beast he is, if you give way to him. I'd no more trust him than I'd trust a cat not to steal. He's deep, he's deep, and he's bossy, and he's selfish through and through, as cold as ice. All he wants is to make use of you. And when you're no more use to him, then I pity you."

"I don't think he's as bad as all that," said March.

"No, because he's been playing up to you. But you'll find out, if you see much of him. Oh, Nellie, I can't bear to think of it."

"Well, it won't hurt you, Jill, darling."

"Won't it! Won't it! I shall never know a moment's peace again while I live, nor a moment's happiness. No, Nellie——" and Banford began to weep bitterly.

The boy outside could hear the stifled sound of the woman's sobbing, and could hear March's soft, deep, tender voice comforting, with wonderful gentleness and tenderness, the weeping woman.

His eyes were so round and wide that he seemed to see the whole night, and his ears were almost jumping off his head. He was frozen stiff. He crept back to bed, but felt as if the top of his head were coming off. He could not sleep. He could not keep still. He rose, quietly dressed himself, and crept out on to the landing once more. The women were silent. He went softly downstairs and out to the kitchen.

Then he put on his boots and his overcoat and took the gun. He did not think to go away from the farm. No, he only took the gun. As softly as possible he unfastened the door and went out into the frosty December night. The air was still, the stars bright, the pine trees seemed to bristle audibly in the sky. He went stealthily away down a fence-side, looking for something to shoot. At the same time he remembered that he ought not to shoot and frighten the women.

So he prowled round the edge of the gorse cover, and through the grove of tall old hollies, to the woodside. There he skirted the fence, peering through the darkness with dilated eyes that seemed to be able to grow black and full of sight in the dark, like a cat's. An owl was slowly and mournfully whooing round a great oak tree. He stepped stealthily with his gun, listening, listening, watching.

As he stood under the oaks of the wood-edge he heard the dogs from the neighbouring cottage up the hill yelling suddenly and startlingly, and the wakened dogs from the farms around barking answer. And suddenly it seemed to him England was little and tight, he felt the landscape was constricted even in the dark, and that there were too many dogs in the night, making a noise like a fence of sound, like the network of English hedges netting the view. He felt the fox didn't have a chance. For it must be the fox that had started all this hullabaloo.

Why not watch for him, anyhow! He would, no doubt, be coming sniffing round. The lad walked downhill to where the farmstead with its few pine trees crouched blackly. In the angle of the long shed, in the black dark, he crouched down. He knew the fox would be coming. It seemed to him it would be the last of the foxes in this loudly-barking, thick-voiced England, tight with innumerable little houses.

He sat a long time with his eyes fixed unchanging upon the open gateway, where a little light seemed to fall from the stars or from the horizon, who knows. He was sitting on a log in a dark corner with the gun across his knees. The pine trees snapped. Once a chicken fell off its perch in the barn with a loud crawk and cackle and commotion that startled him, and he stood up, watching with all his eyes, thinking it might be a rat. But he *felt* it was nothing. So he sat down again with the gun on his knees and his hands tucked in to keep them warm, and his eyes fixed unblinking on the pale reach of the open gateway. He felt he could smell the hot, sickly, rich smell of live chickens on the cold air.

And then—a shadow. A sliding shadow in the gateway. He gathered all his vision into a concentrated spark, and saw the shadow of the fox, the fox creeping on his belly through the gate. There he went, on his belly like a snake. The boy smiled to himself and brought the gun to his shoulder. He knew quite well what would happen. He knew the fox would go to where the fowl door was boarded up and sniff there. He knew he would lie there for a minute, sniffing the fowls within. And then he would start again prowling under the edge of the old barn, waiting to get in.

The fowl door was at the top of a slight incline. Soft, soft as a shadow the fox slid up this incline, and crouched with his nose to the boards. And at the same moment there was the awful crash of a gun reverberating between the old buildings, as if all the night had gone smash. But the boy watched keenly. He saw even the white belly of the fox as the beast beat his paws in death. So he went forward.

There was a commotion everywhere. The fowls were scuffling and crawking, the ducks were quark-quarking, the pony had stamped wildly to his feet. But the fox was on his side, struggling in his last tremors. The boy bent over him and smelt his foxy smell.

There was a sound of a window opening upstairs, then March's voice calling:

"Who is it?"

"It's me," said Henry; "I've shot the fox."

"Oh, goodness! You nearly frightened us to death."

"Did I? I'm awfully sorry."

"Whatever made you get up?"

"I heard him about."

"And have you shot him?"

"Yes, he's here," and the boy stood in the yard holding up the warm, dead brute. "You can't see, can you? Wait a minute." And he took his flash-light from his pocket and flashed it on to the dead animal. He was holding it by the brush. March saw, in the middle of the darkness, just the reddish fleece and the white belly and the white underneath of the pointed chin, and the queer, dangling paws. She did not know what to say.

"He's a beauty," he said. "He will make you a lovely fur."

"You don't catch me wearing a fox fur," she replied.

"Oh!" he said. And he switched off the light.

"Well, I should think you'll come in and go to bed again now," she said.

"Probably I shall. What time is it?"

"What time is it, Jill?" called March's voice. It was a quarter to one.

That night March had another dream. She dreamed that Banford was dead, and that she, March, was sobbing her heart out. Then she had to put Banford into her coffin. And the coffin was the rough wood-box in which the bits of chopped wood were kept in the kitchen, by the fire. This was the coffin, and there was no other, and March was in agony and dazed bewilderment, looking for something to line the box with, something to make it soft with, something to cover up the poor, dead darling. Because she couldn't lay her in there just in her white, thin night-dress, in the horrible wood-box. So she hunted and hunted, and picked up thing after thing, and threw it aside in the agony of dream-frustration. And in her dream-despair all she could find that would do was a fox-skin. She knew that it wasn't right, that this was not what she should have. But it was all she could find. And so she folded the brush of the fox, and laid her darling Jill's head on this, and she brought round the skin of the fox and laid it on the top of the body, so that it seemed to make a whole ruddy, fiery coverlet, and she cried and cried, and woke to find the tears streaming down her face.

The first thing that both she and Banford did in the morning was to go out to see the fox. Henry had hung it up by the heels in the shed, with its poor brush falling backwards. It was a lovely dog-fox in its prime, with a handsome, thick, winter coat: a lovely golden-red colour, with grey as it passed to the belly, and belly all white, and a great full brush with a delicate black and grey and pure white tip.

"Poor brute!" said Banford. "If it wasn't such a thieving wretch, you'd feel sorry for it."

March said nothing, but stood with her foot trailing aside, one hip out; her face was pale and her eyes big and black, watching the dead animal that was suspended upside down. White and soft as snow his belly: white and soft as snow. She passed her hand softly down it. And his wonderful black-glinted brush was full and frictional, wonderful. She passed her hand down this also, and quivered. Time after time she took the full fur of that thick tail between her fingers, and passed her hand slowly downwards. Wonderful, sharp, thick, splendour of a tail. And he was dead! She pursed her lips, and her eyes went black and vacant. Then she took the head in her hand.

Henry was sauntering up, so Banford walked rather pointedly away. March stood there bemused, with the head of the fox in her hand. She was wondering, wondering, wondering over his long, fine muzzle. For some reason it reminded her of a spoon or a spatula. She felt she could not understand it. The beast was a strange beast to her, incomprehensible, out of her range. Wonderful silver whiskers he had, like ice-threads. And pricked ears with hair inside. But that long, long, slender spoon of a nose!—and the marvellous white teeth beneath! It was to thrust forward and bite with, deep, deep, deep into the living prey, to bite and bite the blood.

"He's a beauty, isn't he?" said Henry, standing by.

"Oh yes, he's a fine big fox. I wonder how many chickens he's responsible for," she replied.

"A good many. Do you think he's the same one you saw in the summer?"

"I should think very likely he is," she replied.

He watched her, but he could make nothing of her. Partly she was so shy and virgin, and partly she was so grim, matter-of-fact, shrewish. What she said seemed to him so different from the look of her big, queer, dark eyes.

"Are you going to skin him?" she asked.

"Yes, when I've had breakfast, and got a board to peg him on."

"My word, what a strong smell he's got! Pooo! It'll take some washing off one's hands. I don't know why I was so silly as to handle him." And she looked at her right hand, that had passed down his belly and along his tail, and had even got a tiny streak of blood from one dark place in his fur.

"Have you seen the chickens when they smell him, how frightened they are?" he said.

"Yes, aren't they!"

"You must mind you don't get some of his fleas."

"Oh, fleas!" she replied, nonchalant.

Later in the day she saw the fox's skin nailed flat on a board, as if crucified. It gave her an uneasy feeling.

The boy was angry. He went about with his mouth shut, as if he had swallowed part of his chin. But in behaviour he was polite and affable. He did not say anything about his intention. And he left March alone.

That evening they sat in the dining-room. Banford wouldn't have him in her sitting-room any more. There was a very big log on the fire. And everybody was busy. Banford had letters to write, March was sewing a dress, and he was mending some little contrivance.

Banford stopped her letter-writing from time to time to

look round and rest her eyes. The boy had his head down, his face hidden over his job.

"Let's see," said Banford. "What train do you go by, Henry?"

He looked up straight at her.

"The morning train. In the morning," he said.

"What, the eight-ten or the eleven-twenty?"

"The eleven-twenty, I suppose," he said.

"That is the day after to-morrow?" said Banford.

"Yes, the day after to-morrow."

"Mm!" murmured Banford, and she returned to her writing. But as she was licking her envelope, she asked:

"And what plans have you made for the future, if I may ask?"

"Plans?" he said, his face very bright and angry.

"I mean about you and Nellie, if you are going on with this business. When do you expect the wedding to come off?" She spoke in a jeering tone.

"Oh, the wedding!" he replied. "I don't know."

"Don't you know anything?" said Banford. "Are you going to clear out on Friday and leave things no more settled than they are?"

"Well, why shouldn't I? We can always write letters."

"Yes, of course you can. But I wanted to know because of this place. If Nellie is going to get married all of a sudden, I shall have to be looking round for a new partner."

"Couldn't she stay on here if she were married?" he said. He knew quite well what was coming.

"Oh," said Banford, "this is no place for a married couple. There's not enough work to keep a man going, for one thing. And there's no money to be made. It's quite useless your thinking of staying on here if you marry. Absolutely!"

"Yes, but I wasn't thinking of staying on here," he said.

"Well, that's what I want to know. And what about Nellie, then? How long is *she* going to be here with me, in that case?"

The two antagonists looked at one another.

"That I can't say," he answered.

"Oh, go along," she cried petulantly. "You must have some idea what you are going to do, if you ask a woman to marry you. Unless it's all a hoax."

"Why should it be a hoax? I am going back to Canada."

"And taking her with you?"

"Yes, certainly."

"You hear that, Nellie?" said Banford.

March, who had had her head bent over her sewing, now looked up with a sharp, pink blush on her face, and a queer, sardonic laugh in her eyes and on her twisted mouth.

"That's the first time I've heard that I was going to Canada," she said.

"Well, you have to hear it for the first time, haven't you?" said the boy.

"Yes, I suppose I have," she said nonchalantly. And she went back to her sewing.

"You're quite ready, are you, to go to Canada? Are you, Nellie?" asked Banford.

March looked up again. She let her shoulders go slack, and let her hand that held the needle lie loose in her lap.

"It depends on *how* I'm going," she said. "I don't think I want to go jammed up in the steerage, as a soldier's wife. I'm afraid I'm not used to that way."

The boy watched her with bright eyes.

"Would you rather stay over here while I go first?" he asked.

"I would, if that's the only alternative," she replied.

"That's much the wisest. Don't make it any fixed engagement," said Banford. "Leave yourself free to go or not after he's got back and found you a place, Nellie. Anything else is madness, madness."

"Don't you think," said the youth, "we ought to get married before I go—and then go together, or separate, according to how it happens?"

"I think it's a terrible idea," cried Banford.

But the boy was watching March.

"What do you think?" he asked her.

She let her eyes stray vaguely into space.

"Well, I don't know," she said. "I shall have to think about it."

"Why?" he asked pertinently.

"Why?" She repeated his question in a mocking way and looked at him laughing, though her face was pink again. "I should think there's plenty of reasons why."

He watched her in silence. She seemed to have escaped him. She had got into league with Banford against him. There was again the queer, sardonic look about her; she would mock stoically at everything he said or which life offered.

"Of course," he said, "I don't want to press you to do anything you don't wish to do."

"I should think not, indeed," cried Banford indignantly.

At bed-time Banford said plaintively to March:

"You take my hot bottle up for me, Nellie, will you?"

"Yes, I'll do it," said March, with the kind of willing unwillingness she so often showed towards her beloved but uncertain Jill.

The two women went upstairs. After a time March called from the top of the stairs: "Good-night, Henry. I shan't be coming down. You'll see to the lamp and the fire, won't you?"

The next day Henry went about with the cloud on his brow and his young cub's face shut up tight. He was cogitating all the time. He had wanted March to marry him and go back to Canada with him. And he had been sure she would do it. Why he wanted her he didn't know. But he did want her. He had set his mind on her. And he was convulsed with a youth's fury at being thwarted. To be thwarted, to be thwarted! It made him so furious inside that he did not know what to do with himself. But he kept himself in hand. Because even now things might turn out differently. She might come over to him. Of course she might. It was her business to do so.

Things drew to a tension again towards evening. He and Banford had avoided each other all day. In fact, Banford went in to the little town by the 11.20 train. It was market day. She arrived back on the 4.25. Just as the night was falling Henry saw her little figure in a dark-blue coat and a dark-blue tam-o'-shanter hat crossing the first meadow from the station. He stood under one of the wild pear trees, with the old dead leaves round his feet. And he watched the little blue figure advancing persistently over the rough winter-ragged meadow. She had her arms full of parcels, and advanced slowly, frail thing she was, but with that devilish little certainty which he so detested in her. He stood invisible under the pear tree, watching her every step. And if looks could have affected her, she would have felt a log of iron on each of her ankles as she made her way forward. "You're a nasty little thing, you are," he was saying softly, across the distance. "You're a nasty little thing. I hope you'll be paid back for all the harm you've done me for nothing. I hope you will—you nasty little thing. I hope you'll have to pay for it. You will, if wishes are anything. You nasty little creature that you are."

She was toiling slowly up the slope. But if she had been slipping back at every step towards the Bottomless Pit, he would not have gone to help her with her parcels. Aha, there went March, striding with her long, land stride in her breeches and her short tunic! Striding downhill at a great pace, and even running a few steps now and then, in her great solicitude and desire to come to the rescue of the little Banford. The boy watched her with rage in his heart. See her leap a ditch, and run, run as if a house was on fire, just to get to that creeping, dark little object down there! So, the Banford just stood still and waited. And March strode up and took *all* the parcels except a bunch of yellow chrysanthemums. These the Banford still carried—yellow chrysanthemums!

"Yes, you look well, don't you?" he said softly into the dusk air. "You look well, pottering up there with a bunch of flowers, you do. I'd make you eat them for your tea if you hug them so tight. And I'd give them you for breakfast again, I would. I'd give you flowers. Nothing but flowers."

He watched the progress of the two women. He could hear their voices: March always outspoken and rather scolding in her tenderness, Banford murmuring rather vaguely. They were evidently good friends. He could not hear what they said till they came to the fence of the home meadow, which they must climb. Then he saw March manfully climbing over the bars with all her packages in her arms, and on the still air he heard Banford's fretful:

"Why don't you let me help you with the parcels?" She had a queer, plaintive hitch in her voice. Then came March's robust and reckless:

"Oh, I can manage. Don't you bother about me. You've all you can do to get yourself over."

"Yes, that's all very well," said Banford fretfully. "You say, *Don't you bother about me,* and then all the while you feel injured because nobody thinks of you."

"When do I feel injured?" said March.

"Always. You always feel injured. Now you're feeling injured because I won't have that boy to come and live on the farm."

"I'm not feeling injured at all," said March.

"I know you are. When he's gone you'll sulk over it. I know you will."

"Shall I?" said March. "We'll see."

"Yes, we *shall* see, unfortunately. I can't think how you can make yourself so cheap. I can't *imagine* how you can lower yourself like it."

"I haven't lowered myself," said March.

"I don't know what you call it, then. Letting a boy like that come so cheeky and impudent and make a mug of you. I don't know what you think of yourself. How much respect do you think he's going to have for you afterwards? My word, I wouldn't be in your shoes, if you married him."

"Of course you wouldn't. My boots are a good bit too big for you, and not half dainty enough," said March, with rather a misfire sarcasm.

"I thought you had too much pride, really I did. A woman's got to hold herself high, especially with a youth like that. Why, he's impudent. Even the way he forced himself on us at the start."

"We asked him to stay," said March.

"Not till he'd almost forced us to. And then he's so cocky and self-assured. My word, he puts my back up. I simply can't imagine how you can let him treat you so cheaply."

"I don't let him treat me cheaply," said March. "Don't you worry yourself, nobody's going to treat me cheaply. And even you aren't, either." She had a tender defiance and a certain fire in her voice.

"Yes, it's sure to come back to me," said Banford bitterly. "That's always the end of it. I believe you only do it to spite me."

They went now in silence up the steep, grassy slope and over the brow, through the gorse bushes. On the other side of the hedge the boy followed in the dusk, at some little distance. Now and then, through the huge ancient hedge of hawthorn, risen into trees, he saw the two dark figures creeping up the hill. As he came to the top of the slope he saw the homestead dark in the twilight, with a huge old pear tree leaning from the near gable, and a little yellow light twinkling in the small side windows of the kitchen. He heard the clink of the latch and saw the kitchen door open into light as the two women went indoors. So they were at home.

And so!—this was what they thought of him. It was rather

in his nature to be a listener, so he was not at all surprised
whatever he heard. The things people said about him always
missed him personally. He was only rather surprised at the
women's way with one another. And he disliked the Banford
with an acid dislike. And he felt drawn to the March again.
He felt again irresistibly drawn to her. He felt there was a
secret bond, a secret thread between him and her, something
very exclusive, which shut out everybody else and made him
and her possess each other in secret.

He hoped again that she would have him. He hoped with
his blood suddenly firing up that she would agree to marry
him quite quickly: at Christmas, very likely. Christmas was
not far off. He wanted, whatever else happened, to snatch
her into a hasty marriage and a consummation with him. Then
for the future, they could arrange later. But he hoped it would
happen as he wanted it. He hoped that to-night she would
stay a little while with him, after Banford had gone upstairs.
He hoped he could touch her soft, creamy cheek, her strange,
frightened face. He hoped he could look into her dilated,
frightened dark eyes, quite near. He hoped he might even
put his hand on her bosom and feel her soft breasts under her
tunic. His heart beat deep and powerful as he thought of
that. He wanted very much to do so. He wanted to make
sure of her soft woman's breasts under her tunic. She always
kept the brown linen coat buttoned so close up to her throat.
It seemed to him like some perilous secret, that her soft
woman's breasts must be buttoned up in that uniform. It
seemed to him, moreover, that they were so much softer,
tenderer, more lovely and lovable, shut up in that tunic, than
were the Banford's breasts, under her soft blouses and chiffon
dresses. The Banford would have little iron breasts, he said
to himself. For all her frailty and fretfulness and delicacy, she
would have tiny iron breasts. But March, under her crude,
fast, workman's tunic, would have soft, white breasts, white
and unseen. So he told himself, and his blood burned.

When he went in to tea, he had a surprise. He appeared at
the inner door, his face very ruddy and vivid and his blue
eyes shining, dropping his head forward as he came in, in his
usual way, and hesitating in the doorway to watch the inside
of the room, keenly and cautiously, before he entered. He
was wearing a long-sleeved waistcoat. His face seemed extraordinarily like a piece of the out-of-doors come indoors: as

holly-berries do. In his second of pause in the doorway he took in the two women sitting at table, at opposite ends, saw them sharply. And to his amazement March was dressed in a dress of dull, green silk crape. His mouth came open in surprise. If she had suddenly grown a moustache he could not have been more surprised.

"Why," he said, "do you wear a dress, then?"

She looked up, flushing a deep rose colour, and twisting her mouth with a smile, said:

"Of course I do. What else do you expect me to wear but a dress?"

"A land girl's uniform, of course," said he.

"Oh," she cried, nonchalant, "that's only for this dirty, mucky work about here."

"Isn't it your proper dress, then?" he said.

"No, not indoors it isn't," she said. But she was blushing all the time as she poured out his tea. He sat down in his chair at table, unable to take his eyes off her. Her dress was a perfectly simple slip of bluey-green crape, with a line of gold stitching round the top and round the sleeves, which came to the elbow. It was cut just plain and round at the top, and showed her white, soft throat. Her arms he knew, strong and firm muscled, for he had often seen her with her sleeves rolled up. But he looked her up and down, up and down.

Banford, at the other end of the table, said not a word, but piggled with the sardine on her plate. He had forgotten her existence. He just simply stared at March while he ate his bread and margarine in huge mouthfuls, forgetting even his tea.

"Well, I never knew anything make such a difference!" he murmured, across his mouthfuls.

"Oh, goodness!" cried March, blushing still more. "I might be a pink monkey!"

And she rose quickly to her feet and took the tea-pot to the fire, to the kettle. And as she crouched on the hearth with her green slip about her, the boy stared more wide-eyed than ever. Through the crape her woman's form seemed soft and womanly. And when she stood up and walked he saw her legs move soft within her modernly short skirt. She had on black silk stockings, and small patent shoes with little gold buckles.

No, she was another being. She was something quite

different. Seeing her always in the hard-cloth breeches, wide on the hips, buttoned on the knee, strong as armour, and in the brown puttees and thick boots, it had never occurred to him that she had a woman's legs and feet. Now it came upon him. She had a woman's soft, skirted legs, and she was accessible. He blushed to the roots of his hair, shoved his nose in his tea-cup and drank his tea with a little noise that made Banford simply squirm: and strangely, suddenly he felt a man, no longer a youth. He felt a man, with all a man's grave weight of responsibility. A curious quietness and gravity came over his soul. He felt a man, quiet, with a little of the heaviness of male destiny upon him.

She was soft and accessible in her dress. The thought went home in him like an everlasting responsibility.

"Oh, for goodness' sake, say something, somebody," cried Banford fretfully. "It might be a funeral." The boy looked at her, and she could not bear his face.

"A funeral!" said March, with a twisted smile. "Why, that breaks my dream."

Suddenly she had thought of Banford in the wood-box for a coffin.

"What, have you been dreaming of a wedding?" said Banford sarcastically.

"Must have been," said March.

"Whose wedding?" asked the boy.

"I can't remember," said March.

She was shy and rather awkward that evening, in spite of the fact that, wearing a dress, her bearing was much more subdued than in her uniform. She felt unpeeled and rather exposed. She felt almost improper.

They talked desultorily about Henry's departure next morning, and made the trivial arrangement. But of the matter on their minds, none of them spoke. They were rather quiet and friendly this evening; Banford had practically nothing to say. But inside herself she seemed still, perhaps kindly.

At nine o'clock March brought in the tray with the everlasting tea and a little cold meat which Banford had managed to procure. It was the last supper, so Banford did not want to be disagreeable. She felt a bit sorry for the boy, and felt she must be as nice as she could.

He wanted her to go to bed. She was usually the first. But she sat on in her chair under the lamp, glancing at her book now and then, and staring into the fire. A deep silence had come into the room. It was broken by March asking, in a rather small tone:

"What time is it, Jill?"

"Five past ten," said Banford, looking at her wrist.

And then not a sound. The boy had looked up from the book he was holding between his knees. His rather wide, cat-shaped face had its obstinate look, his eyes were watchful.

"What about bed?" said March at last.

"I'm ready when you are," said Banford.

"Oh, very well," said March. "I'll fill your bottle."

She was as good as her word. When the hot-water bottle was ready, she lit a candle and went upstairs with it. Banford remained in her chair, listening acutely. March came downstairs again.

"There you are, then," she said. "Are you going up?"

"Yes, in a minute," said Banford. But the minute passed, and she sat on in her chair under the lamp.

Henry, whose eyes were shining like a cat's as he watched from under his brows, and whose face seemed wider, more chubbed and cat-like with unalterable obstinacy, now rose to his feet to try his throw.

"I think I'll go and look if I can see the she-fox," he said. "She may be creeping round. Won't you come as well for a minute, Nellie, and see if we see anything?"

"Me!" cried March, looking up with her startled, wondering face.

"Yes. Come on," he said. It was wonderful how soft and warm and coaxing his voice could be, how near. The very sound of it made Banford's blood boil. "Come on for a minute," he said, looking down into her uplifted, unsure face.

And she rose to her feet as if drawn up by his young, ruddy face that was looking down on her.

"I should think you're never going out at this time of night, Nellie!" cried Banford.

"Yes, just for a minute," said the boy, looking round on her, and speaking with an odd, sharp yelp in his voice.

March looked from one to the other, as if confused, vague. Banford rose to her feet for battle.

"Why, it's ridiculous. It's bitter cold. You'll catch your death in that thin frock. And in those slippers. You're not going to do any such thing."

There was a moment's pause. Banford turtled up like a little fighting cock, facing March and the boy.

"Oh, I don't think you need worry yourself," he replied. "A moment under the stars won't do anybody any damage. I'll get the rug off the sofa in the dining-room. You're coming, Nellie."

His voice had so much anger and contempt and fury in it as he spoke to Banford: and so much tenderness and proud authority as he spoke to March, that the latter answered:

"Yes, I'm coming."

And she turned with him to the door.

Banford, standing there in the middle of the room, suddenly burst into a long wail and a spasm of sobs. She covered her face with her poor, thin hands, and her thin shoulders shook in an agony of weeping. March looked back from the door.

"Jill!" she cried in a frantic tone, like someone just coming awake. And she seemed to start towards her darling.

But the boy had March's arm in his grip, and she could not move. She did not know why she could not move. It was as in a dream when the heart strains and the body cannot stir.

"Never mind," said the boy softly. "Let her cry. Let her cry. She will have to cry sooner or later. And the tears will relieve her feelings. They will do her good."

So he drew March slowly through the doorway. But her last look was back to the poor little figure which stood in the middle of the room with covered face and thin shoulders shaken with bitter weeping.

In the dining-room he picked up the rug and said:

"Wrap yourself up in this."

She obeyed—and they reached the kitchen door, he holding her soft and firm by the arm, though she did not know it. When she saw the night outside she started back.

"I must go back to Jill," she said. "I *must*! Oh yes, I must."

Her tone sounded final. The boy let go of her and she turned indoors. But he seized her again and arrested her.

"Wait a minute," he said. "Wait a minute. Even if you go, you're not going yet."

"Leave go! Leave go!" she cried. "My place is at Jill's side. Poor little thing, she's sobbing her heart out."

"Yes," said the boy bitterly. "And your heart too, and mine as well."

"Your heart?" said March. He still gripped her and detained her.

"Isn't it as good as her heart?" he said. "Or do you think it's not?"

"Your heart?" she said again, incredulous.

"Yes, mine! Mine! Do you think I haven't *got* a heart?" And with his hot grasp he took her hand and pressed it under his left breast. "There's my heart," he said, "if you don't believe in it."

It was wonder which made her attend. And then she felt the deep, heavy, powerful stroke of his heart, terrible, like something from beyond. It was like something from beyond, something awful from outside, signalling to her. And the signal paralysed her. It beat upon her very soul, and made her helpless. She forgot Jill. She could not think of Jill any more. She could not think of her. That terrible signalling from outside!

The boy put his arm round her waist.

"Come with me," he said gently. "Come and let us say what we've got to say."

And he drew her outside, closed the door. And she went with him darkly down the garden path. That he should have a beating heart! And that he should have his arm round her, outside the blanket! She was too confused to think who he was or what he was.

He took her to a dark corner of the shed, where there was a tool-box with a lid, long and low.

"We'll sit here a minute," he said.

And obediently she sat down by his side.

"Give me your hand," he said.

She gave him both her hands, and he held them between his own. He was young, and it made him tremble.

"You'll marry me. You'll marry me before I go back, won't you?" he pleaded.

"Why, aren't we both a pair of fools?" she said.

He had put her in the corner, so that she should not look out and see the lighted window of the house across the dark garden. He tried to keep her all there inside the shed with him.

"In what way a pair of fools?" he said. "If you go back to Canada with me, I've got a job and a good wage waiting for me, and it's a nice place, near the mountains. Why shouldn't you marry me? Why shouldn't we marry? I should like to

have you there with me. I should like to feel I'd got somebody there, at the back of me, all my life."

"You'd easily find somebody else who'd suit you better,"
she said.

"Yes, I might easily find another girl. I know I could. But
not one I really wanted. I've never met one I really wanted
for good. You see, I'm thinking of all my life. If I marry, I
want to feel it's for all my life. Other girls: well, they're just
girls, nice enough to go a walk with now and then. Nice
enough for a bit of play. But when I think of my life, then
I should be very sorry to have to marry one of them, I should
indeed."

"You mean they wouldn't make you a good wife."

"Yes, I mean that. But I don't mean they wouldn't do
their duty by me. I mean—I don't know what I mean. Only
when I think of my life, and of you, then the two things go
together."

"And what if they didn't?" she said, with her odd, sardonic
touch.

"Well, I think they would."

They sat for some time silent. He held her hands in his, but
he did not make love to her. Since he had realised that she
was a woman, and vulnerable, accessible, a certain heaviness
had possessed his soul. He did not want to make love to her.
He shrank from any such performance, almost with fear. She
was a woman, and vulnerable, accessible to him finally, and
he held back from that which was ahead, almost with dread.
It was a kind of darkness he knew he would enter finally, but
of which he did not want as yet even to think. She was the
woman, and he was responsible for the strange vulnerability
he had suddenly realised in her.

"No," she said at last, "I'm a fool. I know I'm a fool."

"What for?" he asked.

"To go on with this business."

"Do you mean me?" he asked.

"No, I mean myself. I'm making a fool of myself, and a
big one."

"Why, because you don't want to marry me, really?"

"Oh, I don't know whether I'm against it, as a matter of
fact. That's just it. I don't know."

He looked at her in the darkness, puzzled. He did not in
the least know what she meant.

"And don't you know whether you like to sit here with me this minute or not?" he asked.

"No, I don't really. I don't know whether I wish I was somewhere else, or whether I like being here. I don't know, really."

"Do you wish you were with Miss Banford? Do you wish you'd gone to bed with her?" he asked, as a challenge.

She waited a long time before she answered.

"No," she said at last. "I don't wish that."

"And do you think you would spend all your life with her—when your hair goes white, and you are old?" he said.

"No," she said, without much hesitation. "I don't see Jill and me two old women together."

"And don't you think, when I'm an old man and you're an old woman, we might be together still, as we are now?" he said.

"Well, not as we are now," she replied. "But I could imagine—no, I can't. I can't imagine you an old man. Besides, it's dreadful!"

"What, to be an old man?"

"Yes, of course."

"Not when the time comes," he said. "But it hasn't come. Only it will. And when it does, I should like to think you'd be there as well."

"Sort of old age pensions," she said dryly.

Her kind of witless humour always startled him. He never knew what she meant. Probably she didn't quite know herself.

"No," he said, hurt.

"I don't know why you harp on old age," she said. "I'm not ninety."

"Did anybody ever say you were?" he asked, offended.

They were silent for some time, pulling different ways in the silence.

"I don't want you to make fun of me," he said.

"Don't you?" she replied, enigmatic.

"No, because just this minute I'm serious. And when I'm serious, I believe in not making fun of it."

"You mean nobody else must make fun of you," she replied.

"Yes, I mean that. And I mean I don't believe in making fun of it myself. When it comes over me so that I'm serious, then—there it is, I don't want it to be laughed at."

She was silent for some time. Then she said, in a vague, almost pained voice:

"No, I'm not laughing at you."

A hot wave rose in his heart.

"You believe me, do you?" he asked.

"Yes, I believe you," she replied, with a twang of her old, tired nonchalance, as if she gave in because she was tired. But he didn't care. His heart was hot and clamorous.

"So you agree to marry me before I go?—perhaps at Christmas?"

"Yes, I agree."

"There!" he exclaimed. "That's settled it."

And he sat silent, unconscious, with all the blood burning in all his veins, like fire in all the branches and twigs of him. He only pressed her two hands to his chest, without knowing. When the curious passion began to die down, he seemed to come awake to the world.

"We'll go in, shall we?" he said: as if he realised it was cold.

She rose without answering.

"Kiss me before we go, now you've said it," he said.

And he kissed her gently on the mouth, with a young, frightened kiss. It made her feel so young, too, and frightened, and wondering: and tired, tired, as if she were going to sleep.

They went indoors. And in the sitting-room, there, crouched by the fire like a queer little witch, was Banford. She looked round with reddened eyes as they entered, but did not rise. He thought she looked frightening, unnatural, crouching there and looking round at them. Evil he thought her look was, and he crossed his fingers.

Banford saw the ruddy, elate face on the youth: he seemed strangely tall and bright and looming. And March had a delicate look on her face; she wanted to hide her face, to screen it, to let it not be seen.

"You've come at last," said Banford uglily.

"Yes, we've come," said he.

"You've been long enough for anything," she said.

"Yes, we have. We've settled it. We shall marry as soon as possible," he replied.

"Oh, you've settled it, have you! Well, I hope you won't live to repent it," said Banford.

"I hope so too," he replied.

"Are you going to bed *now*, Nellie?" said Banford.

"Yes, I'm going now."

"Then for goodness' sake come along."

March looked at the boy. He was glancing with his very bright eyes at her and at Banford. March looked at him wistfully. She wished she could stay with him. She wished she had married him already, and it was all over. For oh, she felt suddenly so safe with him. She felt so strangely safe and peaceful in his presence. If only she could sleep in his shelter, and not with Jill. She felt afraid of Jill. In her dim, tender state, it was agony to have to go with Jill and sleep with her. She wanted the boy to save her. She looked again at him.

And he, watching with bright eyes, divined something of what she felt. It puzzled and distressed him that she must go with Jill.

"I shan't forget what you've promised," he said, looking clear into her eyes, right into her eyes, so that he seemed to occupy all herself with his queer, bright look.

She smiled to him faintly, gently. She felt safe again—safe with him.

But in spite of all the boy's precautions, he had a setback. The morning he was leaving the farm he got March to accompany him to the market-town, about six miles away, where they went to the registrar and had their names stuck up as two people who were going to marry. He was to come at Christmas, and the wedding was to take place then. He hoped in the spring to be able to take March back to Canada with him, now the war was really over. Though he was so young, he had saved some money.

"You never have to be without *some* money at the back of you, if you can help it," he said.

So she saw him off in the train that was going West: his camp was on Salisbury Plain. And with big, dark eyes she watched him go, and it seemed as if everything real in life was retreating as the train retreated with his queer, chubby, ruddy face, that seemed so broad across the cheeks, and which never seemed to change its expression, save when a cloud of sulky anger hung on the brow, or the bright eyes fixed themselves in their stare. This was what happened now. He leaned there out of the carriage window as the train drew off, saying goodbye and staring back at her, but his face quite unchanged. There was no emotion on his face. Only his eyes tightened and became fixed and intent in their watching like a cat's when suddenly she sees something and stares. So the boy's eyes stared fixedly as the train drew away, and she was left feeling intensely forlorn. Failing his physical presence, she seemed to have nothing of him. And she had nothing of anything. Only his face was fixed in her mind: the full, ruddy, unchanging cheeks, and the straight snout of a nose and the two eyes staring above. All she could remember was how he suddenly wrinkled his nose when he laughed, as a puppy does when he is playfully growling. But him, himself, and what he was—she knew nothing, she had nothing of him when he left her.

On the ninth day after he had left her he received this letter.

"Dear Henry,

"I have been over it all again in my mind, this business of me and you, and it seems to me impossible. When you aren't there I see what a fool I am. When you are there you seem to blind me to things as they actually are. You make me see things all unreal, and I don't know what. Then when I am alone again with Jill I seem to come to my own senses and realise what a fool I am making of myself, and how I am treating you unfairly. Because it must be unfair to you for me to go on with this affair when I can't feel in my heart that I really love you. I know people talk a lot of stuff and nonsense about love, and I don't want to do that. I want to keep to plain facts and act in a sensible way. And that seems to me what I'm not doing. I don't see on what grounds I am going to marry you. I know I am not head over heels in love with you, as I have fancied myself to be with fellows when I was a young fool of a girl. You are an absolute stranger to me, and it seems to me you will always be one. So on what grounds am I going to marry you? When I think of Jill, she is ten times more real to me. I know her and I'm awfully fond of her, and I hate myself for a beast if I ever hurt her little finger. We have a life together. And even if it can't last for ever, it is a life while it does last. And it might last as long as either of us lives. Who knows how long we've got to live? She is a delicate little thing, perhaps nobody but me knows how delicate. And as for me, I feel I might fall down the well any day. What I don't seem to see at all is you. When I think of what I've been and what I've done with you, I'm afraid I am a few

screws loose. I should be sorry to think that softening of the
brain is setting in so soon, but that is what it seems like. You
are such an absolute stranger, and so different from what I'm
used to, and we don't seem to have a thing in common. As
for love, the very word seems impossible. I know what love
means even in Jill's case, and I know that in this affair with
you it's an absolute impossibility. And then going to Canada.
I'm sure I must have been clean off my chump when I promised
such a thing. It makes me feel fairly frightened of myself. I
feel I might do something really silly that I wasn't responsible
for—and end my days in a lunatic asylum. You may think
that's all I'm fit for after the way I've gone on, but it isn't a
very nice thought for me. Thank goodness Jill is here, and
her being here makes me feel sane again, else I don't know
what I might do; I might have an accident with the gun one
evening. I love Jill, and she makes me feel safe and sane, with
her loving anger against me for being such a fool. Well, what
I want to say is, won't you let us cry the whole thing off? I
can't marry you, and really, I won't do such a thing if it seems
to me wrong. It is all a great mistake. I've made a complete
fool of myself, and all I can do is to apologise to you and ask
you please to forget it, and please to take no further notice of
me. Your fox-skin is nearly ready, and seems all right. I will
post it to you if you will let me know if this address is still
right, and if you will accept my apology for the awful and
lunatic way I have behaved with you, and then let the matter
rest.

"Jill sends her kindest regards. Her mother and father are
staying with us over Christmas.

"Yours very sincerely,

"ELLEN MARCH."

The boy read this letter in camp as he was cleaning his kit.
He set his teeth, and for a moment went almost pale, yellow
round the eyes with fury. He said nothing and saw nothing
and felt nothing but a livid rage that was quite unreasoning.
Balked! Balked again! Balked! He wanted the woman, he
had fixed like doom upon having her. He felt that was his
doom, his destiny, and his reward, to have this woman. She
was his heaven and hell on earth, and he would have none
elsewhere. Sightless with rage and thwarted madness he got
through the morning. Save that in his mind he was lurking

and scheming towards an issue, he would have committed some insane act. Deep in himself he felt like roaring and howling and gnashing his teeth and breaking things. But he was too intelligent. He knew society was on top of him, and he must scheme. So with his teeth bitten together, and his nose curiously slightly lifted, like some creature that is vicious, and his eyes fixed and staring, he went through the morning's affairs drunk with anger and suppression. In his mind was one thing—Banford. He took no heed of all March's outpouring: none. One thorn rankled, stuck in his mind. Banford. In his mind, in his soul, in his whole being, one thorn rankling to insanity. And he would have to get it out. He would have to get the thorn of Banford out of his life, if he died for it.

With this one fixed idea in his mind, he went to ask for twenty-four hours' leave of absence. He knew it was not due to him. His consciousness was supernaturally keen. He knew where he must go—he must go to the captain. But how could he get at the captain? In that great camp of wooden huts and tents he had no idea where his captain was.

But he went to the officers' canteen. There was his captain standing talking with three other officers. Henry stood in the doorway at attention.

"May I speak to Captain Berryman?" The captain was Cornish like himself.

"What do you want?" called the captain.

"May I speak to you, Captain?"

"What do you want?" replied the captain, not stirring from among his group of fellow officers.

Henry watched his superior for a minute without speaking.

"You won't refuse me, sir, will you?" he asked gravely.

"It depends what it is."

"Can I have twenty-four hours' leave?"

"No, you've no business to ask."

"I know I haven't. But I must ask you."

"You've had your answer."

"Don't send me away, Captain."

There was something strange about the boy as he stood there so everlasting in the doorway. The Cornish captain felt the strangeness at once, and eyed him shrewdly.

"Why, what's afoot?" he said, curious.

"I'm in trouble about something. I must go to Blewbury," said the boy.

"Blewbury, eh? After the girls?"

"Yes, it is a woman, Captain." And the boy, as he stood there with his head reaching forward a little, went suddenly terribly pale, or yellow, and his lips seemed to give off pain. The captain saw and paled a little also. He turned aside.

"Go on, then," he said. "But for God's sake don't cause any trouble of any sort."

"I won't, Captain, thank you."

He was gone. The captain, upset, took a gin and bitters. Henry managed to hire a bicycle. It was twelve o'clock when he left the camp. He had sixty miles of wet and muddy cross-roads to ride. But he was in the saddle and down the road without a thought of food.

At the farm, March was busy with a work she had had some time in hand. A bunch of Scotch fir trees stood at the end of the open shed, on a little bank where ran the fence between two of the gorse-shaggy meadows. The farthest of these trees was dead—it had died in the summer, and stood with all its needles brown and sere in the air. It was not a very big tree. And it was absolutely dead. So March determined to have it, although they were not allowed to cut any of the timber. But it would make such splendid firing, in these days of scarce fuel.

She had been giving a few stealthy chops at the trunk for a week or more, every now and then hacking away for five minutes, low down, near the ground, so no one should notice. She had not tried the saw, it was such hard work, alone. Now the tree stood with a great yawning gap in his base, perched, as it were, on one sinew, and ready to fall. But he did not fall.

It was late in the damp December afternoon, with cold mists creeping out of the woods and up the hollows, and darkness waiting to sink in from above. There was a bit of yellowness where the sun was fading away beyond the low woods of the distance. March took her axe and went to the tree. The small thud-thud of her blows resounded rather ineffectual about the wintry homestead. Banford came out wearing her thick coat, but with no hat on her head, so that her thin, bobbed hair blew on the uneasy wind that sounded in the pines and in the wood.

"What I'm afraid of," said Banford, "is that it will fall on the shed and we sh'll have another job repairing that."

"Oh, I don't think so," said March, straightening herself

and wiping her arm over her hot brow. She was flushed red, her eyes were very wide open and queer, her upper lip lifted away from her two white, front teeth with a curious, almost rabbit look.

A little stout man in a black overcoat and a bowler hat came pottering across the yard. He had a pink face and a white beard and smallish, pale-blue eyes. He was not very old, but nervy, and he walked with little short steps.

"What do you think, father?" said Banford. "Don't you think it might hit the shed in falling?"

"Shed, no!" said the old man. "Can't hit the shed. Might as well say the fence."

"The fence doesn't matter," said March, in her high voice.

"Wrong as usual, am I!" said Banford, wiping her straying hair from her eyes.

The tree stood as it were on one spelch of itself, leaning, and creaking in the wind. It grew on the bank of a little dry ditch between the two meadows. On the top of the bank straggled one fence, running to the bushes up-hill. Several trees clustered there in the corner of the field near the shed and near the gate which led into the yard. Towards this gate, horizontal across the weary meadows, came the grassy, rutted approach from the high road. There trailed another rickety fence, long split poles joining the short, thick, wide-apart uprights. The three people stood at the back of the tree, in the corner of the shed meadow, just above the yard gate. The house, with its two gables and its porch, stood tidy in a little grassed garden across the yard. A little, stout, rosy-faced woman in a little red woollen shoulder shawl had come and taken her stand in the porch.

"Isn't it down yet?" she cried, in a high little voice.

"Just thinking about it," called her husband. His tone towards the two girls was always rather mocking and satirical. March did not want to go on with her hitting while he was there. As for him, he wouldn't lift a stick from the ground if he could help it, complaining, like his daughter, of rheumatics in his shoulder. So the three stood there a moment silent in the cold afternoon, in the bottom corner near the yard.

They heard the far-off taps of a gate, and craned to look. Away across, on the green horizontal approach, a figure was just swinging on to a bicycle again, and lurching up and down over the grass, approaching.

"Why, it's one of our boys—it's Jack," said the old man.

"Can't be," said Banford.

March craned her head to look. She alone recognised the khaki figure. She flushed, but said nothing.

"No, it isn't Jack, I don't think," said the old man, staring with little round blue eyes under his white lashes.

In another moment the bicycle lurched into sight, and the rider dropped off at the gate. It was Henry, his face wet and red and spotted with mud. He was altogether a muddy sight.

"Oh!" cried Banford, as if afraid. "Why, it's Henry!"

"What!" muttered the old man. He had a thick, rapid, muttering way of speaking, and was slightly deaf. "What? What? Who is it? Who is it, do you say? That young fellow? That young fellow of Nellie's? Oh! Oh!" And the satiric smile came on his pink face and white eyelashes.

Henry, pushing the wet hair off his steaming brow, had caught sight of them and heard what the old man said. His hot, young face seemed to flame in the cold light.

"Oh, are you all there!" he said, giving his sudden, puppy's little laugh. He was so hot and dazed with cycling he hardly knew where he was. He leaned the bicycle against the fence and climbed over into the corner on to the bank, without going into the yard.

"Well, I must say, we weren't expecting *you*," said Banford laconically.

"No, I suppose not," said he, looking at March.

She stood aside, slack, with one knee drooped and the axe resting its head loosely on the ground. Her eyes were wide and vacant, and her upper lip lifted from her teeth in that helpless, fascinated rabbit look. The moment she saw his glowing, red face it was all over with her. She was as helpless as if she had been bound. The moment she saw the way his head seemed to reach forward.

"Well, who is it? Who is it, anyway?" asked the smiling, satiric old man in his muttering voice.

"Why, Mr. Grenfel, whom you've heard us tell about, father," said Banford coldly.

"Heard you tell about, I should think so. Heard of nothing else practically," muttered the elderly man, with his queer little jeering smile on his face. "How do you do," he added, suddenly reaching out his hand to Henry.

The boy shook hands just as startled. Then the two men fell apart.

"Cycled over from Salisbury Plain, have you?" asked the old man.

"Yes."

"Hm! Longish ride. How long d'it take you, eh? Some time, eh? Several hours, I suppose."

"About four."

"Eh? Four! Yes, I should have thought so. When are you going back, then?"

"I've got till to-morrow evening."

"Till to-morrow evening, eh? Yes. Hm! Girls weren't expecting you, were they?"

And the old man turned his pale-blue, round little eyes under their white lashes mockingly towards the girls. Henry also looked round. He had become a little awkward. He looked at March, who was still staring away into the distance as if to see where the cattle were. Her hand was on the pommel of the axe, whose head rested loosely on the ground.

"What were you doing there?" he asked in his soft, courteous voice. "Cutting a tree down?"

March seemed not to hear, as if in a trance.

"Yes," said Banford. "We've been at it for over a week."

"Oh! And have you done it all by yourselves then?"

"Nellie's done it all, I've done nothing," said Banford.

"Really! You must have worked quite hard," he said, addressing himself in a curious gentle tone direct to March. She did not answer, but remained half averted staring away towards the woods above as if in a trance.

"*Nellie!*" cried Banford sharply. "Can't you answer?"

"What—me?" cried March, starting round and looking from one to the other. "Did anyone speak to me?"

"Dreaming!" muttered the old man, turning aside to smile. "Must be in love, eh, dreaming in the day-time!"

"Did you say anything to me?" said March, looking at the boy as from a strange distance, her eyes wide and doubtful, her face delicately flushed.

"I said you must have worked hard at the tree," he replied courteously.

"Oh, that! Bit by bit. I thought it would have come down by now."

"I'm thankful it hasn't come down in the night, to frighten us to death," said Banford.

"Let me just finish it for you, shall I?" said the boy.

March slanted the axe-shaft in his direction.

"Would you like to?" she said.

"Yes, if you wish it," he said.

"Oh, I'm thankful when the thing's down, that's all," she replied, nonchalant.

"Which way is it going to fall?" said Banford. "Will it hit the shed?"

"No, it won't hit the shed," he said. "I should think it will fall there—quite clear. Though it might give a twist and catch the fence."

"Catch the fence!" cried the old man. "What, catch the fence! When it's leaning at that angle? Why, it's farther off than the shed. It won't catch the fence."

"No," said Henry, "I don't suppose it will. It has plenty of room to fall quite clear, and I suppose it will fall clear."

"Won't tumble backwards on top of *us*, will it?" asked the old man, sarcastic.

"No, it won't do that," said Henry, taking off his short over-coat and his tunic. "Ducks! Ducks! Go back!"

A line of four brown-speckled ducks led by a brown-and-green drake were stemming away downhill from the upper meadow, coming like boats running on a ruffled sea, cockling their way top speed downwards towards the fence and towards the little group of people, and cackling as excitedly as if they brought news of the Spanish Armada.

"Silly things! Silly things!" cried Banford, going forward to turn them off. But they came eagerly towards her, opening their yellow-green beaks and quacking as if they were so excited to say something..

"There's no food. There's nothing here. You must wait a bit," said Banford to them. "Go away. Go away. Go round to the yard."

They didn't go, so she climbed the fence to swerve them round under the gate and into the yard. So off they waggled in an excited string once more, wagging their rumps like the stems of little gondolas, ducking under the bar of the gate. Banford stood on the top of the bank, just over the fence, looking down on the other three.

Henry looked up at her, and met her queer, round-pupilled,

weak eyes staring behind her spectacles. He was perfectly
still. He looked away, up at the weak, leaning tree. And as
he looked into the sky, like a huntsman who is watching a
flying bird, he thought to himself: "If the tree falls in just
such a way, and spins just so much as it falls, then the branch
there will strike her exactly as she stands on top of that bank."

He looked at her again. She was wiping the hair from her
brow again, with that perpetual gesture. In his heart he had
decided her death. A terrible still force seemed in him, and a
power that was just his. If he turned even a hair's breadth in
the wrong direction, he would lose the power.

"Mind yourself, Miss Banford," he said. And his heart held
perfectly still, in the terrible pure will that she should not
move.

"Who, me, mind myself?" she cried, her father's jeering
tone in her voice. "Why, do you think you might hit me
with the axe?"

"No, it's just possible the tree might, though," he answered
soberly. But the tone of his voice seemed to her to imply that
he was only being falsely solicitous, and trying to make her
move because it was his will to move her.

"Absolutely impossible," she said.

He heard her. But he held himself icy still, lest he should
lose his power.

"No, it's just possible. You'd better come down this way."

"Oh, all right. Let us see some crack Canadian tree-felling,"
she retorted.

"Ready, then," he said, taking the axe, looking round to see
he was clear.

There was a moment of pure, motionless suspense, when
the world seemed to stand still. Then suddenly his form
seemed to flash up enormously tall and fearful, he gave two
swift, flashing blows, in immediate succession, the tree was
severed, turning slowly, spinning strangely in the air and
coming down like a sudden darkness on the earth. No one
saw what was happening except himself. No one heard the
strange little cry which the Banford gave as the dark end of
the bough swooped down, down on her. No one saw her
crouch a little and receive the blow on the back of the neck.
No one saw her flung outwards and laid, a little twitching
heap, at the foot of the fence. No one except the boy. And
he watched with intense bright eyes, as he would watch a

wild goose he had shot. Was it winged or dead? Dead!
Immediately he gave a loud cry. Immediately March gave
a wild shriek that went far, far down the afternoon. And the
father started a strange bellowing sound.

The boy leapt the fence and ran to the fringe. The back of
the neck and head was a mass of blood, of horror. He turned
it over. The body was quivering with little convulsions. But
she was dead really. He knew it, that it was so. He knew it
in his soul and his blood. The inner necessity of his life was
fulfilling itself, it was he who was to live. The thorn was
drawn out of his bowels. So he put her down gently. She was
dead.

He stood up. March was standing there petrified and absolutely motionless. Her face was dead white, her eyes big black
pools. The old man was scrambling horribly over the fence.

"I'm afraid it's killed her," said the boy.

The old man was making curious, blubbering noises as he
huddled over the fence. "What!" cried March, starting
electric.

"Yes, I'm afraid," repeated the boy.

March was coming forward. The boy was over the fence
before she reached it.

"What do you say, killed her?" she asked in a sharp voice.

"I'm afraid so," he answered softly.

She went still whiter, fearful. The two stood facing one
another. Her black eyes gazed on him with the last look of
resistance. And then in a last agonised failure she began to
grizzle, to cry in a shivery little fashion of a child that doesn't
want to cry, but which is beaten from within, and gives that
little first shudder of sobbing which is not yet weeping, dry
and fearful.

He had won. She stood there absolutely helpless, shuddering her dry sobs and her mouth trembling rapidly. And then,
as in a child, with a little crash came the tears and the blind
agony of sightless weeping. She sank down on the grass, and
sat there with her hands on her breast and her face lifted in
sightless, convulsed weeping. He stood above her, looking
down on her, mute, pale, and everlasting seeming. He never
moved, but looked down on her. And among all the torture
of the scene, the torture of his own heart and bowels, he was
glad, he had won.

After a long time he stooped to her and took her hands.

"Don't cry," he said softly. "Don't cry."

She looked up at him with tears running from her eyes, a senseless look of helplessness and submission. So she gazed on him as if sightless, yet looking up to him. She would never leave him again. He had won her. And he knew it and was glad, because he wanted her for his life. His life must have her. And now he had won her. It was what his life must have.

But if he had won her, he had not yet got her. They were married at Christmas as he had planned, and he got again ten days' leave. They went to Cornwall, to his own village, on the sea. He realised that it was awful for her to be at the farm any more.

But though she belonged to him, though she lived in his shadow, as if she could not be away from him, she was not happy. She did not want to leave him: and yet she did not feel free with him. Everything round her seemed to watch her, seemed to press on her. He had won her, he had her with him, she was his wife. And she—she belonged to him, she knew it. But she was not glad. And he was still foiled. He realised that though he was married to her and possessed her in every possible way, apparently, and though she *wanted* him to possess her, she wanted it, she wanted nothing else, now, still he did not quite succeed.

Something was missing. Instead of her soul swaying with new life, it seemed to droop, to bleed, as if it were wounded. She would sit for a long time with her hand in his, looking away at the sea. And in her dark, vacant eyes was a sort of wound, and her face looked a little peaked. If he spoke to her, she would turn to him with a faint new smile, the strange, quivering little smile of a woman who has died in the old way of love, and can't quite rise to the new way. She still felt she ought to *do* something, to strain herself in some direction. And there was nothing to do, and no direction in which to strain herself. And she could not quite accept the submergence which his new love put upon her. If she was in love, she ought to *exert* herself, in some way, loving. She felt the weary need of our day to *exert* herself in love. But she knew that in fact she must no more exert herself in love. He would not have the love which exerted itself towards him. It made his brow go black. No, he wouldn't let her exert her love towards him. No, she had to be passive, to acquiesce,

and to be submerged under the surface of love. She had to
be like the seaweeds she saw as she peered down from the
boat, swaying forever delicately under water, with all their
delicate fibrils put tenderly out upon the flood, sensitive,
utterly sensitive and receptive within the shadowy sea, and
never, never rising and looking forth above water while they
lived. Never. Never looking forth from the water until they
died, only then washing, corpses, upon the surface. But while
they lived, always submerged, always beneath the wave. Beneath the wave they might have powerful roots, stronger than
iron; they might be tenacious and dangerous in their soft
waving within the flood. Beneath the water they might be
stronger, more indestructible than resistant oak trees are on
land. But it was always under-water, always under-water.
And she, being a woman, must be like that.

And she had been so used to the very opposite. She had
had to take all the thought for love and for life, and all the
responsibility. Day after day she had been responsible for
the coming day, for the coming year: for her dear Jill's health
and happiness and well-being. Verily, in her own small way,
she had felt herself responsible for the well-being of the world.
And this had been her great stimulant, this grand feeling that,
in her own small sphere, she was responsible for the well-
being of the world.

And she had failed. She knew that, even in her small
way, she had failed. She had failed to satisfy her own
feeling of responsibility. It was so difficult. It seemed so
grand and easy at first. And the more you tried, the more
difficult it became. It had seemed so easy to make one beloved
creature happy. And the more you tried, the worse the failure.
It was terrible. She had been all her life reaching, reaching,
and what she reached for seemed so near, until she had
stretched to her utmost limit. And then it was always
beyond her.

Always beyond her, vaguely, unrealisably beyond her, and
she was left with nothingness at last. The life she reached
for, the happiness she reached for, the well-being she reached
for all slipped back, became unreal, the farther she stretched
her hand. She wanted some goal, some finality—and there
was none. Always this ghastly reaching, reaching, striving for
something that might be just beyond. Even to make Jill happy.
She was glad Jill was dead. For she had realised that she could

never make her happy. Jill would always be fretting herself thinner and thinner, weaker and weaker. Her pains grew worse instead of less. It would be so for ever. She was glad she was dead.

And if Jill had married a man it would have been just the same. The woman striving, striving to make the man happy, striving within her own limits for the well-being of her world. And always achieving failure. Little, foolish successes in money or in ambition. But at the very point where she most wanted success, in the anguished effort to make some one beloved human being happy and perfect, there the failure was almost catastrophic. You wanted to make your beloved happy, and his happiness seemed always achievable. If only you did just this, that and the other. And you did this, that, and the other, in all good faith, and every time the failure became a little more ghastly. You could love yourself to ribbons and strive and strain yourself to the bone, and things would go from bad to worse, bad to worse, as far as happiness went. The awful mistake of happiness.

Poor March, in her good-will and her responsibility, she had strained herself till it seemed to her that the whole of life and everything was only a horrible abyss of nothingness. The more you reach after the fatal flower of happiness, which trembles so blue and lovely in a crevice just beyond your grasp, the more fearfully you become aware of the ghastly and awful gulf of the precipice below you, into which you will inevitably plunge, as into the bottomless pit, if you reach any farther. You pluck flower after flower—it is never *the* flower. The flower itself—its calyx is a horrible gulf, it is the bottomless pit.

That is the whole history of the search for happiness, whether it be your own or somebody else's that you want to win. It ends, and it always ends, in the ghastly sense of the bottomless nothingness into which you will inevitably fall if you strain any farther.

And women?—what goal can any woman conceive, except happiness? Just happiness for herself and the whole world. That, and nothing else. And so, she assumes the responsibility and sets off towards her goal. She can see it there, at the foot of the rainbow. Or she can see it a little way beyond, in the blue distance. Not far, not far.

But the end of the rainbow is a bottomless gulf down which

you can fall forever without arriving, and the blue distance is a void pit which can swallow you and all your efforts into its emptiness, and still be no emptier. You and all your efforts. So, the illusion of attainable happiness!

Poor March, she had set off so wonderfully towards the blue goal. And the farther and farther she had gone, the more fearful had become the realisation of emptiness. An agony, an insanity at last.

She was glad it was over. She was glad to sit on the shore and look westwards over the sea, and know the great strain had ended. She would never strain for love and happiness any more. And Jill was safely dead. Poor Jill, poor Jill. It must be sweet to be dead.

For her own part, death was not her destiny. She would have to leave her destiny to the boy. But then, the boy. He wanted more than that. He wanted her to give herself without defences, to sink and become submerged in him. And she —she wanted to sit still, like a woman on the last milestone, and watch. She wanted to see, to know, to understand. She wanted to be alone: with him at her side.

And he! He did not want her to watch any more, to see any more, to understand any more. He wanted to veil her woman's spirit, as Orientals veil the woman's face. He wanted her to commit herself to him, and to put her independent spirit to sleep. He wanted to take away from her all her effort, all that seemed her very *raison d'être*. He wanted to make her submit, yield, blindly pass away out of all her strenuous consciousness. He wanted to take away her consciousness, and make her just his woman. Just his woman.

And she was so tired, so tired, like a child that wants to go to sleep, but which fights against sleep as if sleep were death. She seemed to stretch her eyes wider in the obstinate effort and tension of keeping awake. She *would* keep awake. She *would* know. She *would* consider and judge and decide. She *would* have the reins of her own life between her own hands. She *would* be an independent woman to the last. But she was so tired, so tired of everything. And sleep seemed near. And there was such rest in the boy.

Yet there, sitting in a niche of the high, wild cliffs of West Cornwall, looking over the westward sea, she stretched her eyes wider and wider. Away to the West, Canada, America. She *would* know and she *would* see what was ahead. And the boy, sitting beside her, staring down at the gulls, had a cloud between his brows and the strain of discontent in his eyes. He wanted her asleep, at peace in him. He wanted her at peace, asleep in him. And *there* she was, dying with the strain of her own wakefulness. Yet she would not sleep: no, never. Sometimes he thought bitterly that he ought to have left her. He ought never to have killed Banford. He should have left Banford and March to kill one another.

But that was only impatience: and he knew it. He was waiting, waiting to go West. He was aching almost in torment to leave England, to go West, to take March away. To leave this shore! He believed that as they crossed the seas, as they left this England which he so hated, because in some way it seemed to have stung him with poison, she would go to sleep. She would close her eyes at last and give in to him.

And then he would have her, and he would have his own life at last. He chafed, feeling he hadn't got his own life. He would never have it till she yielded and slept in him. Then he would have all his own life as a young man and a male, and she would have all her own life as a woman and a female. There would be no more of this awful straining. She would not be a man any more, an independent woman with a man's responsibility. Nay, even the responsibility for her own soul she would have to commit to him. He knew it was so, and obstinately held out against her, waiting for the surrender.

"You'll feel better when once we get over the seas to Canada over there," he said to her as they sat among the rocks on the cliff.

She looked away to the sea's horizon, as if it were not real. Then she looked round at him, with the strained, strange look of a child that is struggling against sleep.

"Shall I?" she said.

"Yes," he answered quietly.

And her eyelids dropped with the slow motion, sleep weighing them unconscious. But she pulled them open again to say:

"Yes, I may. I can't tell. I can't tell what it will be like over there."

"If only we could go soon!" he said, with pain in his voice.

THE CAPTAIN'S DOLL

THE CAPTAIN'S DOLL

I

"Hannele!"

"*Ja—a.*"

"*Wo bist du?*"

"*Hier.*"

"*Wo dann?*"

Hannele did not lift her head from her work. She sat in a low chair under a reading-lamp, a basket of coloured silk pieces beside her, and in her hands a doll, or mannikin, which she was dressing. She was doing something to the knee of the mannikin, so that the poor little gentleman flourished head downwards with arms wildly tossed out. And it was not at all seemly, because the doll was a Scotch soldier in tight-fitting tartan trews.

There was a tap at the door, and the same voice, a woman's, calling:

"Hannele?"

"*Ja—a!*"

"Are you here? Are you alone?" asked the voice in German.

"Yes—come in."

Hannele did not sound very encouraging. She turned round her doll as the door opened, and straightened his coat. A dark-eyed young woman peeped in through the door, with a roguish coyness. She was dressed fashionably for the street, in a thick cape-wrap, and a little black hat pulled down to her ears.

"Quite, quite alone!" said the newcomer, in a tone of wonder. "Where is he, then?"

"That I don't know," said Hannele.

"And you sit here alone and wait for him? But no! That I call courage! Aren't you afraid?" Mitchka strolled across to her friend.

"Why shall I be afraid?" said Hannele curtly.

"But no! And what are you doing? Another puppet? He is a good one, though! Ha—ha—ha! *Him!* It is him! No—

183

no—that is too beautiful! No—that is too beautiful, Hannele. It is him—exactly him. Only the trousers."

"He wears those trousers too," said Hannele, standing her doll on her knee. It was a perfect portrait of an officer of a Scottish regiment, slender, delicately made, with a slight, elegant stoop of the shoulders and close-fitting tartan trousers. The face was beautifully modelled, and a wonderful portrait, dark-skinned, with a little, close-cut, dark moustache, and wide-open dark eyes, and that air of aloofness and perfect diffidence which marks an officer and a gentleman.

Mitchka bent forward, studying the doll. She was a handsome woman with a warm, dark golden skin and clear black eyebrows over her russet-brown eyes.

"No," she whispered to herself, as if awe-struck. "That is him. That is him. Only not the trousers. Beautiful, though, the trousers. Has he really such beautiful fine legs?"

Hannele did not answer.

"Exactly him. Just as finished as he is. Just as complete. He is just like that: finished off. Has he seen it?"

"No," said Hannele.

"What will he say, then?" She started. Her quick ear had caught a sound on the stone stairs. A look of fear came to her face. She flew to the door and out of the room, closing the door to behind her.

"Who is it?" her voice was heard calling anxiously down the stairs.

The answer came in German. Mitchka immediately opened the door again and came back to join Hannele.

"Only Martin," she said.

She stood waiting. A man appeared in the doorway—erect, military.

"Ah! Countess Hannele," he said in his quick, precise way, as he stood on the threshold in the distance. "May one come in?"

"Yes, come in," said Hannele.

The man entered with a quick, military step, bowed, and kissed the hand of the woman who was sewing the doll. Then, much more intimately, he touched Mitchka's hands with his lips.

Mitchka meanwhile was glancing round the room. It was a very large attic, with the ceiling sloping and then bending in two handsome movements towards the walls. The light from the dark-shaded reading-lamp fell softly on the huge white-washed vaulting of the ceiling, on the various objects round the walls, and made a brilliant pool of colour where Hannele sat in her soft, red dress, with her basket of silks.

She was a fair woman with dark-blond hair and a beautiful fine skin. Her face seemed luminous, a certain quick gleam of life about it as she looked up at the man. He was handsome, clean-shaven, with very blue eyes strained a little too wide. One could see the war in his face.

Mitchka was wandering round the room, looking at everything, and saying: "Beautiful! But beautiful! Such good taste! A man, and such good taste! No, they don't need a woman. No, look here, Martin, the Captain Hepburn has arranged all this room himself. Here you have the man. Do you see? So simple, yet so elegant. He needs a woman."

The room was really beautiful, spacious, pale, soft-lighted. It was heated by a large stove of dark-blue tiles, and had very little furniture save large peasant cupboards or presses of painted wood, and a huge writing-table, on which were writing materials and some scientific apparatus and a cactus plant with fine scarlet blossoms. But it was a man's room. Tobacco and pipes were on a little tray, on the pegs in the distance hung military overcoats and belts, and two guns on a bracket. Then there were two telescopes, one mounted on a stand near a window. Various astronomical apparatus lay upon the table.

"And he reads the stars. Only think—he is an astronomer and reads the stars. Queer, queer people, the English!"

"He is Scottish," said Hannele.

"Yes, Scottish," said Mitchka. "But, you know, I am afraid when I am with him. He is at a closed end. I don't know where I can get to with him. Are you afraid of him too, Hannele? Ach, like a closed road!"

"Why should I be?"

"Ah, you! Perhaps you don't know when you should be afraid. But if he were to come and find us here? No, no— let us go. Let us go, Martin. Come, let us go. I don't want the Captain Hepburn to come and find me in his room. Oh no!" Mitchka was busily pushing Martin to the door, and he was laughing with the queer, mad laugh in his strained eyes. "Oh no! I don't like. I don't like it," said Mitchka, trying her

English now. She spoke a few sentences prettily. "Oh no, Sir Captain, I don't want that you come. I don't like it, to be here when you come. Oh no. Not at all. I go. I go, Hannele. I go, my Hannele. And you will really stay here and wait for him? But when will he come? You don't know? Oh dear, I don't like it, I don't like it. I do not wait in the man's room. No, no—Never—*jamais*—*jamais*, *voyez-vous*. Ach, you poor Hannele! And he has got wife and children in England? Nevair! No, nevair shall I wait for him."

She had bustlingly pushed Martin through the door and settled her wrap and taken a mincing, elegant pose, ready for the street, and waved her hand and made wide, scared eyes at Hannele, and was gone. The Countess Hannele picked up the doll again and began to sew its shoe. What living she now had she earned making these puppets.

But she was restless. She pressed her arms into her lap, as if holding them bent had wearied her. Then she looked at the little clock on his writing-table. It was long after dinner-time—why hadn't he come? She sighed rather exasperated. She was tired of her doll.

Putting aside her basket of silks, she went to one of the windows. Outside the stars seemed white, and very near. Below was the dark agglomeration of the roofs of houses, a fume of light came up from beneath the darkness of roofs, and a faint breakage of noise from the town far below. The room seemed high, remote, in the sky.

She went to the table and looked at his letter-clip with letters in it, and at his sealing-wax and his stamp-box, touching things and moving them a little, just for the sake of the contrast, not really noticing what she touched. Then she took a pencil, and in stiff Gothic characters began to write her name—Johanna zu Rassentlow—time after time her own name—and then once, bitterly, curiously, with a curious sharpening of her nose: Alexander Hepburn.

But she threw the pencil down, having no more interest in her writing. She wandered to where the large telescope stood near a farther window, and stood for some minutes with her fingers on the barrel, where it was a little brighter from his touching it. Then she drifted restlessly back to her chair. She had picked up her puppet when she heard him on the stairs. She lifted her face and watched as he entered.

"Hello, you there!" he said quietly, as he closed the door

behind him. She glanced at him swiftly, but did not move nor answer.

He took off his overcoat with quick, quiet movements, and went to hang it up on the pegs. She heard his step, and looked again. He was like the doll, a tall, slender, well-bred man in uniform. When he turned, his dark eyes seemed very wide open. His black hair was growing grey at the temples—the first touch.

She was sewing her doll. Without saying anything, he wheeled round the chair from the writing-table, so that he sat with his knees almost touching her. Then he crossed one leg over the other. He wore fine tartan socks. His ankles seemed slender and elegant, his brown shoes fitted as if they were part of him. For some moments he watched her as she sat sewing. The light fell on her soft, delicate hair, that was full of strands of gold and of tarnished gold and shadow. She did not look up.

In silence he held out his small, naked-looking brown hand for the doll. On his fore-arm were black hairs.

She glanced up at him. Curious how fresh and luminous her face looked in contrast to his.

"Do you want to see it?" she asked, in natural English.

"Yes," he said.

She broke off her thread of cotton and handed him the puppet. He sat with one leg thrown over the other, holding the doll in one hand and smiling inscrutably with his dark eyes. His hair, parted perfectly on one side, was jet black and glossy.

"You've got me," he said at last, in his amused, melodious voice.

"What?" she said.

"You've got me," he repeated.

"I don't care," she said.

"What—— You don't care?" His face broke into a smile. He had an odd way of answering, as if he were only half attending, as if he were thinking of something else.

"You are very late, aren't you?" she ventured.

"Yes. I am rather late."

"Why are you?"

"Well, as a matter of fact, I was talking with the Colonel."

"About me?"

"Yes. It was about you."

She went pale as she sat looking up into his face. But it was impossible to tell whether there was distress on his dark brow or not.

"Anything nasty?" she said.

"Well, yes. It was rather nasty. Not about you, I mean. But rather awkward for me."

She watched him. But still he said no more.

"What was it?" she said.

"Oh, well—only what I expected. They seem to know rather too much about you—about you and me, I mean. Not that anybody cares one bit, you know, unofficially. The trouble is, they are apparently going to have to take official notice."

"Why?"

"Oh, well—it appears my wife has been writing letters to the Major-General. He is one of her family acquaintances—known her all his life. And I suppose she's been hearing rumours. In fact, I know she has. She said so in her letter to me."

"And what do you say to her then?"

"Oh, I tell her I'm all right—not to worry."

"You don't expect *that* to stop her worrying, do you?" she asked.

"Oh, I don't know. Why should she worry?" he said.

"I think she might have some reason," said Hannele. "You've not seen her for a year. And if she adores you——"

"Oh, I don't think she adores me. I think she quite likes me."

"Do you think you matter as little as that to her?"

"I don't see why not. Of course she likes to feel *safe* about me."

"But now she doesn't feel safe?"

"No—exactly. Exactly. That's the point. That's where it is. The Colonel advises me to go home on leave."

He sat gazing with curious, bright, dark, unseeing eyes at the doll which he held by one arm. It was an extraordinary likeness of himself, true even to the smooth parting of his hair and his peculiar way of fixing his dark eyes.

"For how long?" she asked.

"I don't know. For a month," he replied, first vaguely, then definitely.

"For a month!" She watched him, and seemed to see him fade from her eyes.

"And will you go?" she asked.

"I don't know. I don't know." His head remained bent, he seemed to muse rather vaguely. "I don't know," he repeated. "I can't make up my mind what I shall do."

"Would you like to go?" she asked.

He lifted his brows and looked at her. Her heart always melted in her when he looked straight at her with his black eyes and that curious, bright, unseeing look that was more like second sight than direct human vision. She never knew what he saw when he looked at her.

"No," he said simply. "I don't *want* to go. I don't think I've any desire at all to go to England."

"Why not?" she asked.

"I can't say." Then again he looked at her, and a curious white light seemed to shine on his eyes, as he smiled slowly with his mouth, and said: "I suppose you ought to know, if anybody does."

A glad, half-frightened look came on her face.

"You mean you don't want to leave me?" she asked, breathless.

"Yes. I suppose that's what I mean."

"But you aren't sure?"

"Yes, I am, I'm quite sure," he said, and the curious smile lingered on his face, and the strange light shone on his eyes.

"That you don't want to leave me?" she stammered, looking aside.

"Yes, I'm quite sure I don't want to leave you," he repeated. He had a curious, very melodious Scottish voice. But it was the incomprehensible smile on his face that convinced and frightened her. It was almost a gargoyle smile, a strange, lurking, changeless-seeming grin.

She was frightened, and turned aside her face. When she looked at him again, his face was like a mask, with strange, deep-graven lines and a glossy dark skin and a fixed look—as if carved half grotesquely in some glossy stone. His black hair on his smooth, beautifully-shaped head seemed changeless.

"Are you rather tired?" she asked him.

"Yes, I think I am." He looked at her with black, unseeing eyes and a mask-like face. Then he glanced aside as if he heard something. Then he rose with his hand on his belt, saying: "I'll take off my belt and change my coat, if you don't mind."

He walked across the room, unfastening his broad, brown belt. He was in well-fitting, well-cut khaki. He hung up his belt and came back to her wearing an old, light tunic, which he left unbuttoned. He carried his slippers in one hand. When he sat down to unfasten his shoes, she noticed again how black and hairy his fore-arm was, how naked his brown hand seemed. His hair was black and smooth and perfect on his head, like some close helmet, as he stooped down.

He put on his slippers, carried his shoes aside, and resumed his chair, stretching luxuriously.

"There," he said. "I feel better now." And he looked at her. "Well," he said, "and how are you?"

"Me?" she said. "Do I matter?" She was rather bitter.

"Do you matter?" he repeated, without noticing her bitterness. "Why, what a question! Of course you are of the very highest importance. What? Aren't you?" And smiling his curious smile—it made her for a moment think of the fixed sadness of monkeys, of those Chinese carved soapstone apes —he put his hand under her chin, and gently drew his finger along her cheek. She flushed deeply.

"But I'm not as important as you, am I?" she asked defiantly.

"As important as me! Why, bless you, I'm not important a bit. I'm not important a bit!"—the odd, straying sound of his words mystified her. What did he really mean?

"And I'm even less important than that," she said bitterly.

"Oh no, you're not. Oh no, you're not. You're very important. You're very important indeed, I assure you."

"And your wife?"—the question came rebelliously. "Your wife? Isn't she important?"

"My wife? My wife?" He seemed to let the word stray out of him as if he did not quite know what it meant. "Why, yes, I suppose she is important in her own sphere."

"What sphere?" blurted Hannele, with a laugh.

"Why, her own sphere, of course. Her own house, her own home, and her two children: that's her sphere."

"And you?—where do you come in?"

"At present I don't come in," he said.

"But isn't that just the trouble," said Hannele. "If you have a wife and a home, it's your business to belong to it, isn't it?"

"Yes, I suppose it is, if I want to," he replied.

"And you *do* want to?" she challenged.

"No, I don't," he replied.

"Well, then?" she said.

"Yes, quite," he answered. "I admit it's a dilemma."

"But what will you *do*?" she insisted.

"Why, I don't know. I don't know yet. I haven't made up my mind what I'm going to do."

"Then you'd better begin to make it up," she said.

"Yes, I know that. I know that."

He rose and began to walk uneasily up and down the room. But the same vacant darkness was on his brow. He had his hands in his pockets. Hannele sat feeling helpless. She couldn't help being in love with the man: with his hands, with his strange, fascinating physique, with his incalculable presence. She loved the way he put his feet down, she loved the way he moved his legs as he walked, she loved the mould of his loins, she loved the way he dropped his head a little, and the strange, dark vacancy of his brow, his not-thinking. But now the restlessness only made her unhappy. Nothing would come of it. Yet she had driven him to it.

He took his hands out of his pockets and returned to her like a piece of iron returning to a magnet. He sat down again in front of her and put his hands out to her, looking into her face.

"Give me your hands," he said softly, with that strange, mindless, soft, suggestive tone which left her powerless to disobey. "Give me your hands, and let me feel that we are together. Words mean so little. They mean nothing. And all that one thinks and plans doesn't amount to anything. Let me feel that we are together, and I don't care about all the rest."

He spoke in his slow, melodious way, and closed her hands in his. She struggled still for voice.

"But you'll *have* to care about it. You'll *have* to make up your mind. You'll just *have* to," she insisted.

"Yes, I suppose I shall. I suppose I shall. But now that we are together, I won't bother. Now that we are together, let us forget it."

"But when we *can't* forget it any more?"

"Well—then I don't know. But—to-night—it seems to me—we might just as well forget it."

The soft, melodious, straying sound of his voice made her feel helpless. She felt that he never answered her. Words of reply seemed to stray out of him, in the need to say *something*. But he himself never spoke. There he was, a continual blank silence in front of her.

She had a battle with herself. When he put his hand again on her cheek, softly, with the most extraordinary soft half-touch, as a kitten's paw sometimes touches one, like a fluff of living air, then, if it had not been for the magic of that almost indiscernible caress of his hand, she would have stiffened herself and drawn away and told him she could have nothing to do with him, while he was so half-hearted and unsatisfactory. She wanted to tell him these things. But when she began he answered invariably in the same soft, straying voice, that seemed to spin gossamer threads all over her, so that she could neither think nor act nor even feel distinctly. Her soul groaned rebelliously in her. And yet, when he put his hand softly under her chin, and lifted her face and smiled down on her with that gargoyle smile of his—she let him kiss her.

"What are you thinking about to-night?" he said. "What are you thinking about?"

"What did your Colonel say to you, exactly?" she replied, trying to harden her eyes.

"Oh, that!" he answered. "Never mind that. That is of no significance whatever."

"But what *is* of any significance?" she insisted. She almost hated him.

"What is of any significance? Well, nothing to me, outside of this room at this minute. Nothing in time or space matters to me."

"Yes, *this minute!*" she repeated bitterly. "But then there's the future. *I've* got to live in the future."

"The future! The future! The future is used up every day. The future to me is like a big tangle of black thread. Every morning you begin to untangle one loose end—and that's your day. And every evening you break off and throw away what you've untangled, and the heap is so much less: just one thread less, one day less. That's all the future matters to me."

"Then nothing matters to you. And I don't matter to you. As you say, only an end of waste thread," she resisted him.

"No, there you're wrong. You aren't the future to me."

"What am I then?—the past?"

"No, not any of those things. You're nothing. As far as all that goes, you're nothing."

"Thank you," she said sarcastically, "if I'm nothing."

But the very irrelevancy of the man overcame her. He kissed her with half discernible, dim kisses, and touched her throat. And the meaninglessness of him fascinated her and left her powerless. She could ascribe no meaning to him, none whatever. And yet his mouth, so strange in kissing, and his hairy forearms, and his slender, beautiful breast with black hair—it was all like a mystery to her, as if one of the men from Mars were loving her. And she was heavy and spell-bound, and she loved the spell that bound her. But also she didn't love it.

II

Countess zu Rassentlow had a studio in one of the main streets. She was really a refugee. And nowadays you can be a grand-duke and a pauper, if you are a refugee. But Hannele was not a pauper, because she and her friend Mitchka had the studio where they made these dolls, and beautiful cushions of embroidered coloured wools, and such-like objects of feminine art. The dolls were quite famous, so the two women did not starve.

Hannele did not work much in the studio. She preferred to be alone in her own room, which was another fine attic, not quite so large as the captain's, under the same roof. But often she went to the studio in the afternoon, and if purchasers came, then they were offered a cup of tea.

The Alexander doll was never intended for sale. What made Hannele take it to the studio one afternoon, we do not know. But she did so, and stood it on a little bureau. It was a wonderful little portrait of an officer and gentleman, the physique modelled so that it made you hold your breath.

"And *that*—that is genius!" cried Mitchka. "That is a *chef d'œuvre!* That is thy masterpiece, Hannele. That is really marvellous. And beautiful! A beautiful man, what! But no, that is *too* real. I don't understand how you *dare*. I always thought you were *good*, Hannele, so much better-natured than I am. But now you frighten me. I am afraid you are wicked, do you know. It frightens me to think that you are wicked. *Aber nein!* But you won't leave him there?"

"Why not?" said Hannele, satiric.

Mitchka made big dark eyes of wonder, reproach, and fear. "But you *must* not," she said.

"Why not?"

"No, that you *may* not do. You love the man."

"What then?"

"You can't leave his puppet standing there."

"Why can't I?"

"But you are really wicked. *Du bist wirklich bös.* Only think!—and he is an English officer."

"He isn't sacrosanct even then."

"They will expel you from the town. They will deport you."

"Let them, then."

"But no! What will you do? That would be horrible if we had to go to Berlin or to Munich and begin again. Here everything has happened so well."

"I don't care," said Hannele.

Mitchka looked at her friend and said no more. But she was angry. After some time she turned and uttered her ultimatum.

"When you are not there," she said, "I shall put the puppet away in a drawer. I shall show it to nobody, nobody. And I must tell you, it makes me afraid to see it there. It makes me afraid. And you have no right to get me into trouble, do you see. It is not I who look at the English officers. I don't like them, they are too cold and finished off for me. I shall never bring trouble on *myself* because of the English officers."

"Don't be afraid," said Hannele. "They won't trouble *you*. They know everything we do, well enough. They have their spies everywhere. Nothing will happen to you."

"But if they make you go away—and I am planted here with the studio——"

It was no good, however; Hannele was obstinate.

So, one sunny afternoon there was a ring at the door: a little lady in white, with a wrinkled face that still had its prettiness.

"Good afternoon!"—in rather lardy-dardy, middle-class English. "I wonder if I may see your things in your studio."

"Oh yes!" said Mitchka. "Please to come in."

Entered the little lady in her finery and her crumpled prettiness. She would not be very old: perhaps younger than fifty.

And it was odd that her face had gone so crumpled, because her figure was very trim, her eyes were bright, and she had pretty teeth when she laughed. She was very fine in her clothes: a dress of thick knitted white silk, a large ermine scarf with the tails only at the ends, and a black hat over which dripped a trail of green feathers of the osprey sort. She wore rather a lot of jewellery, and two bangles tinkled over her white kid gloves as she put up her fingers to touch her hair, whilst she stood complacently and looked round.

"You've got a *charming* studio—*charming*—perfectly delightful! I couldn't imagine anything more delightful."

Mitchka gave a slight ironic bow, and said in her odd, plangent English:

"Oh yes. We like it very much also."

Hannele, who had dodged behind a screen, now came quickly forth.

"Oh, how do you do!" smiled the elderly lady. "I heard there were two of you. Now which is which, if I may be so bold? This"—and she gave a winsome smile and pointed a white kid finger at Mitchka—"is the——?"

"Annamaria von Prielau-Carolath," said Mitchka, slightly bowing.

"Oh!"—and the white kid finger jerked away. "Then this——"

"Johanna zu Rassentlow," said Hannele, smiling.

"Ah, yes! Countess von Rassentlow! And this is Baroness von—von—but I shall never remember even if you tell me, for I'm awful at names. Anyhow, I shall call one *Countess* and the other *Baroness*. That will do, won't it, for poor me! Now I should like awfully to see your things, if I may. I want to buy a little present to take back to England with me. I suppose I shan't have to pay the world in duty on things like these, shall I?"

"Oh no," said Mitchka. "No duty. Toys, you know, they—there is——" Her English stammered to an end, so she turned to Hannele.

"They don't charge duty on toys, and the embroideries they don't notice," said Hannele.

"Oh, well. Then I'm all right," said the visitor. "I hope I can buy something really nice! I see a perfectly lovely jumper over there, perfectly delightful. But a little too gay for me, I'm afraid. I'm not quite so young as I was, alas." She smiled her winsome little smile, showing her pretty teeth and the old pearls in her ears shook.

"I've heard so much about your dolls. I hear they're perfectly exquisite, quite works of art. May I see some, please?"

"Oh yes," came Mitchka's invariable answer, this exclamation being the foundation-stone of all her English.

There were never more than three or four dolls in stock. This time there were only two. The famous captain was hidden in his drawer.

"Perfectly beautiful! Perfectly wonderful!" murmured the little lady, in an artistic murmur. "I think they're perfectly delightful. It's wonderful of you, Countess, to make them. It is you who make them, is it not? Or do you both do them together?"

Hannele explained, and the inspection and the rhapsody went on together. But it was evident that the little lady was a cautious buyer. She went over the things very carefully, and thought more than twice. The dolls attracted her—but she thought them expensive, and hung fire.

"I do wish," she said wistfully, "there had been a larger selection of the dolls. I feel, you know, there might have been one which I *just loved*. Of course these are *darlings*—darlings they are: and worth every *penny*, considering the work there is in them. And the art, of course. But I have a feeling, don't you know how it is, that if there had been just one or two more, I should have found one which I *absolutely* couldn't live without. Don't you know how it is? One is so foolish, of course. What does Goethe say—'*Dort wo du nicht bist . . .*'? My German isn't even a beginning, so you must excuse it. But it means you always feel you would be happy somewhere else, and not just where you are. Isn't that it? Ah, well, it's so very often true—so very often. But not always, thank goodness." She smiled an odd little smile to herself, pursed her lips, and resumed: "Well now, that's how I feel about the dolls. If only there had been one or two more. Isn't there a single one?"

She looked winsomely at Hannele.

"Yes," said Hannele, "there is one. But it is ordered. It isn't for sale."

"Oh, do you think I might see it? I'm sure it's lovely. Oh, I'm dying to see it. You know what woman's curiosity is, don't you?"—she laughed her tinkling little laugh. "Well,

I'm afraid I'm all woman, unfortunately. One is so much harder if one has a touch of the man in one, don't you think, and more able to bear things. But I'm afraid I'm all woman." She sighed and became silent.

Hannele went quietly to the drawer and took out the captain. She handed him to the little woman. The latter looked frightened. Her eyes became round and childish, her face went yellowish. Her jewels tinkled nervously as she stammered:

"Now *that*—isn't that——" and she laughed a little, hysterical laugh.

She turned round, as if to escape.

"Do you mind if I sit down," she said. "I think the standing——" and she subsided into a chair. She kept her face averted. But she held the puppet fast, her small, white fingers with their heavy jewelled rings clasped round his waist.

"You know," rushed in Mitchka, who was terrified. "You know, that is a life picture of one of the Englishmen, of a gentleman, you know. A life picture, you know."

"A portrait," said Hannele brightly.

"Yes," murmured the visitor vaguely. "I'm sure it is. I'm sure it is a very clever portrait indeed."

She fumbled with a chain, and put up a small gold lorgnette before her eyes, as if to screen herself. And from behind the screen of her lorgnette she peered at the image in her hand.

"But," she said, "none of the English officers, or rather Scottish, wear the close-fitting tartan trews any more—except for fancy dress."

Her voice was vague and distant.

"No, they don't now," said Hannele. "But that is the correct dress. I think they are so handsome, don't you?"

"Well. I don't know. It depends"—and the little woman laughed shakily.

"Oh yes," said Hannele. "It needs well-shapen legs."

"Such as the original of your doll must have had—quite," said the lady.

"Oh yes," said Hannele. "I think his legs are very handsome."

"Quite!" said the lady. "Judging from his portrait, as you call it. May I ask the name of the gentleman—if it is not too indiscreet?"

"Captain Hepburn," said Hannele.

"Yes, of course it is. I knew him at once. I've known him for many years."

"Oh, please," broke in Mitchka. "Oh, please, do not tell him you have seen it! Oh, please! Please do not tell anyone!"

The visitor looked up with a grey little smile.

"But why not?" she said. "Anyhow, I can't tell him at once, because I hear he is away at present. You don't happen to know when he will be back?"

"I believe to-morrow," said Hannele.

"To-morrow!"

"And please!" pleaded Mitchka, who looked lovely in her pleading distress, "please not to tell anybody that you have seen it."

"Must I promise?" smiled the little lady wanly. "Very well, then, I won't tell him I've seen it. And now I think I must be going. Yes, I'll just take the cushion-cover, thank you. Tell me again how much it is, please."

That evening Hannele was restless. He had been away on some duty for three days. He was returning that night—should have been back in time for dinner. But he had not arrived, and his room was locked and dark. Hannele had heard the servant light the stove some hours ago. Now the room was locked and blank as it had been for three days.

Hannele was most uneasy because she seemed to have forgotten him in the three days whilst he had been away. He seemed to have quite disappeared out of her. She could hardly even remember him. He had become so insignificant to her she was dazed.

Now she wanted to see him again, to know if it was really so. She felt that he was coming. She felt that he was already putting out some influence towards her. But what? And was he real? Why had she made his doll? Why had his doll been so important, if he was nothing? Why had she shown it to that funny little woman this afternoon? Why was she herself such a fool, getting herself into tangles in this place where it was so unpleasant to be entangled? Why was she entangled, after all? It was all so unreal. And particularly *he* was unreal: as unreal as a person in a dream, whom one has never heard of in actual life. In actual life, her own German friends were real. Martin was real: German men were real to her. But this other, he was simply not there. He didn't really exist.

He was a nullus, in reality. A nullus—and she had somehow got herself complicated with him.

Was it possible? Was it possible she had been so closely entangled with an absolute nothing? Now he was absent she couldn't even *imagine* him. He had gone out of her imagination, and even when she looked at his doll she saw nothing but a barren puppet. And yet for this dead puppet she had been compromising herself, now, when it was so risky for her to be compromised.

Her own German friends—her own German men—they were men, they were real beings. But this English officer, he was neither fish, flesh, fowl, nor good red herring, as they say. He was just a hypothetical presence. She felt that if he never came back, she would be just as if she had read a rather peculiar but false story, a *tour de force* which works up one's imagination all falsely.

Nevertheless, she was uneasy. She had a lurking suspicion that there might be something else. So she kept uneasily wandering out to the landing, and listening to hear if he might be coming.

Yes—there was a sound. Yes, there was his slow step on the stairs, and the slow, straying purr of his voice. And instantly she heard his voice she was afraid again. She knew there *was* something there. And instantly she felt the reality of his presence, she felt the unreality of her own German men friends. The moment she heard the peculiar, slow melody of his foreign voice everything seemed to go changed in her, and Martin and Otto and Albrecht, her German friends, seemed to go pale and dim as if one could almost see through them, like unsubstantial things.

This was what she had to reckon with, this recoil from one to the other. When he was present, he seemed so terribly real. When he was absent he was completely vague, and her own men of her own race seemed so absolutely the only reality.

But he was talking. Who was he talking to? She heard the steps echo up the hollows of the stone staircase slowly, as if wearily, and voices slowly, confusedly mingle. The slow, soft trail of his voice—and then the peculiar, quick tones—yes, of a woman. And not one of the maids, because they were speaking English. She listened hard. The quick, and yet slightly hushed, slightly sad-sounding voice of a woman who talks a good deal, as if talking to herself. Hannele's quick ears caught the sound of what she was saying: "Yes, I thought the Baroness a perfectly beautiful creature, perfectly lovely. But so extraordinarily like a Spaniard. Do you remember, Alec, at Malaga? I always thought they fascinated you then, with their mantillas. Perfectly lovely she would look in a mantilla. Only perhaps she is too open-hearted, too impulsive, poor thing. She lacks the Spanish reserve. Poor thing, I feel sorry for her. For them both, indeed. It must be very hard to have to do these things for a living, after you've been accustomed to be made much of for your own sake, and for your aristocratic title. It's very hard for them, poor things. Baroness, Countess, it sounds just a little ridiculous, when you're buying woollen embroideries from them. But I suppose, poor things, they can't help it. Better drop the titles altogether, I think——"

"Well, they do, if people will let them. Only English and American people find it so much easier to say Baroness or Countess than Fräulein von Prielau-Carolath, or whatever it is."

"They could say simply Fräulein, as we do to our governesses—or as we used to, when we *had* German governesses," came the voice of *her*.

"Yes, we *could*," said his voice.

"After all, what is the good, what is the good of titles if you have to sell dolls and woollen embroideries—not so very beautiful, either."

"Oh, quite! Oh, quite! I think titles are perhaps a mistake, anyhow. But they've always had them," came his slow, musical voice, with its sing-song note of hopeless indifference. He sounded rather like a man talking out of his sleep.

Hannele caught sight of the tail of blue-green crane feathers veering round a turn in the stairs away below, and she beat a hasty retreat.

III

There was a little platform out on the roof, where he used sometimes to stand his telescope and observe the stars or the moon: the moon when possible. It was not a very safe platform, just a little ledge of the roof, outside the window at the end of the top corridor: or rather, the top landing, for it was only the space between the attics. Hannele had the one attic-room at the back, he had the room we have seen, and a little bedroom which was really only a lumber-room. Before he came, Hannele had been alone under the roof. His rooms were then lumber-room and laundry-room, where the clothes were dried. But he had wanted to be high up, because of his stars, and this was the place that pleased him.

Hannele heard him quite late in the night, wandering about. She heard him also on the ledge outside. She could not sleep. He disturbed her. The moon was risen, large and bright in the sky. She heard the bells from the cathedral slowly strike two: two great drops of sound in the livid night. And again, from outside on the roof, she heard him clear his throat. Then a cat howled.

She rose, wrapped herself in a dark wrap, and went down the landing to the window at the end. The sky outside was full of moonlight. He was squatted like a great cat peering up his telescope, sitting on a stool, his knees wide apart. Quite motionless he sat in that attitude, like some leaden figure on the roof. The moonlight glistened with a gleam of plumbago on the great slope of black tiles. She stood still in the window, watching. And he remained fixed and motionless at the end of the telescope.

She tapped softly on the window-pane. He looked round, like some tom-cat staring round with wide night eyes. Then he reached down his hand and pulled the window open.

"Hello," he said quietly. "You not asleep?"

"Aren't *you* tired?" she replied, rather resentful.

"No, I was as wide awake as I could be. *Isn't* the moon fine to-night! What? Perfectly amazing. Wouldn't you like to come up and have a look at her?"

"No, thank you," she said hastily, terrified at the thought.

He resumed his posture, peering up the telescope.

"Perfectly amazing," he said, murmuring. She waited for some time, bewitched likewise by the great October moon and the sky full of resplendent white-green light. It seemed like another sort of day-time. And there he straddled on the roof like some cat! It was exactly like day in some other planet.

At length he turned round to her. His face glistened faintly, and his eyes were dilated like a cat's at night.

"You know I had a visitor?" he said.

"Yes."

"My wife."

"Your *wife!*"—she looked up really astonished. She had thought it might be an acquaintance—perhaps his aunt—or even an elder sister. "But she's years older than you," she added.

"Eight years," he said. "I'm forty-one."

There was a silence.

"Yes," he mused. "She arrived suddenly, by surprise, yesterday, and found me away. She's staying in the hotel, in the Vier Jahreszeiten."

There was a pause.

"Aren't you going to stay with her?" asked Hannele.

"Yes, I shall probably join her to-morrow."

There was a still longer pause.

"Why not to-night?" asked Hannele.

"Oh, well—I put it off for to-night. It meant all the bother of my wife changing her room at the hotel—and it was late—and I was all mucky after travelling."

"But you'll go to-morrow?"

"Yes, I shall go to-morrow. For a week or so. After that I'm not sure what will happen."

There was quite a long pause. He remained seated on his stool on the roof, looking with dilated, blank, black eyes at nothingness. She stood below in the open window space, pondering.

"Do you want to go to her at the hotel?" asked Hannele.

"Well, I don't, particularly. But I don't mind, really. We're very good friends. Why, we've been friends for eighteen years—we've been married seventeen. Oh, she's a nice little woman. I don't want to hurt her feelings. I wish her no harm, you know. On the contrary, I wish her all the good in the world."

He had no idea of the blank amazement in which Hannele listened to these stray remarks.

"But——" she stammered. "But doesn't she expect you to make *love* to her?"

"Oh yes, she expects that. You bet she does: woman-like."

"And you?"—the question had a dangerous ring.

"Why, I don't mind, really, you know, if it's only for a

short time. I'm used to her. I've always been fond of her, you know—and so if it gives her any pleasure—why, I like her to get what pleasure out of life she can."

"But *you*—you *yourself*! Don't *you* feel anything?" Hannele's amazement was reaching the point of incredulity. She began to feel that he was making it up. It was all so different from her own point of view. To sit there so quiet and to make such statements in all good faith: no, it was impossible.

"I don't consider I count," he said naïvely.

Hannele looked aside. If that wasn't lying, it was imbecility, or worse. She had for the moment nothing to say. She felt he was a sort of psychic phenomenon like a grasshopper or a tadpole or an ammonite. Not to be regarded from a human point of view. No, he just wasn't normal. And she had been fascinated by him! It was only sheer, amazed curiosity that carried her on to her next question.

"But do you *never* count, then?" she asked, and there was a touch of derision, of laughter in her tone. He took no offence.

"Well—very rarely," he said. "I count very rarely. That's how life appears to me. One matters so *very* little."

She felt quite dizzy with astonishment. And he called himself a man!

"But if you matter so very little, what do you do anything at all for?" she asked.

"Oh, one has to. And then, why not? Why not do things, even if oneself hardly matters. Look at the moon. It doesn't matter in the least to the moon whether I exist or whether I don't. So why should it matter to me?"

After a blank pause of incredulity she said:

"I could die with laughter. It seems to me all so ridiculous—no, I can't believe it."

"Perhaps it is a point of view," he said.

There was a long and pregnant silence: we should not like to say pregnant with what.

"And so I don't mean anything to you at all?" she said.

"I didn't say that," he replied.

"Nothing means anything to you," she challenged.

"I don't say that."

"Whether it's your wife—or me—or the moon—*toute la même chose*."

"No—no—that's hardly the way to look at it."

She gazed at him in such utter amazement that she felt something would really explode in her if she heard another word. Was this a man?—or what was it? It was too much for her, that was all.

"Well, good-bye," she said. "I hope you will have a nice time at the Vier Jahreszeiten."

So she left him still sitting on the roof.

"I suppose," she said to herself, "that is love *a l'anglaise*. But it's more than I can swallow."

IV

"Won't you come and have tea with me—do! Come right along now. Don't you find it bitterly cold? Yes—well now—come in with me and we'll have a cup of nice, hot tea in our little sitting-room. The weather changes so suddenly, and really one needs a little reinforcement. But perhaps you don't take tea?"

"Oh yes. I got so used to it in England," said Hannele.

"Did you now! Well now, were you long in England?"

"Oh yes——"

The two women had met in the Domplatz. Mrs. Hepburn was looking extraordinarily like one of Hannele's dolls, in a funny little cape of odd striped skins, and a little dark-green skirt, and a rather fuzzy sort of hat. Hannele looked almost huge beside her.

"But now you will come in and have tea, won't you? Oh, please do. Never mind whether it's *de rigueur* or not. I *always* please myself *what* I do. I'm afraid my husband gets some shocks sometimes—but that we can't help. I won't have anybody laying down the law to me." She laughed her winsome little laugh. "So now come along in, and we'll see if there aren't hot scones as well. I love a hot scone for tea in cold weather. And I hope you do. That is, if there are any. We don't know yet." She tinkled her little laugh. "My husband may or may not be in. But that makes no difference to you and me, does it? There, it's just striking half-past four. In England we always have tea at half-past. My husband *adores* his tea. I don't suppose our man is five minutes off the half-past, ringing the gong for tea, not once in twelve months. My husband doesn't mind at all if dinner is a little late. But he gets—quite—well, quite 'ratty' if tea is late." She tinkled a laugh. "Though I shouldn't say that. He is the soul of kindness and patience. I don't think I've ever known him do an unkind thing—or hardly say an unkind word. But I doubt if he will be in to-day."

He *was* in, however, standing with his feet apart and his hands in his trouser pockets in the little sitting-room upstairs in the hotel. He raised his eyebrows the smallest degree, seeing Hannele enter.

"Ah, Countess Hannele—my wife has brought you along! Very nice, very nice! Let me take your wrap. Oh yes, certainly . . ."

"Have you rung for tea, dear?" asked Mrs. Hepburn.

"Er—yes. I said as soon as you came in they were to bring it."

"Yes—well. Won't you ring again, dear, and say for *three*."

"Yes—certainly. Certainly."

He rang, and stood about with his hands in his pockets waiting for tea.

"Well now," said Mrs. Hepburn, as she lifted the teapot, and her bangles tinkled, and her huge rings of brilliants twinkled, and her big ear-rings of clustered seed-pearls bobbed against her rather withered cheek, "isn't it charming of Countess zu— Countess zu——"

"Rassentlow," said he. "I believe most people say Countess Hannele. I know we always do among ourselves. We say Countess Hannele's shop."

"Countess Hannele's shop! Now, isn't that perfectly delightful: such a romance in the very sound of it. You take cream?"

"Thank you," said Hannele.

The tea passed in a cloud of chatter, while Mrs. Hepburn manipulated the tea-pot, and lit the spirit-flame, and blew it out, and peeped into the steam of the tea-pot, and couldn't see whether there was any more tea or not—and—"At home I *know*—I was going to say to a teaspoonful—how much tea there is in the pot. But this tea-pot—I don't know what it's made of—it isn't silver, I know that—it is so heavy in itself that it's deceived me several times already. And my husband is a greedy man, a greedy man—he likes at least three cups— and four if he can get them, or five! Yes, dear, I've plenty of tea to-day. You shall have even five, if you don't mind the last two weak. Do let me fill your cup, Countess Hannele. I think it's a *charming* name."

"There's a play called *Hannele*, isn't there?" said he.

When he had had his five cups, and his wife had got her cigarette perched in the end of a long, long, slim, white holder, and was puffing like a little Chinawoman from the distance, there was a little lull.

"Alec, dear," said Mrs. Hepburn. "You won't forget to leave that message for me at Mrs. Rackham's. I'm so afraid it will be forgotten."

"No, dear, I won't forget. Er—would you like me to go round now?"

Hannele noticed how often he said 'er' when he was beginning to speak to his wife. But they *were* such good friends, the two of them.

"Why, if you *would*, dear, I should feel perfectly comfortable. But I don't want you to hurry one bit."

"Oh, I may as well go now."

And he went. Mrs. Hepburn detained her guest.

"He *is* so charming to me," said the little woman. "He's really wonderful. And he always has been the same—invariably. So that if he *did* make a little slip—well, you know, I don't have to take it so seriously."

"No," said Hannele, feeling as if her ears were stretching with astonishment.

"It's the war. It's just the war. It's had a terribly deteriorating effect on the men."

"In what way?" said Hannele.

"Why, morally. Really, there's hardly one man left the same as he was before the war. Terribly degenerated."

"Is that so?" said Hannele.

"It is indeed. Why, isn't it the same with the German men and officers?"

"Yes, I think so," said Hannele.

"And I'm sure so, from what I hear. But of course it is the women who are to blame in the first place. We poor women! We are a guilty race, I am afraid. But I never throw stones. I know what it is myself to have temptations. I have to flirt a little—and when I was younger—well, the men didn't escape me, I assure you. And I was *so* often scorched. But never *quite* singed. My husband never minded. He knew I was *really* safe. Oh yes, I have always been faithful to him.

But still—I have been *very* near the flame." And she laughed her winsome little laugh.

Hannele put her fingers to her ears to make sure they were not falling off.

"Of course during the war it was terrible. I know that in a certain hospital it was quite impossible for a girl to stay on if she kept straight. The matrons and sisters just turned her out. They wouldn't have her unless she was one of themselves. And you know what that means. Quite like the convent in Balzac's story—you know which I mean, I'm sure." And the laugh tinkled gaily.

"But then, what can you expect, when there aren't enough men to go round! Why, I had a friend in Ireland. She and her husband had been an ideal couple, an *ideal* couple. Real playmates. And you can't say more than that, can you? Well, then, he became a major during the war. And she was so looking forward, poor thing, to the perfectly lovely times they would have together when he came home. She is like me, and is lucky enough to have a little income of her own—not a great fortune—but—well—— Well now, what was I going to say? Oh yes, she was looking forward to the perfectly lovely times they would have when he came home: building on her dreams, poor thing, as we unfortunate women always do. I suppose we shall never be cured of it." A little tinkling laugh. "Well now, not a bit of it. Not a bit of it." Mrs. Hepburn lifted her heavily-jewelled little hand in a motion of protest. It was curious, her hands were pretty and white, and her neck and breast, now she wore a little tea-gown, were also smooth and white and pretty, under the medley of twinkling little chains and coloured jewels. Why should her face have played her this nasty trick of going all crumpled? However, it was so.

"Not one bit of it," reiterated the little lady. "He came home quite changed. She said she could hardly recognise him for the same man. Let me tell you one little incident. Just a trifle, but significant. He was coming home—this was some time after he was free from the army—he was coming home from London, and he told her to meet him at the boat: gave her the time and everything. Well, she went to the boat, poor thing, and he didn't come. She waited, and no word of explanation or anything. So she couldn't make up her mind whether to go next day and meet the boat again. However, she decided she wouldn't. So of course, on that boat he arrived. When he got home, he said to her: 'Why didn't you meet the boat?' 'Well,' she said, 'I went yesterday, and you didn't come.' 'Then why didn't you meet it again to-day?' Imagine it, the sauce! And they had been real playmates. Heart-breaking, isn't it? 'Well,' she said in self-defence, 'why didn't you come yesterday?' 'Oh,' he said, 'I met a woman in town whom I liked, and she asked me to spend the night with her, so I did.' Now what do you think of that? Can you conceive of such a thing?"

"Oh no," said Hannele. "I call that unnecessary brutality."

"Exactly! So terrible to say such a thing to her! The brutality of it! Well, that's how the world is to-day. I'm thankful my husband isn't that sort. I don't say he's perfect. But whatever else he did, he'd never be unkind, and he *couldn't* be brutal. He just couldn't. He'd never tell me a lie—I know *that*. But callous brutality, no, thank goodness, he hasn't a spark of it in him. I'm the wicked one, if either of us is wicked." The little laugh tinkled. "Oh, but he's been perfect to me, perfect. Hardly a cross word. Why, on our wedding night, he kneeled down in front of me and promised, with God's help, to make my life happy. And I must say, as far as possible, he's kept his word. It has been his one aim in life, to make my life happy."

The little lady looked away with a bright, musing look towards the window. She was being a heroine in a romance. Hannele could see her being a heroine, playing the chief part in her own life romance. It is such a feminine occupation, that no woman takes offence when she is made audience.

"I'm afraid I've more of the woman than the mother in my composition," resumed the little heroine. "I adore my two children. The boy is at Winchester, and my little girl is in a convent in Brittany Oh, they are perfect darlings, both of them. But the man is first in my mind, I'm afraid. I fear I'm rather old-fashioned. But never mind. I can see the attractions in other men—can't I indeed! There was a perfectly exquisite creature—he was a very clever engineer—but much, much more than *that*. But never mind." The little heroine sniffed as if there were perfume in the air, folded her jewelled hands, and resumed: "However—I know what it is myself to flutter round the flame. You know I'm Irish myself, and we Irish can't help it. Oh, I wouldn't be English for anything.

Just that little touch of imagination, you know . . ." The little laugh tinkled. "And that's what makes me able to sympathise with my husband even when, perhaps, I shouldn't. Why, when he was at home with me, he never gave a thought, not a thought to another woman. I must say, he used to make *me* feel a little guilty sometimes. But there! I don't think he ever thought of another woman as being flesh and blood, after he knew me. I could tell. Pleasant, courteous, charming— but other women were not flesh and blood to him, they were just people, callers—that kind of thing. It used to amaze me, when some perfectly lovely creature came, whom I should have been head over heels in love with in a minute—and he, he was charming, delightful; he could see her points, but she was no more to him than, let me say, a pot of carnations or a beautiful old piece of *punto di Milano*. Not flesh and blood. Well, perhaps one can feel too safe. Perhaps one needs a tiny pinch of salt of jealousy. I believe one does. And I have not had one jealous moment for seventeen years. So that, *really*, when I heard a whisper of something going on here, I felt almost pleased. I felt exonerated for my own little pecca-dilloes, for one thing. And I felt he was perhaps a little more human. Because, after all, it is nothing but human to fall in love, if you are alone for a long time and in the company of a beautiful woman—and if you're an attractive man yourself."

Hannele sat with her eyes propped open and her ears buttoned back with amazement, expecting the next revela-tions.

"Why, of course," she said, knowing she was expected to say something.

"Yes, of course," said Mrs. Hepburn, eyeing her sharply. "So I thought I'd better come and see how far things had gone. I had nothing but a hint to go on. I knew no name— nothing. I had just a hint that she was German, and a refugee aristocrat—and that he used to call at the studio." The little lady eyed Hannele sharply, and gave a breathless little laugh, clasping her hands nervously. Hannele sat absolutely blank: really dazed.

"Of course," resumed Mrs. Hepburn, "that was enough. That was quite a sufficient clue. I'm afraid my intentions when I called at the studio were not as pure as they might have been. I'm afraid I wanted to see something more than the dolls. But when you showed me *his* doll, then I knew. Of course there wasn't a shadow of doubt after that. And I saw at once that she loved him, poor thing. She was *so* agitated. And no idea who I was. And you were so unkind to show me the doll. Of course, you had no idea who you were showing it to. But for her, poor thing, it was such a trial. I could see how she suffered. And I must say she's very lovely—she's very, very lovely, with her golden skin and her reddish amber eyes and her beautiful, beautiful carriage. And such a naïve, impulsive nature. Gives everything away in a minute. And then her deep voice—'*Oh yes—Oh, please!*'—such a child. And such an aristocrat, that lovely turn of her head, and her simple, elegant dress. Oh, she's very charming. And she's just the type I always knew would attract him, if he hadn't got me. I've thought about it many a time—many a time. When a woman is older than a man, she does think these things—especially if he has his attractive points too. And when I've dreamed of the woman he would love if he hadn't got me, it has always been a Spanish type. And the Baroness is extraordinarily Spanish in her appearance. She must have had some noble Spanish ancestor. Don't you think so?"

"Oh yes," said Hannele. "There were such a lot of Spaniards in Austria, too, with the various emperors."

"With Charles V, exactly. Exactly. That's how it must have been. And so she has all the Spanish beauty, and all the German feeling. Of course, for myself, I miss the *reserve*, the haughtiness. But she's very, very lovely, and I'm sure I could never *hate* her. I couldn't even if I tried. And I'm not going to try. But I think she's much too dangerous for my husband to see much of her. Don't you agree, now?"

"Oh, but really," stammered Hannele. "There's nothing in it, really."

"Well," said the little lady, cocking her head shrewdly aside, "I shouldn't like there to be any *more* in it."

And there was a moment's dead pause. Each woman was reflecting. Hannele wondered if the little lady was just fooling her.

"Anyhow," continued Mrs. Hepburn, "the spark is there, and I don't intend the fire to spread. I am going to be very, very careful, myself, not to fan the flames. The last thing I should think of would be to make my husband scenes. I believe it would be fatal."

"Yes," said Hannele, during the pause.

"I am going very carefully. You think there isn't much in it—between him and the Baroness?"

"No—no—I'm sure there isn't," cried Hannele, with a full voice of conviction. She was almost indignant at being slighted so completely herself, in the little lady's suspicions.

"Hm!—mm!" hummed the little woman, sapiently nodding her head slowly up and down. "I'm not so sure! I'm not so sure that it hasn't gone pretty far."

"Oh no!" cried Hannele, in real irritation of protest.

"Well," said the other. "In any case, I don't intend it to go any farther."

There was dead silence for some time.

"There's more in it than you say. There's more in it than you say," ruminated the little woman. "I know him, for one thing. I know he's got a cloud on his brow. And I know it hasn't left his brow for a single minute. And when I told him I had been to the studio, and showed him the cushion-cover, I knew he felt guilty. I am not so easily deceived. We Irish all have a touch of second sight, I believe. Of course I haven't challenged him. I haven't even mentioned the doll. By the way, who ordered the doll? Do you mind telling me?"

"No, it wasn't ordered," confessed Hannele.

"Ah—I thought not—I thought not!" said Mrs. Hepburn, lifting her finger. "At least, I knew no outsider had ordered it. Of course I knew." And she smiled to herself.

"So," she continued, "I had too much sense to say anything about it. I don't believe in stripping wounds bare. I believe in gently covering them and letting them heal. But I did say I thought her a lovely creature." The little lady looked brightly at Hannele.

"Yes," said Hannele.

"And he was very vague in his manner. 'Yes, not bad,' he said. I thought to myself: Aha, my boy, you don't deceive me with your not bad. She's very much more than not bad. I said so, too. I wanted, of course, to let him know I had a suspicion."

"And do you think he knew?"

"Of course he did. Of course he did. 'She's much too dangerous,' I said, 'to be in a town where there are so many strange men: married and unmarried.' And then he turned round to me and gave himself away, oh, so plainly. 'Why?' he said. But such a haughty, distant tone. I said to myself:

'It's time, my dear boy, you were removed out of the danger zone.' But I answered him: Surely somebody is bound to fall in love with her. Not at all, he said, she keeps to her own countrymen. You don't tell *me*, I answered him, with her pretty broken English! It is a wonder the two of them are allowed to stay in the town. And then again he rounded on me. Good gracious! he said. Would you have them turned out just because they're beautiful to look at, when they have nowhere else to go, and they make their bit of a livelihood here? I assure you, he hasn't rounded on me in that over-bearing way, not once before, in all our married life. So I just said quietly: I should like to protect *our own men*. And he didn't say anything more. But he looked at me under his brows and went out of the room."

There was a silence. Hannele waited with her hands in her lap, and Mrs. Hepburn mused, with her hands in *her* lap. Her face looked yellow, and *very* wrinkled.

"Well now," she said, breaking again suddenly into life. "What are we to do? I mean what is to be done? You are the Baroness's nearest friend. And I wish her *no* harm, none whatever."

"What can we do?" said Hannele, in the pause.

"I have been urging my husband for some time to get his discharge from the army," said the little woman. "I know he could have it in three months' time. But like so many more men, he has no income of his own, and he doesn't want to feel dependent. Perfect nonsense! So he says he wants to stay on in the army. I have never known him before go against my real wishes."

"But it *is* better for a man to be independent," said Hannele.

"I know it is. But it is also better for him to be *at home*. And I could get him a post in one of the observatories. He could do something in meteorological work."

Hannele refused to answer any more.

"Of course," said Mrs. Hepburn, "if he *does* stay on here, it would be much better if the Baroness left the town."

"I'm sure she will never leave of her own choice," said Hannele.

"I'm sure she won't either. But she might be made to see that it would be very much *wiser* of her to move of her own free will."

"Why?" said Hannele.

"Why, because she might any time be removed by the British authorities."

"Why should she?" said Hannele.

"I think the women who are a menace to our men should be removed."

"But she is *not* a menace to your men."

"Well, I have my own opinion on that point."

Which was a decided deadlock.

"I'm sure I've kept you an awful long time with my chatter," said Mrs. Hepburn. "But I did want to make everything as simple as possible. As I said before, I can't feel any ill-will against her. Yet I can't let things just go on. Heaven alone knows when they may end. Of course if I can persuade my husband to resign his commission and come back to England—anyhow, we will see. I'm sure I am the last person in the world to bear malice."

The tone in which she said it conveyed a dire threat.

Hannele rose from her chair.

"Oh, and one other thing," said her hostess, taking out a tiny lace handkerchief and touching her nose delicately with it. "Do you think"—dab, dab—"that I might have that *doll*—you know——?"

"That——?"

"Yes, of my husband"—the little lady rubbed her nose with her kerchief.

"The price is three guineas," said Hannele.

"Oh, indeed!"—the tone was very cold. "I thought it was not for sale."

Hannele put on her wrap.

"You'll send it round—will you?—if you will be so kind."

"I must ask my friend first."

"Yes, of course. But I'm sure she will be so kind as to send it me. It is a little—er—indelicate, don't you think!"

"No," said Hannele. "No more than a painted portrait."

"Don't you?" said her hostess coldly. "Well, even a painted portrait I think I should like in my own possession. This *doll*——"

Hannele waited, but there was no conclusion.

"Anyhow," she said, "the price is three guineas: or the equivalent in marks."

"Very well," said the little lady, "you shall have your three guineas when I get the doll."

V

Hannele went her way pondering. A man never is quite such an abject specimen as his wife makes him look, talking about 'my husband'. Therefore, if any woman wishes to rescue her husband from the clutches of another female, let her only invite this female to tea and talk quite sincerely about 'my husband, you know'. Every man has made a ghastly fool of himself with a woman at some time or other. No woman ever forgets. And most women will give the show away, with real pathos, to another woman. For instance, the picture of Alec at his wife's feet on his wedding night, vowing to devote himself to her life-long happiness—this picture strayed across Hannele's mind time after time, whenever she thought of her dear captain. With disastrous consequences to the captain. Of course if he had been at her own feet, then Hannele would have thought it almost natural: almost a necessary part of the show of love. But at the feet of that other little woman! And what was that other little woman wearing? Her wedding night! Hannele hoped before heaven it wasn't some awful little nightie of frail flowered silk. Imagine it, that little lady! Perhaps in a chic little boudoir cap of *punto di Milano*, and this slip of frail flowered silk: and the man, perhaps, in his braces! Oh, merciful heaven, save us from other people's indiscretions. No, let us be sure it was in proper evening dress—twenty years ago—very low cut, with a full skirt gathered behind and trailing a little, and a little feather erection in her high-dressed hair, and all those jewels: pearls of course: and he in a dinner-jacket and a white waistcoat: probably in an hotel bedroom in Lugano or Biarritz. And she? Was she standing with one small hand on his shoulder?—or was she seated on the couch in the bedroom? Oh, dreadful thought! And yet it was almost inevitable, that scene. Hannele had never been married, but she had come quite near enough to the realisation of the event to know that such a scene *was* practically inevitable. An indispensable part of any honeymoon. Him on his knees, with his heels up!

And how black and tidy his hair must have been then! and no grey at the temples at all. Such a good-looking bridegroom. Perhaps with a white rose in his button-hole still. And she could see him kneeling there, in his new black trousers and a

wing collar. And she could see his head bowed. And she could
hear his plangent, musical voice saying: "With God's help, I
will make your life happy. I will live for that and for nothing
else." And then the little lady must have had tears in her
eyes, and she must have said, rather superbly: "Thank you,
dear. I'm perfectly sure of it."

Ach! Ach! Husbands should be left to their own wives:
and wives should be left to their own husbands. And *no*
stranger should ever be made a party to these terrible bits of
connubial staging. Nay, thought Hannele, that scene was
really true. It actually took place. And with the man of that
scene I have been in love! With the devoted husband of that
little lady. Oh God, oh God, how was it possible! Him on
his knees, on his knees, with his heels up!

Am I a perfect fool? she thought to herself. Am I really
just an idiot, gaping with love for him? How *could* I? How
could I? The very way he says: "Yes, dear!" to her! The
way he does what she tells him! The way he fidgets about
the room with his hands in his pockets! The way he goes off
when she sends him away because she wants to talk to me.
And he knows she wants to talk to me. And he knows what
she *might* have to say to me. Yet he goes off on his errand
without a question, like a servant. "I will do whatever you
wish, darling." He must have said those words time after
time to the little lady. And fulfilled them, also. Performed
all his pledges and his promises.

Ach! Ach! Hannele wrung her hands to think of *herself*
being mixed up with him. And he had seemed to her so manly.
He seemed to have so much silent male passion in him. And
yet—the little lady! "My husband has *always* been *perfectly
sweet* to me." Think of it! On his knees too. And his "Yes,
dear! Certainly. Certainly." Not that he was afraid of the
little lady. He was just committed to her, as he might have
been committed to gaol, or committed to paradise.

Had she been dreaming, to be in love with him? Oh, she
wished so much she had never been. She *wished* she had
never given herself away. To him!—given herself away to
him!—and so abjectly. Hung upon his words and his motions,
and looked up to him as if he were Cæsar. So he had seemed
to her: like a mute Cæsar. Like Germanicus. Like—she did
not know what.

How had it all happened? What had taken her in? Was it

just his good looks? No, not really. Because they were the kind of staring good looks she didn't really care for. He must have had charm. He must have charm. Yes, he *had* charm. When it worked.

His charm had not worked on her now for some time— never since that evening after his wife's arrival. Since then he had seemed to her—rather awful. Rather awful—stupid—an ass—a limited, rather vulgar person. That was what he seemed to her when his charm wouldn't work. A limited, rather inferior person. And in a world of *Schiebers* and profiteers and vulgar, pretentious persons, this was the worst thing possible. A limited, inferior, slightly pretentious individual! The husband of the little lady! And oh heaven, she was so deeply implicated with him! He had not, however, spoken with her in private since his wife's arrival. Probably he would never speak with her in private again. She hoped to heaven, never again. The awful thing was the past, that which had been between him and her. She shuddered when she thought of it The husband of the little lady!

But surely there was something to account for it! Charm, just charm. He had a charm. And then, oh, heaven, when the charm left off working! It had left off so completely at this moment, in Hannele's case, that her very mouth tasted salt. What *did* it all amount to?

What was his charm, after all? How could it have affected her? She began to think of him again, at his best: his presence, when they were alone high up in that big, lonely attic near the stars. His room!—the big white-washed walls, the first scent of tobacco, the silence, the sense of the stars being near, the telescopes, the cactus with fine scarlet flowers: and above all, the strange, remote, insidious silence of his presence, that was so congenial to her also. The curious way he had of turning his head to listen—to listen to what?— as if he heard something in the stars. The strange look, like destiny, in his wide-open, almost staring black eyes. The beautiful lines of his brow, that seemed always to have a certain cloud on it. The slow elegance of his straight, beautiful legs as he walked, and the exquisiteness of his dark, slender chest! Ah, she could feel the charm mounting over her again. She could feel the snake biting her heart. She could feel the arrows of desire rankling.

But then—and she turned from her thoughts back to this

last little tea-party in the Vier Jahreszeiten. She thought of his voice: "Yes, dear. Certainly. Certainly I will." And she thought of the stupid, inferior look on his face. And the something of a servant-like way in which he went out to do his wife's bidding.

And then the charm was gone again, as the glow of sunset goes off a burning city and leaves it a sordid industrial hole. So much for charm!

So much for charm. She had better have stuck to her own sort of men, Martin, for instance, who was a gentleman and a daring soldier, and a queer soul and pleasant to talk to. Only he hadn't any *magic*. Magic? The very word made her writhe. Magic? Swindle. Swindle, that was all it amounted to. Magic!

And yet—let us not be too hasty. If the magic had *really* been there, on those evenings in that great lofty attic. Had it? Yes. Yes, she was bound to admit it. There had been magic. If there had been magic in his presence and in his contact, the husband of the little lady—— But the distaste was in her mouth again.

So she started afresh, trying to keep a tight hold on the tail of that all-too-evanescent magic of his. Dear, it slipped so quickly into disillusion. Nevertheless. If it had existed it did exist. And if it did exist, it was worth having. You could call it an illusion if you liked. But an illusion which is a real experience is worth having. Perhaps this disillusion was a greater illusion than the illusion itself. Perhaps all this disillusion of the little lady and the husband of the little lady was falser than the illusion and magic of those few evenings. Perhaps the long disillusion of life was falser than the brief moments of real illusion. After all—the delicate darkness of his breast, the mystery that seemed to come with him as he trod slowly across the floor of his room, after changing his tunic—— Nay, nay, if she could keep the illusion of his charm, she would give all disillusion to the devils. Nay, only let her be under the spell of his charm. Only let the spell be upon her. It was all she yearned for. And the thing she had to fight was the vulgarity of disillusion. The vulgarity of the little lady, the vulgarity of the husband of the little lady, the vulgarity of his insincerity, his "Yes, dear. Certainly! Certainly!"—this was what she had to fight. He *was* vulgar and horrible, then. But also, the queer figure that sat alone on the roof watching the stars! The wonderful red flower of the cactus. The mystery that advanced with him as he came across the room after changing his tunic. The glamour and sadness of him, his silence, as he stooped unfastening his boots. And the strange gargoyle smile, fixed, when he caressed her with his hand under the chin! Life is all a choice. And if she chose the glamour, the magic, the charm, the illusion, the spell! Better death than that other, the husband of the little lady. When all was said and done, was he as much the husband of the little lady as he was that queer, delicate-breasted Cæsar of her own knowledge? Which was he?

No, she was *not* going to send her the doll. The little lady should never have the doll.

What a doll she would make herself! Heavens, what a wizened jewel!

VI

Captain Hepburn still called occasionally at the house for his post. The maid always put his letters in a certain place in the hall, so that he should not have to climb the stairs.

Among his letters—that is to say, along with another letter, for his correspondence was very meagre—he one day found an envelope with a crest. Inside this envelope two letters.

"Dear Captain Hepburn,

"I had the enclosed letter from Mrs. Hepburn. I don't intend her to have the doll which is your portrait, so I shall not answer this note. Also I don't see why she should try to turn us out of the town. She talked to me after tea that day, and it seems she believes that Mitchka is your lover. I didn't say anything at all—except that it wasn't true. But she needn't be afraid of me. I don't want you to trouble yourself. But you may as well *know* how things are.

"Johanna z. R."

The other letter was on his wife's well-known heavy paper, and in her well-known large, 'aristocratic' hand.

"My dear Countess,

"I wonder if there has been some mistake, or some misunderstanding. Four days ago you said you would send round that *doll* we spoke of, but I have seen no sign of it yet. I thought of calling at the studio, but did not wish to disturb the Baroness. I should be very much obliged if you could send the doll at once, as I do not feel easy while it is out of my possession. You may rely on having a cheque by return.

"Our old family friend, Major-General Barlow, called on me yesterday, and we had a most interesting conversation on our *Tommies*, and the protection of their morals here. It seems we have full power to send away any person or persons deemed undesirable, with twenty-four hours' notice to leave. But of course all this is done as quietly and with the intention of causing as little scandal as possible.

"Please let me have the doll by to-morrow, and perhaps some hint as to your future intentions.

"With very best wishes from one who only seeks to be your friend.

"Yours very sincerely,
"EVANGELINE HEPBURN."

VII

And then a dreadful thing happened: really a very dreadful thing. Hannele read of it in the evening newspaper of the town—the *Abendblatt*. Mitchka came rushing up with the paper at ten o'clock at night, just when Hannele was going to bed.

Mrs. Hepburn had fallen out of her bedroom window, from the third floor of the hotel, down on to the pavement below, and was killed. She was dressing for dinner. And apparently she had in the morning washed a certain little camisole, and put it on the window-sill to dry. She must have stood on a chair reaching for it when she fell out of the window. Her husband, who was in the dressing-room, heard a queer little noise, a sort of choking cry, and came into her room to see what it was. And she wasn't there. The window was open, and the chair by the window. He looked round, and thought she had left the room for a moment, so returned to his shaving. He was half shaved when one of the maids rushed in. When he looked out of the window down into the street he fainted, and would have fallen too if the maid had not pulled him in in time.

The very next day the captain came back to his attic.

Hannele did not know, until quite late at night when he tapped on her door. She knew his soft tap immediately.

"Won't you came over for a chat?" he said.

She paused for some moments before she answered. And then perhaps surprise made her agree: surprise and curiosity.

"Yes, in a minute," she said, closing her door in his face.

She found him sitting quite still, not even smoking, in his quiet attic. He did not rise, but just glanced round with a faint smile. And she thought his face seemed different, more flexible. But in the half-light she could not tell. She sat at some little distance from him.

"I suppose you've heard," he said.

"Yes."

After a long pause, he resumed:

"Yes. It seems an impossible thing to have happened. Yet it *has* happened."

Hannele's ears were sharp. But strain them as she might, she could not catch the meaning of his voice.

"A terrible thing. A *very* terrible thing," she said.

"Yes."

"Do you think she fell quite accidentally?" she said.

"Must have done. The maid was in just a minute before, and she seemed as happy as possible. I suppose reaching over that broad window-ledge, her brain must suddenly have turned. I can't imagine why she didn't call me. She could never bear even to look out of a high window. Turned her ill instantly if she saw a space below her. She used to say she couldn't really look at the moon, it made her feel as if she would fall down a dreadful height. She never dared do more than glance at it. She always had the feeling, I suppose, of the awful space beneath her, if she were on the moon."

Hannele was not listening to his words, but to his voice. There was something a little automatic in what he said. But then that is always so when people have had a shock.

"It must have been terrible for you too," she said.

"Ah, yes. At the time it was awful. Awful. I felt the smash right inside me, you know."

"Awful!" she repeated.

"But now," he said, "I feel very strangely happy about it. I feel happy about it. I feel happy for her sake, if you can understand that. I feel she has got out of some great tension. I feel she's free now for the first time in her life. She was a gentle soul, and an original soul, but she was like a fairy who is condemned to live in houses and sit on furniture and all that, don't you know. It was never her nature."

"No?" said Hannele, herself sitting in blank amazement.

"I always felt she was born in the wrong period—or on the wrong planet. Like some sort of delicate creature you take out of a tropical forest the moment it is born, and from the first moment teach it to perform tricks. You know what I mean. All her life she performed the tricks of life, clever little monkey she was at it too. Beat me into fits. But her own poor little soul, a sort of fairy soul, those queer Irish creatures, was cooped up inside her all her life, tombed in. There it was, tombed in, while she went through all the tricks of life that you have to go through if you are born to-day."

"But," stammered Hannele, "what would she have done if she *had* been free?"

"Why, don't you see, there *is* nothing for her to do in the world to-day. Take her language, for instance. She never ought to have been speaking English. I don't know what language she ought to have spoken. Because if you take the Irish language, they only learn it back from English. They think in English, and just put Irish words on top. But English was never her language. It bubbled off her lips, so to speak. And she had no other language. Like a starling that you've made talk from the very beginning, and so it can only shout these talking noises, don't you know. It can't whistle its own whistling to save its life. Couldn't do it. It's lost it. All its own natural mode of expressing itself has collapsed, and it can only be artificial."

There was a long pause.

"Would she have been wonderful, then, if she had been able to talk in some unknown language?" said Hannele jealously.

"I don't say she would have been wonderful. As a matter of fact, we think a talking starling is much more wonderful than an ordinary starling. I don't myself, but most people do. And she would have been a sort of starling. And she would have had her own language and her own ways. As it was, poor thing, she was always arranging herself and fluttering and chattering inside a cage. And she never knew she was in the cage, any more than we know we are inside our own skins."

"But," said Hannele, with a touch of mockery, "how do you

know you haven't made it all up—just to console yourself?"

"Oh, I've thought it long ago," he said.

"Still," she blurted, "you may have invented it all—as a sort of consolation for—for—for your life."

"Yes, I may," he said. "But I don't think so. It was her eyes. Did you ever notice her eyes? I often used to catch her eyes. And she'd be talking away, all the language bubbling off her lips. And her eyes were so clear and bright and different. Like a child's that is listening to something, and is going to be frightened. She was always listening—and waiting—for something else. I tell you what, she was exactly like that fairy in the Scotch song, who is in love with a mortal, and sits by the high road in terror waiting for him to come, and hearing the plovers and the curlews. Only nowadays motor-lorries go along the moor roads, and the poor thing is struck unconscious, and carried into our world in a state of unconsciousness, and when she comes round, she tries to talk our language and behave as we behave, and she can't remember anything else, so she goes on and on, till she falls with a crash, back to her own world."

Hannele was silent, and so was he.

"You loved her then?" she said at length.

"Yes. But in this way. When I was a boy I caught a bird, a black-cap, and I put it in a cage. And I loved that bird. I don't know why, but I loved it. I simply loved that bird. All the gorse, and the heather, and the rock, and the hot smell of yellow gorse blossom, and the sky that seemed to have no end to it, when I was a boy, everything that I almost was *mad* with, as boys are, seemed to me to be in that little, fluttering black-cap. And it would peck its seed as if it didn't quite know what else to do; and look round about, and begin to sing. But in quite a few days it turned its head aside and died. Yes, it died. I never had the feeling again that I got from that black-cap when I was a boy—not until I saw her. And then I felt it all again. I felt it all again. And it was the same feeling. I knew, quite soon I knew, that she would die. She would peck her seed and look round in the cage just the same. But she would die in the end. Only it would last much longer. But she would die in the cage, like the black-cap."

"But she loved the cage. She loved her clothes and her jewels. She must have loved her house and her furniture and all that with a perfect frenzy."

"She did. She did. But like a child with play-things. Only they were big, marvellous play-things to her. Oh yes, she was never away from them. She never forgot her things—her trinkets and her furs and her furniture. She never got away from them for a minute. And everything in her mind was mixed up with them."

"Dreadful!" said Hannele.

"Yes, it was dreadful," he answered.

"Dreadful," repeated Hannele.

"Yes, quite. Quite! And it got worse. And her way of talking got worse. As if it bubbled off her lips. But her eyes never lost their brightness, they never lost that faery look. Only I used to see fear in them. Fear of everything—even all the things she surrounded herself with. Just like my black-cap used to look out of his cage—so bright and sharp, and yet as if he didn't know that it was just the cage that was between him and the outside. He thought it was inside himself, the barrier. He thought it was part of his own nature to be shut in. And she thought it was part of her own nature. And so they both died."

"What I can't see," said Hannele, "is what she would have done outside her cage. What other life could she have, except her *bibelots* and her furniture and her talk?"

"Why, none. There *is* no life outside for human beings."

"Then there's nothing," said Hannele.

"That's true. In a great measure, there's nothing."

"Thank you," said Hannele.

There was a long pause.

"And perhaps I was to blame. Perhaps I ought to have made some sort of a move. But I didn't know what to do. For my life, I didn't know what to do, except try to make her happy. She had enough money—and I didn't think it mattered if she shared it with me. I always had a garden—and the astronomy. It's been an immense relief to me watching the moon. It's been wonderful. Instead of looking inside the cage, as I did at my bird, or at her—I look right out—into freedom—into freedom."

"The moon, you mean?" said Hannele.

"Yes, the moon."

"And that's your freedom?"

"That's where I've found the greatest sense of freedom," he said.

"Well, I'm not going to be jealous of the moon," said Hannele at length.

"Why should you? It's not a thing to be jealous of."

In a little while, she bade him good-night and left him.

VIII

The chief thing that the captain knew, at this juncture, was that a hatchet had gone through the ligatures and veins that connected him with the people of his affection, and that he was left with the bleeding ends of all his vital human relationships. Why it should be so he did not know. But then one never can know the whys and the wherefores of one's passional changes.

He only knew that it was so. The emotional flow between him and all the people he knew and cared for was broken, and for the time being he was conscious only of the cleavage. The cleavage that had occurred between him and his fellowmen, the cleft that was now between him and them. It was not the fault of anybody or anything. He could neither reproach himself nor them. What had happened had been preparing for a long time. Now suddenly the cleavage. There had been a long, slow weaning away: and now this sudden silent rupture.

What it amounted to principally was that he did not want even to see Hannele. He did not want to think of her even. But neither did he want to see anybody else, or to think of anybody else. He shrank with a feeling almost of disgust from his friends and acquaintances, and their expressions of sympathy. It affected him with instantaneous disgust when anybody wanted to share emotions with him. He did not want to share emotions or feelings of any sort. He wanted to be by himself, essentially, even if he was moving about among other people.

So he went to England to settle his own affairs, and out of duty to see his children. He wished his children all the well in the world—everything except any emotional connection with himself. He decided to take his girl away from the convent at once, and to put her into a jolly English school. His boy was all right where he was.

The captain had now an income sufficient to give him his independence, but not sufficient to keep up his wife's house.

So he prepared to sell the house and most of the things in it. He decided also to leave the army as soon as he could be free. And he thought he would wander about for a time, till he came upon something he wanted.

So the winter passed, without his going back to Germany. He was free of the army. He drifted along, settling his affairs. They were of no very great importance. And all the time he never wrote once to Hannele. He could not get over his disgust that people insisted on his sharing their emotions. He could not bear their emotions, neither their activities. Other people might have all the emotions and feelings and earnestness and busy activities they liked. Quite nice even that they had such a multifarious commotion for themselves. But the moment they approached him to spread their feelings over him or to entangle him in their activities a helpless disgust came up in him, and until he could get away he felt sick, even physically.

This was no state of mind for a lover. He could not even think of Hannele. Anybody else he felt he need not think about. He was deeply, profoundly thankful that his wife was dead. It was an end of pity now; because, poor thing, she had escaped and gone her own way into the void, like a flown bird.

IX

Nevertheless, a man hasn't finished his life at forty. He may, however, have finished one great phase of his life.

And Alexander Hepburn was not the man to live alone. All our troubles, says somebody wise, come upon us because we cannot be alone. And that is all very well. We must all be *able* to be alone, otherwise we are just victims. But when we *are* able to be alone, then we realise that the only thing to do is to start a new relationship with another—or even the same —human being. That people should all be stuck up apart, like so many telegraph-poles, is nonsense.

So with our dear captain. He had his convulsion into a sort of telegraph-pole isolation: which was absolutely necessary for him. But then he began to bud with a new yearning for— for what? For love?

It was a question he kept nicely putting to himself. And really, the nice young girls of eighteen or twenty attracted him very much: so fresh, so impulsive, and looking up to him as if he were something wonderful. If only he could have married two or three of them, instead of just one!

Love! When a man has no particular ambition, his mind turns back perpetually, as a needle towards the pole. That tiresome word Love. It means so many things. It meant the feeling he had had for his wife. He had loved her. But he shuddered at the thought of having to go through such love again. It meant also the feeling he had for the awfully nice young things he met here and there: fresh, impulsive girls ready to give all their hearts away. Oh yes, he could fall in love with half a dozen of them. But he knew he'd better not.

At last he wrote to Hannele: and got no answer. So he wrote to Mitchka and still got no answer. So he wrote for information—and there was none forthcoming, except that the two women had gone to Munich.

For the time being he left it at that. To him, Hannele did not exactly represent rosy love. Rather a hard destiny. He did not adore her. He did not feel one bit of adoration for her. As a matter of fact, not all the beauties and virtues of woman put together with all the gold in the Indies would have tempted him into the business of adoration any more. He had gone on his knees once, vowing with faltering tones to try and make the adored one happy. And now—never again. Never.

The temptation this time was to be adored. One of those fresh young things would have adored him as if he were a god. And there was something *very* alluring about the thought. Very—very alluring. To be god-almighty in your own house, with a lovely young thing adoring you, and you giving off beams of bright effulgence like a Gloria! Who wouldn't be tempted: at the age of forty? And this was why he dallied.

But in the end he suddenly took the train to Munich. And when he got there he found the town beastly uncomfortable, the Bavarians rude and disagreeable, and no sign of the missing females, not even in the Café Stéphanie. He wandered round and round.

And then one day, oh heaven, he saw his doll in a shop window: a little art shop. He stood and stared quite spellbound.

"Well, if that isn't the devil," he said. "Seeing yourself in a shop window!"

He was so disgusted that he would not go into the shop.

Then, every day for a week did he walk down that little street and look at himself in the shop window. Yes, there he stood, with one hand in his pocket. And the figure had one hand in its pocket. There he stood, with his cap pulled rather low over his brow. And the figure had its cap pulled low over its brow. But, thank goodness, his own cap now was a civilian tweed. But there he stood, his head rather forward, gazing with fixed dark eyes. And himself in little, that wretched figure, stood there with its head rather forward, staring with fixed dark eyes. It was such a real little *man* that it fairly staggered him. The oftener he saw it, the more it staggered him. And the more he hated it. Yet it fascinated him, and he came again to look.

And it was always there. A lonely little individual lounging there with one hand in its pocket, and nothing to do, among the bric-à-brac and the *bibelots*. Poor devil, stuck so incongruously in the world. And yet losing none of his masculinity.

A male little devil, for all his forlornness. But such an air of isolation, or not-belonging. Yet taut and male, in his tartan trews. And what a situation to be in!—lounging with his back against a little Japanese lacquer cabinet, with a few old pots on his right hand and a tiresome brass ink-tray on his left, while pieces of not-very-nice filet lace hung their length up and down the background. Poor little devil: it was like a deliberate satire.

And then one day it was gone. There was the cabinet and the filet lace and the tiresome ink-stand tray: and the little gentleman wasn't there. The captain at once walked into the shop.

"Have you sold that doll?—that unknown soldier?" he added, without knowing quite what he was saying.

The doll was sold.

"Do you know who bought it?"

The girl looked at him very coldly, and did not know.

"I once knew the lady who made it. In fact, the doll was *me*," he said.

The girl now looked at him with sudden interest.

"Don't you think it was like me?" he said.

"Perhaps"—she began to smile.

"It was me. And the lady who made it was a friend of mine. Do you know her name?"

"Yes."

"Gräfin zu Rassentlow," he cried, his eyes shining.

"Oh yes. But her dolls are famous."

"Do you know where she is? Is she in Munich?"

"That I don't know."

"Could you find out?"

"I don't know. I can ask."

"Or the Baroness von Prielau-Carolath."

"The Baroness is dead."

"Dead!"

"She was shot in a riot in Salzburg. They say a lover——"

"How do you know?"

"From the newspapers."

"Dead! Is it possible. Poor Hannele."

There was a pause.

"Well," he said, "if you would enquire about the address—I'll call again."

Then he turned back from the door.

"By the way, do you mind telling me how much you sold the doll for?"

The girl hesitated. She was by no means anxious to give away any of her trade details. But at length she answered reluctantly:

"Five hundred marks."

"So cheap," he said. "Good-day. Then I will call again."

X

Then again he got a trace. It was in the Chit-Chat column of the *Muenchener Neue Zeitung*: under Studio-Comments. "Theodor Worpswede's latest picture is a still-life, containing an entertaining group of a doll, two sunflowers in a glass jar, and a poached egg on toast. The contrast between the three substances is highly diverting and instructive, and this is perhaps one of the most interesting of Worpswede's works. The doll, by the way, is one of the creations of our fertile Countess Hannele. It is the figure of an English, or rather Scottish, officer in the famous tartan trousers which, clinging closely to the legs of the lively Gaul, so shocked the eminent Julius

Cæsar and his cohorts. We, of course, are no longer shocked, but full of admiration for the creative genius of our dear Countess. The doll itself is a masterpiece, and has begotten another masterpiece in Theodor Worpswede's Still-life. We have heard, by the way, a rumour of Countess zu Rassentlow's engagement. Apparently the Herr Regierungsrat von Poldi, of that most beautiful of summer resorts, Kaprun, in the Tyrol, is the fortunate man——"

XI

The captain bought the Still-life. This new version of himself along with the poached egg and the sunflowers was rather frightening. So he packed up for Austria, for Kaprun, with his picture, and had a fight to get the beastly thing out of Germany, and another fight to get it into Austria. Fatigued and furious he arrived in Salzburg, seeing no beauty in anything. Next day he was in Kaprun.

It was an elegant and fashionable watering-place before the war: a lovely little lake in the midst of the Alps, an old Tyrolese town on the water-side, green slopes sheering up opposite, and away beyond a glacier. It was still crowded and still elegant. But alas, with a broken, bankrupt, desperate elegance, and almost empty shops.

The captain felt rather dazed. He found himself in an hotel full of Jews of the wrong, rich sort, and wondered what next. The place was beautiful, but the life wasn't.

XII

The Herr Regierungsrat was not at first sight prepossessing. He was approaching fifty, and had gone stout and rather loose, as so many men of his class and race do. Then he wore one of those dreadful full-bottom coats, a kind of poor relation to our full-skirted frock-coat: it would best be described as a family coat. It flapped about him as he walked, and he looked at first glance lower middle-class.

But he wasn't. Of course, being in office in the collapsed Austria, he was a republican. But by nature he was a monarchist, nay, an imperialist, as every true Austrian is. And he was a true Austrian. And as such he was much finer and subtler than he looked. As one got used to him, his rather fat face, with its fine nose and slightly bitter, pursed mouth, came to have a resemblance to the busts of some of the late Roman emperors. And as one was with him, one came gradually to realise that out of all his baggy bourgeois appearance came something of a *grand geste*. He could not help it. There was something sweeping and careless about his soul: big, rather assertive, and ill-bred-seeming; but, in fact, not ill-bred at all, only a little bitter and a good deal indifferent to his surroundings. He looked at first sight so common and *parvenu*. And then one had to realise that he was a member of a big, old empire, fallen into a sort of epicureanism, and a little bitter. There was no littleness, no meanness, and no real coarseness. But he was a great talker, and relentless towards his audience.

Hannele was attracted to him by his talk. He began as soon as dinner appeared: and he went on, carrying the decanter and the wine-glass with him out on to the balcony of the villa, over the lake, on and on until midnight. The summer night was still and warm: the lake lay deep and full, and the old town twinkled away across. There was the faintest tang of snow in the air, from the great glacier-peaks that were hidden in the night opposite. Sometimes a boat with a lantern twanged a guitar. The clematis flowers were quite black, like leaves, dangling from the terrace.

It was so beautiful, there in the very heart of the Tyrol. The hotels glittered with lights: electric light was still cheap. There seemed a fullness and a loveliness in the night. And yet for some reason it was all terrible and devastating: the life-spirit seemed to be squirming, bleeding all the time.

And on and on talked the Herr Regierungsrat, with all the witty volubility of the more versatile Austrian. He was really very witty, very human, and with a touch of salty cynicism that reminded one of a real old Roman of the Empire. That subtle stoicism, that unsentimental epicureanism, that kind of reckless hopelessness, of course, fascinated the women. And particularly Hannele. He talked on and on—about his work before the war, when he held an important post and was one of the governing class—then about the war—then about the hopelessness of the present: and in it all there seemed a big-ness, a carelessness based on indifference and hopelessness that laughed at its very self. The real old Austria had always fascinated Hannele. As represented in the witty, bitter-indifferent Herr Regierungsrat it carried her away.

And he, of course, turned instinctively to her, talking in his rapid, ceaseless fashion, with a laugh and a pause to drink and a new start taken. She liked the sound of his Austrian speech: its racy carelessness, its salty indifference to standards of correctness. Oh yes, here was the *grand geste* still lingering.

He turned his large breast towards her, and made a quick gesture with his fat, well-shapen hand, blurted out another subtle, rough-seeming romance, pursed his mouth, and emptied his glass once more. Then he looked at his half-forgotten cigar and started again.

There was something almost boyish and impulsive about him: the way he turned to her, and the odd way he seemed to open his big breast to her. And again he seemed almost eternal, sitting there in his chair with knees planted apart. It was as if he would never rise again, but would remain sitting for ever, and talking. He seemed as if he had no legs, save to sit with. As if to stand on his feet and walk would not be natural to him.

Yet he rose at last, and kissed her hand with the grand gesture that France or Germany have never acquired: carelessness, profound indifference to other people's standards, and then such a sudden stillness, as he bent and kissed her hand. Of course she felt a queen in exile.

And perhaps it is more dangerous to feel yourself a queen in exile than a queen *in situ*. She fell in love with him, with this large, stout, loose widower of fifty, with two children. He had no money except some Austrian money that was worth nothing outside Austria. He could not even go to Germany. There he was, fixed in this hollow in the middle of the Tyrol.

But he had an ambition still, old Roman of the decadence that he was. He had year by year and without making any fuss collected the material for a very minute and thorough history of his own district: the Chiemgau and the Pinzgau. Hannele found that his fund of information on this subject was inexhaustible, and his intelligence was so delicate, so human, and his scope seemed so wide, that she felt a touch of reverence for him. He wanted to write this history. And she wanted to help him.

For, of course, as things were he would never write it. He was Regierungsrat: that is, he was the petty local governor of his town and immediate district. The Amthaus was a great old building, and there young ladies in high heels flirted among masses of papers with bare-kneed young gentlemen in Tyrolese costume, and occasionally they parted to take a pleasant, interesting attitude and write a word or two, after which they fluttered together for a little more interesting diversion. It was extraordinary how many finely built, handsome young people of an age fitted for nothing but love-affairs ran the governmental business of this department. And the Herr Regierungsrat sailed in and out of the big, old room, his wide coat flying like wings and making the papers flutter, his rather wine-reddened, old-Roman face smiling with its bitter look. And of course it was a witticism he uttered first, even if Hungary was invading the frontier or cholera was in Vienna.

When he was on his legs, he walked nimbly, briskly, and his coat-bottoms always flew. So he waved through the town, greeting somebody at every few strides and grinning, and yet with a certain haughty reserve. Oh yes, there was a certain salty *hauteur* about him which made the people trust him. And he spoke the vernacular so racily.

Hannele felt she would like to marry him. She would like to be near him. She would like him to write his history. She would like him to make her feel a queen in exile. No one had ever *quite* kissed her hand as he kissed it: with that sudden stillness and strange, chivalric abandon of himself. How he would abandon himself to her!—terribly—wonderfully—perhaps a little horribly. His wife, whom he had married late, had died after seven years of marriage. Hannele could understand that too. One or the other must die.

She became engaged. But something made her hesitate before marriage. Being in Austria was like being on a wrecked ship that *must* sink after a certain short length of time. And marrying the Herr Regierungsrat was like marrying the doomed captain of the doomed ship. The sense of fatality was part of the attraction.

And yet she hesitated. The summer weeks passed. The strangers flooded in and crowded the town, and ate up the food like locusts. People no longer counted the paper money, they weighed it by the kilogram. Peasants stored it in a corner of the meal-bin, and mice came and chewed holes in it. Nobody knew where the next lot of food was going to come from: yet it always came. And the lake teemed with bathers. When the captain arrived he looked with amazement on the crowds of strapping, powerful fellows who bathed all day long, magnificent blond flesh of men and women. No wonder the old Romans stood in astonishment before the huge blond limbs of the savage Germans.

Well, the life was like a madness. The hotels charged fifteen hundred kronen a day: the women, old and young, paraded in the peasant costume, in flowery cotton dresses with gaudy, expensive silk aprons: the men wore the Tyrolese costume, bare knees and little short jackets. And for the men, the correct thing was to have the leathern hose and the blue linen jacket as old as possible. If you had a hole in your leathern seat, so much the better.

Everything so physical. Such magnificent naked limbs and naked bodies, and in the streets, in the hotels, everywhere, bare, white arms of women and bare, brown, powerful knees and thighs of men. The sense of flesh everywhere, and the endless ache of flesh. Even in the peasants who rowed across the lake, standing and rowing with a slow, heavy, gondolier motion at the one curved oar, there was the same endless ache of physical yearning.

XIII

It was August when Alexander met Hannele. She was walking under a chintz parasol, wearing a dress of blue cotton with little red roses, and a red silk apron. She had no hat, her arms were bare and soft, and she had white stockings under her short dress. The Herr Regierungsrat was at her side, large, nimble, and laughing with a new witticism.

Alexander, in a light summer suit and Panama hat, was just coming out of the bank, shoving twenty thousand kronen into his pocket. He saw her coming across from the Amtsgericht, with the Herr Regierungsrat at her side, across the space of sunshine. She was laughing, and did not notice him.

She did not notice till he had taken off his hat and was saluting her. Then what she saw was the black, smooth, shining head, and she went pale. His black, smooth, close

head—and all the blue Austrian day seemed to shrivel before
her eyes.

"How do you do, Countess! I hoped I should meet you."

She heard his slow, sad-clanging, straying voice again, and
she pressed her hand with the umbrella stick against her
breast. She had forgotten it—forgotten his peculiar, slow
voice. And now it seemed like a noise that sounds in the
silence of night. Ah, how difficult it was, that suddenly the
world could split under her eyes, and show this darkness inside. She wished he had not come.

She presented him to the Herr Regierungsrat, who was stiff
and cold. She asked where the captain was staying. And
then, not knowing what else to say, she said:

"Won't you come to tea?"

She was staying in a villa across the lake. Yes, he would
come to tea.

He went. He hired a boat and a man to row him across. It
was not far. There stood the villa, with its brown balconies
one above the other, the bright red geraniums and white
geraniums twinkling all round, the trees of purple clematis
tumbling at one corner. All the green window doors were
open: but nobody about. In the little garden by the water's
edge the rose trees were tall and lank, drawn up by the dark
green trees of the background. A white table with chairs and
garden seats stood under the shadow of a big willow tree,
and a hammock with cushions swung just behind. But no
one in sight. There was a little landing bridge on to the
garden: and a fairly large boat-house at the garden end.

The captain was not sure that the boat-house belonged to
the villa. Voices were shouting and laughing from the water's
surface, bathers swimming. A tall, naked youth with a little
red cap on his head and a tiny red loin-cloth round his slender
young hips was standing on the steps of the boat-house calling to the three women who were swimming near. The dark-
haired woman with the white cap swam up to the steps and
caught the boy by the ankle. He cried and laughed and
remonstrated, and poked her in the breast with his foot.

"*Nein, nein, Hardu!*" she cried as he tickled her with his
toe. "*Hardu! Hardu! Hör' auf!*—Leave off!"—and she fell
with a crash back into the water. The youth laughed a loud,
deep laugh of a lad whose voice is newly broken.

"*Was macht er dann?*" cried a voice from the waters.

"What is he doing?" It was a dark-skinned girl swimming swiftly, her big dark eyes watching amused from the water surface.

"*Jetze Hardu hör' auf. Nein. Jetzt ruhig!* Now leave off! Now be quiet." And the dark-skinned woman was climbing out in the sunshine on to the pale, raw-wood steps of the boat-house, the water glistening on her dark-blue, stockinette, soft-moulded back and loins: while the boy, with his foot stretched out, was trying to push her back into the water. She clambered out, however, and sat on the steps in the sun, panting slightly. She was dark and attractive-looking, with a mature beautiful figure, and handsome, strong woman's legs.

In the garden appeared a black-and-white maid-servant with a tray.

"*Kaffee, gnädige Frau!*"

The voice came so distinct over the water.

"*Hannele! Hannele! Kaffee!*" called the woman on the steps of the bathing-house.

"*Tante Hannele! Kaffee!*" called the dark-eyed girl, turning round in the water, then swimming for home.

"*Kaffee! Kaffee!*" roared the youth, in anticipation.

"*Ja—a! Ich kom—mm,*" sang Hannele's voice from the water.

The dark-eyed girl, her hair tied up in a silk bandana, had reached the steps and was climbing out, a slim young fish in her close dark suit. The three stood clustered on the steps, the elder woman with one arm over the naked shoulders of the youth, the other arm over the shoulders of the girl. And all in chorus sang:

"*Hannele! Hannele! Hannele! Wir warten auf dich.*"

The boatman had left off rowing, and the boat was drifting slowly in. The family became quiet, because of the intrusion. The attractive-looking woman turned and picked up her blue bath-robe, of a mid-blue colour that became her. She swung it round her as if it were an opera cloak. The youth stared at the boat.

The captain was watching Hannele. With a white kerchief tied round her silky, brownish hair, she was swimming home. He saw her white shoulders and her white, wavering legs below in the clear water. Round the boat fishes were suddenly jumping.

The three on the steps beyond stood silent, watching the

intruding boat with resentment. The boatman twisted his head round and watched them. The captain, who was facing them, watched Hannele. She swam slowly and easily up, caught the rail of the steps, and stooping forward, climbed slowly out of the water. Her legs were large and flashing white and looked rich, the rich, white thighs with the blue veins behind, and the full, rich softness of her sloping loins.

"*Ach! Schön! 'S war schön! Das Wasser ist gut,*" her voice was heard, half singing as she took her breath. "It was lovely."

"*Heiss,*" said the woman above. "*Zu warm.* Too warm."

The youth made way for Hannele, who drew herself erect at the top of the steps, looking round, panting a little and putting up her hands to the knot of her kerchief on her head. Her legs were magnificent and white.

"*Kuck de Leut, die da bleiben,*" said the woman in the blue wrap, in a low voice. "Look at the people stopping there."

"*Ja!*" said Hannele negligently. Then she looked. She started as if in fear, looked round, as if to run away, looked back again, and met the eyes of the captain, who took off his hat.

She cried in a loud, frightened voice:

"Oh, but—I thought it was *to-morrow!*"

"No—to-day," came the quiet voice of the captain over the water.

"*To-day!* Are you sure?" she cried, calling to the boat.

"Quite sure. But we'll make it to-morrow if you like," he said.

"To-day! To-day!" she repeated in bewilderment. "No! Wait a minute." And she ran into the boat-house.

"*Was ist es?*" asked the dark woman, following her. "What is it?"

"A friend—a visitor—Captain Hepburn," came Hannele's voice.

The boatman now rowed slowly to the landing-stage. The dark woman, huddled in her blue wrap as in an opera-cloak, walked proudly and unconcernedly across the background of the garden and up the steps to the first balcony. Hannele, her feet slip-slopping in loose slippers, clutching an old yellow wrap round her, came to the landing-stage and shook hands.

"I am so sorry. It is so stupid of me. I was sure it was to-morrow," she said.

"No, it was to-day. But I wish for your sake it had been to-morrow," he replied.

"No. No. It doesn't matter. You won't mind waiting a minute, will you? You mustn't be angry with me for being so stupid."

So she went away, the heelless slippers flipping up to her naked heels. Then the big-eyed, dusky girl stole into the house: and then the naked youth, who went with sangfroid. He would make a fine, handsome man: and he knew it.

XIV

Hepburn and Hannele were to make a small excursion to the glacier which stood there always in sight, coldly grinning in the sky. The weather had been very hot, but this morning there were loose clouds in the sky. The captain rowed over the lake soon after dawn. Hannele stepped into the little craft, and they pulled back to the town. There was a wind ruffling the water, so that the boat leaped and chuckled. The glacier, in a recess among the folded mountains, looked cold and angry. But morning was very sweet in the sky, and blowing very sweet with a faint scent of the second hay from the low lands at the head of the lake. Beyond stood naked grey rock like a wall of mountains, pure rock, with faint, thin slashes of snow. Yesterday it had rained on the lake. The sun was going to appear from behind the Breitsteinhorn, the sky with its clouds floating in blue light and yellow radiance was lovely and cheering again. But dark clouds seemed to spout up from the Pinzgau valley. And once across the lake, all was shadow, when the water no longer gave back the sky-morning.

The day was a feast day, a holiday. Already so early three young men from the mountains were bathing near the steps of the Badeanstalt. Handsome, physical fellows, with good limbs rolling and swaying in the early morning water. They seemed to enjoy it too. But to Hepburn it was always as if a dark wing were stretched in the sky, over these mountains, like a doom. And these three young, lusty, naked men swimming and rolling in the shadow.

Hepburn's was the first boat stirring. He made fast in the hotel boat-house, and he and Hannele went into the little town. It was deep in shadow, though the light of the sky, curdled with cloud, was bright overhead. But dark and chill and heavy lay the shadow in the black-and-white town, like a sediment.

The shops were all shut, but peasants from the hills were already strolling about in their holiday dress: the men in their short leather trousers, like football drawers, and bare brown knees and great boots: their little grey jackets faced with green, and their green hats with the proud chamois-brush behind. They seemed to stray about like lost souls, and the proud chamois-brush behind their hats, this proud, cocky, perking-up tail, like a mountain-buck with his tail up, was belied by the lost-soul look of the men, as they loitered about with their hands shoved in the front pockets of their trousers. Some women also were creeping about: peasant women, in the funny little black hats that had thick gold under the brim and long black streamers of ribbon, broad, black, water-wave ribbon starting from a bow under the brim behind and streaming right to the bottom of the skirt. These women, in their thick, dark dresses with tight bodices and massive, heavy, full skirts, and bright or dark aprons, strode about with the heavy stride of the mountain women, the heavy, quick, forward-leaning motion. They were waiting for the town-day to begin.

Hepburn had a knapsack on his back, with food for the day. But bread was wanting. They found the door of the bakery open, and got a loaf: a long, hot loaf of pure white bread, beautiful sweet bread. It cost seventy kronen. To Hepburn it was always a mystery where this exquisite bread came from, in a lost land.

In the little square where the clock stood were bunches of people, and a big motor-omnibus, and a motor-car that would hold about eight people. Hepburn had paid his seven hundred kronen for the two tickets. Hannele tied up her head in a thin scarf and put on her thick coat. She and Hepburn sat in front by the peaked driver. And at seven o'clock away went the car, swooping out of the town, past the handsome old Tyrolese Schloss, or manor, black-and-white, with its little black spires pricking up, past the station, and under the trees by the lake-side. The road was not good, but they ran at a great speed, out past the end of the lake, where the reeds grew, out into the open valley mouth, where the mountains opened in two clefts. It was cold in the car. Hepburn buttoned himself up to the throat and pulled his hat down on his ears.

Hannele's scarf fluttered. She sat without saying anything, erect, her face fine and keen, watching ahead. From the deep Pinzgau Valley came the river roaring and raging, a glacier river of pale, seething ice-water. Over went the car, over the log bridge, darting towards the great slopes opposite. And then a sudden immense turn, a swerve under the height of the mountain-side, and again a darting lurch forward, under the pear trees of the high-road, past the big old ruined castle that so magnificently watched the valley mouth, and the foaming river; on, rushing under the huge roofs of the balconied peasant houses of a village, then swinging again to take another valley mouth, there where a little village clustered all black and white on a knoll, with a white church that had a black steeple, and a white castle with black spines, and clustering, ample black-and-white houses of the Tyrol. There is a grandeur even in the peasant houses, with their great wide passage halls where the swallows build, and where one could build a whole English cottage.

So the motor-car darted up this new, narrow, wilder, more sinister valley. A herd of almost wild young horses, handsome reddish things, burst around the car, and one great mare with full flanks went crashing up the road ahead, her heels flashing to the car, while her foal whinneyed and screamed from behind. But no, she could not turn from the road. On and on she crashed, forging ahead, the car behind her. And then at last she did swerve aside, among the thin alder trees by the wild river-bed.

"If it isn't a cow, it's a horse," said the driver, who was thin and weaselish and silent, with his ear-flaps over his ears.

But the great mare had shaken herself in a wild swerve, and screaming and whinneying was plunging back to her foal. Hannele had been frightened.

The car rushed on, through water-meadows, along a naked, white bit of mountain road. Ahead was a darkness of mountain front and pine trees. To the right was the stony, furious, lion-like river, tawny-coloured here, and the slope up beyond. But the road for the moment was swinging fairly level through the stunned water-meadows of the savage valley. There were gates to open, and Hepburn jumped down to open them, as if he were the foot-boy. The heavy Jews of the wrong sort, seated behind, of course did not stir.

At a house on a knoll the driver sounded his horn, and out

rushed children crying Papa! Papa!—then a woman with a
basket. A few brief words from the weaselish man, who
smiled with warm, manly blue eyes at his children, then the
car leaped forward. The whole bearing of the man was so
different when he was looking at his own family. He could
not even say thank you when Hepburn opened the gates. He
hated and even despised his human cargo of middle-class
people. Deep, deep is class-hatred, and it begins to swallow
all human feeling in its abyss. So, stiff, silent, thin, capable,
and neuter towards his fares, sat the little driver with the
flaps over his ears, and his thin nose cold.

The car swept round, suddenly, into the trees: and into the
ravine. The river shouted at the bottom of a gulf. Bristling
pine trees stood around. The air was black and cold and for
ever sunless. The motor-car rushed on, in this blackness,
under the rock-walls and the fir trees.

Then it suddenly stopped. There was a huge motor-omnibus ahead, drab and enormous-looking. Tourists and trippers
of last night coming back from the glacier. It stood like a
great rock. And the smaller motor-car edged past, tilting into
the rock gutter under the face of stone.

So, after a while of this valley of the shadow of death,
lurching in steep loops upwards, the motor-car scrambling
wonderfully, struggling past trees and rock upwards, at last
they came to the end. It was a huge inn or tourist hotel of
brown wood: and here the road ended in a little wide bay
surrounded and overhung by trees. Beyond was a garage and
a bridge over a roaring river: and always the overhung darkness of trees and the intolerable steep slopes immediately
above.

Hannele left her big coat. The sky looked blue above the
gloom. They set out across the hollow-sounding bridge, over
the everlasting mad rush of ice-water, to the immediate up-
slope of the path, under dark trees. But a little old man in a
sort of sentry-box wanted fifty or sixty kronen: apparently
for the upkeep of the road, a sort of toll.

The other tourists were coming—some stopping to have a
drink first. The second omnibus had not yet arrived. Hannele
and Hepburn were the first two, treading slowly up that dark
path, under the trees. The grasses hanging on the rock face
were still dewy. There were a few wild raspberries, and a
tiny tuft of bilberries with black berries here and there, and

a few tufts of unripe cranberries. The many hundreds of tourists who passed up and down did not leave much to pick. Some mountain harebells, like bells of blue water, hung coldly glistening in their darkness. Sometimes the hairy mountain-bell, pale-blue and bristling, stood alone, curving his head right down, stiff and taut. There was an occasional big, moist, lolling daisy.

So the two climbed slowly up the steep ledge of a road. This valley was just a mountain cleft, cleft sheer in the hard, living rock, with black trees like hair flourishing in this secret, naked place of the earth. At the bottom of the open wedge for ever roared the rampant, insatiable water. The sky from above was like a sharp wedge forcing its way into the earth's cleavage, and that eternal ferocious water was like the steel edge of the wedge, the terrible tip biting in into the rocks' intensity. Who could have thought that the soft sky of light, and the soft foam of water could thrust and penetrate into the dark, strong earth? But so it was. Hannele and Hepburn, toiling up the steep little ledge of a road that hung half-way down the gulf, looked back, time after time, back down upon the brown timbers and shingle roofs of the hotel, that now, away below, looked damp and wedged in like boulders. Then back at the next tourists struggling up. Then down at the water, that rushed like a beast of prey. And then, as they rose higher, they looked up also at the livid great sides of rock, livid, bare rock that sloped from the sky-ridge in a hideous sheer swerve downwards.

In his heart of hearts Hepburn hated it. He hated it, he loathed it, it seemed almost obscene, this livid, naked slide of rock, unthinkably huge and massive, sliding down to this gulf where bushes grew like hair in the darkness and water roared. Above, there were thin slashes of snow.

So the two climbed slowly on, up the eternal side of that valley, sweating with the exertion. Sometimes the sun, now risen high, shone full on their side of the gulley. Tourists were trickling downhill too: two maidens with bare arms and bare heads and huge boots: men tourists with great knapsacks and edelweiss in their hats: giving *Bergheil* for a greeting. But the captain said Good-day. He refused this *Bergheil* business. People swarming touristy on these horrible mountains made him feel almost sick.

He and Hannele also were not in good company together.

There was a sort of silent hostility between them. She hated the effort of climbing; but the high air, the cold in the air, the savage cat-howling sound of the water, those awful flanks of livid rock, all this thrilled and excited her to another sort of savageness. And he, dark, rather slender and feline, with something of the physical suavity of a delicate-footed race, he hated beating his way up the rock, he hated the sound of the water, it frightened him, and the high air bit him in his chest, like a viper.

"Wonderful! Wonderful!" she cried, taking great breaths in her splendid chest.

"Yes. And horrible. Detestable," he said.

She turned with a flash, and the high strident sound of the mountain in her voice.

"If you don't like it," she said, rather jeering, "why ever did you come?"

"I had to try," he said.

"And if you don't like it," she said, "why should you try to spoil it for me?"

"I hate it," he answered.

They were climbing more into the height, more into the light, into the open, in the full sun. The valley cleft was sinking below them. Opposite was only the sheer, livid slide of the naked rock, tipping from the pure sky. At a certain angle they could see away beyond the lake lying far off and small, the wall of those other rocks like a curtain of stone, dim and diminished to the horizon. And the sky with curdling clouds and blue sunshine intermittent.

"Wonderful, wonderful, to be high up," she said, breathing great breaths.

"Yes," he said. "It *is* wonderful. But very detestable. I want to live near the sea-level. I am no mountain-topper."

"Evidently not," she said.

"*Bergheil!*" cried a youth with bare arms and bare chest, bare head, terrific fanged boots, a knapsack and an alpenstock, and all the bronzed wind and sun of the mountain snow in his skin and his faintly bleached hair. With his great heavy knapsack, his rumpled thick stockings, his ghastly fanged boots, Hepburn found him repulsive.

"*Guten Tag,*" he answered coldly.

"*Grüss Gott,*" said Hannele.

And the young Tannhäuser, the young Siegfried, this young

Balder beautiful strode climbing down the rocks, marching and swinging with his alpenstock. And immediately after the youth came a maiden, with hair on the wind and her shirt-breast open, striding in corduroy breeches, rumpled worsted stockings, thick boots, a knapsack and an alpenstock. She passed without greeting. And our pair stopped in angry silence and watched her dropping down the mountain-side.

XV

Ah, well, everything comes to an end, even the longest up-climb. So, after much sweat and effort and crossness, Hepburn and Hannele emerged on to the rounded bluff where the road wound out of that hideous great valley cleft into upper regions. So they emerged more on the level, out of the trees as out of something horrible, on to a naked, great bank of rock and grass.

"Thank the Lord!" said Hannele.

So they trudged on round the bluff, and then in front of them saw what is always, always wonderful, one of those shallow, upper valleys, naked, where the first waters are rocked. A flat, shallow, utterly desolate valley, wide as a wide bowl under the sky, with rock slopes and grey stone-slides and precipices all round, and the zig-zag of snow-stripes and ice-roots descending, and then rivers, streams and rivers rushing from many points downwards, down out of the ice-roots and the snow-dagger-points, waters rushing in newly-liberated frenzy downwards, down in waterfalls and cascades and threads, down into the wide, shallow bed of the valley, strewn with rocks and stones innumerable, and not a tree, not a visible bush.

Only, of course, two hotels or restaurant places. But these no more than low, sprawling, peasant-looking places lost among the stones, with stones on their roofs so that they seemed just a part of the valley bed. There was the valley, dotted with rock and rolled-down stone, and these two house-places, and woven with innumerable new waters, and one hoarse stone-tracked river in the desert, and the thin road-track winding along the desolate flat, past first one house, then the other, over one stream, then another, on to the far rock-face above which the glacier seemed to loll like some awful great tongue put out.

"Ah, it is wonderful!" he said, as if to himself.

And she looked quickly at his face, saw the queer, blank, sphinx-look with which he gazed out beyond himself. His eyes were black and set, and he seemed so motionless, as if he were eternal facing these upper facts.

She thrilled with triumph. She felt he was overcome.

"It *is* wonderful," she said.

"Wonderful. And forever wonderful," he said.

"Ah, in *winter*——" she cried.

His face changed, and he looked at her.

"In winter you couldn't get up here," he said.

They went on. Up the slopes cattle were feeding: came that isolated tong-tong-tong of cow-bells, dropping like the slow clink of ice on the arrested air. The sound always woke in him a primeval, almost hopeless melancholy. Always made him feel *navré*. He looked round. There was no tree, no bush, only great grey rocks and pale boulders scattered in place of trees and bushes. But yes, clinging on one side like a dark, close beard were the alpenrose shrubs.

"In May," he said, "that side there must be all pink with alpenroses."

"I *must* come. I *must* come!" she cried.

There were tourists dotted along the road: and two tiny low carts drawn by silky, long-eared mules. These carts went right down to meet the motor-cars, and to bring up provisions for the Glacier Hotel: for there was still another big hotel ahead. Hepburn was happy in that upper valley, that first rocking cradle of early water. He liked to see the great fangs and slashes of ice and snow thrust down into the rock, as if the ice had bitten into the flesh of the earth. And from the fang-tips the hoarse water crying its birth-cry, rushing down.

By the turfy road and under the rocks were many flowers: wonderful harebells, big and cold and dark, almost black, and seeming like purple-dark ice: then little tufts of tiny pale-blue bells, as if some fairy frog had been blowing spume-bubbles out of the ice: then the bishops-crosier of the stiff, bigger, hairy mountain-bell: then many stars of pale-lavender gentian, touched with earth colour: and then monkshood, yellow, primrose yellow monkshood and sudden places full of dark monkshood. That dark-blue, black-blue, terrible colour of the strange rich monkshood made Hepburn look and look and look again. How did the ice come by that lustrous blue-purple intense darkness?—and by that royal poison?—that laughing-snake gorgeousness of much monkshood.

XVI

By one of the loud streams, under a rock in the sun, with scented minty or thyme flowers near, they sat down to eat some lunch. It was about eleven o'clock. A thin bee went in and out the scented flowers and the eyebright. The water poured with all the lust and greed of unloosed water over the stones. He took a cupful for Hannele, bright and icy, and she mixed it with the red Hungarian wine.

Down the road strayed the tourists like pilgrims, and at the closed end of the valley they could be seen, quite tiny, climbing the cut-out road that went up like a stairway. Just by their movements you perceived them. But on the valley-bed they went like rolling stones, little as stones. A very elegant mule came stepping by, following a middle-aged woman in tweeds and a tall, high-browed man in knickerbockers. The mule was drawing a very amusing little cart, a chair, rather like a round office-chair upholstered in red velvet, and mounted on two wheels. The red velvet had gone gold and orange and like fruit-juice, being old: really a lovely colour. And the muleteer, a little shabby creature, waddled beside excitedly.

"*Ach,*" cried Hannele, "that looks almost like before the war: almost as peaceful."

"Except that the chair is too shabby, and that they all feel exceptional," he remarked.

There in that upper valley there was no sense of peace. The rush of the waters seemed like weapons, and the tourists all seemed in a sort of frenzy, in a frenzy to be happy, or to be thrilled. It was a feeling that desolated the heart.

The two sat in the changing sunshine under their rock, with the mountain flowers scenting the snow-bitter air, and they ate their eggs and sausage and cheese, and drank the bright-red Hungarian wine. It seemed lovely: almost like before the war: almost the same feeling of eternal holiday, as if the world was made for man's everlasting holiday. But not quite. Never again quite the same. The world is not made for man's everlasting holiday.

As Alexander was putting the bread back into his shoulder-sack, he exclaimed:

"Oh, look here!"

She looked, and saw him drawing out a flat package wrapped in paper: evidently a picture.

"A picture!" she cried.

He unwrapped the thing and handed it to her. It was Theodor Worpswede's Stillleben: not very large, painted on a board.

Hannele looked at it and went pale.

"It's *good*," she cried, in an equivocal tone.

"Quite good," he said.

"Especially the poached egg," she said.

"Yes, the poached egg is almost living."

"But where did you find it?"

"Oh, I found it in the artist's studio." And he told her how he had traced her.

"How extraordinary!" she cried. "But why did you buy it?"

"I don't quite know."

"Did you *like* it?"

"No, not quite that."

"You could *never* hang it up."

"No, never," he said.

"But do you think it is good as a work of art?"

"I think it is quite clever as a painting. I don't like the spirit of it, of course. I'm too catholic for that."

"No. No," she faltered. "It's rather horrid really. That's why I wonder why you bought it."

"Perhaps to prevent anyone else's buying it," he said.

"Do you mind very much, then?" she asked.

"No, I don't mind very much. I didn't quite like it that you sold the doll," he said.

"I needed the money," she said quietly.

"Oh, quite."

There was a pause for some moments.

"I felt you'd sold *me*," she said, quiet and savage.

"When?"

"When your wife appeared. And when you *disappeared*."

Again there was a pause: his pause this time.

"I did write to you," he said.

"When?"

"Oh—March, I believe."

"Oh yes. I had that letter." Her voice was just as quiet, and even savager.

So there was a pause that belonged to both of them. Then she rose.

"I want to be going," she said. "We shall never get to the glacier at this rate."

He packed up the picture, slung on his knapsack, and they set off. She stooped now and then to pick the starry, earth-lavender gentians from the roadside. As they passed the second of the valley hotels, they saw the man and wife sitting at a little table outside eating bread and cheese, while the mule-chair with its red velvet waited aside on the grass. They passed a whole grove of black-purple nightshade on the left, and some long, low cattle-huts which, with the stones on their roofs, looked as if they had grown up as stones grow in such places through the grass. In the wild, desert place some black pigs were snouting.

So they wound into the head of the valley, and saw the steep face ahead, and high up, like vapour or foam dripping from the fangs of a beast, waterfalls vapouring down from the deep fangs of ice. And there was one end of the glacier, like a great bluey-white fur just slipping over the slope of the rock.

As the valley closed in again the flowers were very lovely, especially the big, dark, icy bells, like harebells, that would sway so easily, but which hung dark and with that terrible motionlessness of upper mountain flowers. And the road turned to get on to the long slant in the cliff face, where it climbed like a stair. Slowly, slowly the two climbed up. Now again they saw the valley below, behind. The mule-chair was coming, hastening, the lady seated tight facing backwards, as the chair faced, and wrapped in rugs. The tall, fair, middle-aged husband in knickerbockers strode just behind, bare-headed.

Alexander and Hannele climbed slowly, slowly up the slant, under the dripping rock-face where the white and veined flowers of the grass of Parnassus still rose straight and chilly in the shadow, like water which had taken on itself white flower-flesh. Above they saw the slipping edge of the glacier, like a terrible great paw, bluey. And from the skyline dark grey clouds were fuming up, fuming up as if breathed black and icily out from some ice-cauldron.

"It is going to rain," said Alexander.

"Not much," said Hannele shortly.

"I hope not," said he.

And still she would not hurry up that steep slant, but insisted on standing to look. So the dark, ice-black clouds fumed solid, and the rain began to fly on a cold wind. The mule-chair hastened past, the lady sitting comfortably with her back to the mule, a little pheasant-trimming in her tweed hat, while her Tannhäuser husband reached for his dark, cape-frilled mantle.

Alexander had his dust-coat, but Hannele had nothing but a light knitted jersey-coat, such as women wear indoors. Over the hollow crest above came the cold, steel rain. They pushed on up the slope. From behind came another mule, and a little old man hurrying, and a little cart like a hand-barrow, on which were hampers with cabbage and carrots and peas and joints of meat, for the hotel above.

"Wird es viel sein?" asked Alexander of the little gnome. "Will it be much?"

"Was meint der Herr?" replied the other. "What does the gentleman say?"

"Der Regen, wird es lang dauern? Will the rain last long?"

"Nein. Nein. Dies ist kein langer Regen."

So, with his mule which had to stand exactly at that spot to make droppings, the little man resumed his way, and Hannele and Alexander were the last on the slope. The air smelt steel-cold of rain, and of hot droppings. Alexander watched the rain beat on the shoulders and on the blue skirt of Hannele.

"It is a pity you left your big coat down below," he said.

"What good is it saying so now!" she replied, pale at the nose with anger.

"Quite," he said, as his eyes glowed and his brow blackened. "What good suggesting anything at any time, apparently?"

She turned round on him in the rain, as they stood perched nearly at the summit of that slanting cliff-climb, with a glacier-paw hung almost invisible above, and waters gloating aloud in the gulf below. She faced him, and he faced her.

"What have you ever suggested to me?" she said, her face naked as the rain itself with an ice-bitter fury. "What have you ever suggested to me?"

"When have you ever been open to suggestion?" he said, his face dark and his eyes curiously glowing.

"I? I? Ha! Haven't I waited for you to suggest something? And all you can do is to come here with a picture to reproach me for having sold your doll. Ha! I'm glad I sold it. A foolish barren effigy it was too, a foolish staring thing. What should I do but sell it. Why should I keep it, do you imagine?"

"Why do you come here with me to-day, then?"

"Why do I come here with you to-day?" she replied. "I come to see the mountains, which are wonderful, and give me strength. And I come to see the glacier. Do you think I come here to see *you*? Why should I? You are always in some hotel or other away below."

"You came to see the glacier and the mountains *with* me," he replied.

"Did I? Then I made a mistake. You can do nothing but find fault even with God's mountains."

A dark flame suddenly went over his face.

"Yes," he said, "I hate them, I hate them. I hate their snow and their affectations."

"*Affectation!*" she laughed. "Oh! Even the mountains are affected for you, are they?"

"Yes," he said. "Their loftiness and their uplift. I hate their uplift. I hate people prancing on mountain-tops and feeling exalted. I'd like to make them all stop up there, on their mountain-tops, and chew ice to fill their stomachs. I wouldn't let them down again, I wouldn't. I hate it all, I tell you; I hate it."

She looked in wonder on his dark, glowing, ineffectual face. It seemed to her like a dark flame burning in the daylight and in the ice-rains: very ineffectual and unnecessary.

"You must be a little mad," she said superbly, "to talk like that about the mountains. They are so much bigger than you."

"No," he said. "No! They are not."

"What!" she laughed aloud. "The mountains are not bigger than you? But you are extraordinary."

"They are not bigger than me," he cried. "Any more than you are bigger than me if you stand on a ladder. They are not bigger than me. They are less than me."

"Oh! Oh!" she cried in wonder and ridicule. "The mountains are less than you."

"Yes," he cried, "they are less."

He seemed suddenly to go silent and remote as she watched him. The speech had gone out of his face again, he seemed to be standing a long way off from her, beyond some border-line. And in the midst of her indignant amazement she watched him with wonder and a touch of fascination. To what country did he belong then?—to what dark, different atmosphere.

"You must suffer from megalomania," she said. And she said what she felt.

But he only looked at her out of dark, dangerous, haughty eyes.

They went on their way in the rain in silence. He was filled with a passionate silence and imperiousness, a curious, dark, masterful force that supplanted thought in him. And she, who always pondered, went pondering: "Is he mad? What does he mean? Is he a madman? He wants to bully me. He wants to bully me into something. What does he want to bully me into? Does he want me to love him?"

At this final question she rested. She decided that what he wanted was that she should love him. And this thought flattered her vanity and her pride and appeased her wrath against him. She felt quite mollified towards him.

But what a way he went about it! He wanted her to love him. Of this she was sure. He had always wanted her to love him, even from the first. Only he had not made up his *mind* about it. He had not made up his mind. After his wife had died he had gone away to make up his mind. Now he had made it up. He wanted her to love him. And he was offended, mortally offended because she had sold his doll.

So, this was the conclusion to which Hannele came. And it pleased her, and it flattered her. And it made her feel quite warm towards him, as they walked in the rain. The rain, by the way, was abating. The spume over the hollow crest to which they were approaching was thinning considerably. They could again see the glacier paw hanging out a little beyond. The rain was going to pass. And they were not far now from the hotel, and the third level of Lammerboden.

He wanted her to love him. She felt again quite glowing and triumphant inside herself, and did not care a bit about the rain on her shoulders. He wanted her to love him. Yes, that was how she had to put it. He didn't want to *love* her. No. He wanted *her* to love *him*.

But then, of course, woman-like, she took his love for granted. So many men had been so very ready to love her. And this one—to her amazement, to her indignation, and rather to her secret satisfaction—just blackly insisted that *she* must love *him*. Very well—she would give him a run for his money. That was it: he blackly insisted that *she* must love *him*. What he felt was not to be considered. *She* must love *him*. And be bullied into it. That was what it amounted to. In his silent, black, overbearing soul, he wanted to compel her, he wanted to have power over her. He wanted to make her love him so that he had power over her. He wanted to bully her, physically, sexually, and from the inside.

And she! Well, she was just as confident that she was not going to be bullied. She would love him: probably she would: most probably she did already. But she was not going to be bullied by him in any way whatsoever. No, he must go down on his knees to her if he wanted her love. And then she would love him. Because she *did* love him. But a dark-eyed little master and bully she would never have.

And this was her triumphant conclusion. Meanwhile the rain had almost ceased, they had almost reached the rim of the upper level, towards which they were climbing, and he was walking in that silent diffidence which made her watch him because she was not sure what he was feeling, what he was thinking, or even what he was. He was a puzzle to her: eternally incomprehensible in his feelings and even his sayings. There seemed to her no logic and no reason in what he felt and said. She could never tell what his next mood would come out of. And this made her uneasy, made her watch him. And at the same time it piqued her attention. He had some of the fascination of the incomprehensible. And his curious inscrutable face—it wasn't really only a meaningless mask, because she had seen it half an hour ago melt with a quite incomprehensible and rather, to her mind, foolish passion. Strange, black, inconsequential passion. Asserting with that curious dark ferocity that he was bigger than the mountains. Madness! Madness! Megalomania.

But because he gave himself away, she forgave him and even liked him. And the strange passion of his, that gave out incomprehensible flashes, *was* rather fascinating to her. She felt just a tiny bit sorry for him. But she wasn't going to be bullied by him. She wasn't going to give in to him and his black passion. No, never. It must be love on equal terms or nothing. For love on equal terms she was quite ready. She only waited for him to offer it.

XVII

In the hotel was a buzz of tourists. Alexander and Hannele sat in the restaurant drinking hot coffee and milk, and watching the maidens in cotton frocks and aprons and bare arms, and the fair youths with maidenly necks and huge voracious boots, and the many Jews of the wrong sort and the wrong shape. These Jews were all being very Austrian, in Tyrol costume that didn't sit on them, assuming the whole gesture and intonation of aristocratic Austria, so that you might think they *were* Austrian aristocrats, if you weren't properly listening, or if you didn't look twice. Certainly they were lords of the Alps, or at least lords of the Alpine hotels this summer, let prejudice be what it might. Jews of the wrong sort. And yet even they imparted a wholesome breath of sanity, disillusion, unsentimentality to the excited '*Bergheil*' atmosphere. Their dark-eyed, sardonic presence seemed to say to the maidenly-necked mountain youths: "Don't sprout wings of the spirit too much, my dears."

The rain had ceased. There was a wisp of sunshine from a grey sky. Alexander left the knapsack, and the two went out into the air. Before them lay the last level of the up-climb, the Lammerboden. It was a rather gruesome hollow between the peaks, a last shallow valley about a mile long. At the end the enormous static stream of the glacier poured in from the blunt mountain-top of ice. The ice was dull, sullen-coloured, melted on the surface by the very hot summer: and so it seemed a huge, arrested, sodden flood, ending in a wave-wall of stone-speckled ice upon the valley bed of rocky débris. A gruesome descent of stone and blocks of rock, the little valley bed, with a river raving through. On the left rose the grey rock, but the glacier was there, sending down great paws of ice. It was like some great, deep-furred ice-bear lying spread upon the top heights, and reaching down terrible paws of ice into the valley: like some immense sky-bear fishing in the earth's solid hollows from above. Hepburn it just filled with terror. Hannele too it scared, but it gave her a sense of ecstasy. Some of the immense, furrowed paws of ice held down between the rock were vivid blue in colour, but of a frightening, poisonous blue, like crystal copper sulphate. Most of the ice was a sullen, semi-translucent greeny grey.

The two set off to walk through the massy, desolate stone-bed, under rocks and over waters, to the main glacier. The flowers were even more beautiful on this last reach. Particularly the dark harebells were large and almost black and ice-metallic: one could imagine they gave a dull ice-chink. And the grass of Parnassus stood erect, white-veined big cups held terribly naked and open to their ice air.

From behind the great blunt summit of ice that blocked the distance at the end of the valley, a pale-grey, woolly mist or cloud was fusing up, exhaling huge, like some grey-dead aura into the sky, and covering the top of the glacier. All the way along the valley people were threading, strangely insignificant, among the grey dishevel of stone and rock, like insects. Hannele and Alexander went ahead quickly, along the tiring track.

"Are you glad now that you came?" she said, looking at him triumphant.

"Very glad I came," he said. His eyes were dilated with excitement that was ordeal or mystic battle rather than the *Bergheil* ecstasy. The curious vibration of his excitement made the scene strange, rather horrible to her. She too shuddered. But it still seemed to her to hold the key to all glamour and ecstasy, the great silent, living glacier. It seemed to her like a grand beast.

As they came near they saw the wall of ice: the glacier end, thick crusted and speckled with stone and dirt débris. From underneath, secret in stones, water rushed out. When they came quite near, they saw the great monster was sweating all over, trickles and rivulets of sweat running down his sides of pure, slush-translucent ice. There it was, the glacier, ending abruptly in the wall of ice under which they stood. Near to, the ice was pure, but water-logged, all the surface rather rotten from the hot summer. It was sullenly translucent, and of a watery, darkish bluey-green colour. But near the earth it became again bright coloured, gleams of green like jade, gleams of blue like thin, pale sapphire, in little caverns above the wet stones where the walls trickled for ever.

Alexander wanted to climb on to the glacier. It was his one desire—to stand upon it. So under the pellucid wet wall they toiled among rocks upwards, to where the guide-track mounted the ice. Several other people were before them—mere day tourists—and all uncertain about venturing any farther. For the ice-slope rose steep and slithery, pure, sunlocked, sweating ice. Still, it was like a curved back. One could scramble on to it, and on up to the first level, like the flat on top of some huge paw.

There stood the little cluster of people, facing the uphill of sullen, pure, sodden-looking ice. They were all afraid: naturally. But being human, they all wanted to go beyond their fear. It was strange that the ice looked so pure, like flesh. Not bright, because the surface was soft like a soft, deep epidermis. But pure ice away down to immense depths.

Alexander, after some hesitation, began gingerly to try the ice. He was frightened of it. And he had no stick, and only smooth-soled boots. But he had a great desire to stand on the glacier. So, gingerly and shakily, he began to struggle a few steps up the pure slope. The ice was soft on the surface, he could kick his heel in it and get a little sideways grip. So, staggering and going sideways he got up a few yards, and was on the naked ice-slope.

Immediately the youths and the fat man below began to tackle it too: also two maidens. For some time, however, Alexander gingerly and scramblingly led the way. The slope of ice was steeper, and rounded, so that it was difficult to stand up in any way. Sometimes he slipped, and was clinging with burnt finger-ends to the soft ice mass. Then he tried throwing his coat down, and getting a foot-hold on that. Then he went quite quickly by bending down and getting a little grip with his fingers, and going ridiculously as on four legs.

Hannele watched from below, and saw the ridiculous exhibition, and was frightened and amused, but more frightened. And she kept calling, to the great joy of the Austrians down below:

"Come back. Do come back."

But when he got on to his feet again he only waved his hand at her, half crossly, as she stood away down there in her blue frock. The other fellows with sticks and nail-boots had now taken heart and were scrambling like crabs past our hero, doing better than he.

He had come to a rift in the ice. He sat near the edge and looked down. Clean, pure ice, fused with pale colour, and fused into intense copper-sulphate blue away down in the crack. It was not like crystal, but fused as one fuses a borax bead under a blow-flame. And keenly, wickedly blue in the depths of the crack.

He looked upwards. He had not half mounted the slope. So on he went, upon the huge body of the soft-fleshed ice, slanting his way sometimes on all fours, sometimes using his coat, usually hitting-in with the side of his heel. Hannele down below was crying him to come back. But two other youths were now almost level with him.

So he struggled on till he was more or less over the brim. There he stood and looked at the ice. It came down from above in a great hollow world of ice. A world, a terrible place of hills and valleys and slopes, all motionless, all of ice. Away above the grey mist-cloud was looming bigger. And near at hand were long, huge cracks, side by side, like gills in the ice. It would seem as if the ice breathed through these great ridged gills. One could look down into the series of gulfs, fearful depths, and the colour burning that acid, intense blue, intenser as the crack went deeper. And the crests of the open gills ridged and grouped pale blue above the crevices. It seemed as if the ice breathed there.

The wonder, the terror, and the bitterness of it. Never a warm leaf to unfold, never a gesture of life to give off. A world sufficient unto itself in lifelessness, all this ice.

He turned to go down, though the youths were passing beyond him. And seeing the naked translucent ice heaving downwards in a vicious curve, always the same dark translucency underfoot, he was afraid. If he slipped, he would certainly slither the whole way down, and break some of his bones. Even when he sat down he had to cling with his finger-nails in the ice, because if he had started to slide he would have slid the whole way down on his trouser-seat, precipitously, and have landed heaven knows how.

Hannele was watching from below. And he was frightened, perched, seated on the shoulder of ice and not knowing how to get off. Above he saw the great blue gills of ice ridging the air. Down below were two blue cracks—then the last wet level claws of ice upon the stones. And there stood Hannele and the three or four people who had got so far.

However, he found that by striking in his heels sideways with sufficient sharpness he could keep his footing, no matter how steep the slope. So he started to jerk his way zig-zag downwards.

As he descended, arrived a guide with a black beard and all the paraphernalia of ropes and pole and bristling boots. He and his gentlemen began to strike their way up the ice. With those bristling nails like teeth in one's boots, it was quite easy: and a pole to press on to.

Hannele, who had got sick of waiting, and who was also frightened, had gone scuttling on the return journey. He hurried after her, thankful to be off the ice, but excited and gratified. Looking round, he saw the guide and the man on the ice watching the ice-world and the weather. Then they too turned to come down. The day wasn't safe.

XVIII

Pondering, rather thrilled, they threaded their way through the desert of rock and rushing water back to the hotel. The sun was shining warmly for a moment, and he felt happy, though his finger-ends were bleeding a little from the ice.

"But one day," said Hannele, "I should love to go with a guide right up, high, right into the glacier."

"No," said he. "I've been far enough. I prefer the world where cabbages will grow on the soil. Nothing grows on glaciers."

"They say there are glacier fleas, which only live on glaciers," she said.

"Well, to me the ice didn't look good to eat, even for a flea."

"You never know," she laughed. "But you're glad you've been, aren't you?"

"Very glad. Now I need never go again."

"But you *did* think it wonderful?"

"Marvellous. And awful, to my mind."

XIX

They ate venison and spinach in the hotel, then set off down again. Both felt happier. She gathered some flowers and put them in her handkerchief so they should not die. And again they sat by the stream, to drink a little wine.

But the fume of cloud was blowing up again, thick from

behind the glacier. Hannele was uneasy. She wanted to get down. So they went fairly quickly. Many other tourists were hurrying downwards also. The rain began—a sharp handful of drops flung from beyond the glacier. So Hannele and he did not stay to rest, but dropped easily down the steep, dark valley towards the motor-car terminus.

There they had tea, rather tired but comfortably so. The big hotel restaurant was hideous, and seemed sordid. So in the gloom of a grey, early twilight they went out again and sat on a seat, watching the tourists and the trippers and the motor-car men. There were three Jews from Vienna: and the girl had a huge white woolly dog, as big as a calf, and white and woolly and silky and amiable as a toy. The men, of course, came patting it and admiring it, just as men always do, in life and in novels. And the girl, holding the leash, posed and leaned backwards in the attitude of heroines on novel-covers. She said the white cool monster was a Siberian steppe-dog. Alexander wondered what the steppes made of such a wuffer. And the three Jews pretended they were elegant Austrians out of popular romances.

"Do you think," said Alexander, "you will marry the Herr Regierungsrat?"

She looked round, making wide eyes.

"It looks like it, doesn't it!" she said.

"Quite," he said.

Hannele watched the woolly white dog. So of course it came wagging its ever-amiable hindquarters towards her. She looked at it still, but did not touch it.

"What makes you ask such a question?" she said.

"I can't say. But even so, you haven't really answered. Do you really fully intend to marry the Herr Regierungsrat? Is that your final intention at this moment?"

She looked at him again.

"But before I answer," she said, "oughtn't I to know why you ask?"

"Probably you know already," he said.

"I assure you I don't."

He was silent for some moments. The huge, woolly dog stood in front of him and breathed enticingly, with its tongue out. He only looked at it blankly.

"Well," he said, "if you were not going to marry the Herr Regierungsrat, I should suggest that you marry me."

She stared away at the auto-garage, a very faint look of amusement, or pleasure, or ridicule on her face: or all three. And a certain shyness.

"But why?" she said.

"Why what?" he returned.

"Why should you suggest that I should marry you?"

"*Why?*" he replied, in his lingering tones. "*Why?* Well, for what purpose does a man usually ask a woman to marry him?"

"For what *purpose!*" she repeated, rather haughtily.

"For what reason, then!" he corrected.

She was silent for some moments. Her face was closed and a little numb-looking, her hands lay very still in her lap. She looked away from him, across the road.

"There is usually only one reason," she replied, in a rather small voice.

"Yes?" he replied curiously. "What would you say that was?"

She hesitated. Then she said, rather stiffly:

"Because he really loved her, I suppose. That seems to me the only excuse for a man asking a woman to marry him."

Followed a dead silence, which she did not intend to break. He knew he would have to answer, and for some reason he didn't want to say what was obviously the thing to say.

"Leaving aside the question of whether you love me or I love you——" he began.

"I certainly *won't* leave it aside," she said.

"And I certainly won't consider it," he said, just as obstinately.

She turned now and looked full at him, with amazement, ridicule, and anger in her face.

"I really think you must be mad," she said.

"I doubt if you do think that," he replied. "It is only a method of retaliation, that is. I think you understand my point very clearly."

"Your point!" she cried. "Your point! Oh, so you have a point in all this palavering?"

"Quite!" said he.

She was silent with indignation for some time. Then she said angrily:

"I assure you I do *not* see your point. I don't see any point at all. I see only impertinence."

"Very good," he replied. "The point is whether we marry on a basis of love."

"Indeed! Marry! We, marry! I don't think that is by any means the point."

He took his knapsack from under the seat between his feet. And from the knapsack he took the famous picture.

"When," he said, "we were supposed to be in love with one another, you made that doll of me, didn't you?" And he sat looking at the odious picture.

"I never for one moment deluded myself that you *really* loved me," she said bitterly.

"Take the other point, whether *you* loved *me* or not," said he.

"How could I love you when I couldn't believe in your love for me?" she cried.

He put the picture down between his knees again.

"All this about love," he said, "is very confusing and very complicated."

"Very! In *your* case. Love to me is simple enough," she said.

"Is it? Is it? And was it simple love which made you make that doll of me?"

"Why shouldn't I make a doll of you? Does it do you any harm? And *weren't* you a doll, good heavens! You *were* nothing but a doll. So what hurt does it do you?"

"Yes, it does. It does me the greatest possible damage," he replied.

She turned on him with wide-open eyes of amazement and rage.

"Why? Pray why? Can you tell me why?"

"Not quite, I can't," he replied, taking up the picture and holding it in front of him. She turned her face from it as a cat turns its nose away from a lighted cigarette. "But when I look at it—when I look at this—then I *know* that there's no love between you and me."

"Then why are you talking at me in this shameful way?" she flashed at him, tears of anger and mortification rising to her eyes. "You want your little revenge on me, I suppose, because I made that doll of you."

"That may be so, in a small measure," he said.

"That is *all*. That is all and everything," she cried. "And that is all you came back to me for—for this petty revenge. Well, you've had it now. But please don't speak to me any more. I shall see if I can go home in the big omnibus."

She rose and walked away. He saw her hunting for the
motor-bus conductor. He saw her penetrate into the yard of
the garage. And he saw her emerge again, after a time, and
take the path to the river. He sat on in front of the hotel.
There was nothing else to do.

The tourists who had arrived in the big bus now began to
collect. And soon the huge, drab vehicle itself rolled up and
stood big as a house before the hotel door. The passengers
began to scramble into their seats. The two men of the white
dog were going: but the woman of the white dog, and the
dog, were staying behind. Hepburn wondered if Hannele had
managed to get herself transferred. He doubted it, because he
knew the omnibus was crowded.

Moreover, he had her ticket.

The passengers were packed in. The conductor was collecting the tickets. And at last the great bus rolled away. The
bay of the road-end seemed very empty. Even the woman
with the white dog had gone. Soon the other car, the Luxus,
so-called, must appear. Hepburn sat and waited. The evening
was falling chilly, the trees looked gruesome.

At last Hannele sauntered up again, unwillingly.

"I think," she said, "you have my ticket."

"Yes, I have," he replied.

"Will you give it me, please?"

He gave it to her. She lingered a moment. Then she walked
away.

There was the sound of a motor-car. With a triumphant
purr the Luxus came steering out of the garage yard and drew
up at the hotel door. Hannele came hastening also. She went
straight to one of the hinder doors—she and Hepburn had
their seats in front, beside the driver. She had her foot on
the step of the back seat. And then she was afraid. The little
sharp-faced driver—there was no conductor—came round
looking at the car. He looked at her with his sharp, metallic
eye of a mechanic.

"Are all the people going back who came?" she asked,
shrinking.

"*Jawohl.*"

"It is full—this car?"

"*Jawohl.*"

"There's no other place?"

"*Nein.*"

Hannele shrank away. The driver was absolutely laconic. Six of the passengers were here: four were already seated. Hepburn sat still by the hotel door, Hannele lingered in the road by the car, and the little driver, with a huge woollen muffler round his throat, was running round and in and out looking for the two missing passengers. Of course there were two missing passengers. No, he could not find them. And off he trotted again, silently, like a weasel after two rabbits. And at last, when everybody was getting cross, he unearthed them and brought them scuttling to the car.

Now Hannele took her seat, and Hepburn beside her. The driver snapped up the tickets and climbed in past them. With a vindictive screech the car glided away down the ravine. Another beastly trip was over, another infernal joyful holiday done with.

"I think," said Hepburn, "I may as well finish what I had to say."

"What?" cried Hannele, fluttering in the wind of the rushing car.

"I may as well finish what I had to say," shouted he, his breath blown away.

"Finish then," she screamed, the ends of her scarf flickering behind her.

"When my wife died," he said loudly, "I knew I couldn't love any more."

"Oh—h!" she screamed ironically.

"In fact," he shouted, "I realised that, as far as I was concerned, love was a mistake."

"*What* was a mistake?" she screamed.

"Love," he bawled.

"Love!" she screamed. "A mistake?" Her tone was derisive.

"For me personally," he said, shouting.

"Oh, only for you personally," she cried, with a pouf of laughter.

The car gave a great swerve, and she fell on the driver. Then she righted herself. It gave another swerve, and she fell on Alexander. She righted herself angrily. And now they ran straight on: and it seemed a little quieter.

"I realised," he said, "that I had always made a mistake, undertaking to love."

"It must have been an undertaking for *you*," she cried.

"Yes, I'm afraid it was. I never really wanted it. But I thought I did. And that's where I made my mistake."

"Whom have you ever loved?—even as an undertaking?" she asked.

"To begin with, my mother: and that was a mistake. Then my sister: and that was a mistake. Then a girl I had known all my life: and that was a mistake. Then my wife: and that was my most terrible mistake. And then I began the mistake of loving you."

"Undertaking to love me, you mean," she said. "But then you never did properly undertake it. You never really *undertook* to love me."

"Not quite, did I?" said he.

And she sat feeling angry that he had never made the undertaking.

"No," he continued. "Not quite. That is why I came back to you. I don't want to love you. I don't want marriage on a basis of love."

"On a basis of what, then?"

"I think you know without my putting it into words," he said.

"Indeed, I assure you I don't. You are much too mysterious," she replied.

Talking in a swiftly-running motor-car is a nerve-wracking business. They both had a pause, to rest, and to wait for a quieter stretch of road.

"It isn't very easy to put it into words," he said. "But I tried marriage once on a basis of love, and I must say it was a ghastly affair in the long run. And I believe it would be so, for me, *whatever* woman I had."

"There must be something wrong with you, then," said she.

"As far as love goes. And yet I want marriage. I want marriage. I want a woman to honour and obey me."

"If you are quite reasonable and *very* sparing with your commands," said Hannele. "And very careful how you give your orders."

"In fact, I want a sort of patient Griselda. I want to be honoured and obeyed. I don't want love."

"How Griselda managed to honour that fool of a husband of hers, even if she obeyed him, is more than I can say," said Hannele. "I'd like to know what she *really* thought of him. Just what any woman thinks of a bullying fool of a husband."

"Well," said he, "that's no good to me."

They were silent now until the car stopped at the station. There they descended and walked on under the trees by the lake.

"Sit on a seat," he said, "and let us finish."

Hannele, who was really anxious to hear what he should say, and who, woman-like, was fascinated by a man when he began to give away his own inmost thoughts—no matter how much she might jeer afterwards—sat down by his side. It was a grey evening, just falling dark. Lights twinkled across the lake, the hotel over there threaded its strings of light. Some little boats came rowing quietly to shore. It was a grey, heavy evening, with that special sense of dreariness with which a public holiday usually winds up.

"Honour and obedience: and the proper physical feelings," he said. "To me that is marriage. Nothing else."

"But what are the proper physical feelings but love?" asked Hannele.

"No," he said. "A woman wants you to adore her, and be in love with her—and I shan't. I will not do it again, if I live a monk for the rest of my days. I will neither adore you nor be in love with you."

"You won't get a chance, thank you. And what do you call the proper physical feelings, if you are not in love? I think you want something vile."

"If a woman honours me—absolutely from the bottom of her nature honours me—and obeys me because of that, I take it, my desire for her goes very much deeper than if I was in love with her, or if I adored her."

"It's the same thing. If you love, then everything is there— all the lot: your honour and obedience and everything. And if love isn't there, nothing is there," she said.

"That isn't true," he replied. "A woman may love you, she may adore you, but she'll never honour you nor obey you. The most loving and adoring woman to-day could any minute start and make a doll of her husband—as you made of me."

"Oh, that eternal doll! What makes it stick so in your mind?"

"I don't know. But there it is. It wasn't malicious. It was

flattering, if you like. But it just sticks in me like a thorn: like a thorn. And there it is, in the world, in Germany somewhere. And you can say what you like, but *any* woman, today, no matter *how* much she loves her man—she could start any minute and make a doll of him. And the doll would be her hero: and her hero would be no more than her doll. My wife might have done it. She did do it, in her mind. She had her doll of me right enough. Why, I heard her talk about me to other women. And her doll was a great deal sillier than the one you made. But it's all the same. If a woman loves you, she'll make a doll out of you. She'll never be satisfied till she's made your doll. And when she's got your doll, that's all she wants. And that's what love means. And so, I won't be loved. And I won't love. I won't have anybody loving me. It is an insult. I feel I've been insulted for forty years: by love, and the women who've loved me. I won't be loved. And I won't love. I'll be honoured and I'll be obeyed: or nothing."

"Then it'll most probably be nothing," said Hannele sarcastically. "For I assure you I've nothing but love to offer."

"Then keep your love," said he.

She laughed shortly.

"And you?" she cried. "You! Even suppose you *were* honoured and obeyed. I suppose all you've got to do is to sit there like a sultan and sup it up."

"Oh no, I have many things to do. And woman or no woman, I'm going to start to do them."

"What, pray?"

"Why, nothing very exciting. I'm going to East Africa to join a man who's breaking his neck to get his three thousand acres of land under control. And when I've done a few more experiments and observations, and got all the necessary facts, I'm going to do a book on the moon. Woman or no woman, I'm going to do that."

"And the woman?—supposing you get the poor thing."

"Why, she'll come along with me, and we'll set ourselves up out there."

"And she'll do all the honouring and obeying and housekeeping incidentally, while you ride about in the day and stare at the moon in the night."

He did not answer. He was staring away across the lake.

"What will you do for the woman, poor thing, while she's

racking herself to pieces honouring you and obeying you and
doing frightful housekeeping in Africa: because I know it can
be *awful:* awful."

"Well," he said slowly, "she'll be my wife, and I shall treat
her as such. If the marriage service says love and cherish—
well, in that sense I shall do so."

"Oh!" cried Hannele. "What, *love* her? Actually love the
poor thing?"

"Not in that sense of the word, no. I shan't adore her or be
in love with her. But she'll be my wife, and I shall love and
cherish her as such."

"Just because she's your wife. Not because she's herself.
Ghastly fate for any miserable woman," said Hannele.

"I don't think so. I think it's her highest fate."

"To be your wife?"

"To be a wife—and to be loved and shielded as a wife—not
as a flirting woman."

"To be loved and cherished just because you're his wife!
No, thank you. All I can admire is the conceit and impudence
of it."

"Very well, then—there it is," he said, rising.

She rose too, and they went on towards where the boat
was tied.

As they were rowing in silence over the lake, he said:

"I shall leave to-morrow."

She made no answer. She sat and watched the lights of the
villa draw near. And then she said:

"I'll come to Africa with you. But I won't promise to
honour and obey you."

"I don't want you otherwise," he said, very quietly.

The boat was drifting to the little landing-stage. Hannele's
friends were hallooing to her from the balcony.

"Hallo!" she cried. *"Ja. Da bin ich. Ja, 's war wunderschön."*

Then to him she said:

"You'll come in?"

"No," he said, "I'll row straight back."

From the villa they were running down the steps to meet
Hannele.

"But won't you have me even if I love you?" she asked him.

"You must promise the other," he said. "It comes in the
marriage service."

"Hat's geregnet? Wie war das Wetter? Warst du auf dem Gletscher?" cried the voices from the garden.

"Nein—kein Regen. Wunderschön! Ja, er war ganz auf dem Gletscher," cried Hannele in reply. And to him, *sotto voce:*

"Don't be a solemn ass. Do come in."

"No," he said, "I don't want to come in."

"Do you want to go away to-morrow? Go if you *do*. But, anyway, I won't say it *before* the marriage service. I needn't, need I?"

She stepped from the boat on to the plank.

"Oh," she said, turning round, "give me that picture, please, will you? I want to burn it."

He handed it to her.

"And come to-morrow, will you?" she said.

"Yes, in the morning."

He pulled back quickly into the darkness.